President & Publisher
Mike Richardson

Editors
Brendan Wright
Daniel Chabon

Assistant Editor
Cardner Clark

Designer
Justin Couch

Digital Art Technician
Allyson Haller

Published by
Dark Horse Books
A division of Dark Horse Comics, Inc.
10956 SE Main Street
Milwaukie, OR 97222

DarkHorse.com

First edition: June 2016 | ISBN 978-1-61655-943-4 | 10 9 8 7 6 5 4 3 2 1

To find a comics shop in your area, call the Comic Shop Locator Service toll-free at 1-888-266-4226.
International Licensing: (503) 905-2377

Neil Hankerson, Executive Vice President; Tom Weddle, Chief Financial Officer; Randy Stradley, Vice President of Publishing; Michael Martens, Vice President of Book Trade Sales; Matt Parkinson, Vice President of Marketing; David Scroggy, Vice President of Product Development; Dale LaFountain, Vice President of Information Technology; Cara Niece, Vice President of Production and Scheduling; Nick McWhorter, Vice President of Media Licensing; Ken Lizzi, General Counsel; Dave Marshall, Editor in Chief; Davey Estrada, Editorial Director; Scott Allie, Executive Senior Editor; Chris Warner, Senior Books Editor; Cary Grazzini, Director of Print and Development; Lia Ribacchi, Art Director; Mark Bernardi, Director of Digital Publishing; Michael Gombos, Director of International Publishing and Licensing

POPPY! AND THE LOST LAGOON

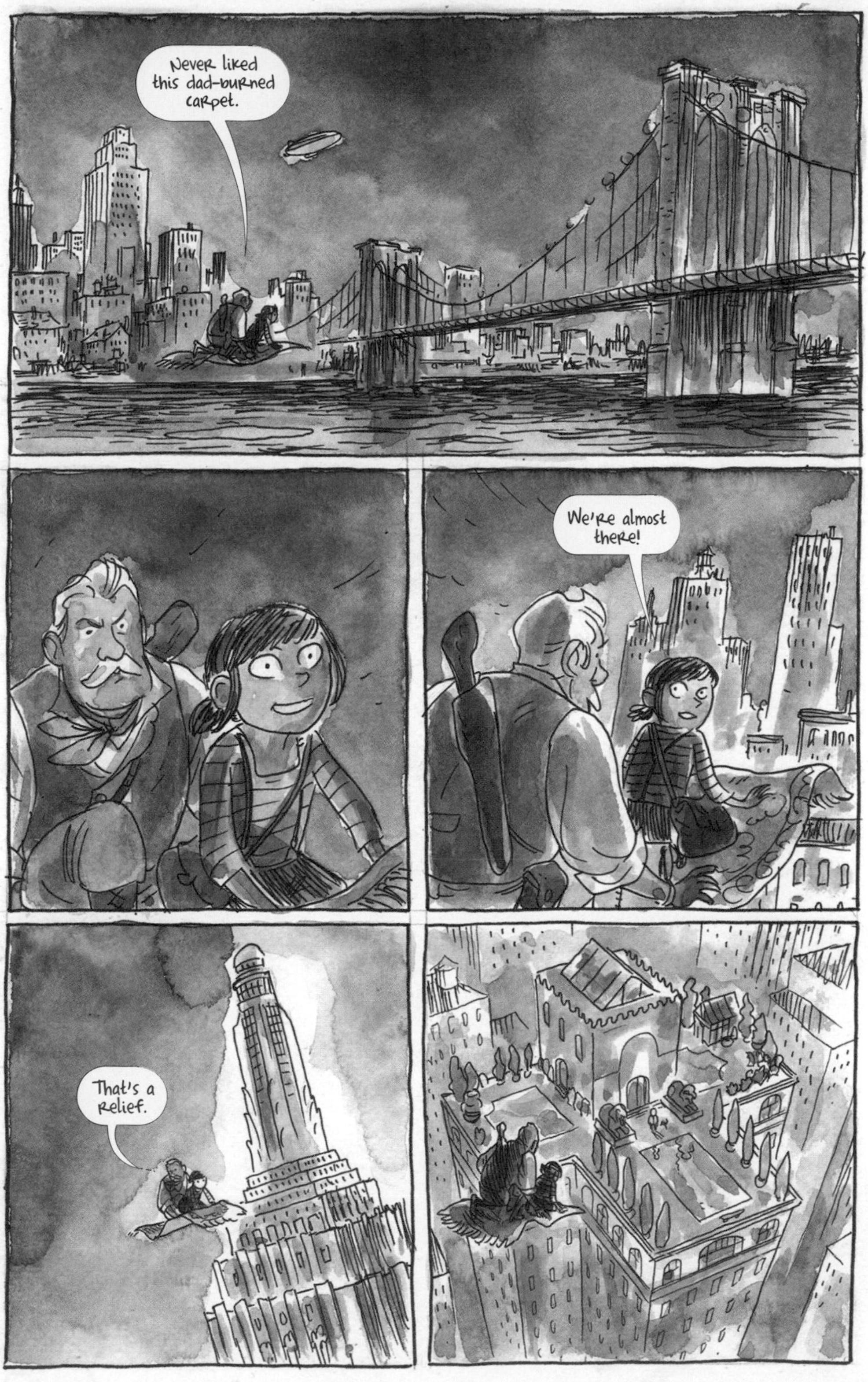
Never liked this dad-burned carpet.
We're almost there!
That's a relief.

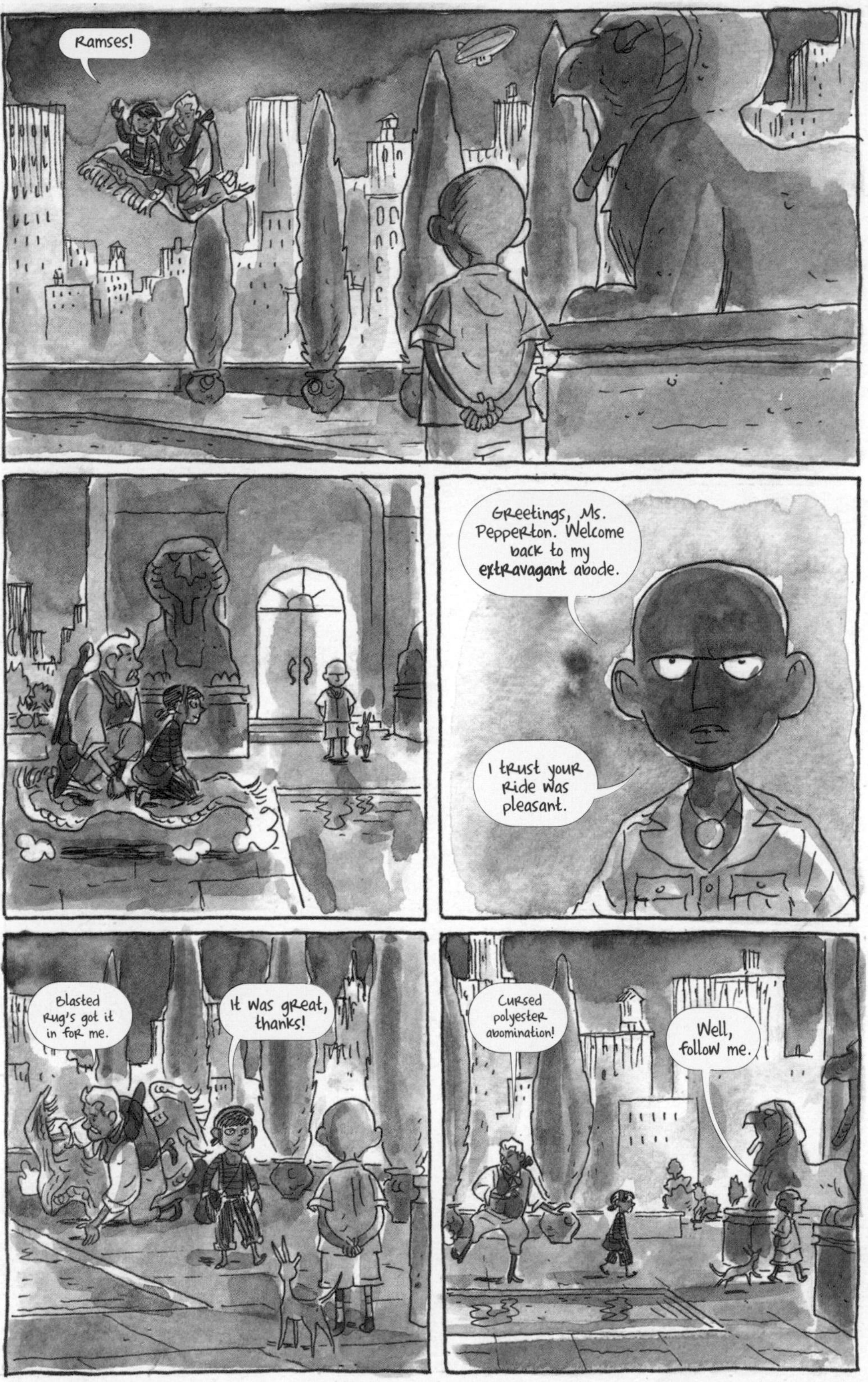
Ramses!
Greetings, Ms. Pepperton. Welcome back to my extravagant abode.
I trust your ride was pleasant.
Blasted Rug's got it in for me.
It was great, thanks!
Cursed polyester abomination!
Well, follow me.

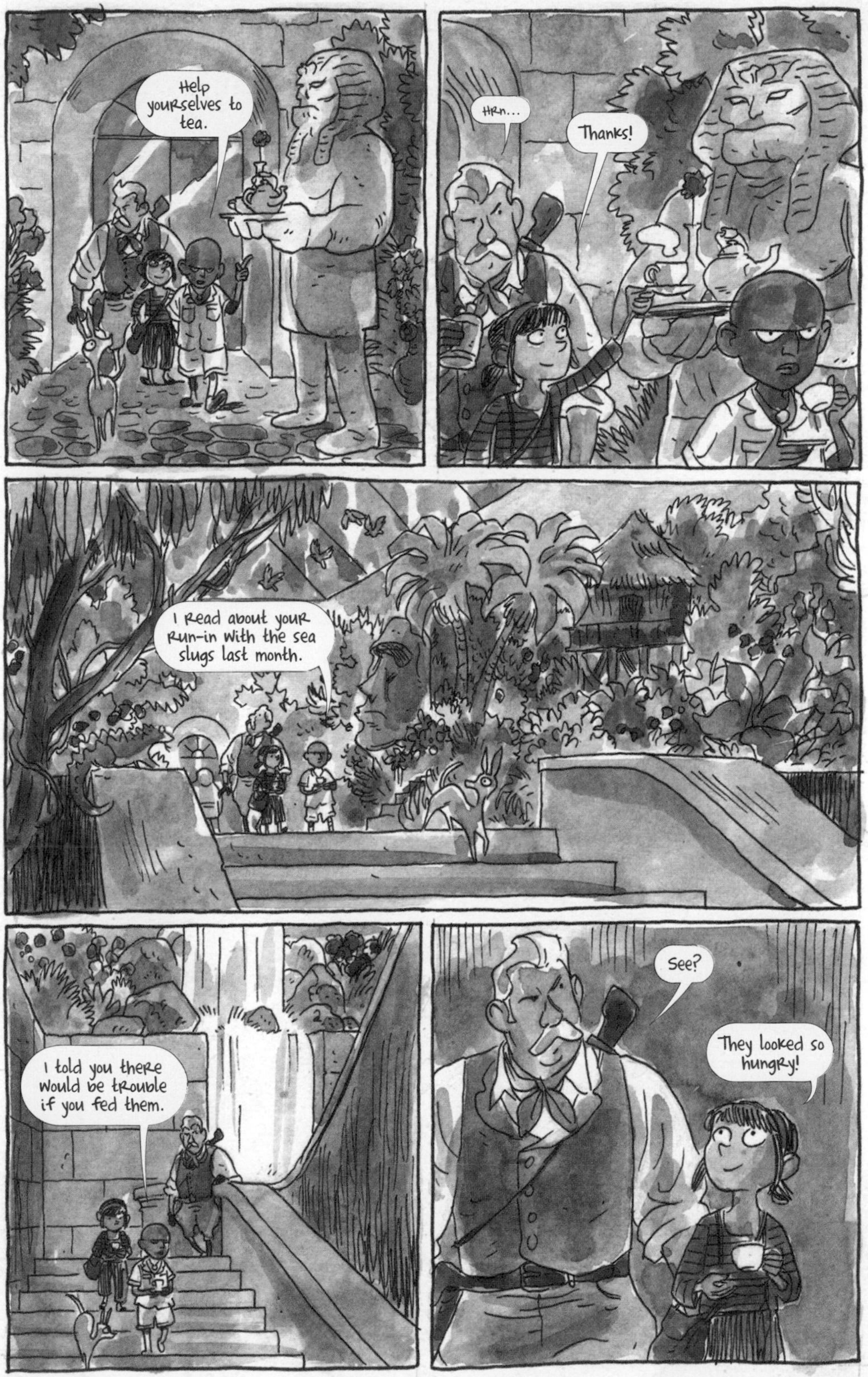
Help yourselves to tea.
HRn...
Thanks!
I Read about your Run-in with the sea slugs last month.
I told you there would be trouble if you fed them.
See?
They looked so hungRy!

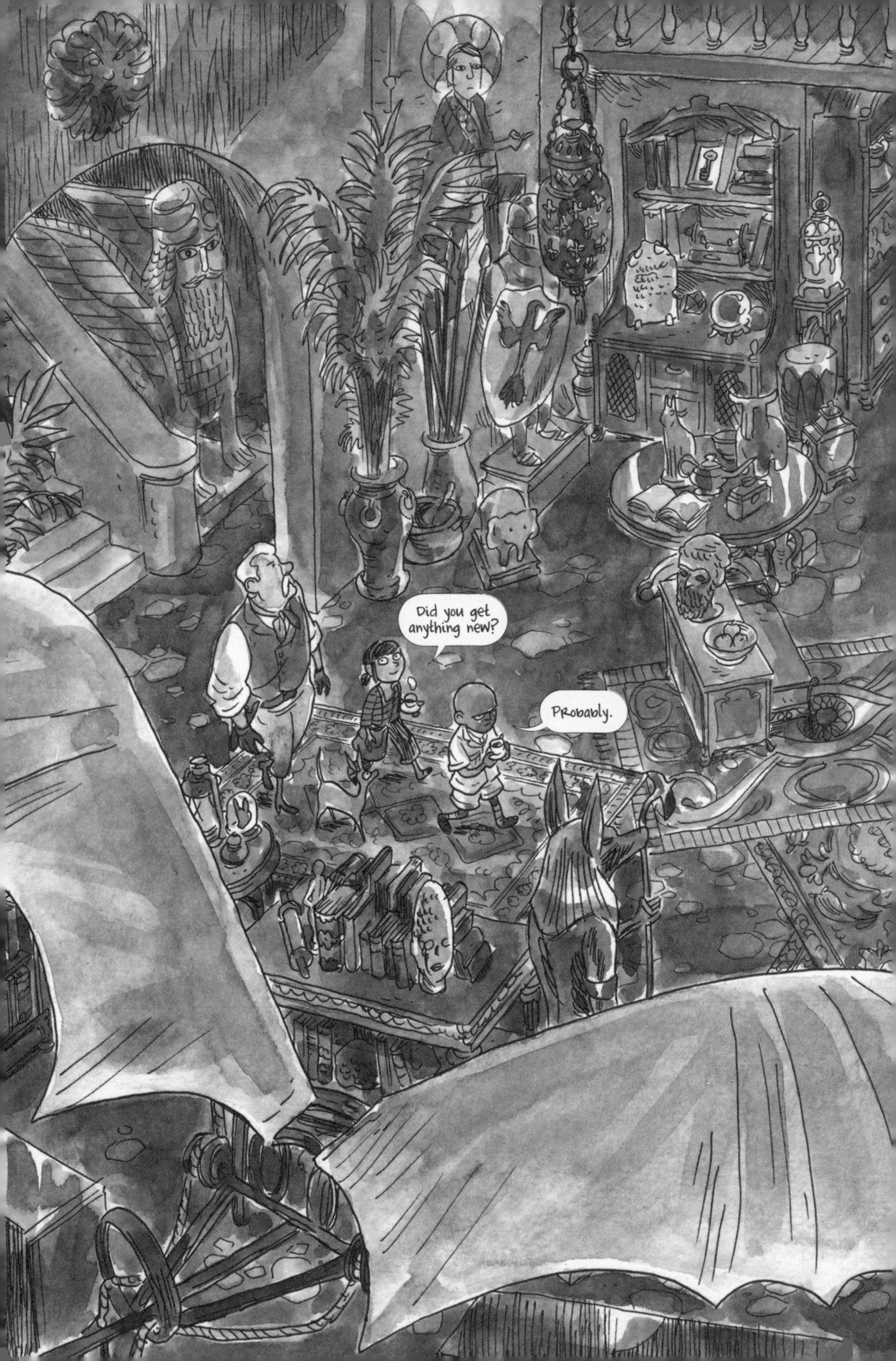
Did you get anything new?
Probably.

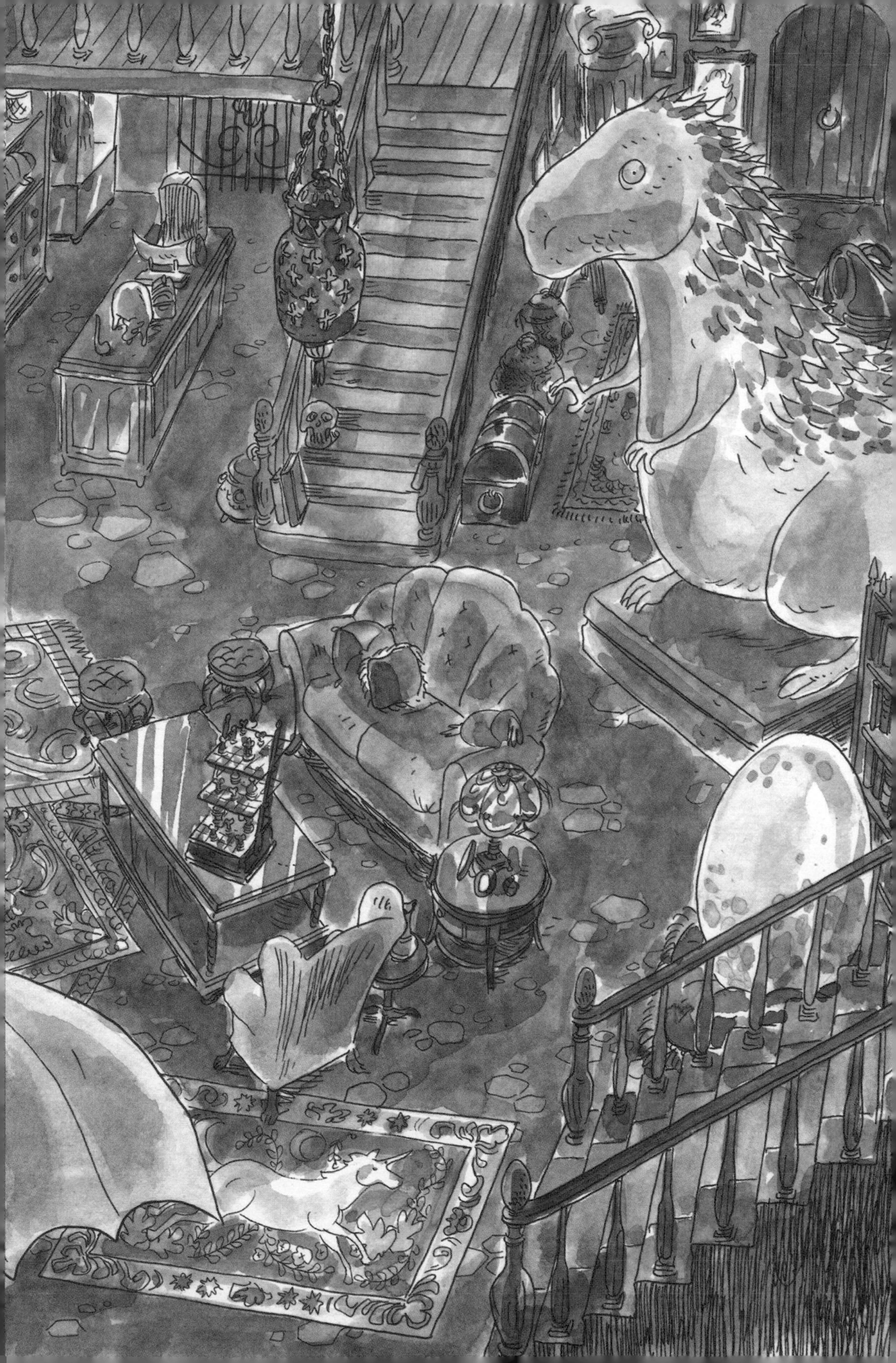

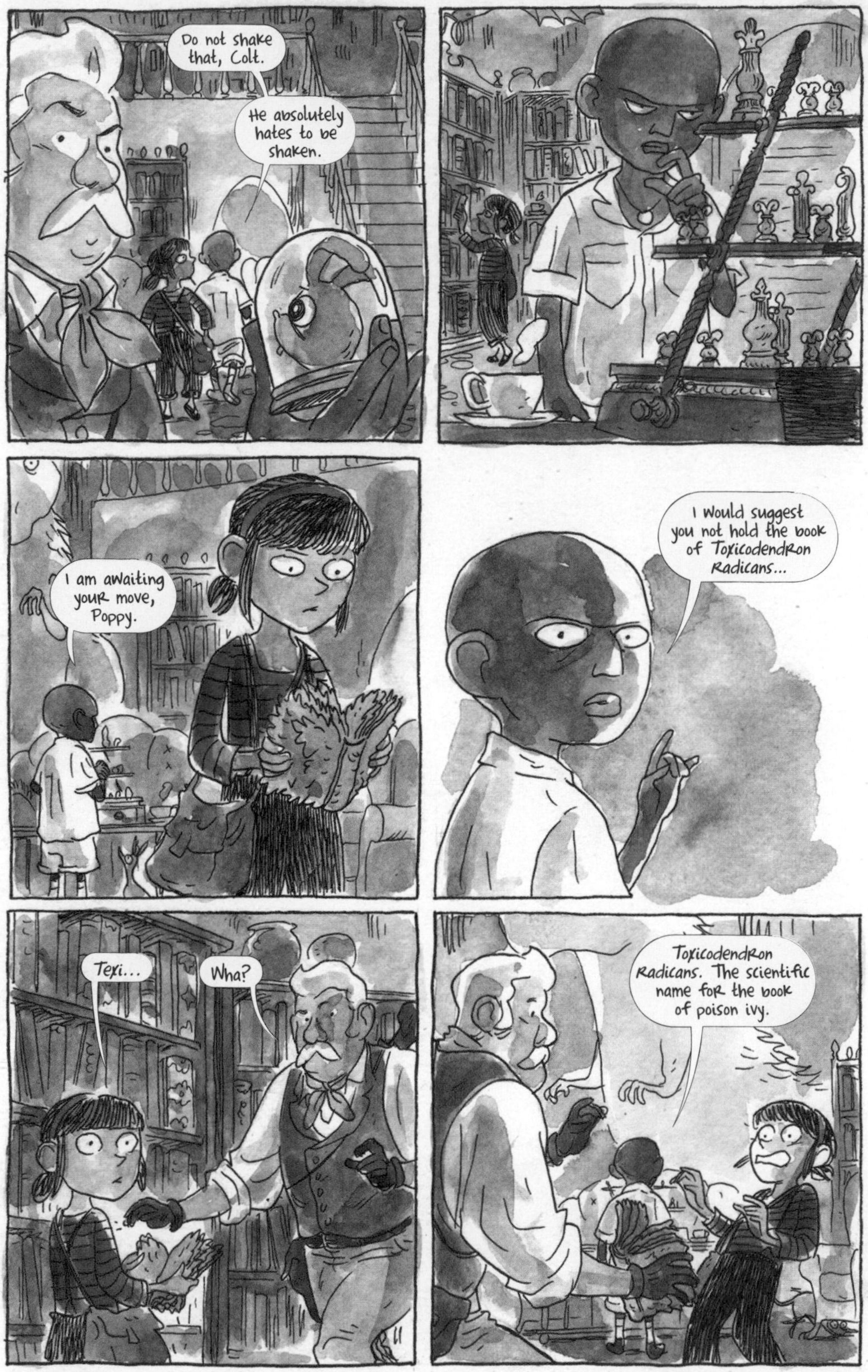
Do not shake that, Colt.
He absolutely hates to be shaken.
I am awaiting your move, Poppy.
I would suggest you not hold the book of Toxicodendron Radicans...
Toxi...
Wha?
Toxicodendron Radicans. The scientific name for the book of poison ivy.

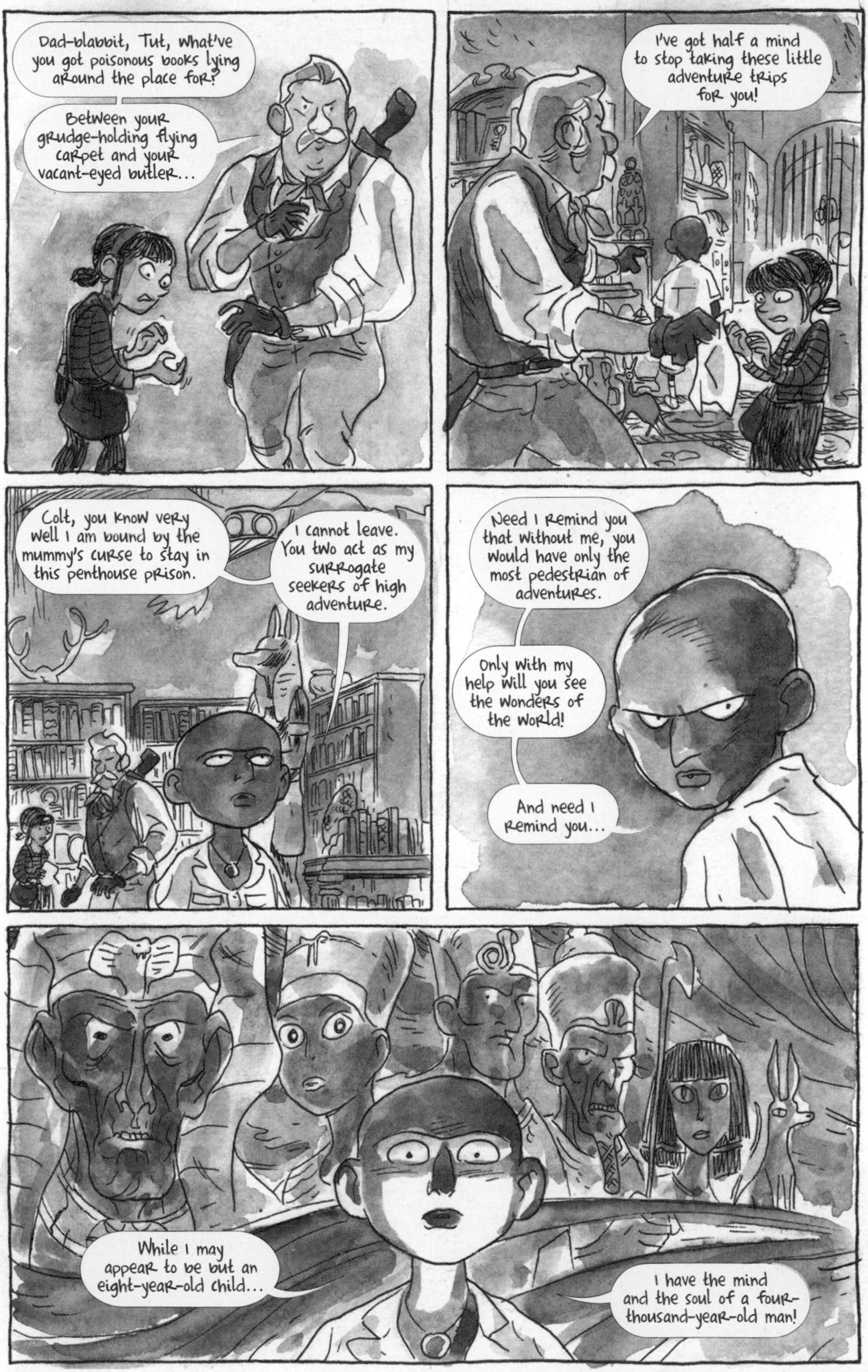

Dad-blabbit, Tut, what've you got poisonous books lying around the place for?
Between your grudge-holding flying carpet and your vacant-eyed butler...
I've got half a mind to stop taking these little adventure trips for you!
Colt, you know very well I am bound by the mummy's curse to stay in this penthouse prison.
I cannot leave. You two act as my surrogate seekers of high adventure.
Need I remind you that without me, you would have only the most pedestrian of adventures.
Only with my help will you see the wonders of the world!
And need I remind you...
While I may appear to be but an eight-year-old child...
I have the mind and the soul of a four-thousand-year-old man!

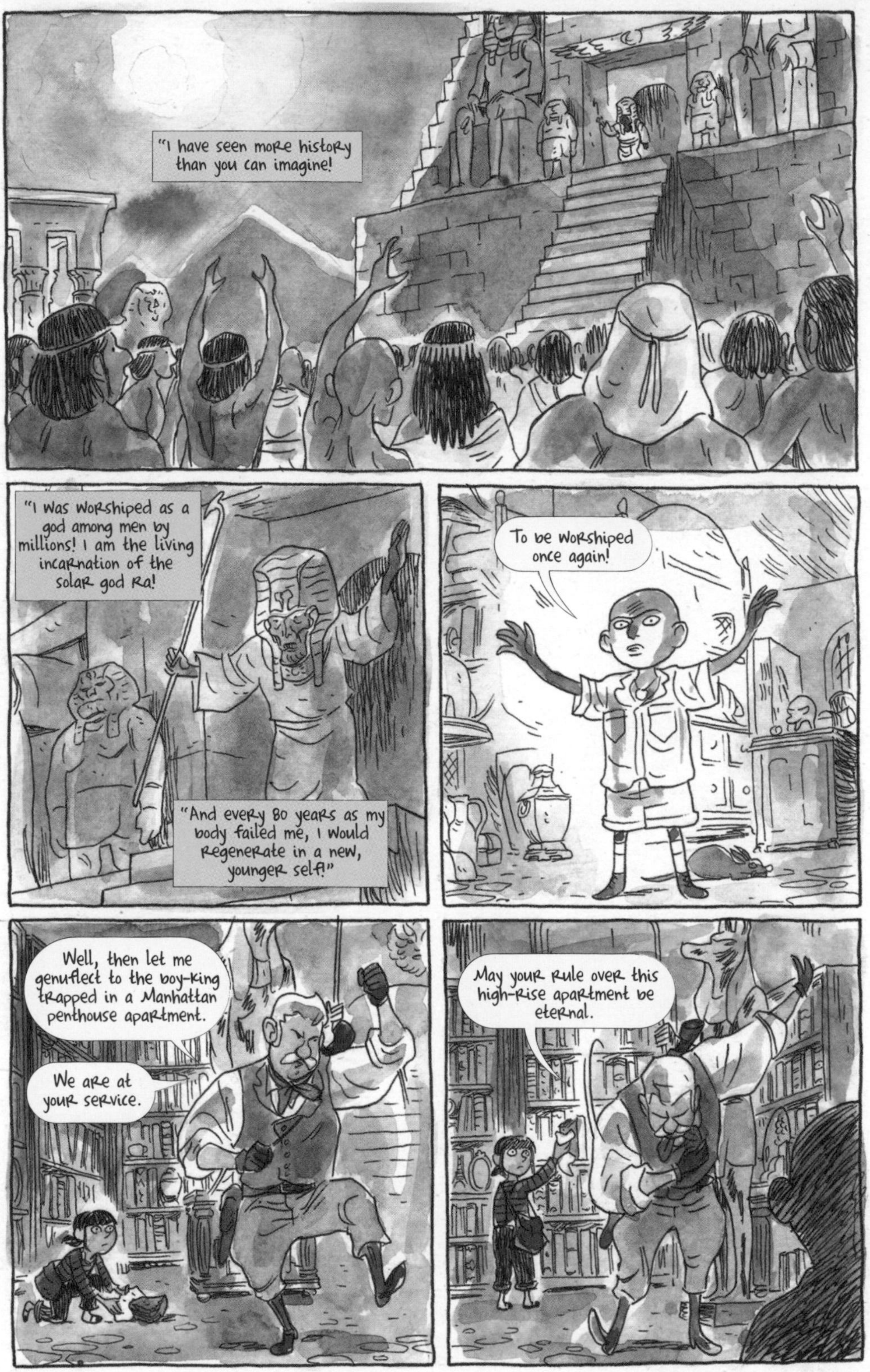

"I have seen more history than you can imagine!
"I was worshiped as a god among men by millions! I am the living incarnation of the solar god Ra!
"And every 80 years as my body failed me, I would regenerate in a new, younger self!"
To be worshiped once again!
Well, then let me genuflect to the boy-king trapped in a Manhattan penthouse apartment.
We are at your service.
May your rule over this high-rise apartment be eternal.

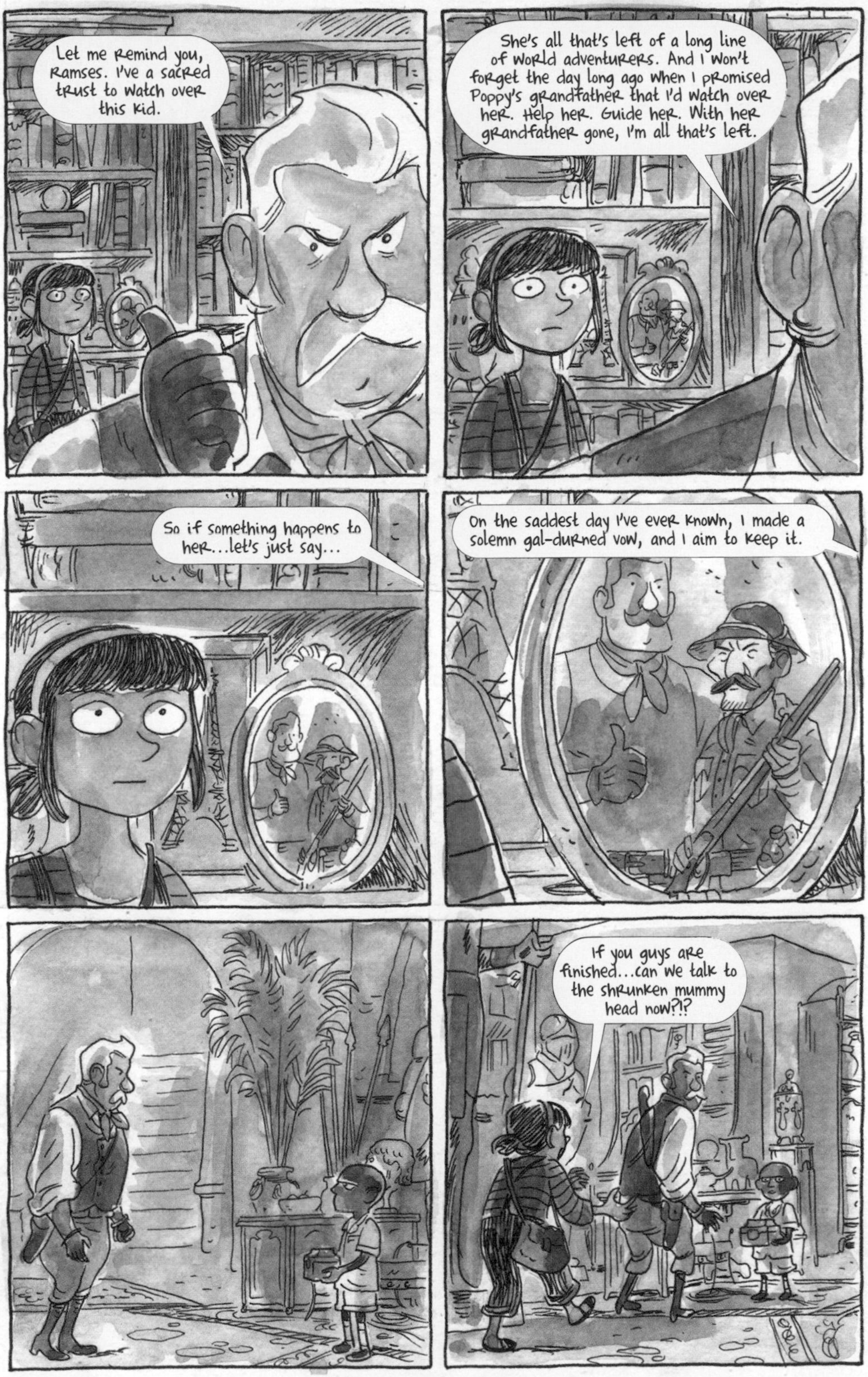
Let me remind you, Ramses. I've a sacred trust to watch over this kid.
She's all that's left of a long line of world adventurers. And I won't forget the day long ago when I promised Poppy's grandfather that I'd watch over her. Help her. Guide her. With her grandfather gone, I'm all that's left.
So if something happens to her...let's just say...
On the saddest day I've ever known, I made a solemn gal-durned vow, and I aim to keep it.
If you guys are finished...can we talk to the shrunken mummy head now?!?

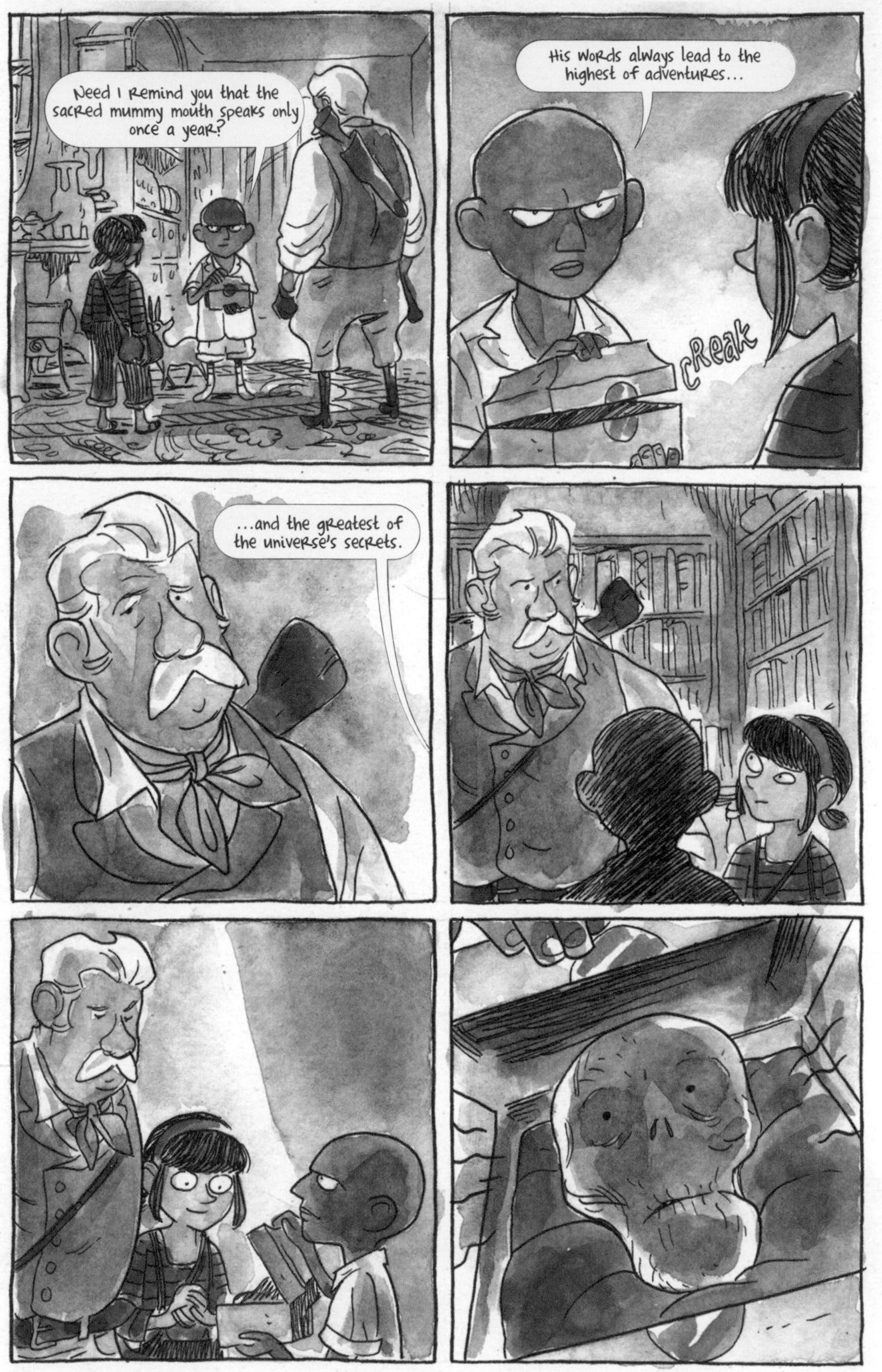
Need I remind you that the sacred mummy mouth speaks only once a year?
His words always lead to the highest of adventures...
cReak
...and the greatest of the universe's secrets.

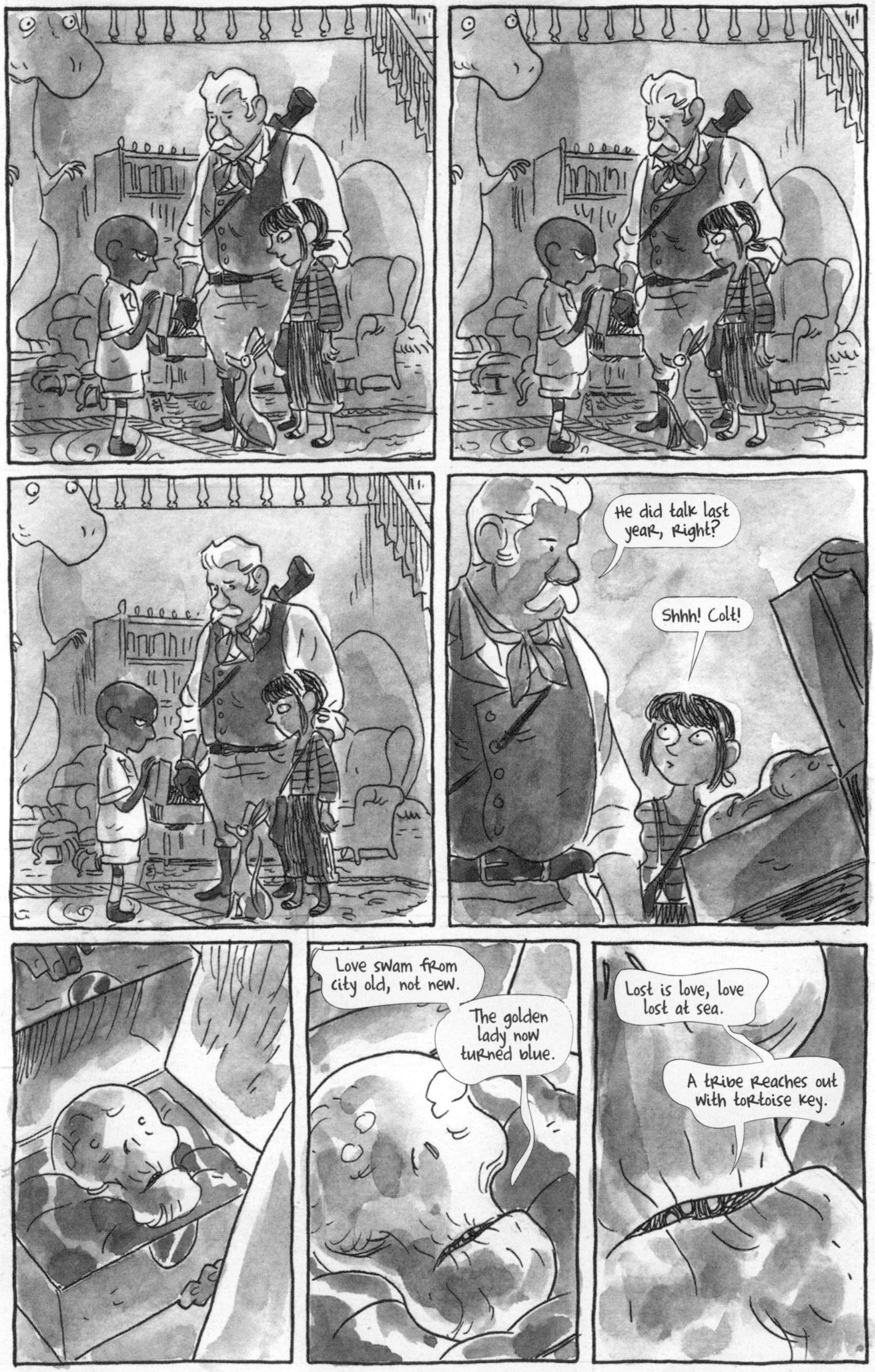
He did talk last year, right?
Shhh! Colt!
Love swam from city old, not new.
The golden lady now turned blue.
Lost is love, love lost at sea.
A tribe reaches out with tortoise key.

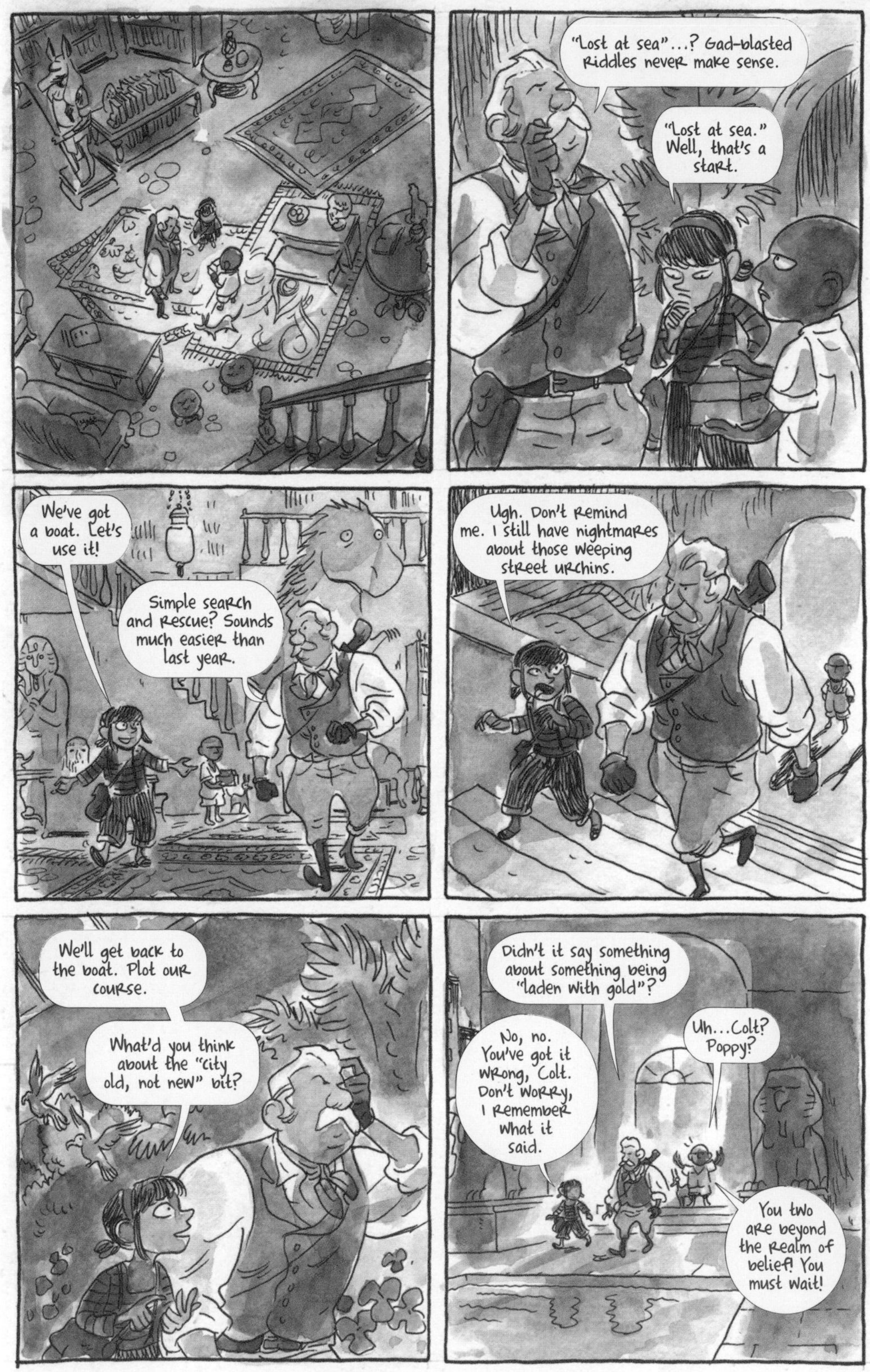
"Lost at sea"...? Gad-blasted Riddles never make sense.
"Lost at sea." Well, that's a start.
We've got a boat. Let's use it!
Simple search and Rescue? Sounds much easier than last year.
Ugh. Don't Remind me. I still have nightmares about those weeping street urchins.
We'll get back to the boat. Plot our course.
What'd you think about the "city old, not new" bit?
Didn't it say something about something being "laden with gold"?
No, no. You've got it wRong, Colt. Don't woRRy, I RememBeR what it said.
Uh...Colt? Poppy?
You two are beyond the Realm of belief! You must wait!

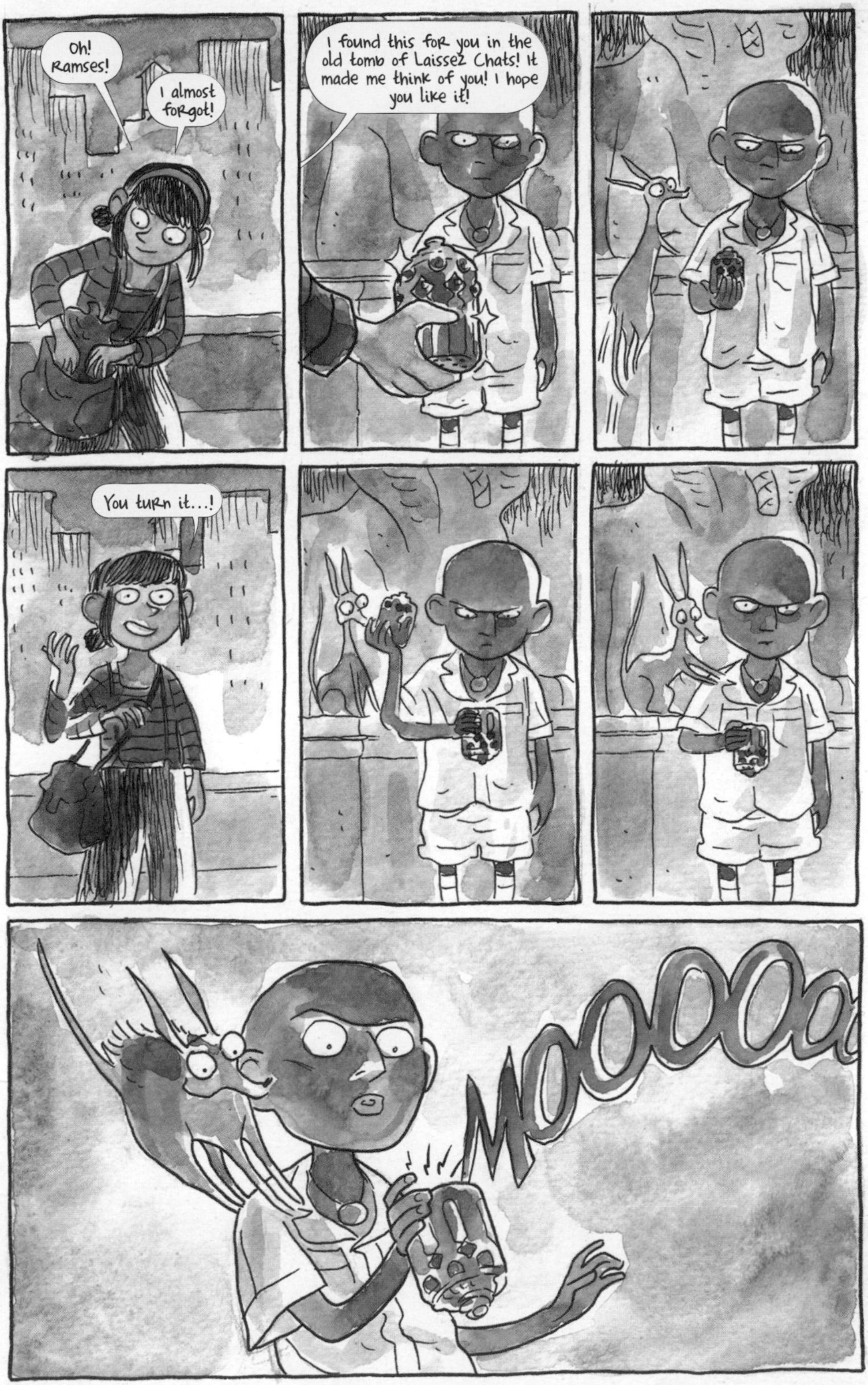
Oh! Ramses!
I almost forgot!
I found this for you in the old tomb of Laissez Chats! It made me think of you! I hope you like it!
You turn it...!
MOOOOa

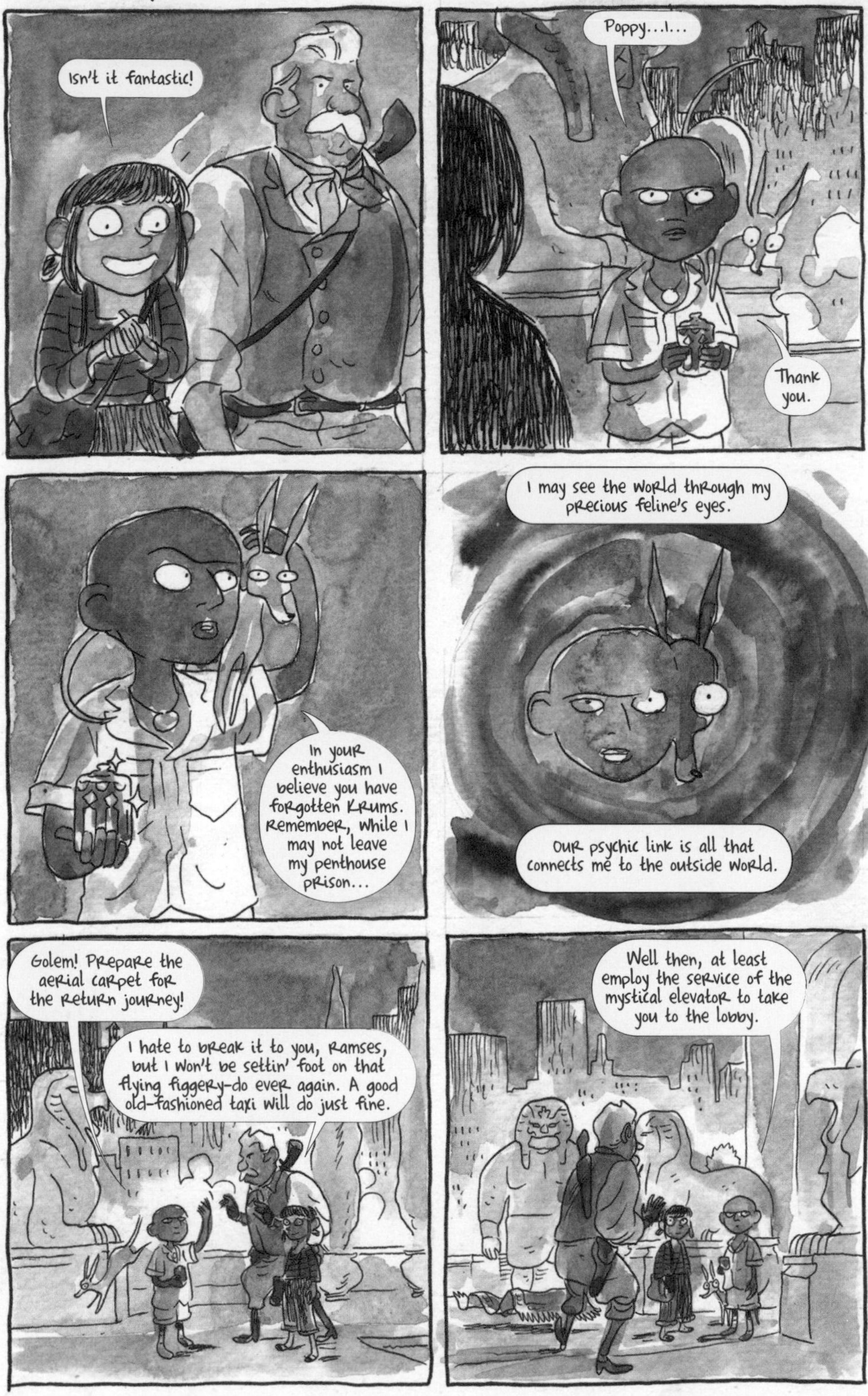
Isn't it fantastic!
Poppy...I...
Thank you.
In your enthusiasm I believe you have forgotten Krums. Remember, while I may not leave my penthouse prison...
I may see the world through my precious feline's eyes.
Our psychic link is all that connects me to the outside world.
Golem! Prepare the aerial carpet for the return journey!
I hate to break it to you, Ramses, but I won't be settin' foot on that flying figgery-do ever again. A good old-fashioned taxi will do just fine.
Well then, at least employ the service of the mystical elevator to take you to the lobby.

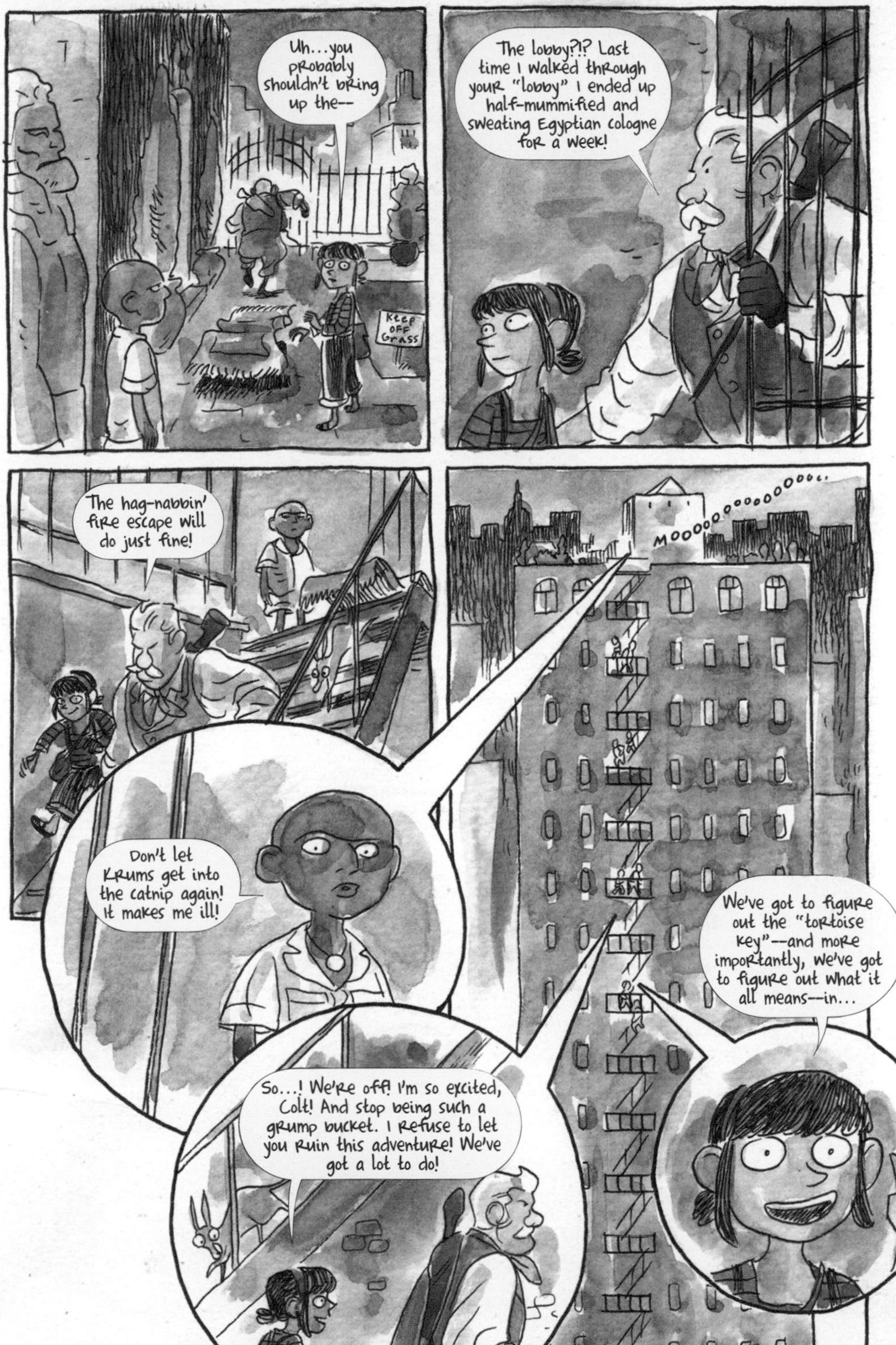
Uh...you probably shouldn't bring up the--
The lobby?!? Last time I walked through your "lobby" I ended up half-mummified and sweating Egyptian cologne for a week!
Keep off Grass
The hag-nabbin' fire escape will do just fine!
MOOOOOOOOOOOOOOooo...
Don't let Krums get into the catnip again! It makes me ill!
We've got to figure out the "tortoise key"--and more importantly, we've got to figure out what it all means--in...
So...! We're off! I'm so excited, Colt! And stop being such a grump bucket. I refuse to let you ruin this adventure! We've got a lot to do!

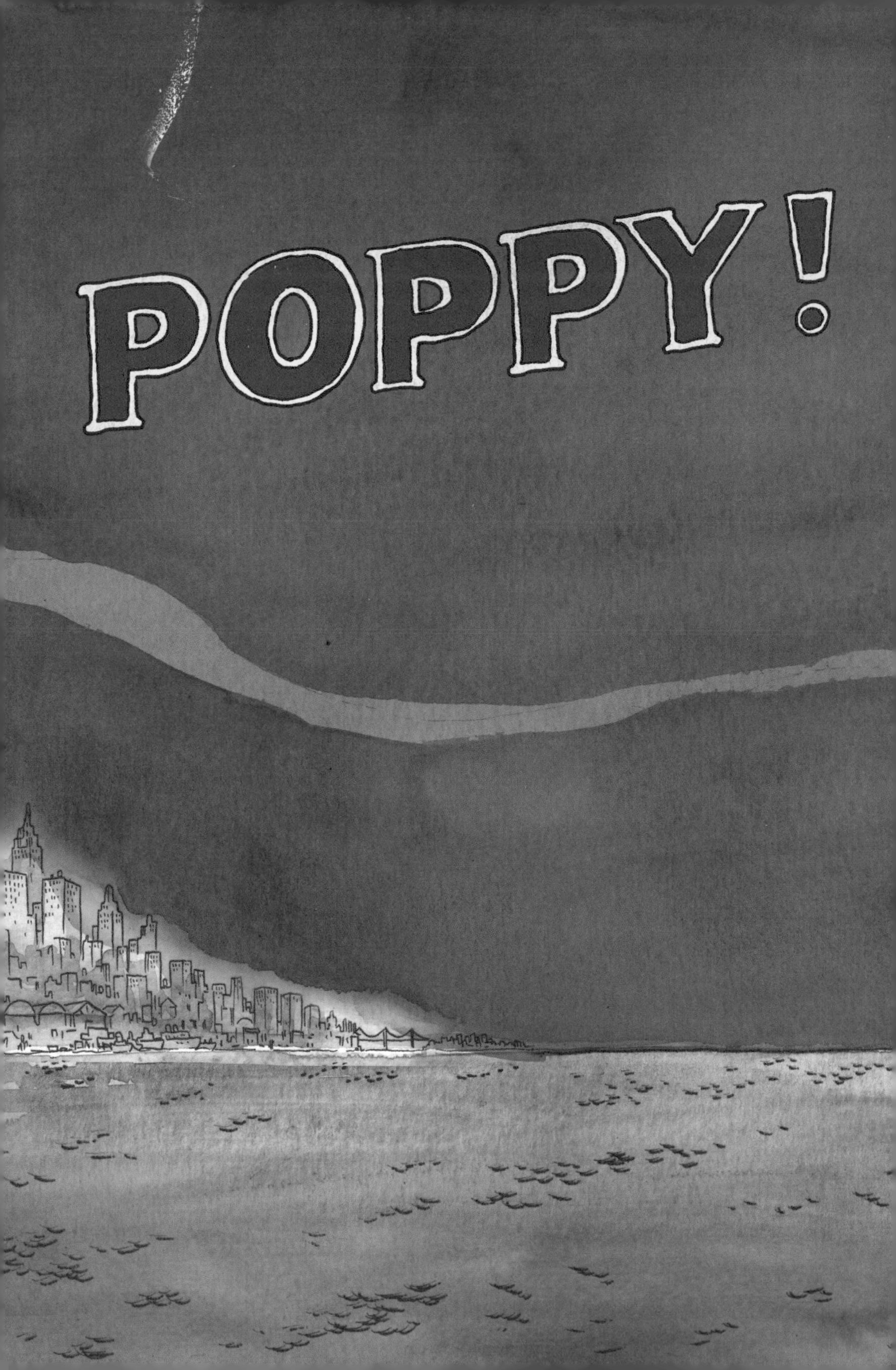
POPPY!

and the Lost Lagoon™

Story
Matt Kindt
Brian Hurtt

Script and Colors
Matt Kindt

Art
Brian Hurtt

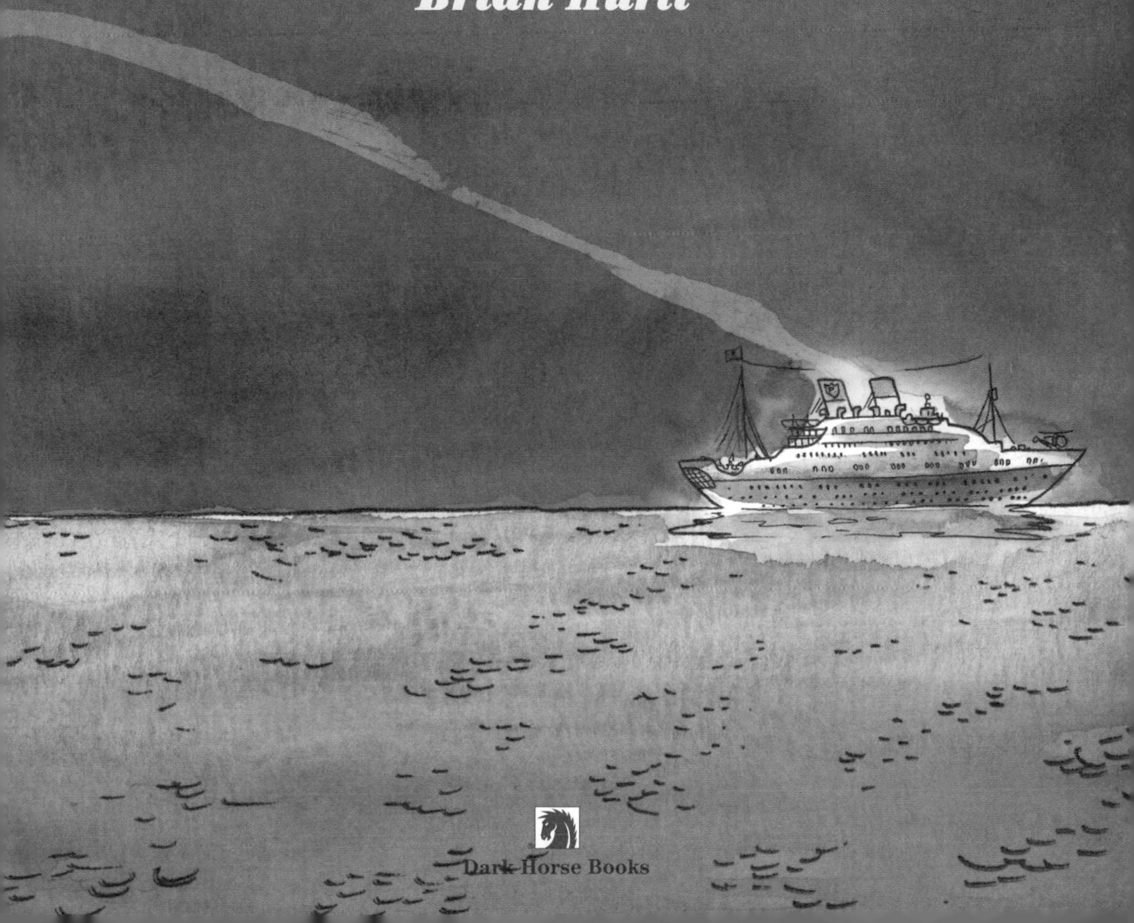

Dark Horse Books

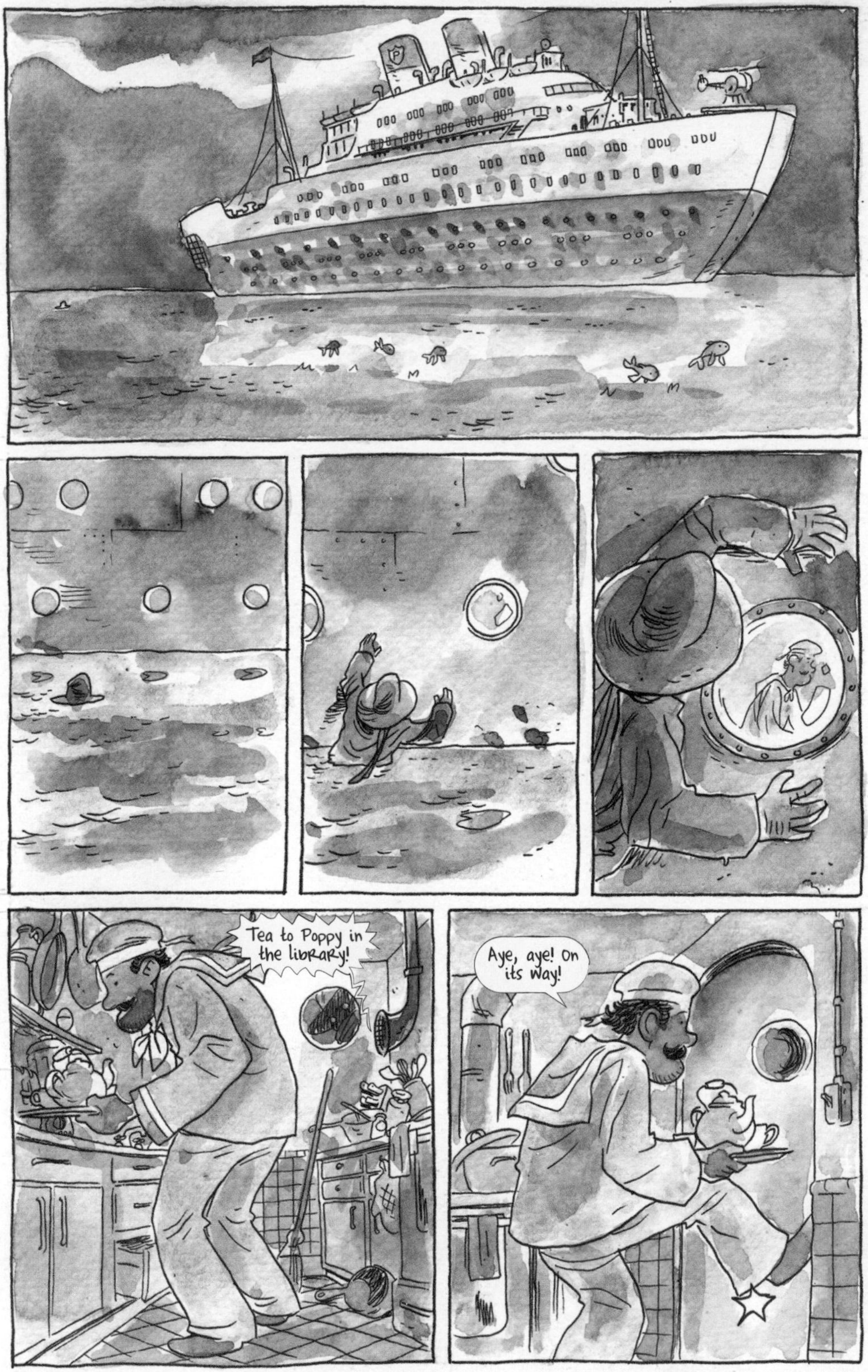
Tea to Poppy in the library!
Aye, aye! On its way!

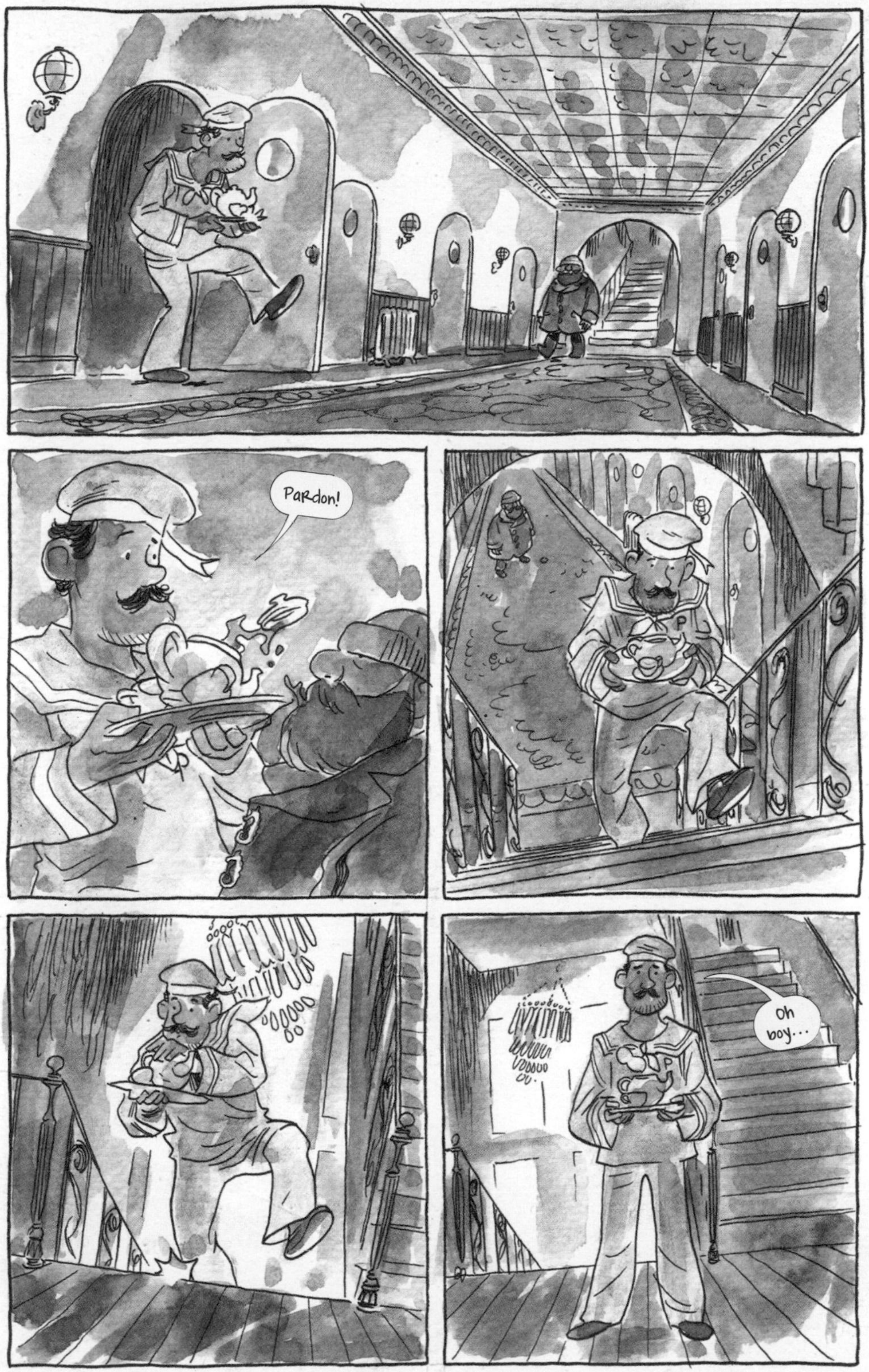
Pardon!
Oh boy...

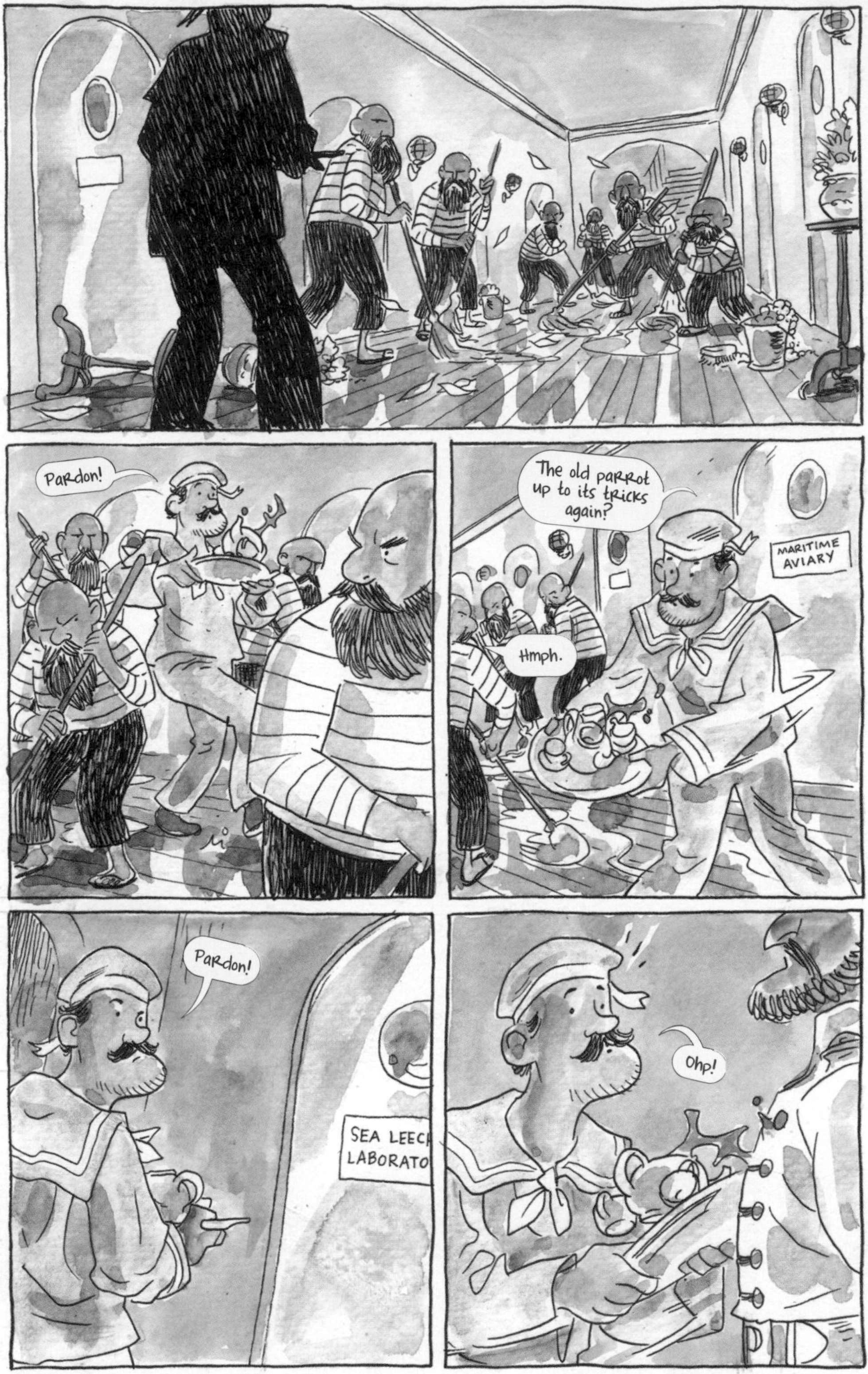
Pardon!
The old parrot up to its tricks again?
MARITIME AVIARY
Hmph.
Pardon!
SEA LEECH
LABORATO
Ohp!

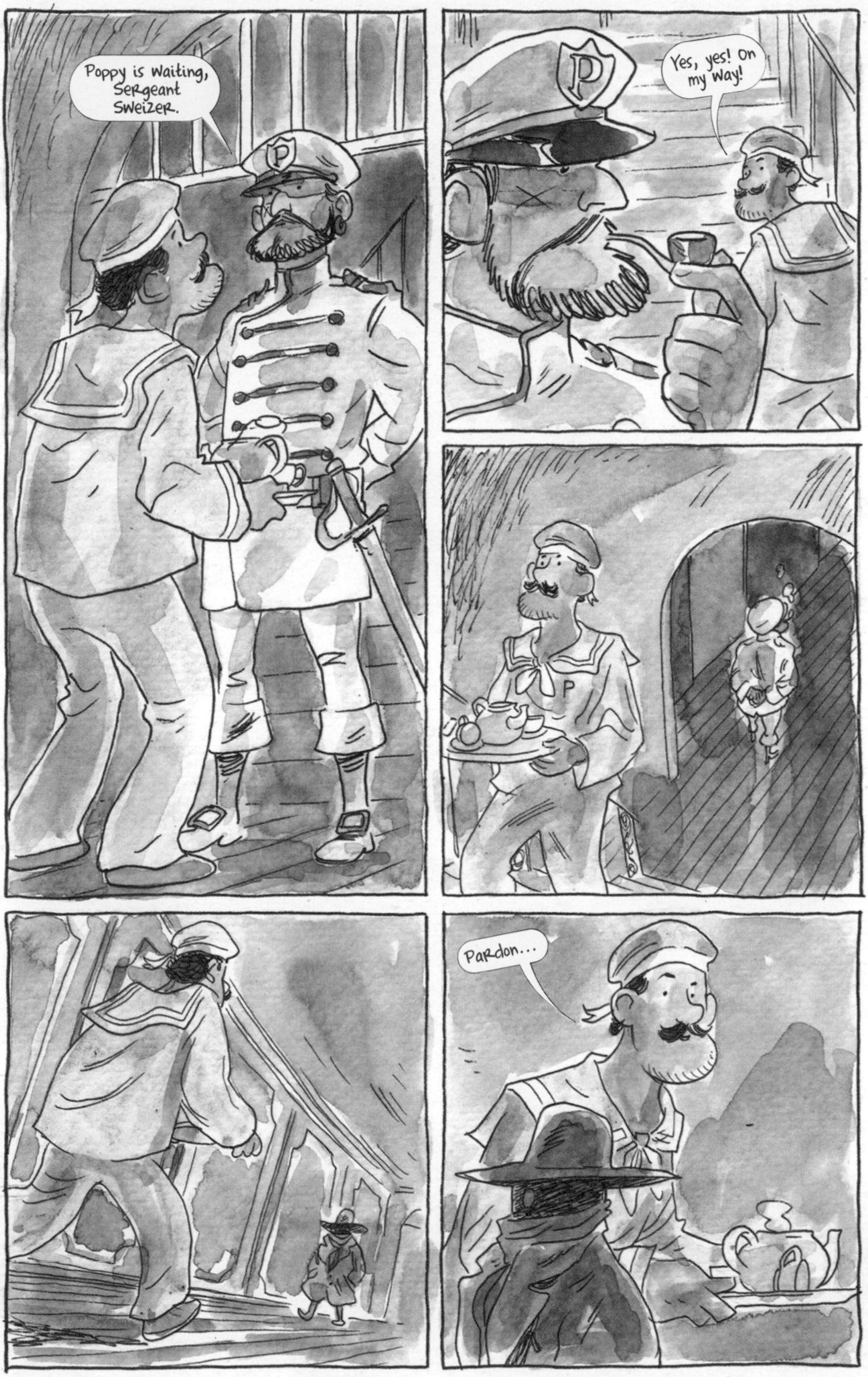
Poppy is Waiting, Sergeant Sweizer.
Yes, yes! On my way!
Pardon...

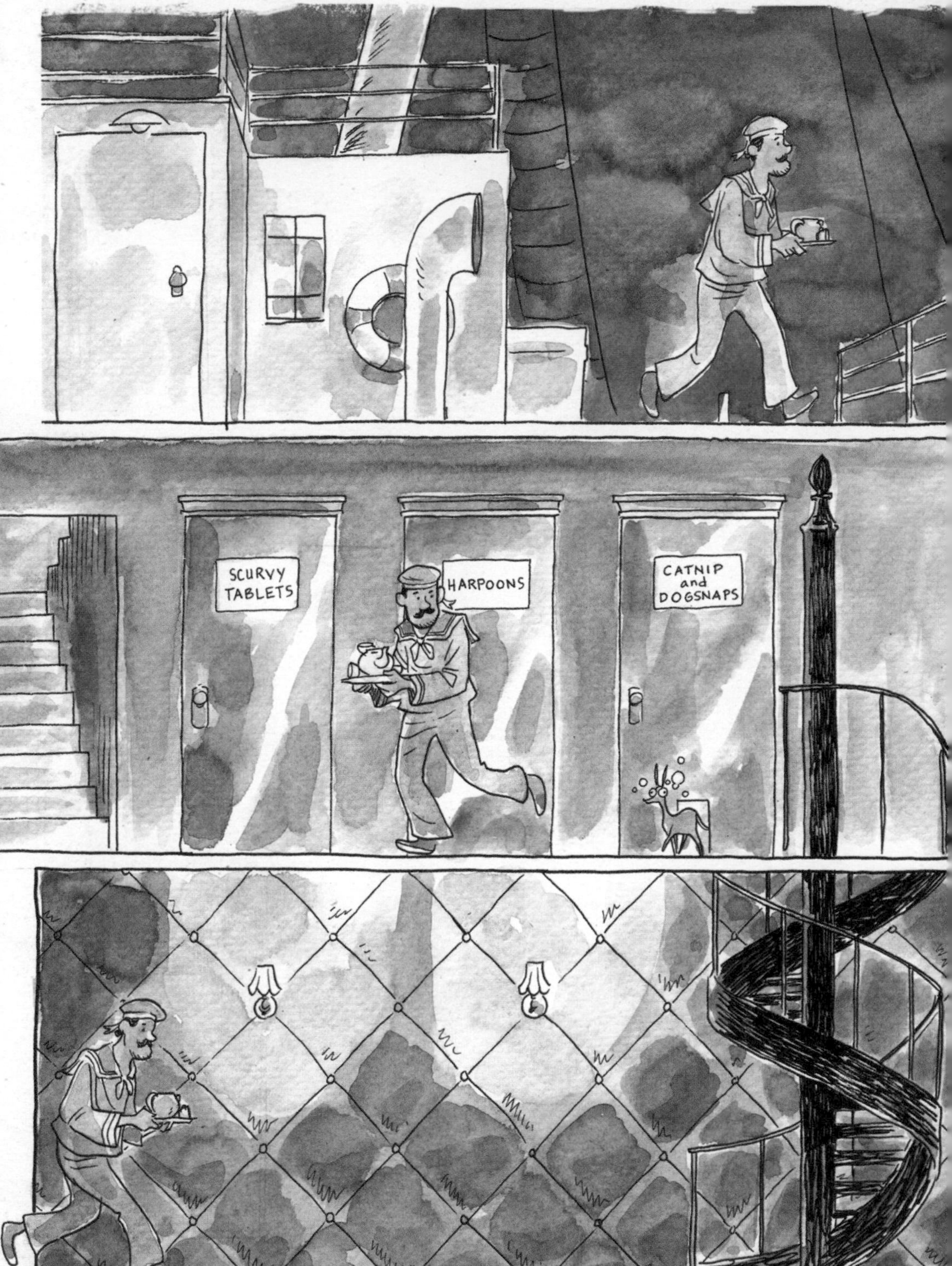
SCURVY TABLETS
HARPOONS
CATNIP and DOGSNAPS

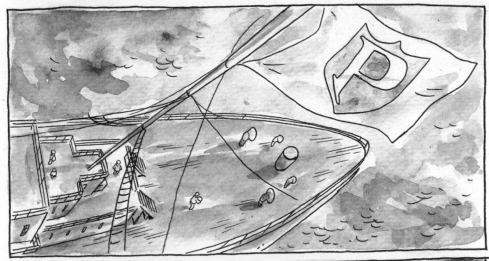

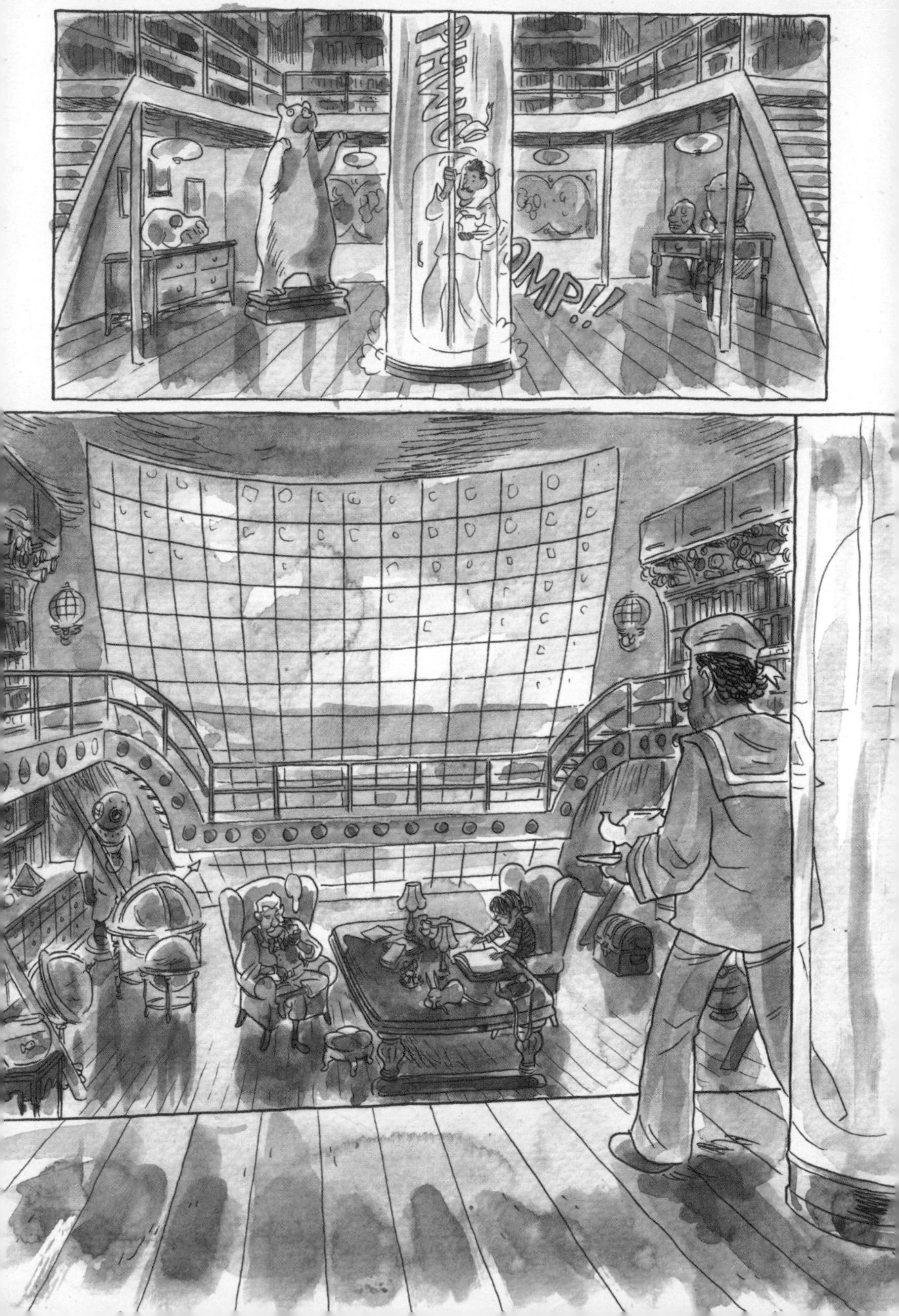
OMP!!

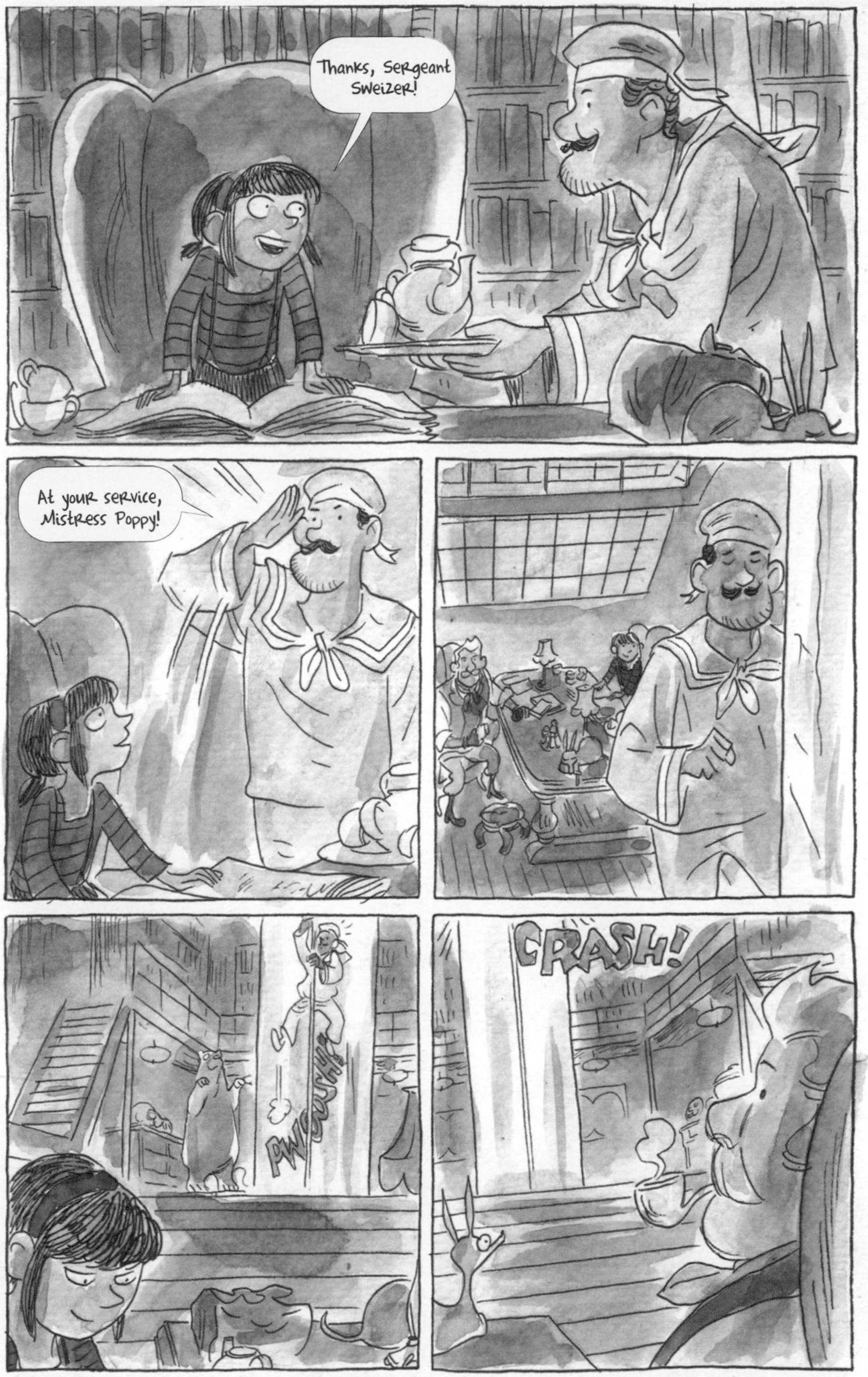
Thanks, Sergeant Sweizer!
At your service, Mistress Poppy!
CRASH!

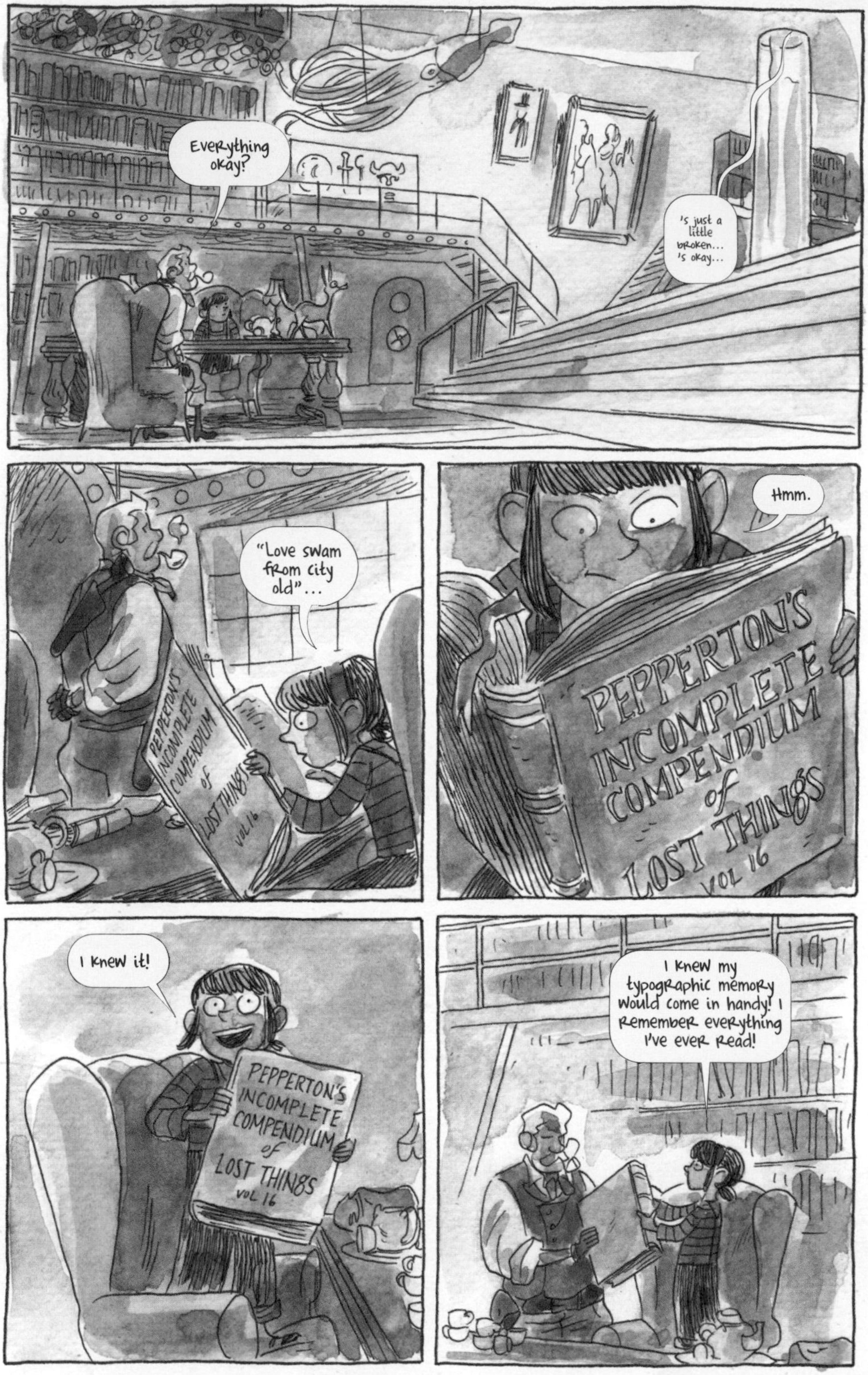
Everything okay?
'S just a little broken... 'S okay...
"Love swam from city old"...
PEPPERTON'S INCOMPLETE COMPENDIUM of LOST THINGS VOL 16
Hmm.
PEPPERTON'S INCOMPLETE COMPENDIUM of LOST THINGS VOL 16
I knew it!
PEPPERTON'S INCOMPLETE COMPENDIUM of LOST THINGS VOL 16
I knew my typographic memory would come in handy! I remember everything I've ever read!

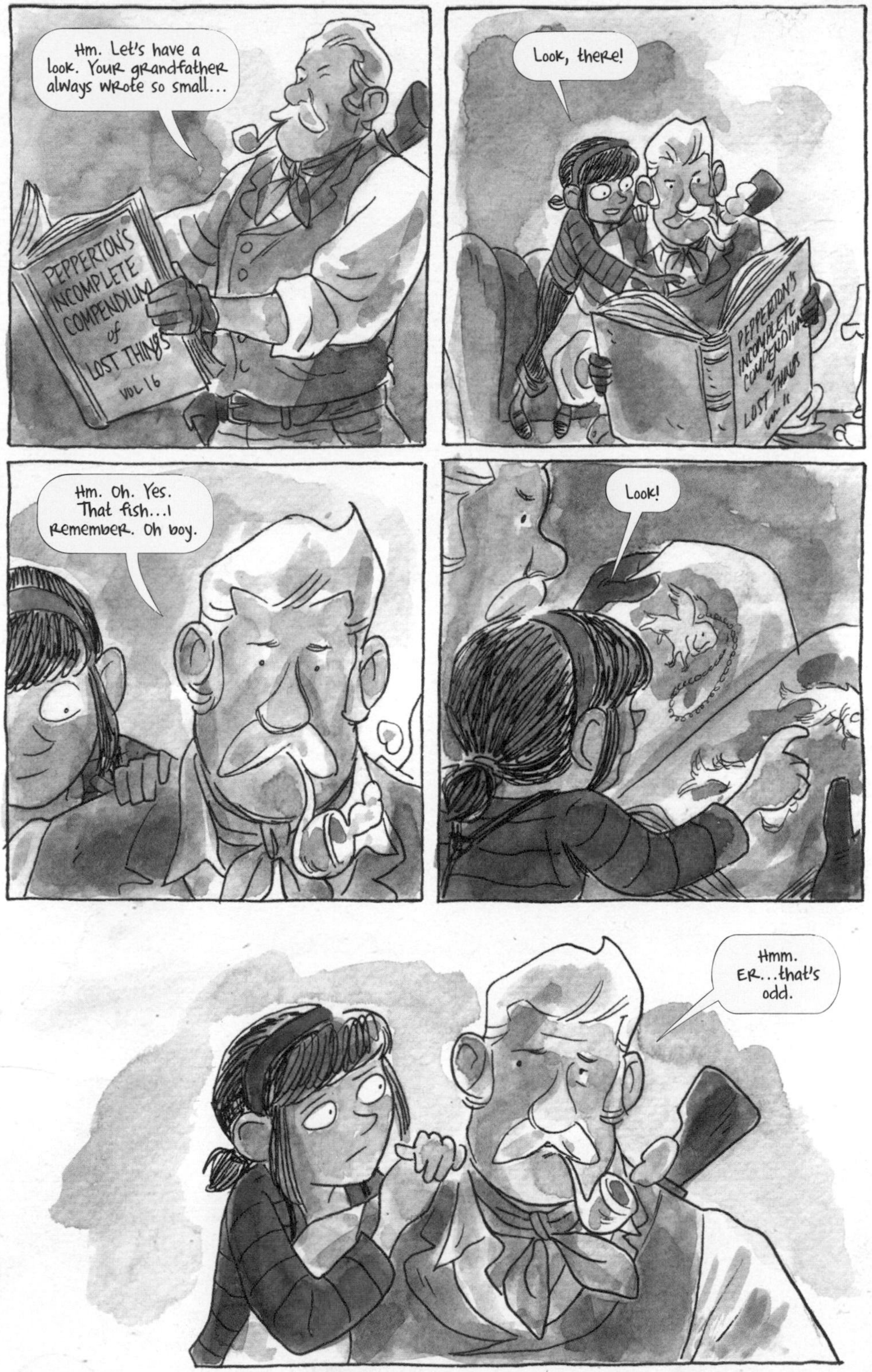
Hm. Let's have a look. Your grandfather always wrote so small...
PEPPERTON'S INCOMPLETE COMPENDIUM of LOST THINGS
VOL 16
Look, there!
PEPPERTON'S INCOMPLETE COMPENDIUM of LOST THINGS
Hm. Oh. Yes. That fish...I remember. Oh boy.
Look!
Hmm. Er...that's odd.

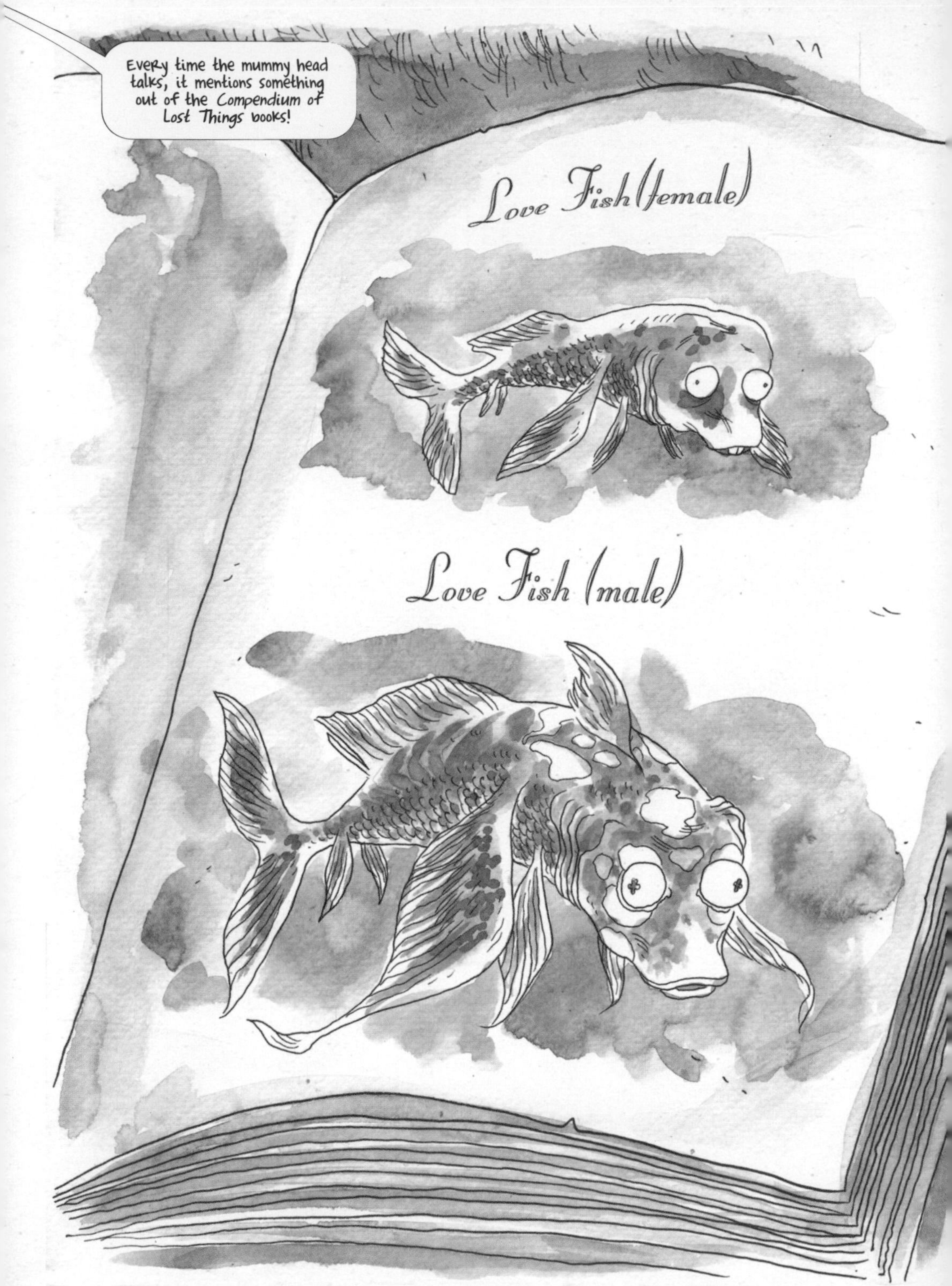
Every time the mummy head talks, it mentions something out of the Compendium of Lost Things books!
Love Fish (female)
Love Fish (male)

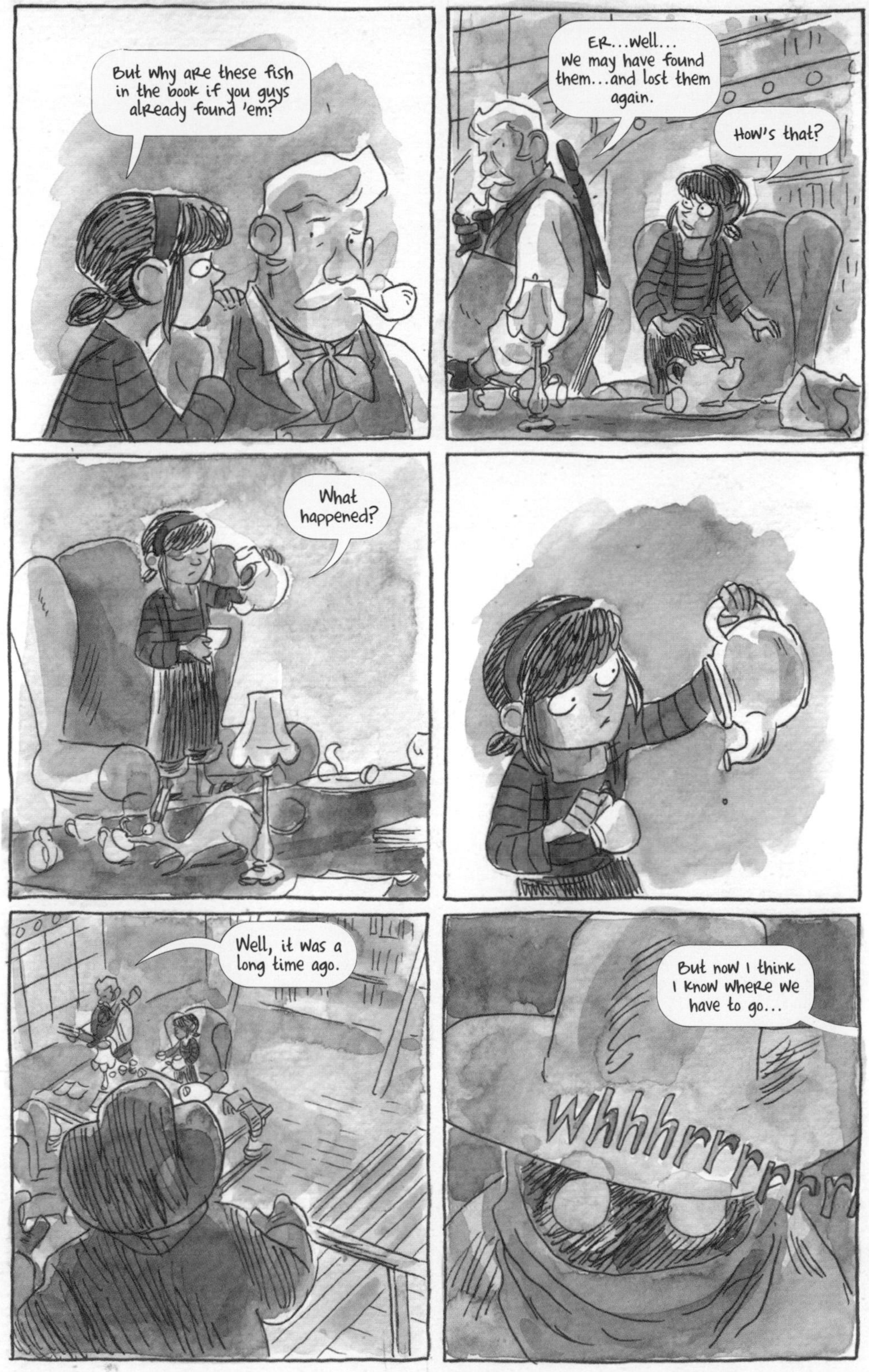
But why are these fish in the book if you guys already found 'em?
Er...well... we may have found them...and lost them again.
How's that?
What happened?
Well, it was a long time ago.
But now I think I know where we have to go...
Whhhrrrrrr

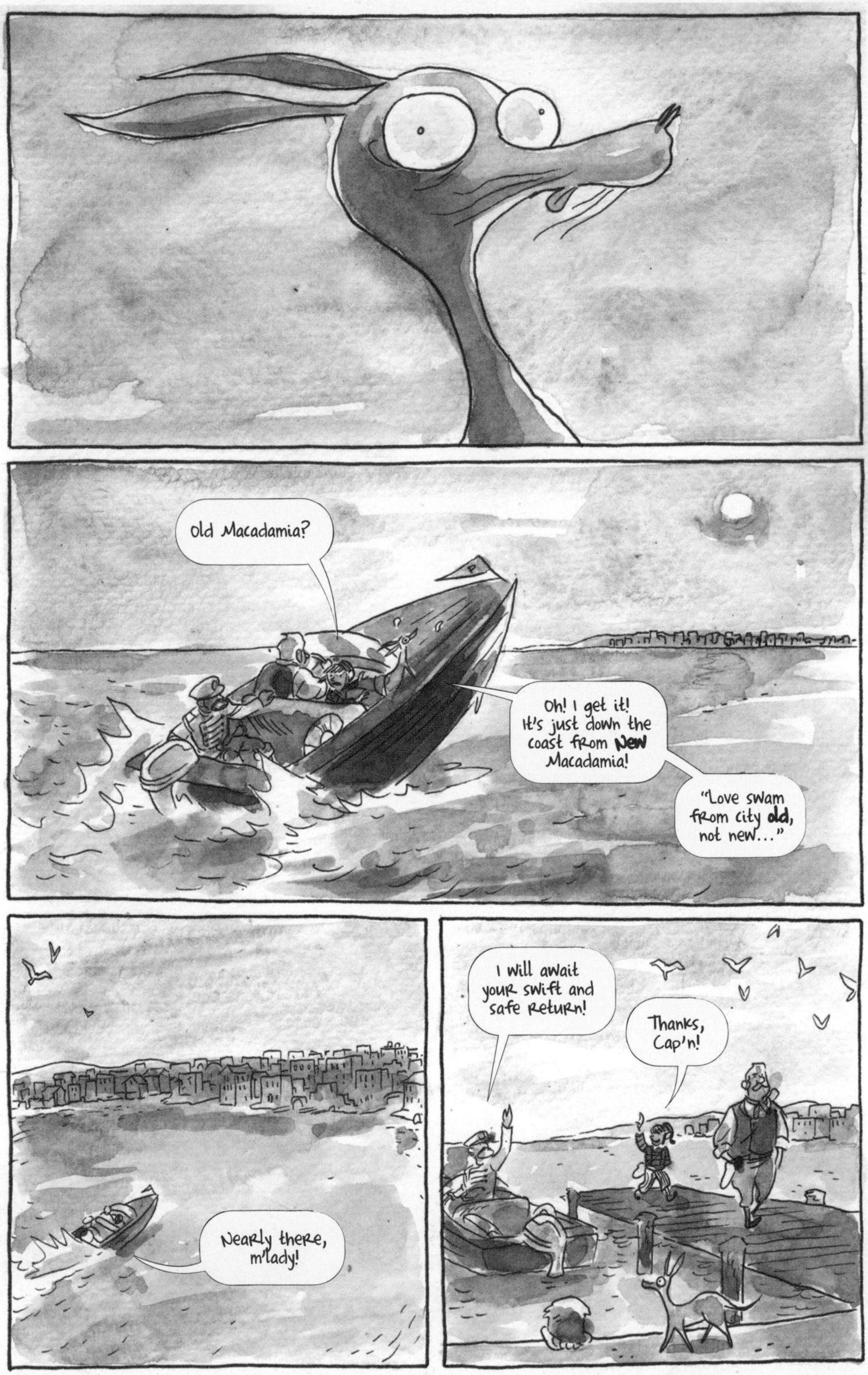

Old Macadamia?
Oh! I get it! It's just down the coast from NEW Macadamia!
"Love swam from city old, not new..."
Nearly there, m'lady!
I will await your swift and safe return!
Thanks, Cap'n!

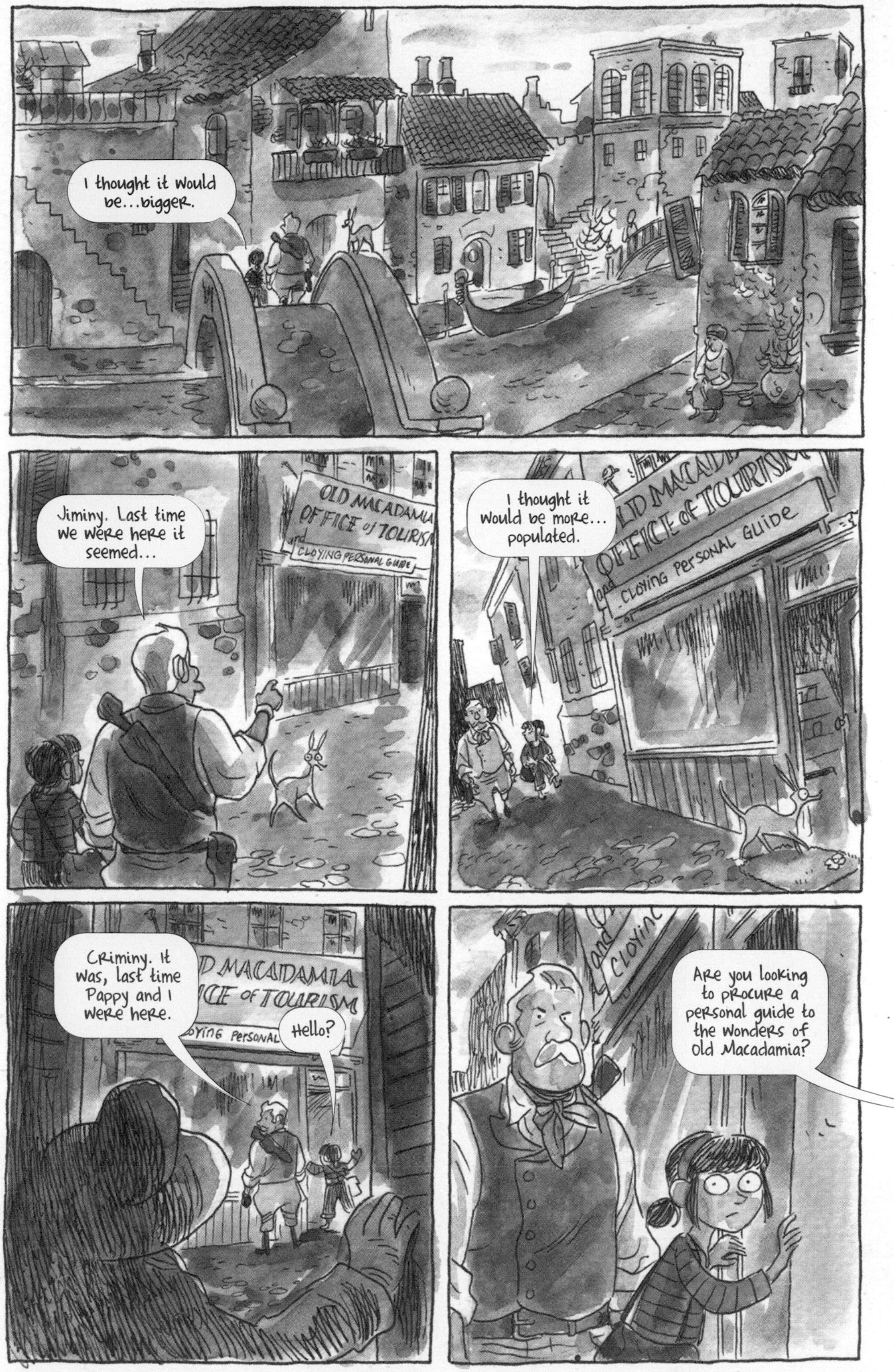
I thought it would be...bigger.
OLD MACADAMIA
OFFICE of TOURISM
and
CLOYING PERSONAL GUIDE
Jiminy. Last time we were here it seemed...
I thought it would be more... populated.
OFFICE of TOURISM
CLOYING PERSONAL GUIDE
Criminy. It was, last time Pappy and I were here.
Hello?
Are you looking to procure a personal guide to the wonders of Old Macadamia?

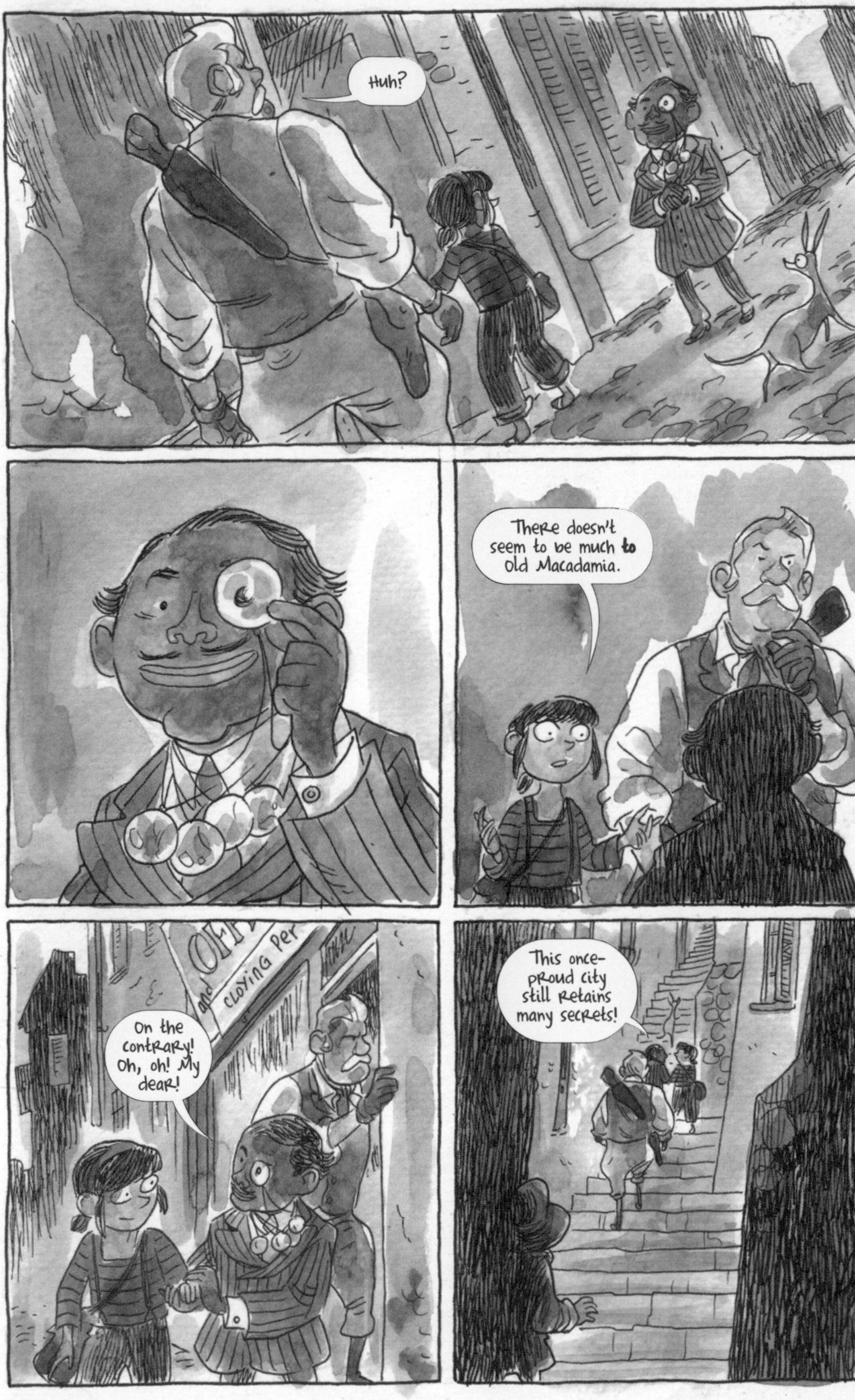
Huh?
There doesn't seem to be much to Old Macadamia.
On the contrary! Oh, oh! My dear!
This once-proud city still retains many secrets!

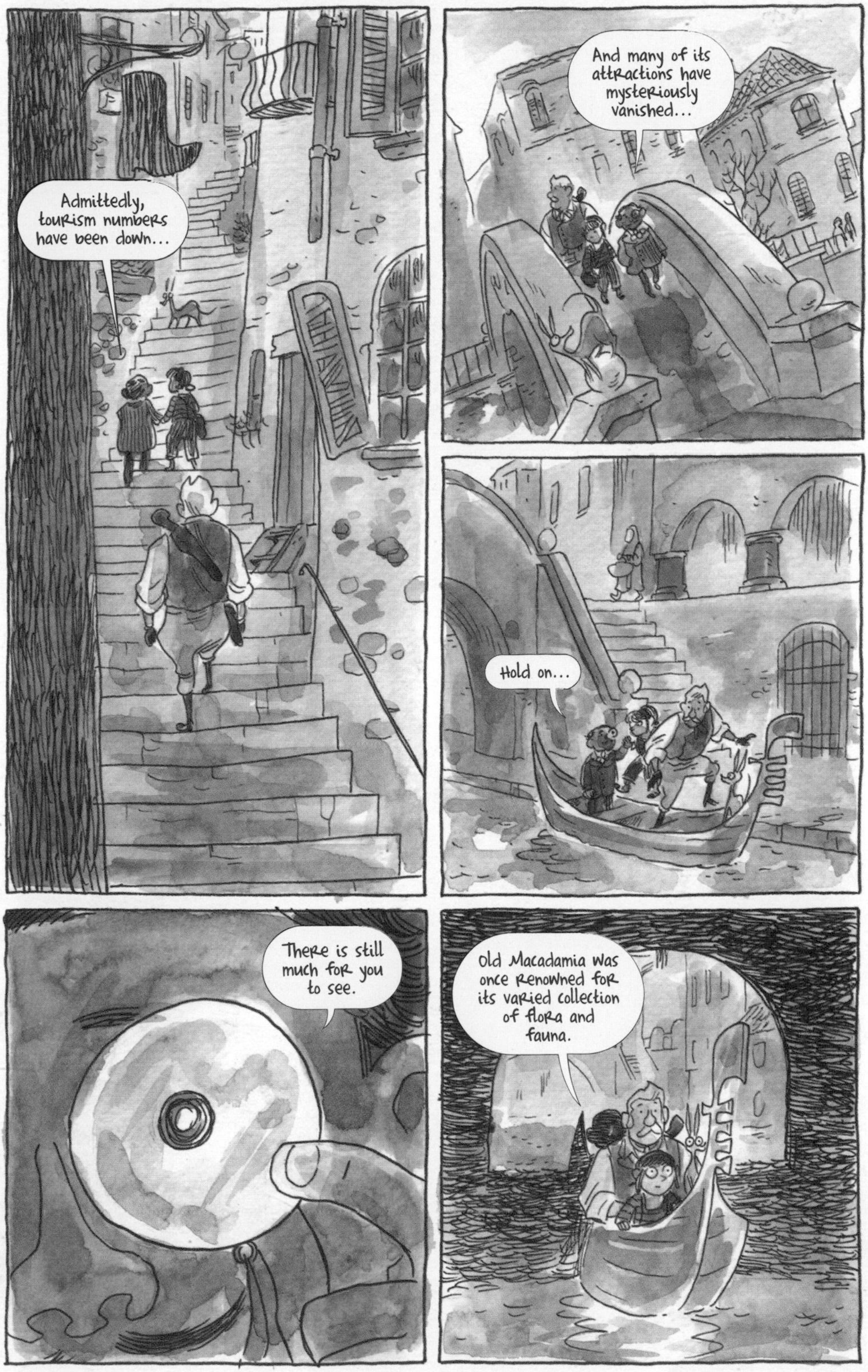
Admittedly, tourism numbers have been down...
And many of its attractions have mysteriously vanished...
Hold on...
There is still much for you to see.
Old Macadamia was once renowned for its varied collection of flora and fauna.

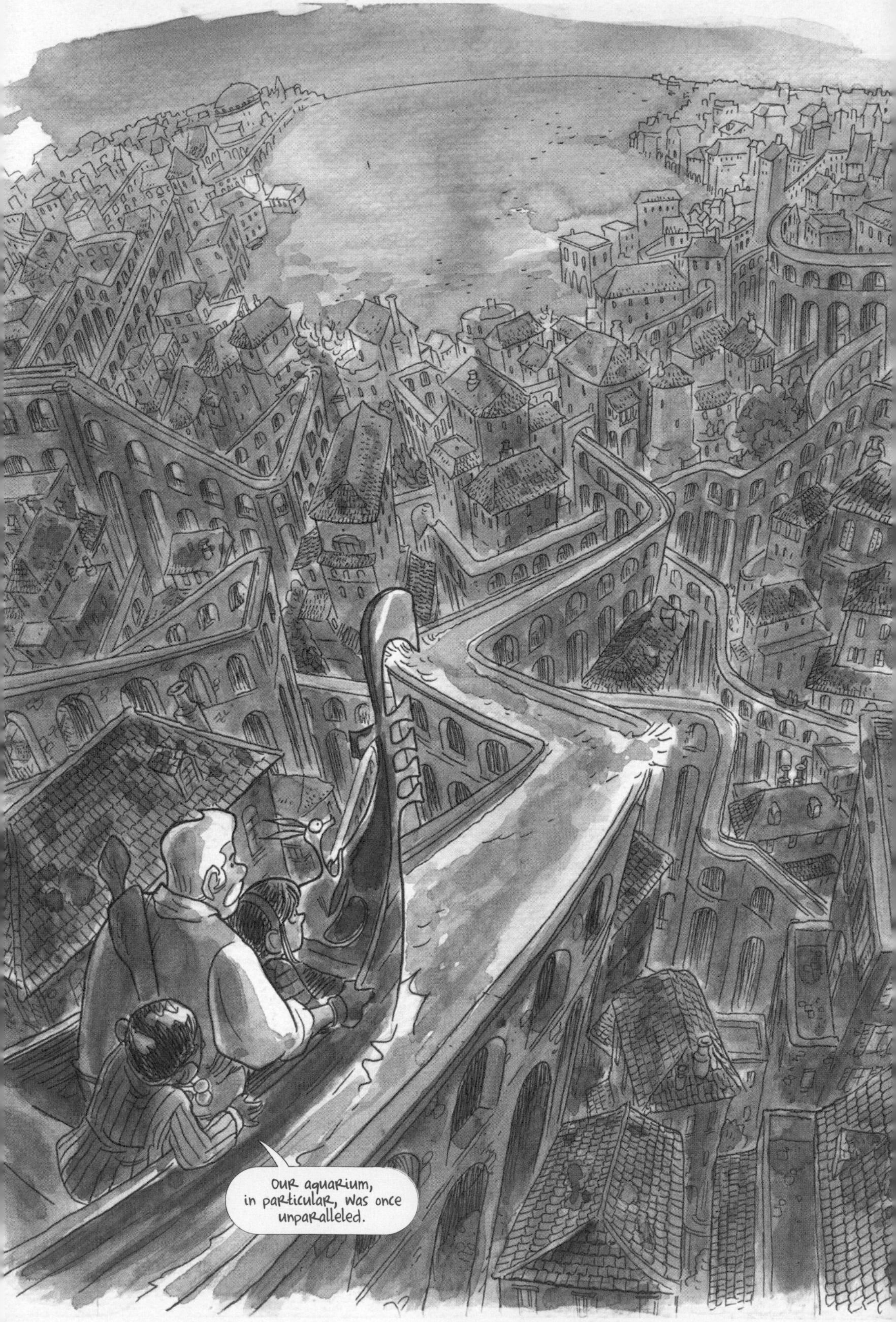
Our aquarium, in particular, was once unparalleled.

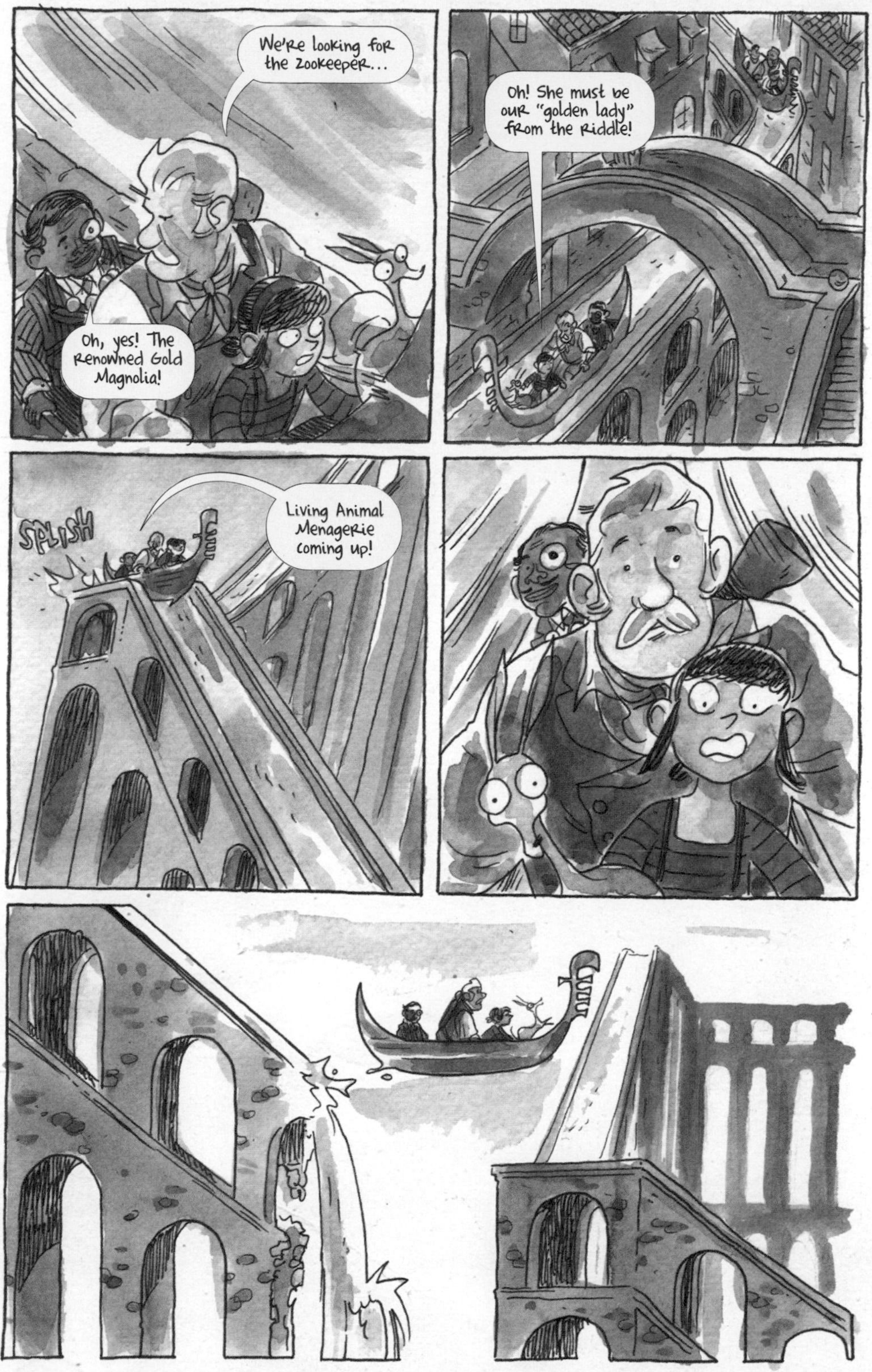
We're looking for the zookeeper...
Oh, yes! The renowned Gold Magnolia!
Oh! She must be our "golden lady" from the riddle!
SPLISH
Living Animal Menagerie coming up!

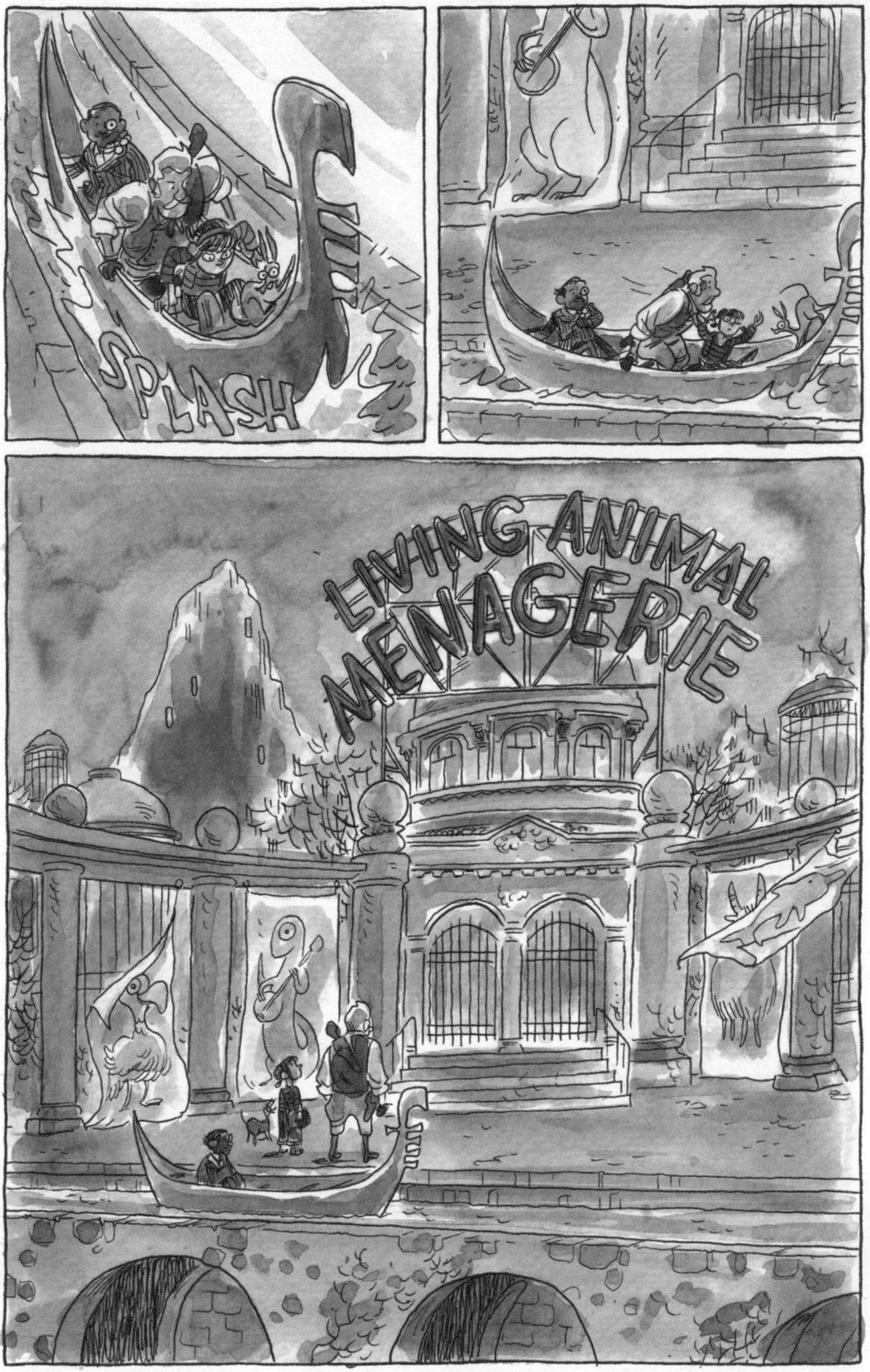
SPLASH
LIVING ANIMAL
MENAGERIE

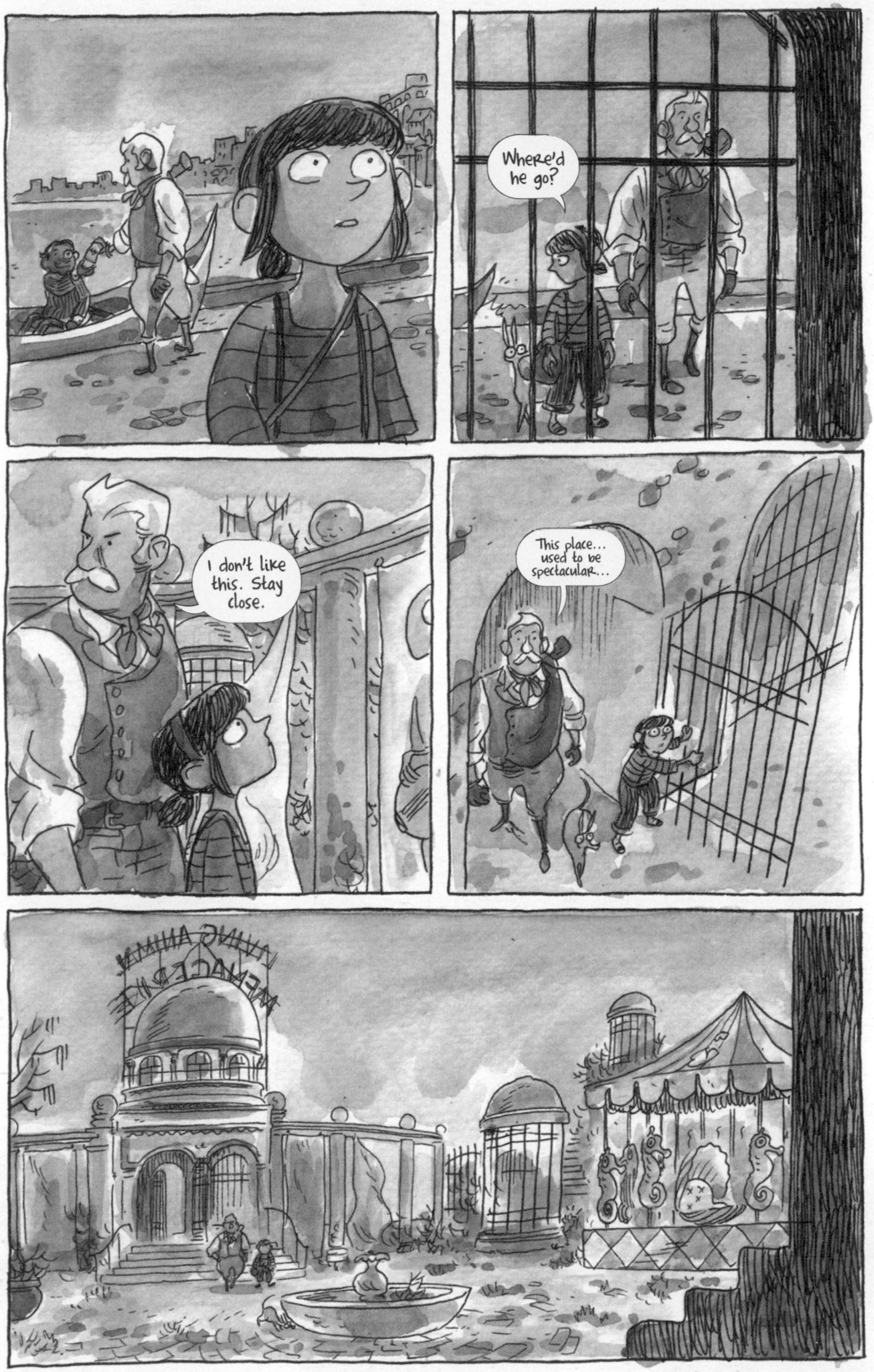
Where'd he go?
I don't like this. Stay close.
This place... used to be spectacular...

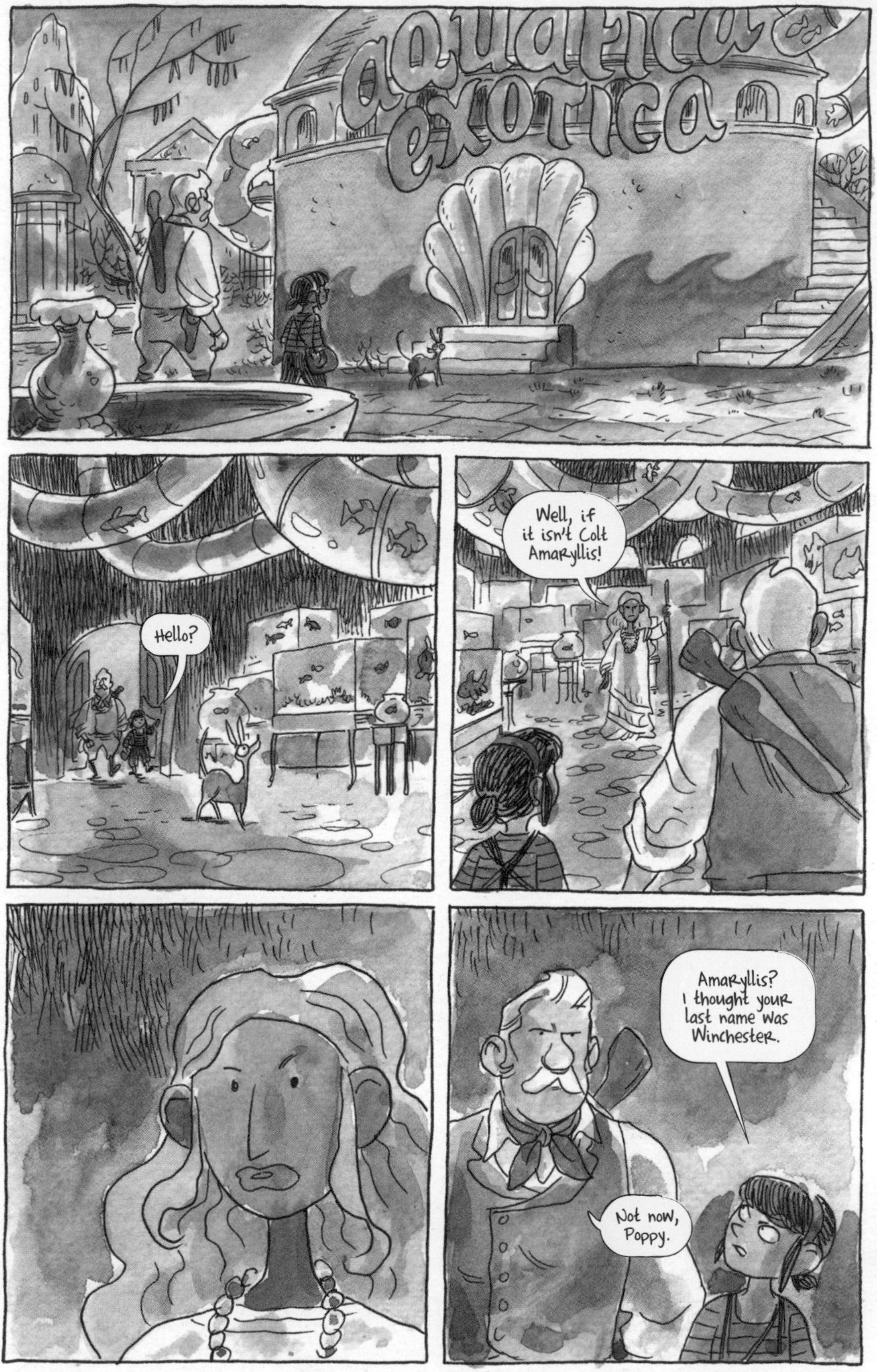
aquatica exotica
Hello?
Well, if it isn't Colt Amaryllis!
Amaryllis? I thought your last name was Winchester.
Not now, Poppy.

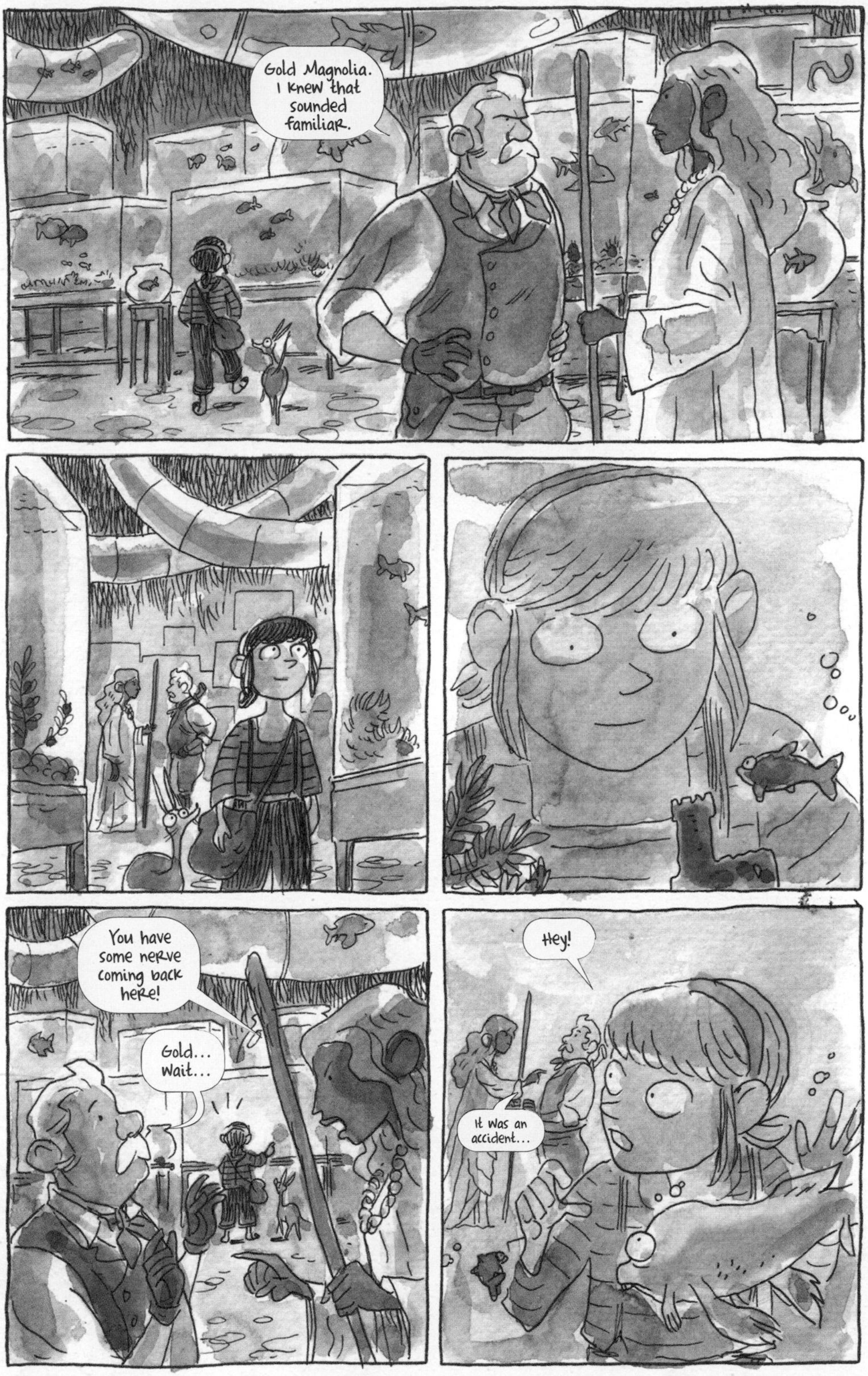
Gold Magnolia. I knew that sounded familiar.
You have some nerve coming back here!
Gold... Wait...
Hey!
It was an accident...

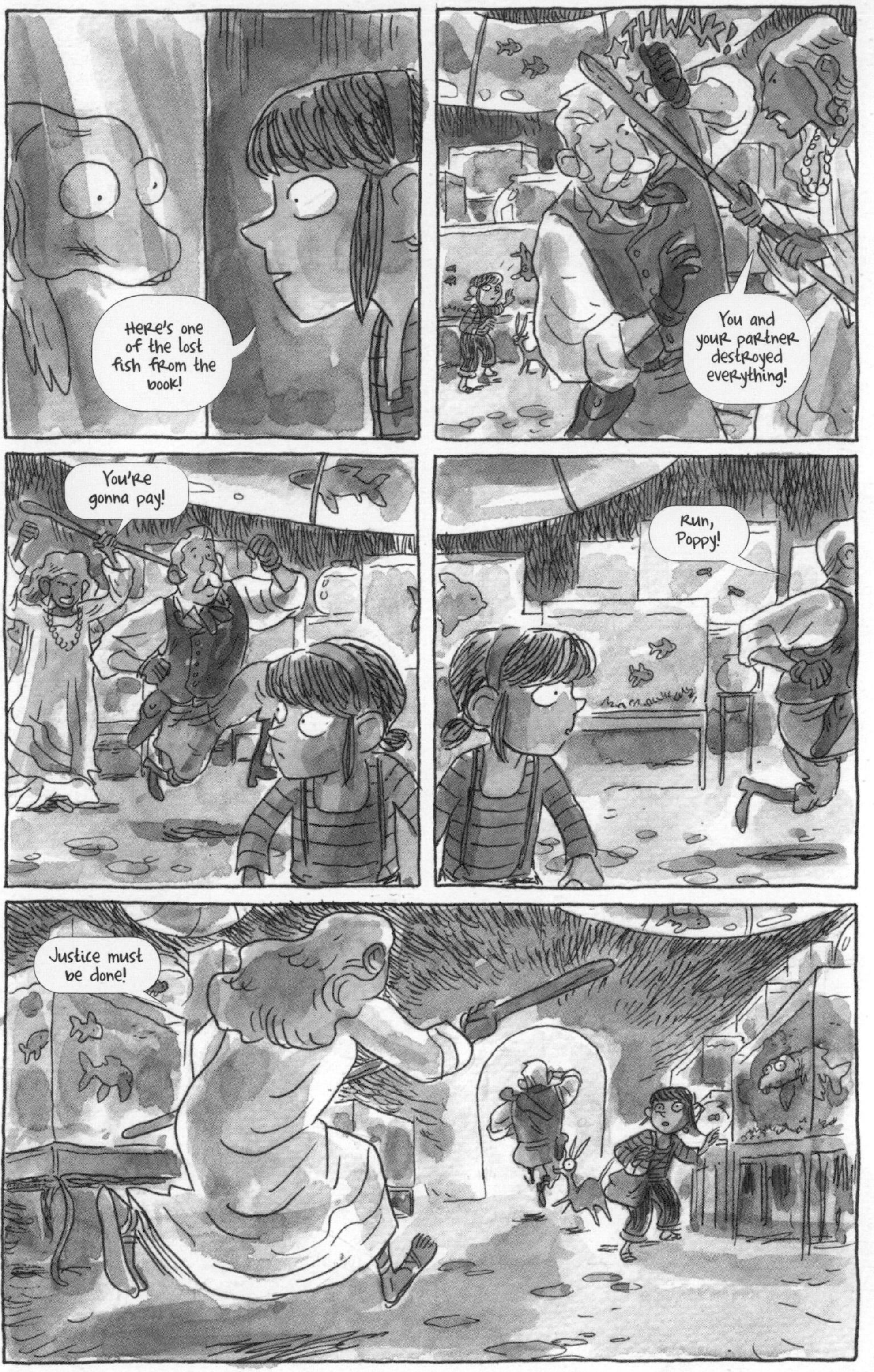
Here's one of the lost fish from the book!
THWAK!
You and your partner destroyed everything!
You're gonna pay!
Run, Poppy!
Justice must be done!

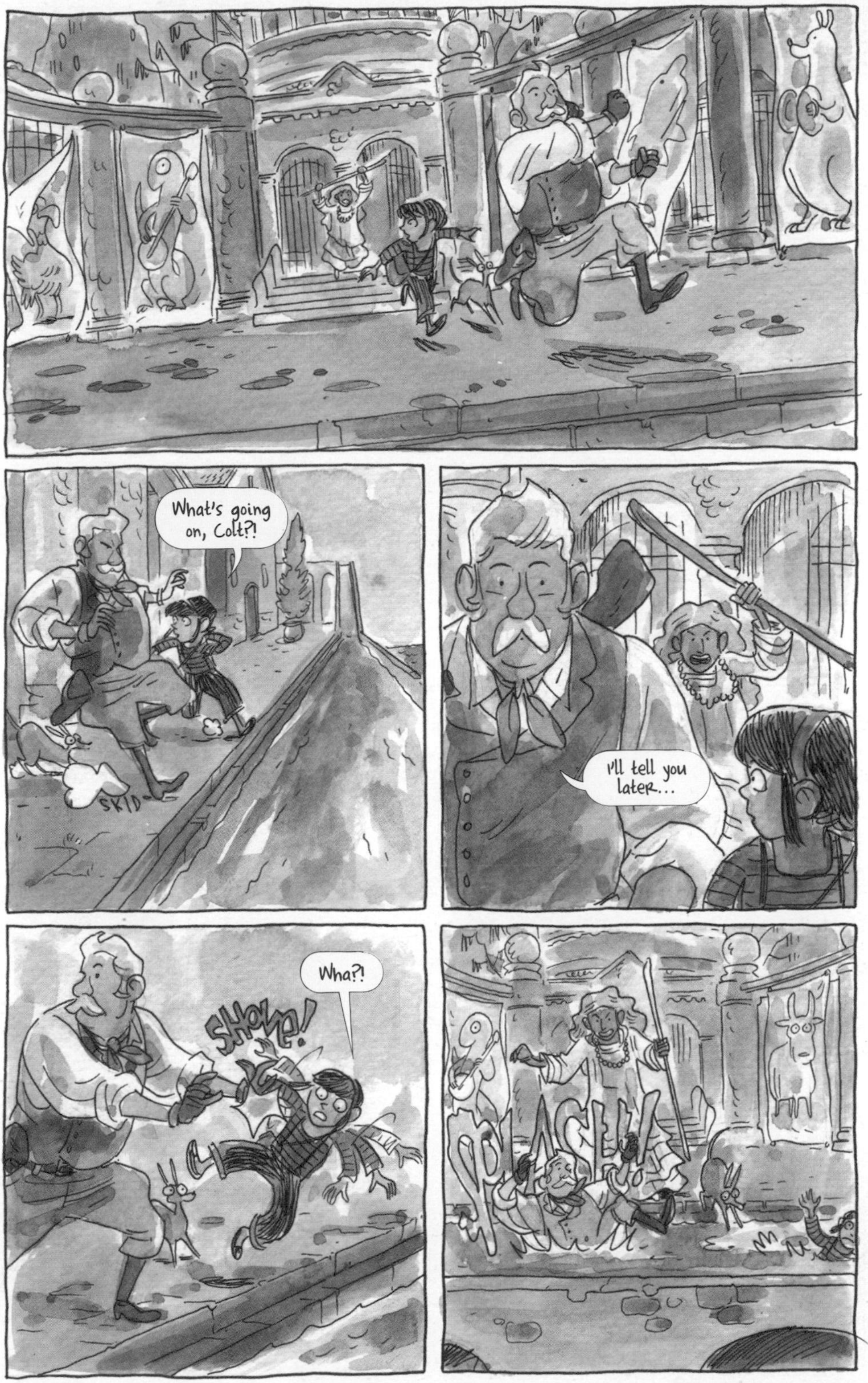
What's going on, Colt?!
SKID
I'll tell you later...
SHOVE!
Wha?!
SPLASH!

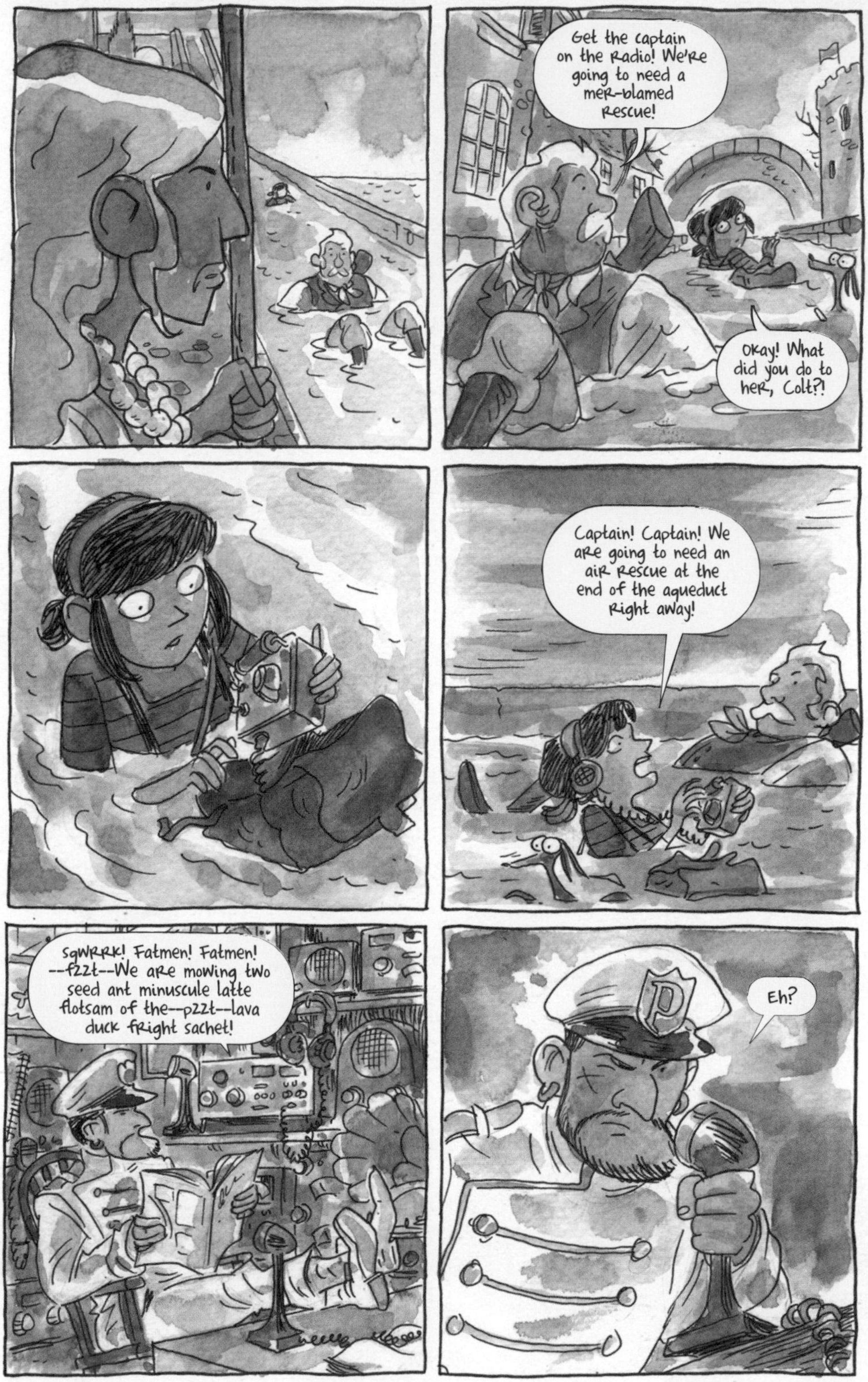
Get the captain on the Radio! We're going to need a mer-blamed Rescue!
Okay! What did you do to her, Colt?!
Captain! Captain! We are going to need an air rescue at the end of the aqueduct right away!
sgwrrk! Fatmen! Fatmen! --fzzt--We are mowing two seed ant minuscule latte flotsam of the--pzzt--lava duck fright sachet!
Eh?

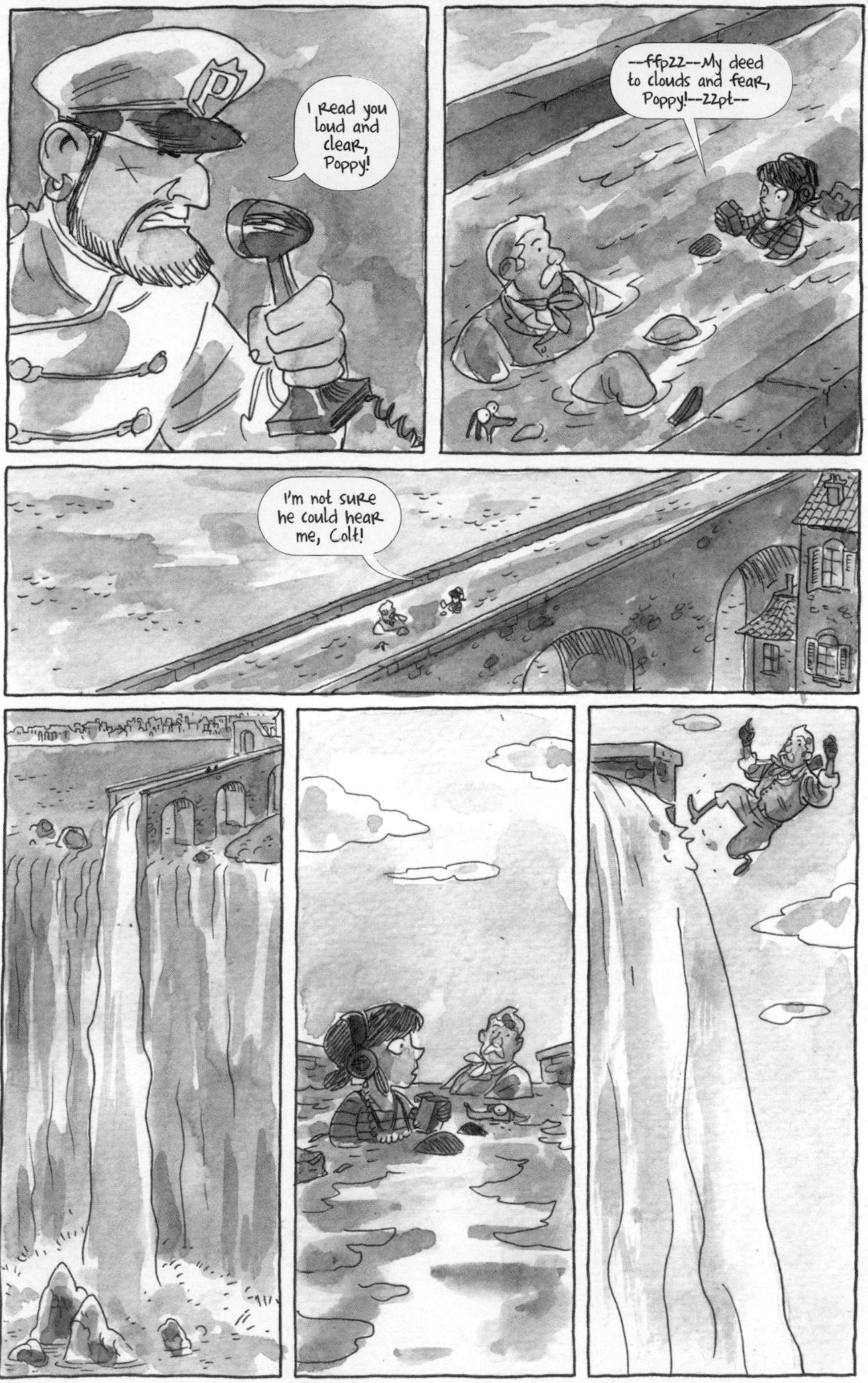
I Read you loud and clear, Poppy!
--ffpzz--My deed to clouds and fear, Poppy!--zzpt--
I'm not sure he could hear me, Colt!

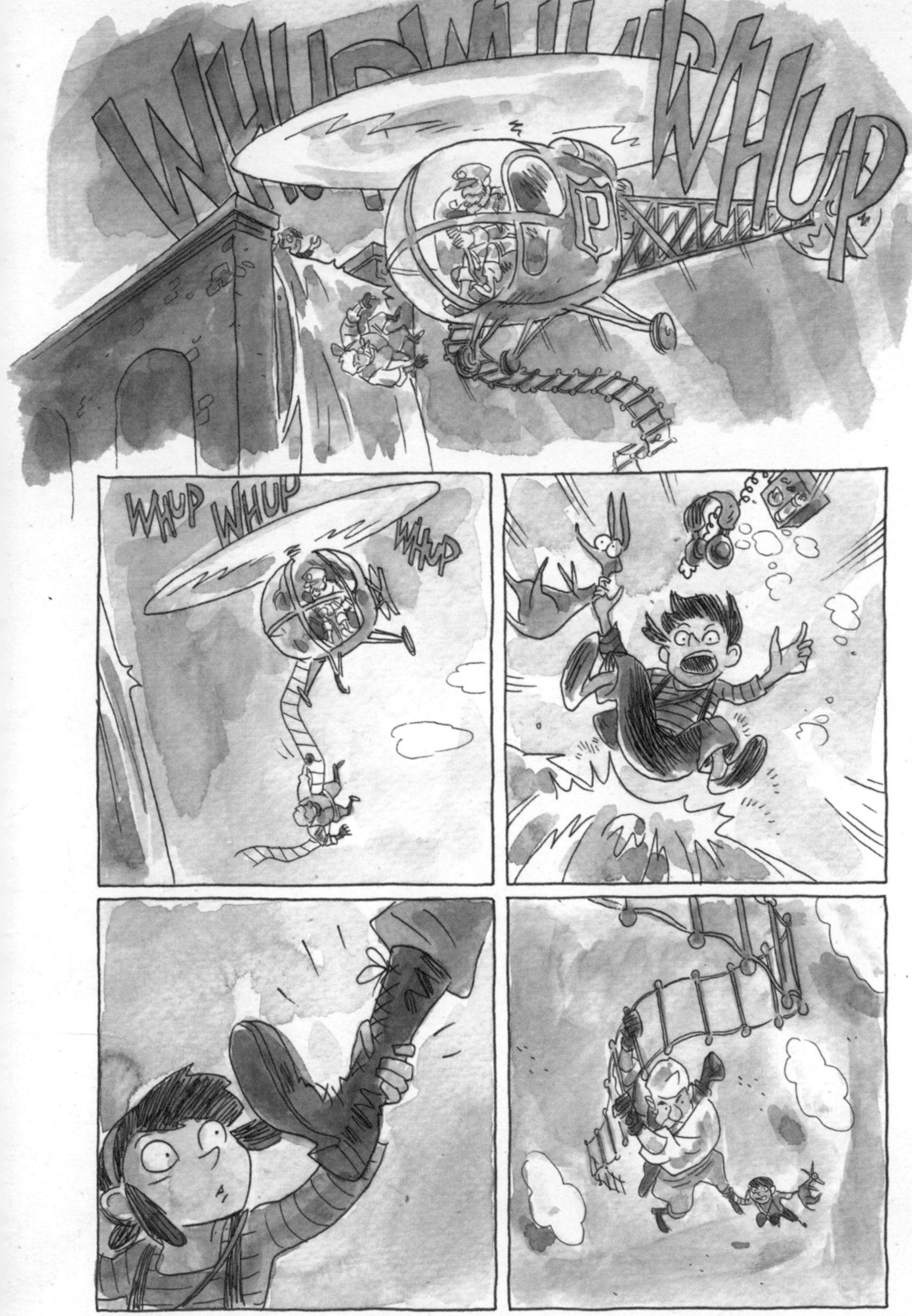
P
WHUP
WHUP WHUP
WHUP

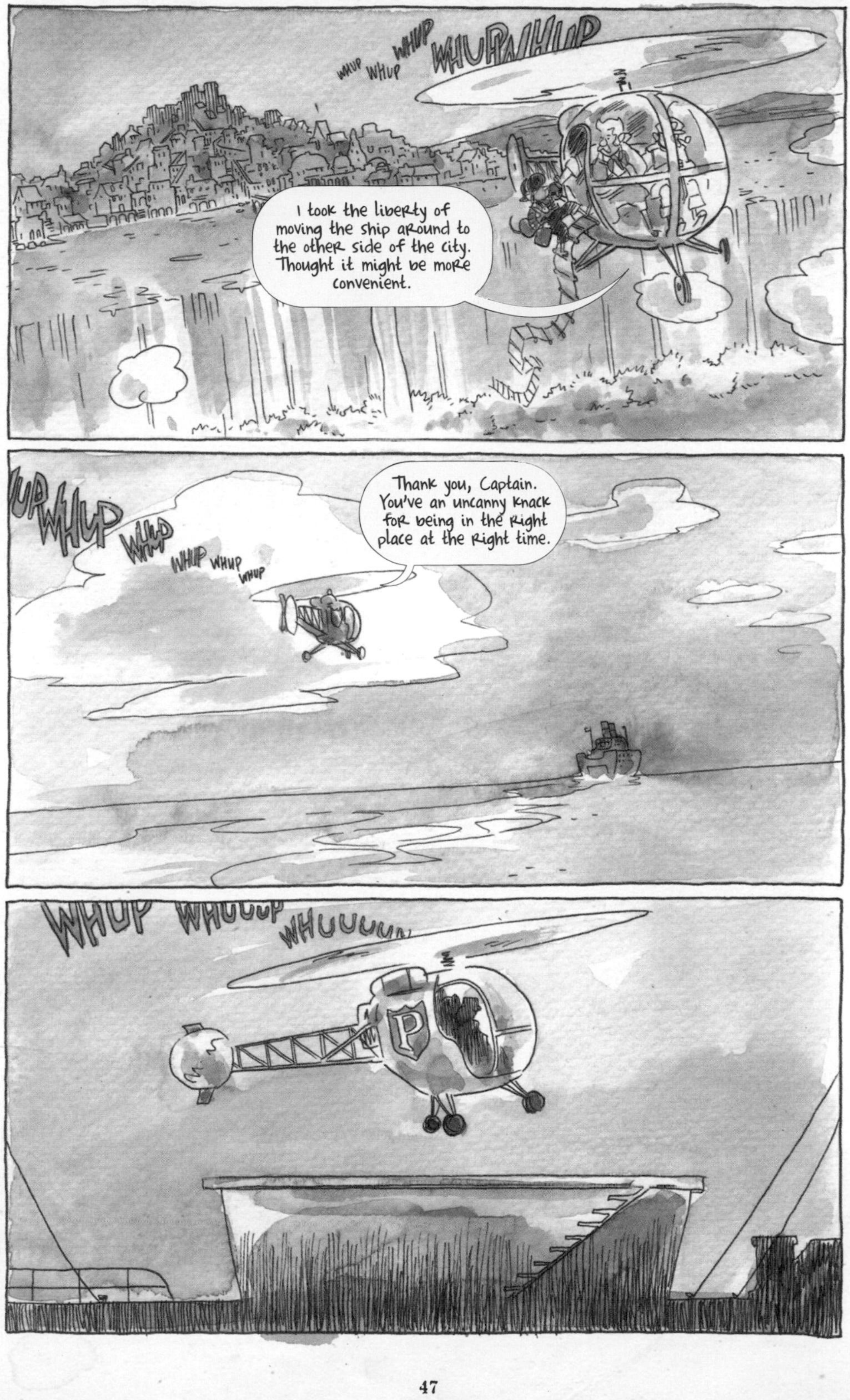
WHUP WHUP WHUP WHUPWHUP
I took the liberty of moving the ship around to the other side of the city. Thought it might be more convenient.
WHUP WHUP WHUP WHUP WHUP
Thank you, Captain. You've an uncanny knack for being in the right place at the right time.
WHUP WHUUUP

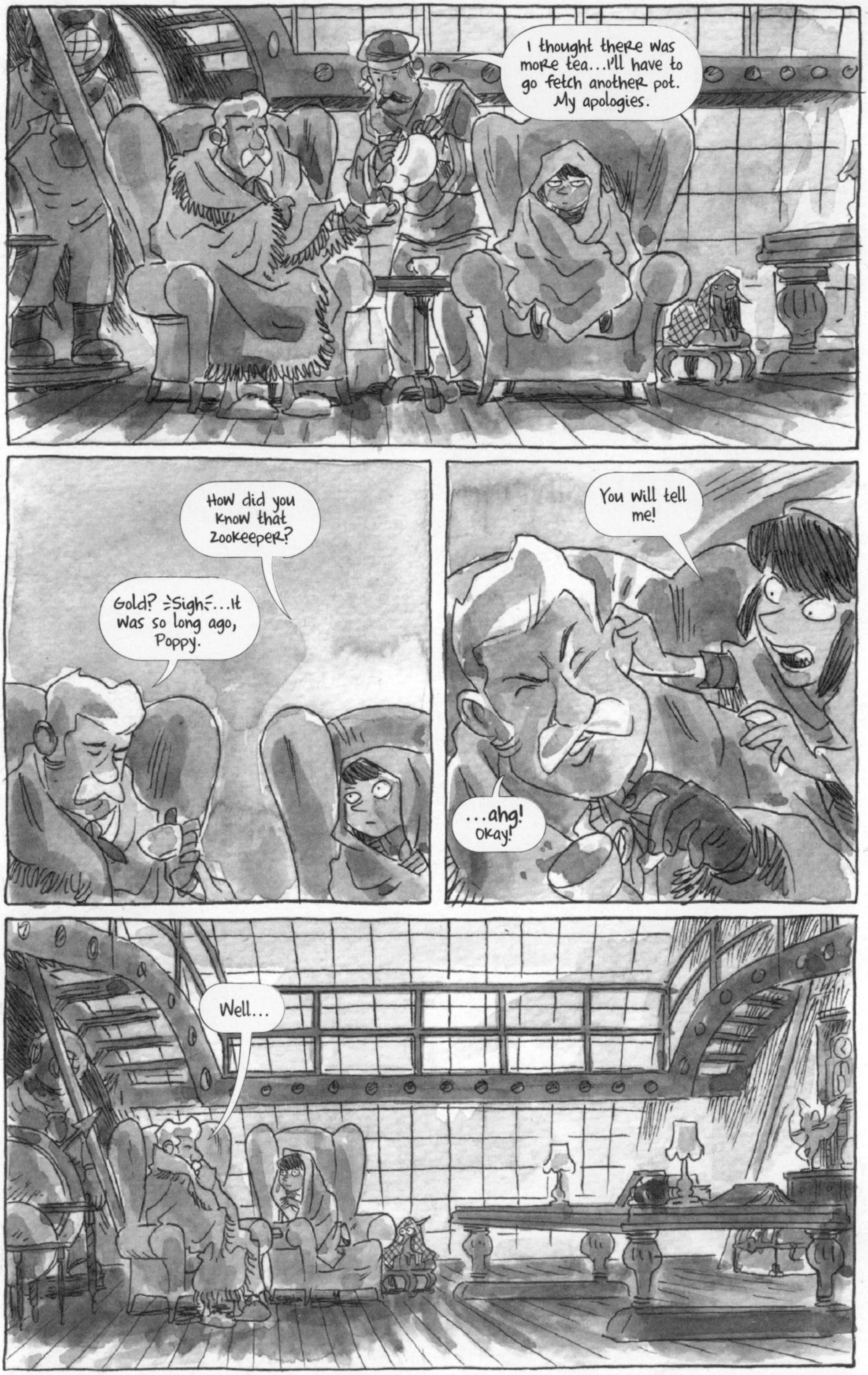

I thought there was more tea...I'll have to go fetch another pot. My apologies.
How did you know that Zookeeper?
Gold? ⪢Sigh⪡...It was so long ago, Poppy.
You will tell me!
...ahg! Okay!
Well...

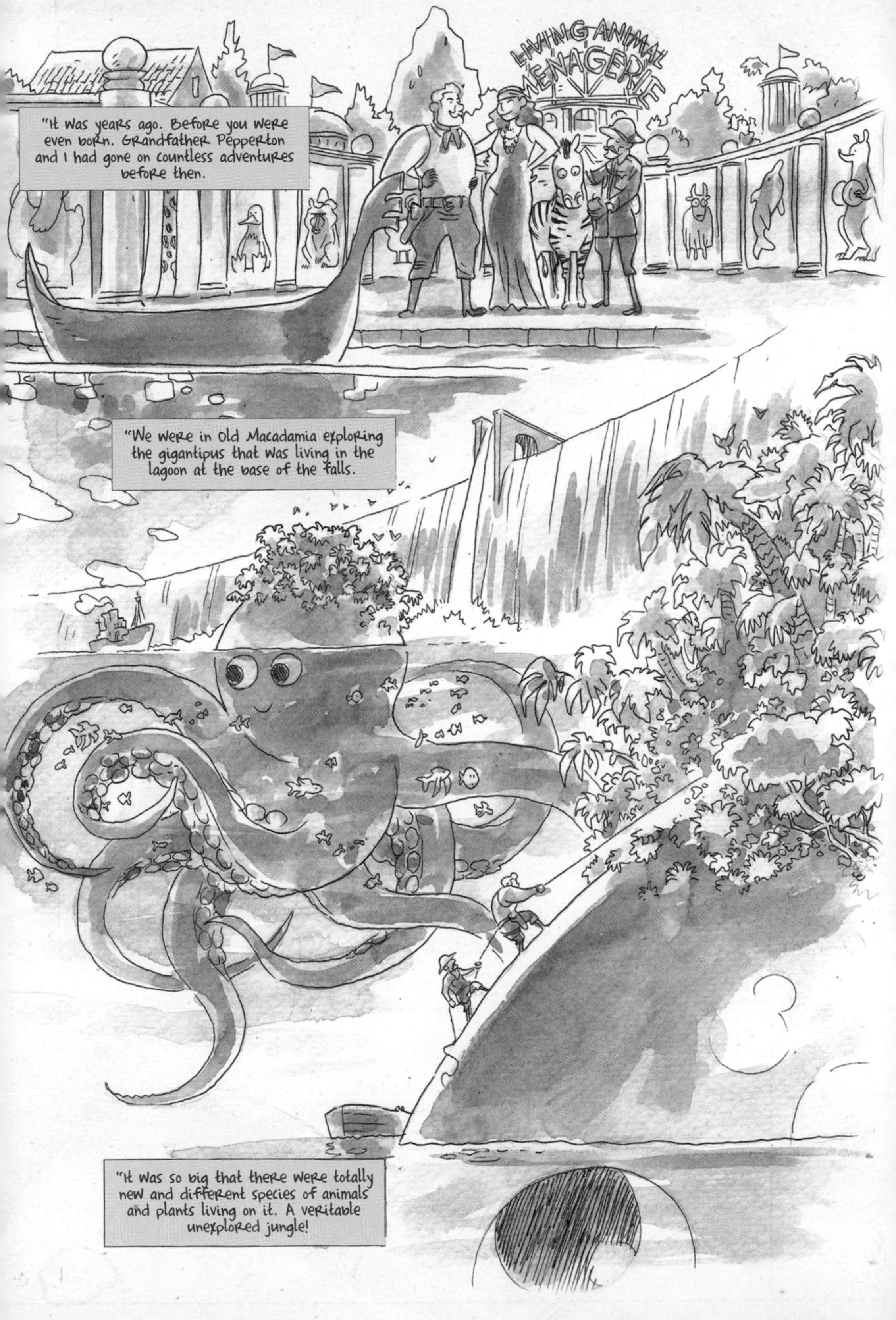
LIVING ANIMAL MENAGERIE
"It was years ago. Before you were even born. Grandfather Pepperton and I had gone on countless adventures before then.
"We were in Old Macadamia exploring the gigantipus that was living in the lagoon at the base of the falls.
"It was so big that there were totally new and different species of animals and plants living on it. A veritable unexplored jungle!

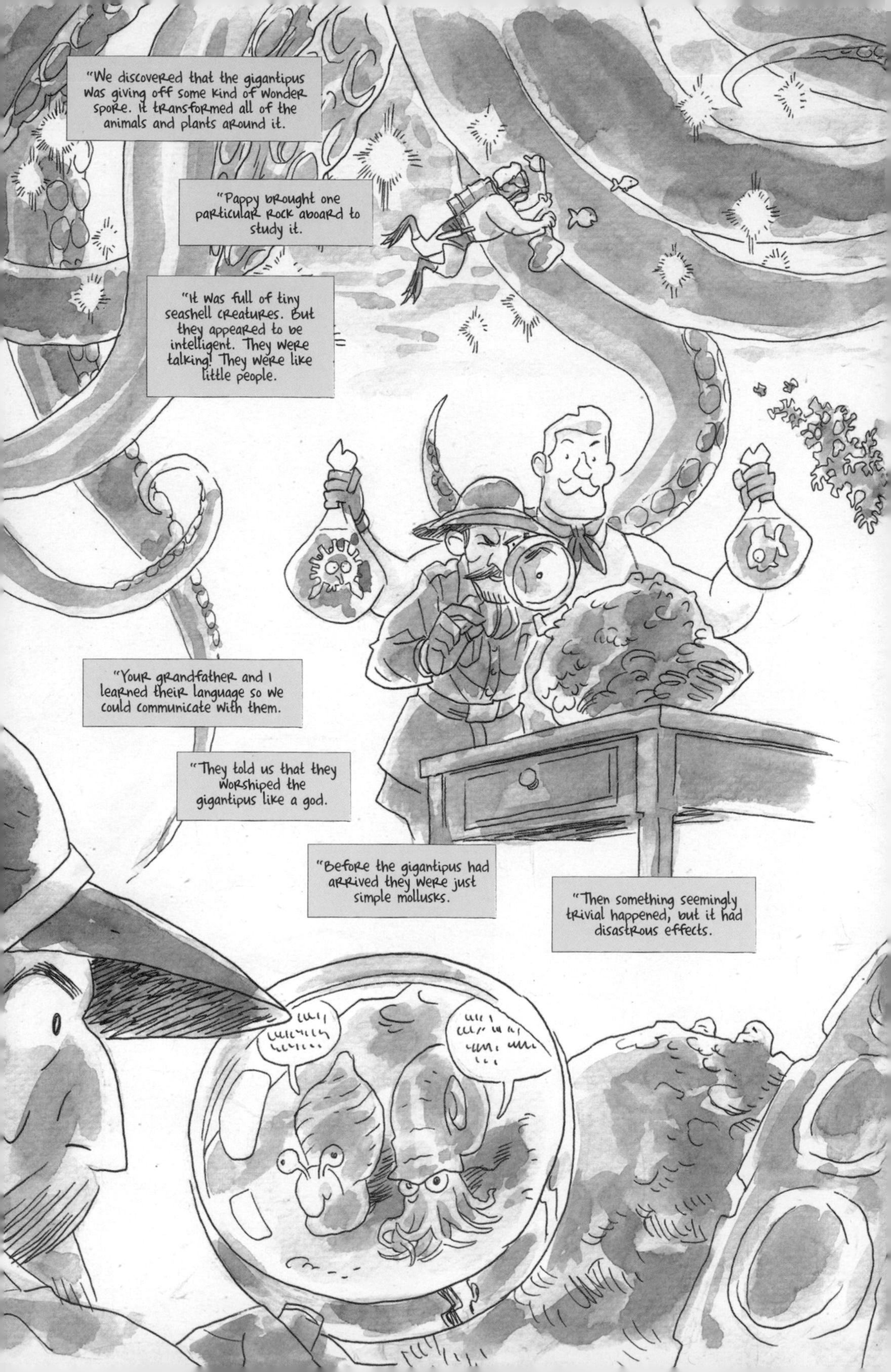
"We discovered that the gigantipus was giving off some kind of wonder spore. It transformed all of the animals and plants around it.
"Pappy brought one particular rock aboard to study it.
"It was full of tiny seashell creatures. But they appeared to be intelligent. They were talking! They were like little people.
"Your grandfather and I learned their language so we could communicate with them.
"They told us that they worshiped the gigantipus like a god.
"Before the gigantipus had arrived they were just simple mollusks.
"Then something seemingly trivial happened, but it had disastrous effects.

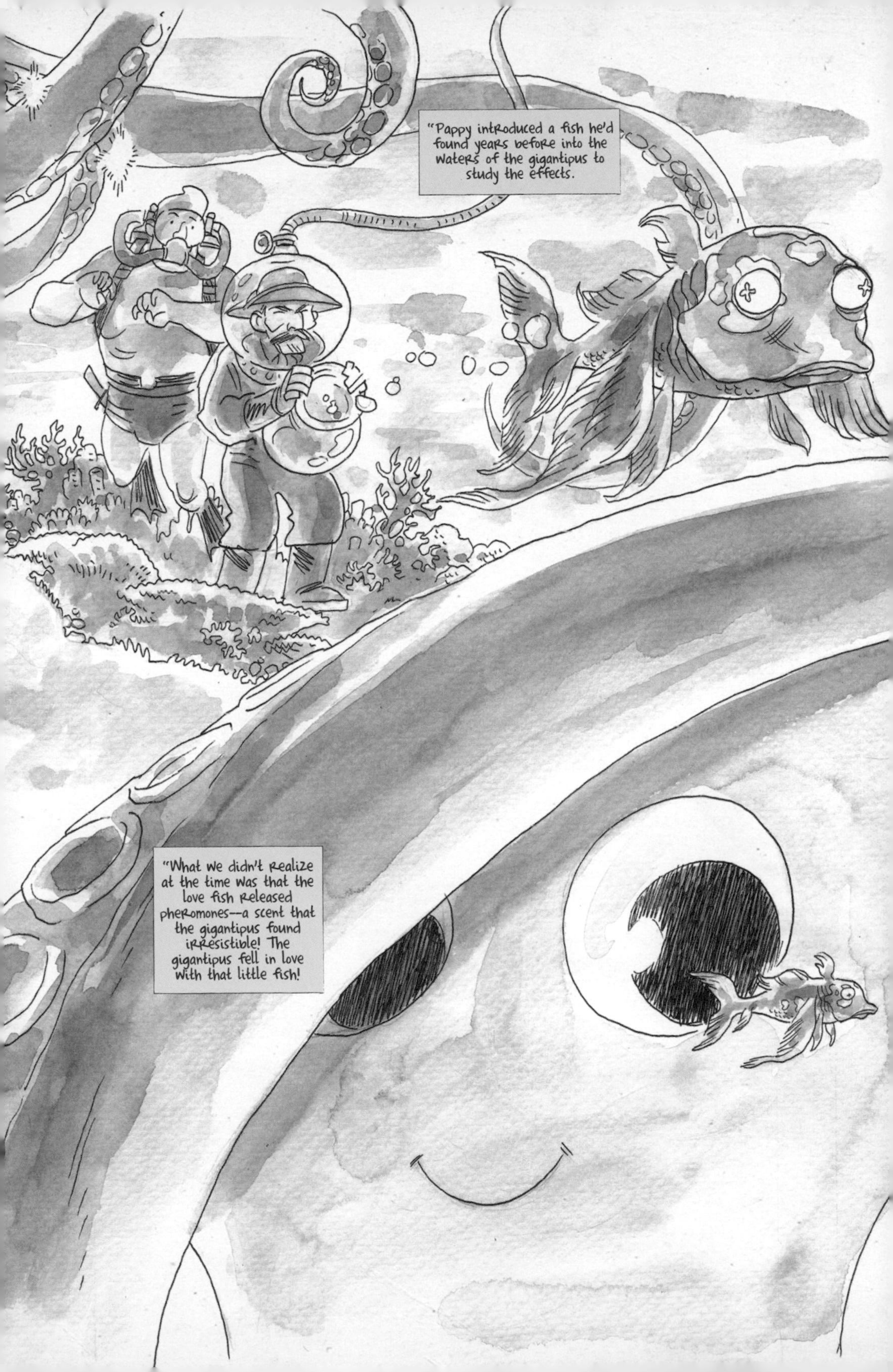
"Pappy introduced a fish he'd found years before into the waters of the gigantipus to study the effects.
"What we didn't realize at the time was that the love fish released pheromones--a scent that the gigantipus found irresistible! The gigantipus fell in love with that little fish!

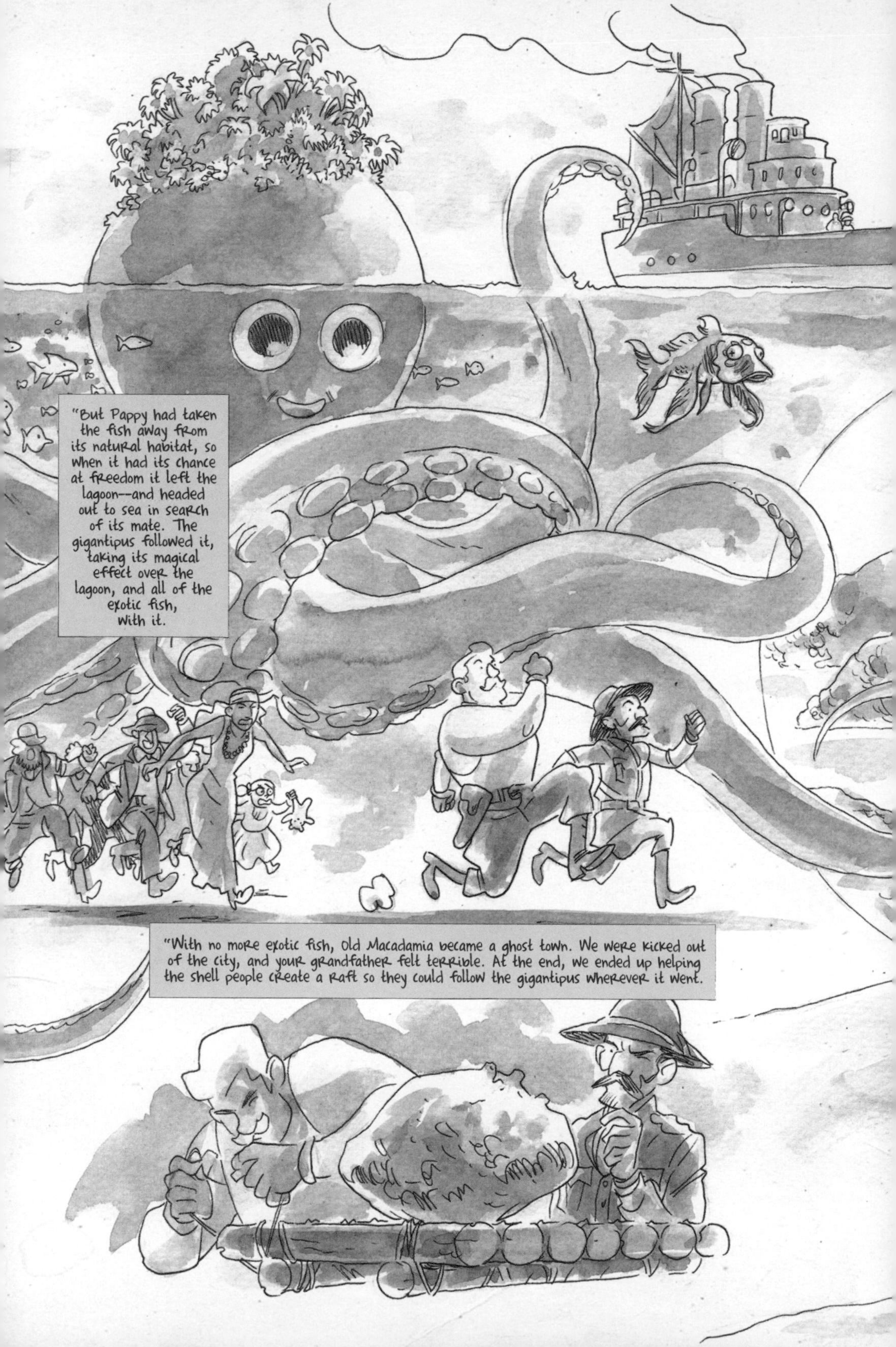
"But Pappy had taken the fish away from its natural habitat, so when it had its chance at freedom it left the lagoon--and headed out to sea in search of its mate. The gigantipus followed it, taking its magical effect over the lagoon, and all of the exotic fish, with it.
"With no more exotic fish, Old Macadamia became a ghost town. We were kicked out of the city, and your grandfather felt terrible. At the end, we ended up helping the shell people create a raft so they could follow the gigantipus wherever it went.

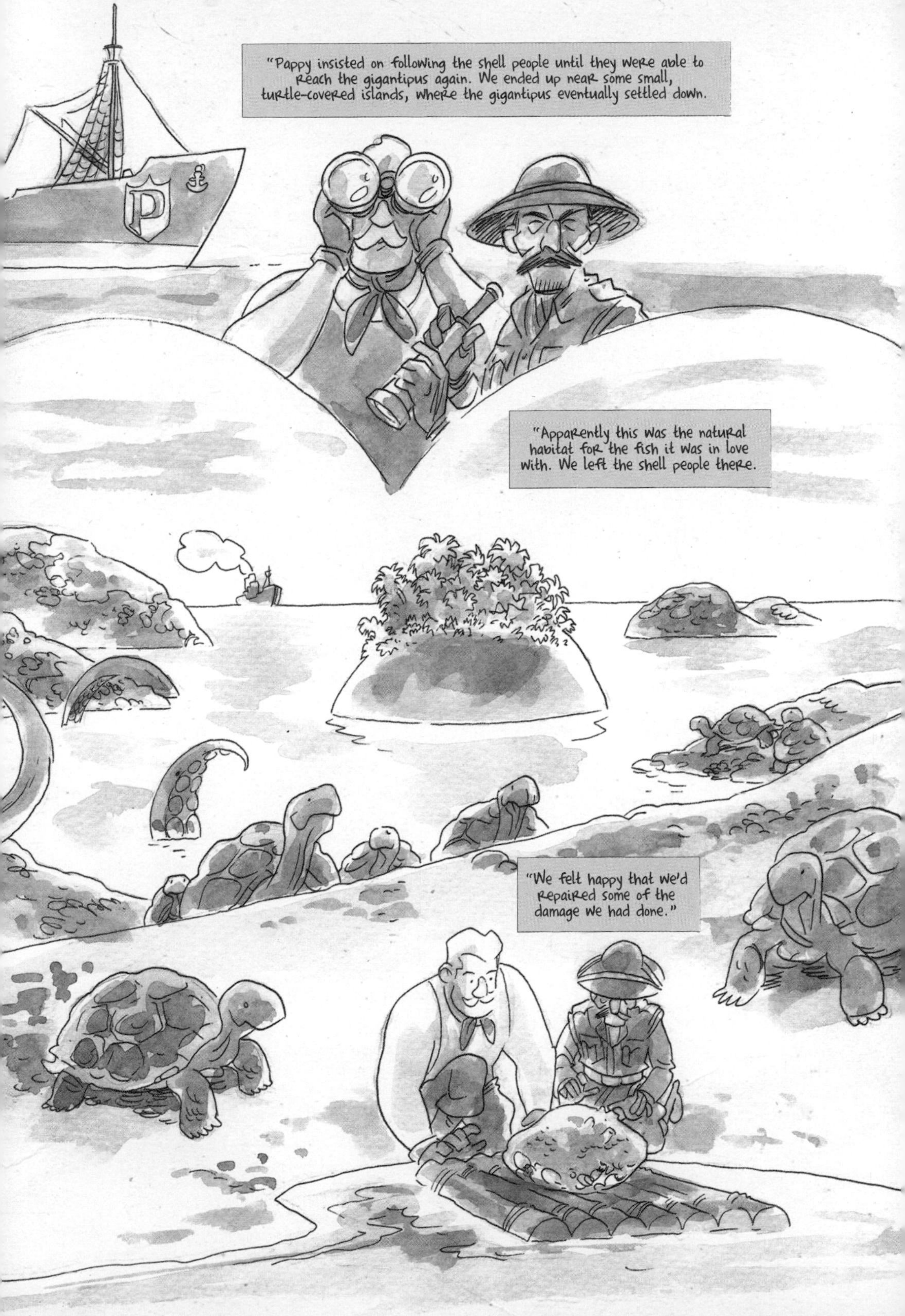
"Pappy insisted on following the shell people until they were able to reach the gigantipus again. We ended up near some small, turtle-covered islands, where the gigantipus eventually settled down.
"Apparently this was the natural habitat for the fish it was in love with. We left the shell people there.
"We felt happy that we'd repaired some of the damage we had done."

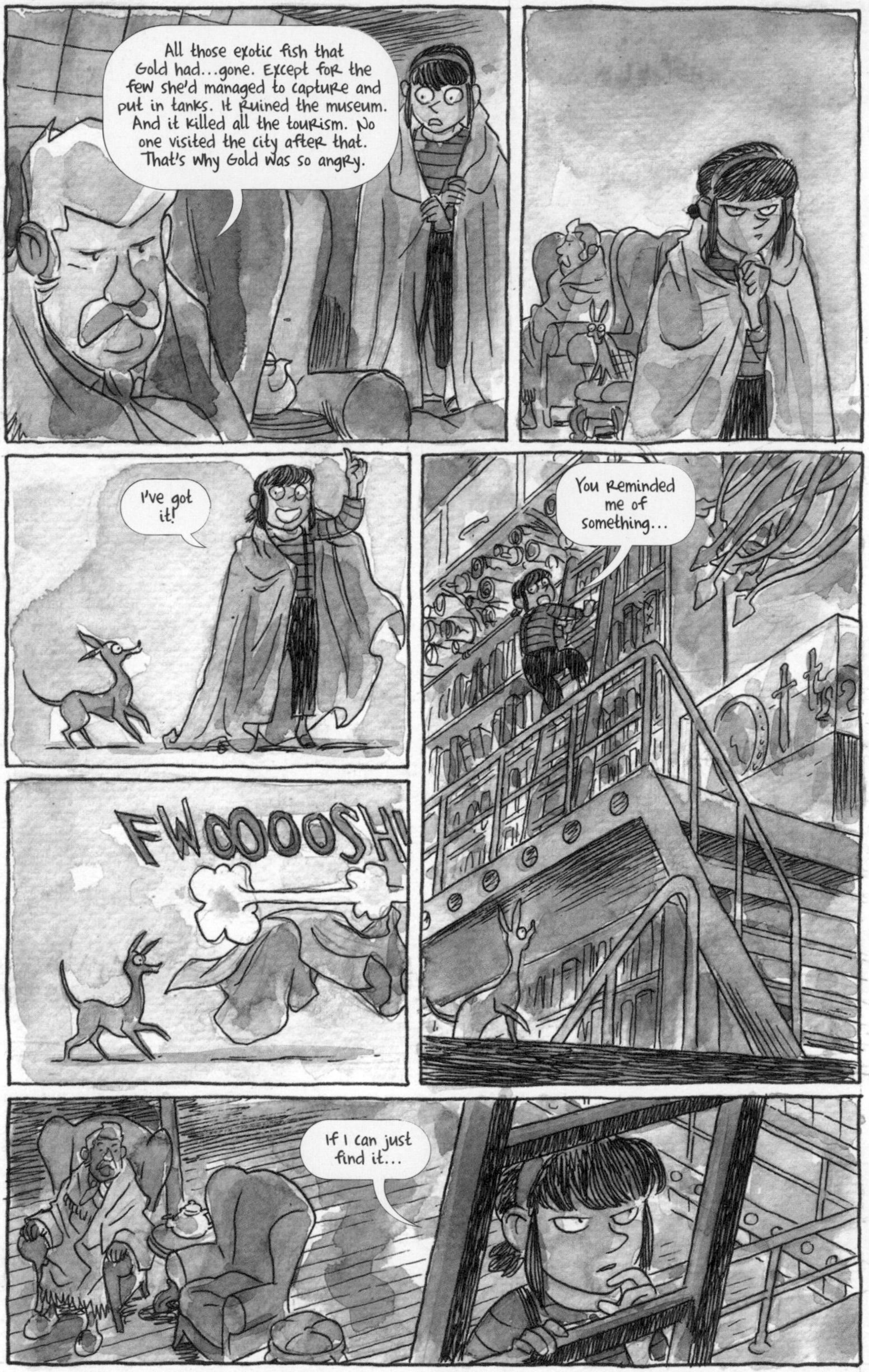
All those exotic fish that Gold had...gone. Except for the few she'd managed to capture and put in tanks. It ruined the museum. And it killed all the tourism. No one visited the city after that. That's why Gold was so angry.
I've got it!
You reminded me of something...
FWOOOOSH!
If I can just find it...

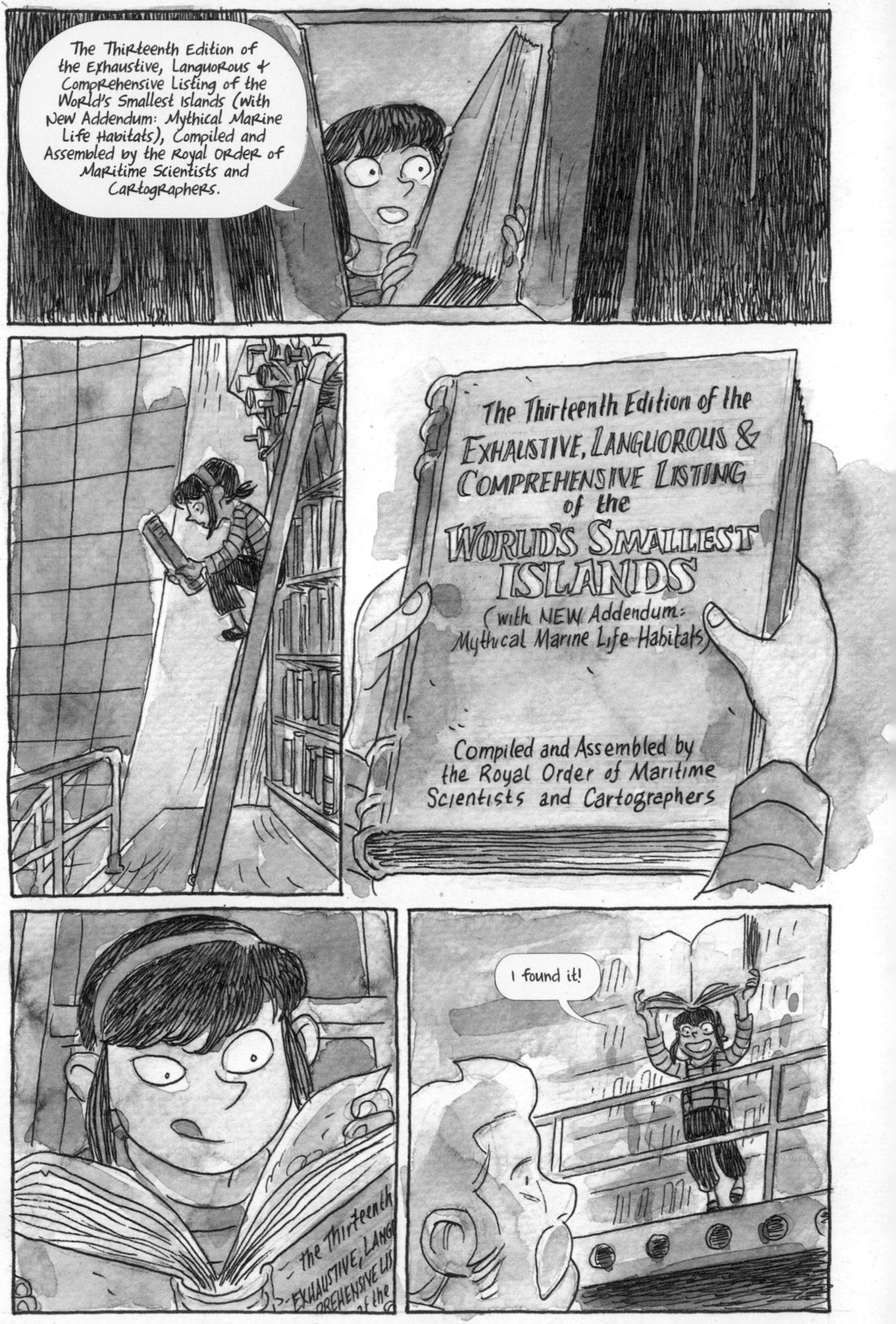
The Thirteenth Edition of the Exhaustive, Languorous & Comprehensive Listing of the World's Smallest Islands (With New Addendum: Mythical Marine Life Habitats), Compiled and Assembled by the Royal Order of Maritime Scientists and Cartographers.
The Thirteenth Edition of the
EXHAUSTIVE, LANGUOROUS &
COMPREHENSIVE LISTING
of the
WORLD'S SMALLEST ISLANDS
(with NEW Addendum: Mythical Marine Life Habitats)
Compiled and Assembled by the Royal Order of Maritime Scientists and Cartographers
the Thirteenth
EXHAUSTIVE, LANG
PREHENSIVE LIS
of the
I found it!

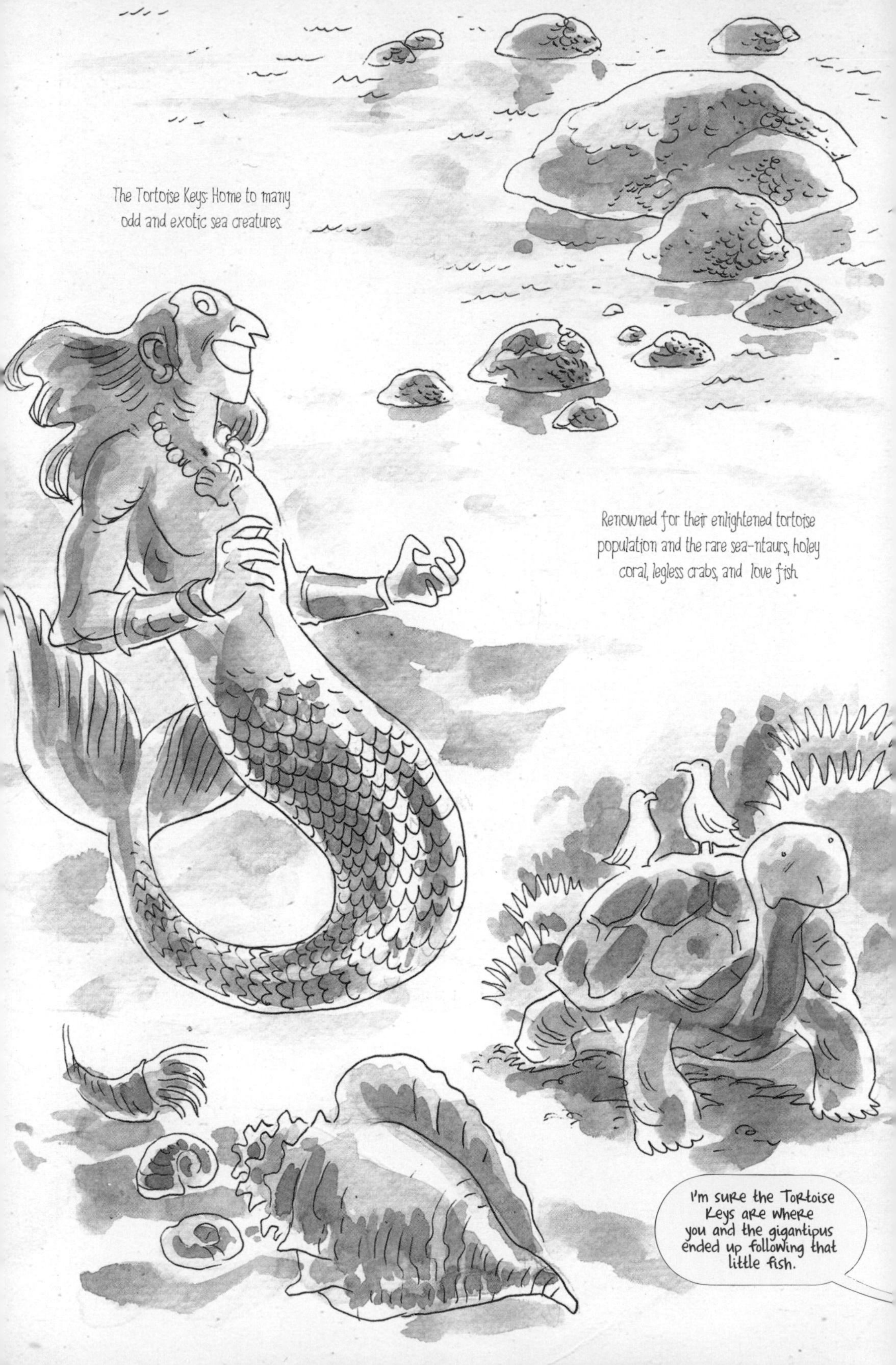
The Tortoise Keys: Home to many odd and exotic sea creatures.
Renowned for their enlightened tortoise population and the rare sea-ntaurs, holey coral, legless crabs, and love fish.
I'm sure the Tortoise Keys are where you and the gigantipus ended up following that little fish.

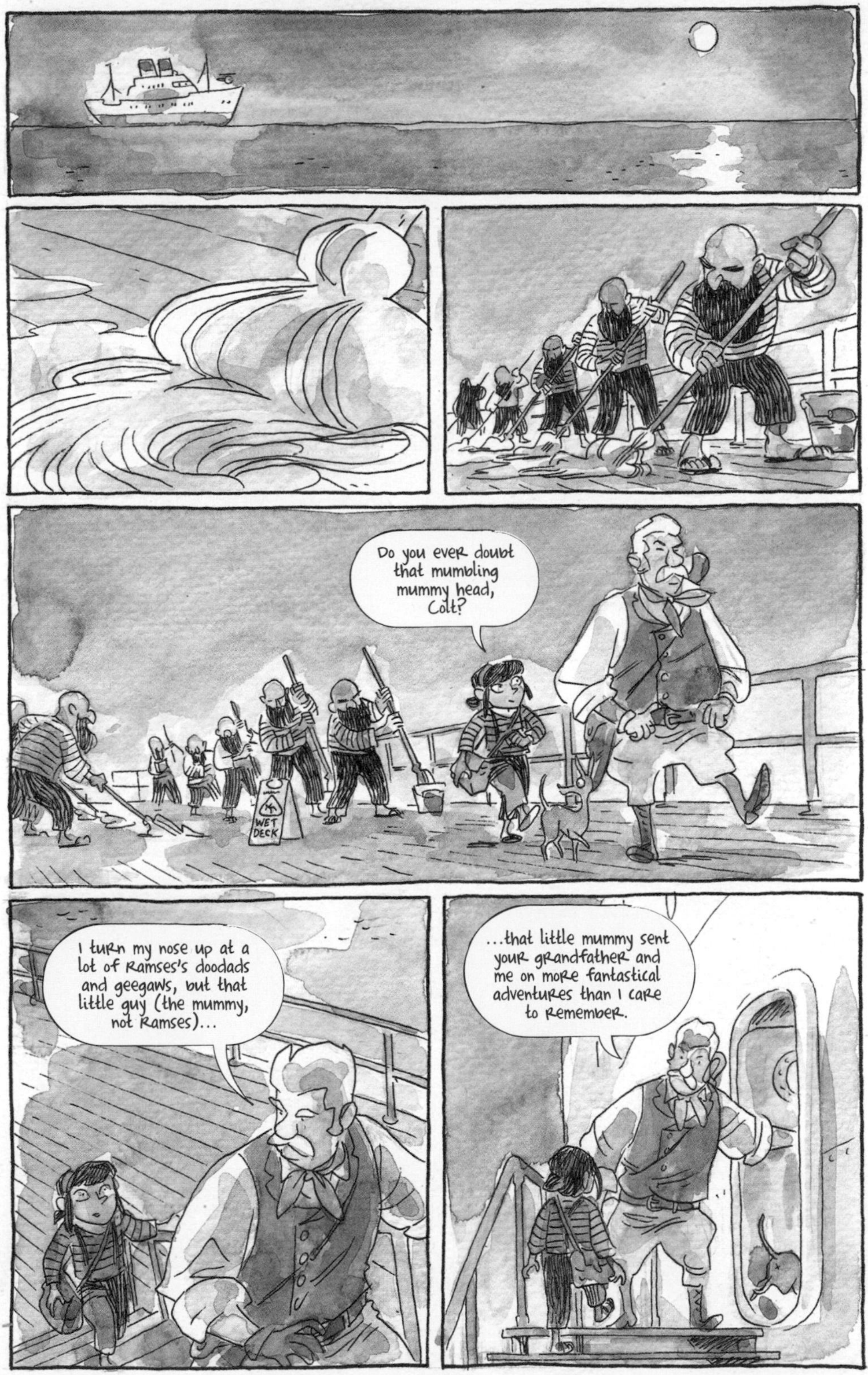

WET DECK
Do you ever doubt that mumbling mummy head, Colt?
I turn my nose up at a lot of Ramses's doodads and geegaws, but that little guy (the mummy, not Ramses)...
...that little mummy sent your grandfather and me on more fantastical adventures than I care to remember.

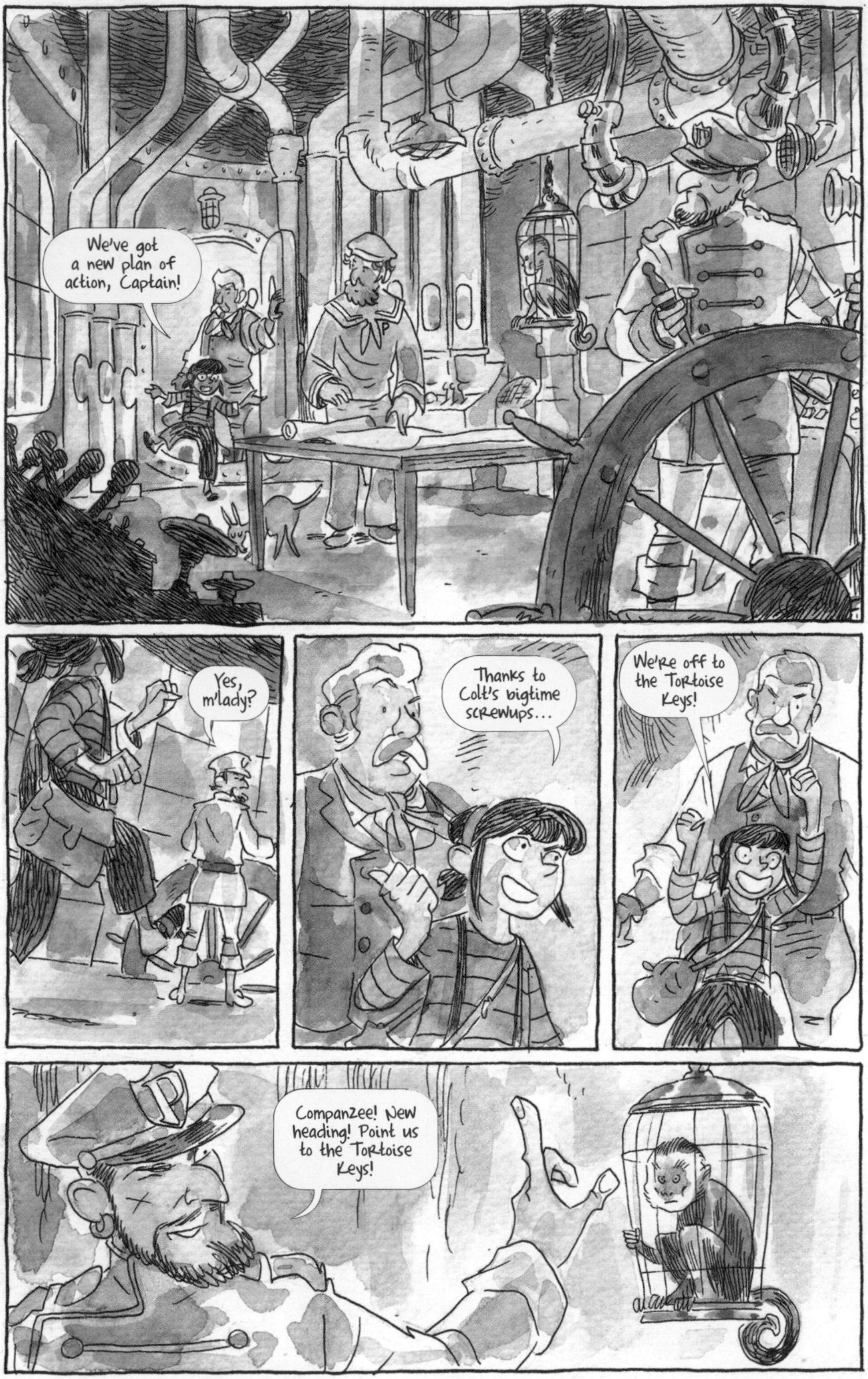
We've got a new plan of action, Captain!
Yes, m'lady?
Thanks to Colt's bigtime screwups...
We're off to the Tortoise Keys!
Companzee! New heading! Point us to the Tortoise Keys!

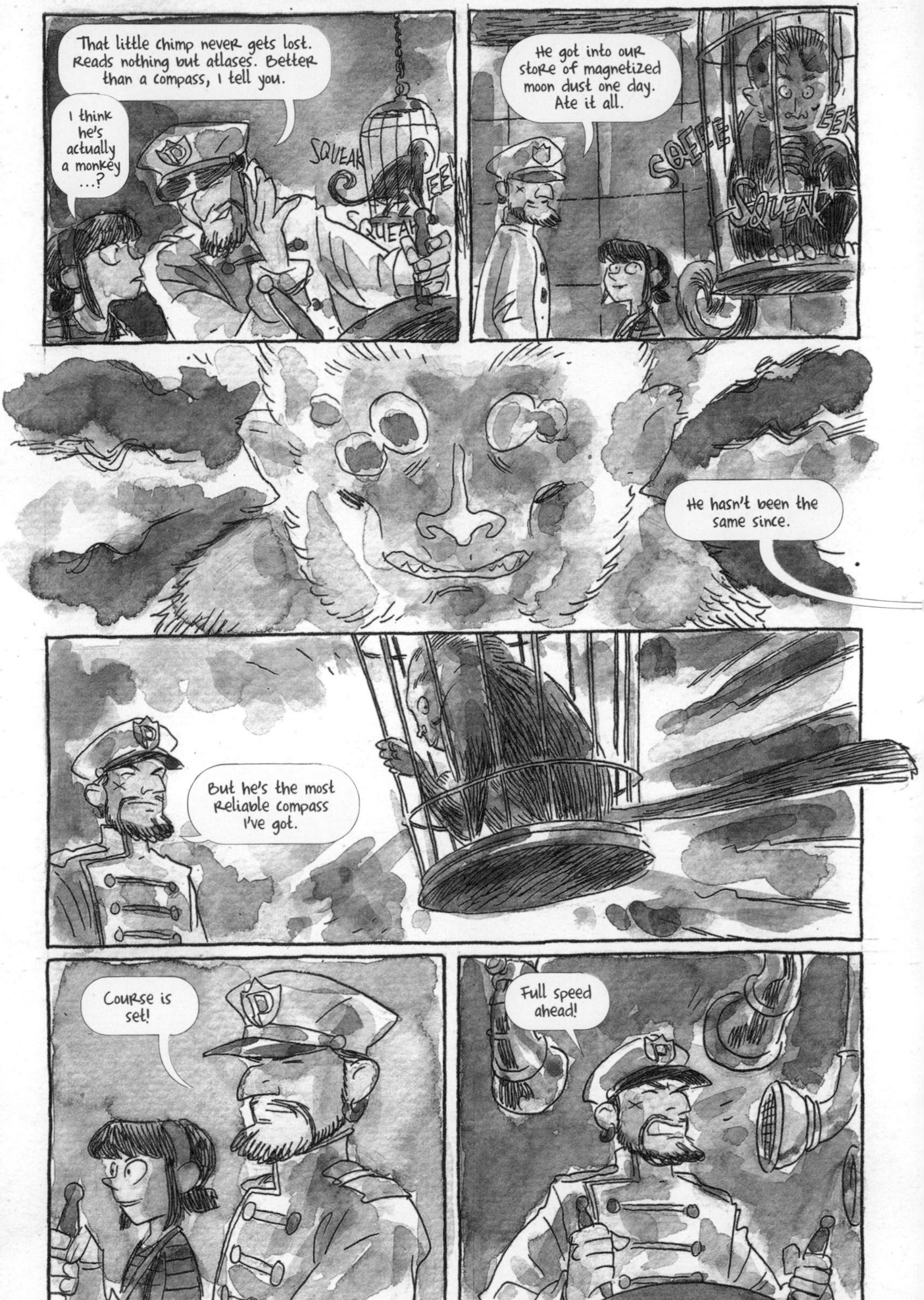
That little chimp never gets lost. Reads nothing but atlases. Better than a compass, I tell you.
I think he's actually a monkey ...?
SQUEAK
EEK
SQUEAK
He got into our store of magnetized moon dust one day. Ate it all.
EEK
SQUEAK
He hasn't been the same since.
But he's the most reliable compass I've got.
Course is set!
Full speed ahead!

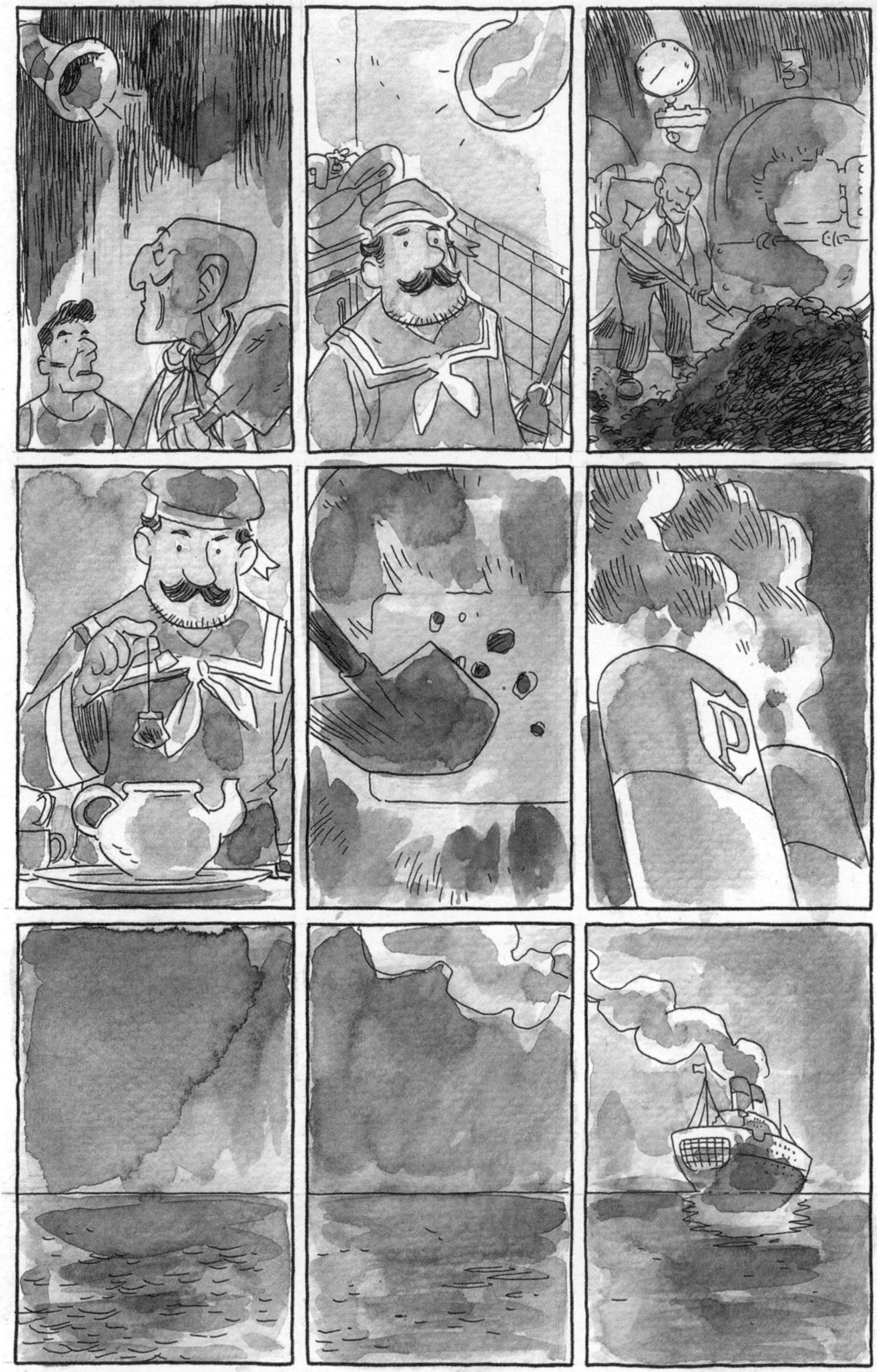

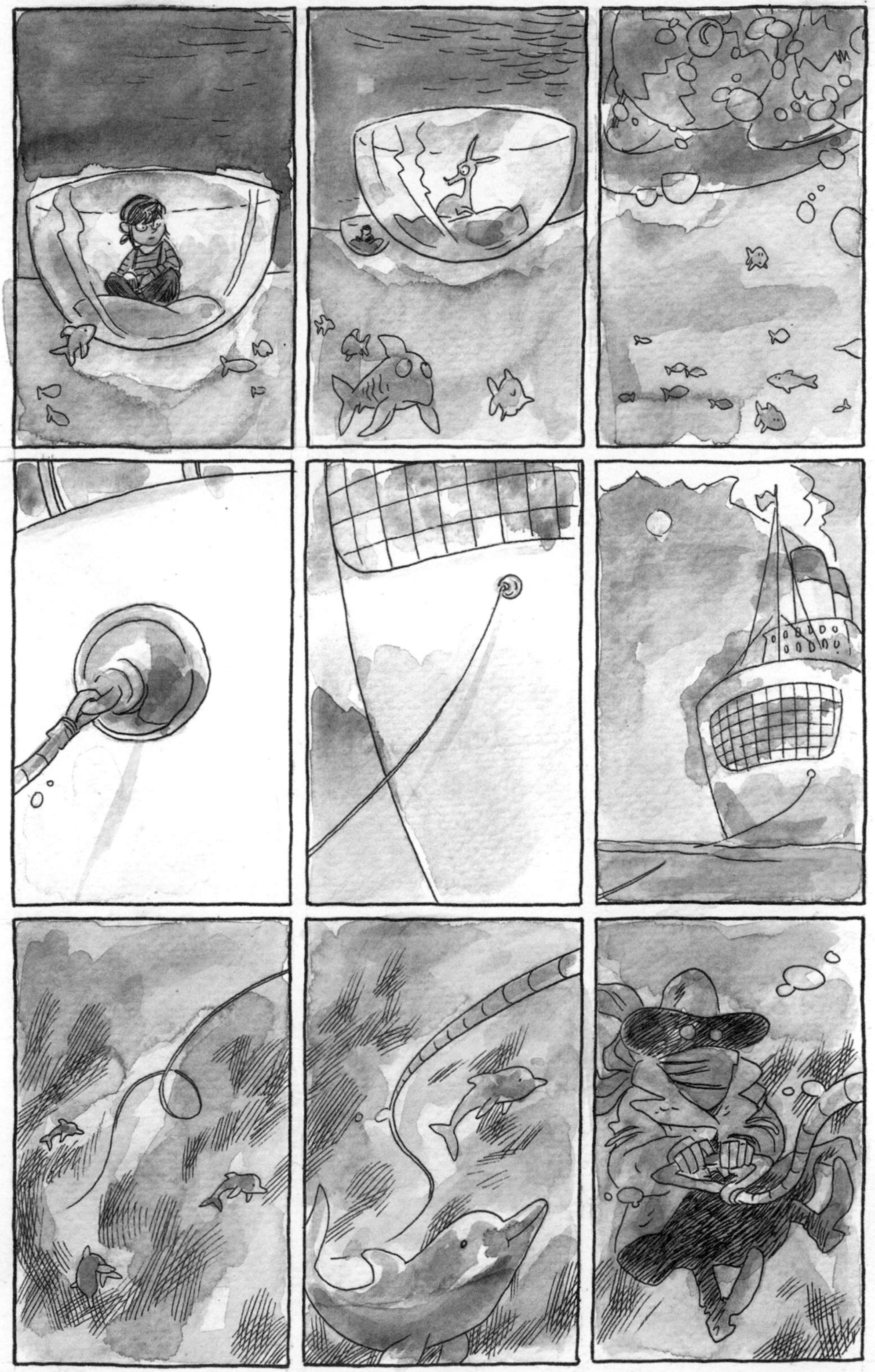

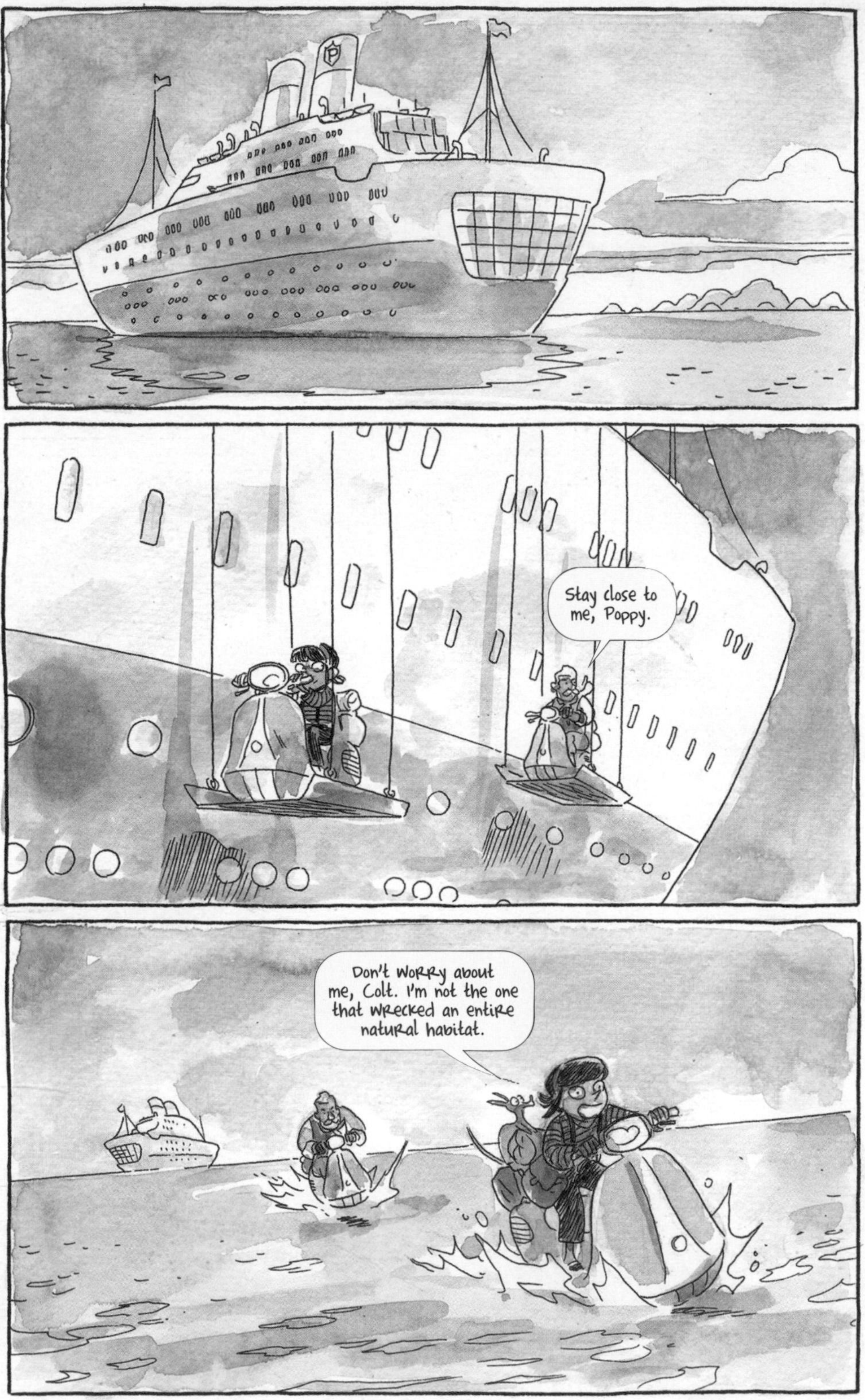
Stay close to me, Poppy.
Don't worry about me, Colt. I'm not the one that wrecked an entire natural habitat.

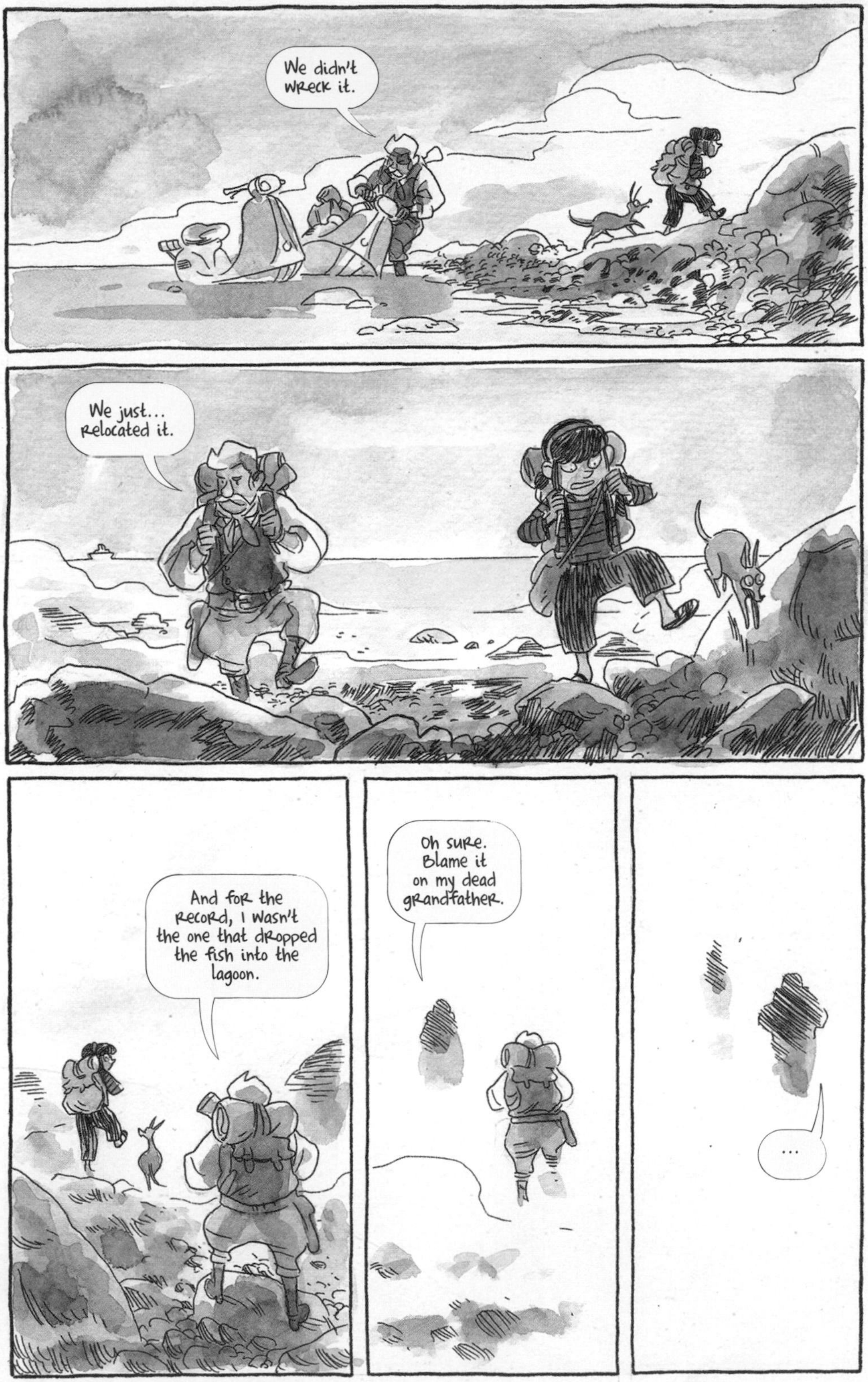
We didn't wreck it.
We just... relocated it.
And for the record, I wasn't the one that dropped the fish into the lagoon.
Oh sure. Blame it on my dead grandfather.
...

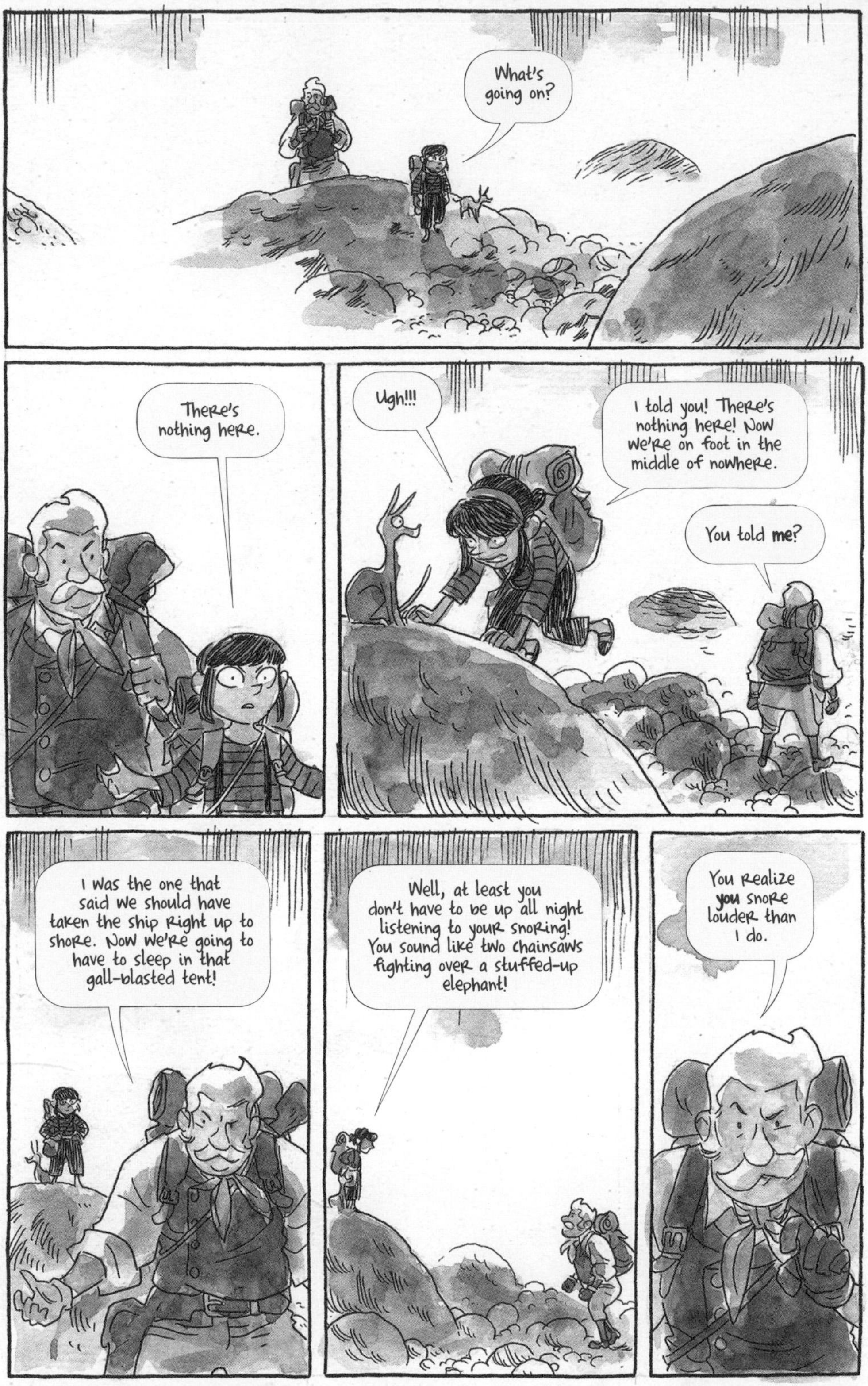
What's going on?
There's nothing here.
Ugh!!!
I told you! There's nothing here! Now we're on foot in the middle of nowhere.
You told **me**?
I was the one that said we should have taken the ship right up to shore. Now we're going to have to sleep in that gall-blasted tent!
Well, at least you don't have to be up all night listening to your snoring! You sound like two chainsaws fighting over a stuffed-up elephant!
You realize **you** snore louder than I do.

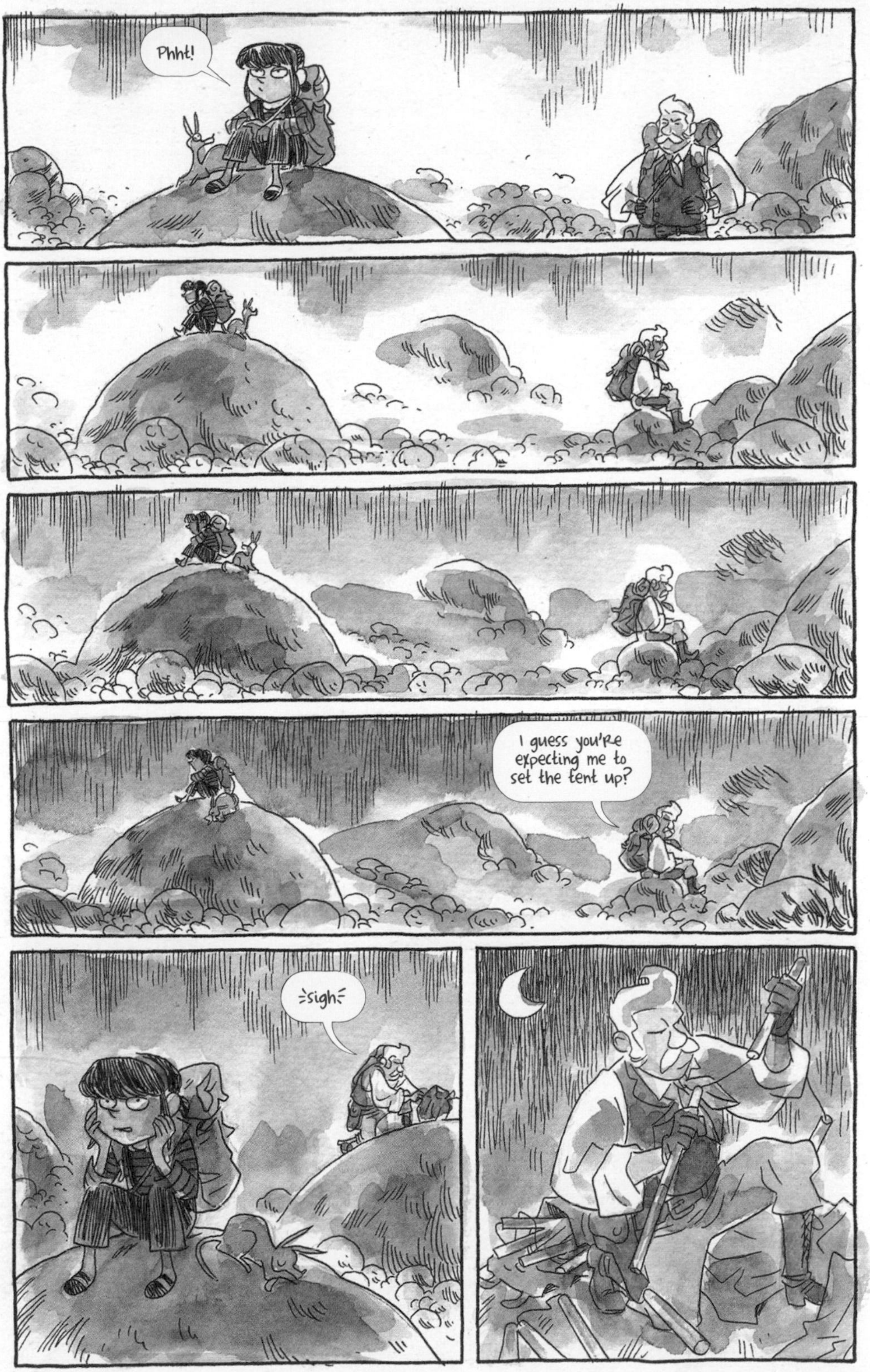
Phht!
I guess you're expecting me to set the tent up?
sigh

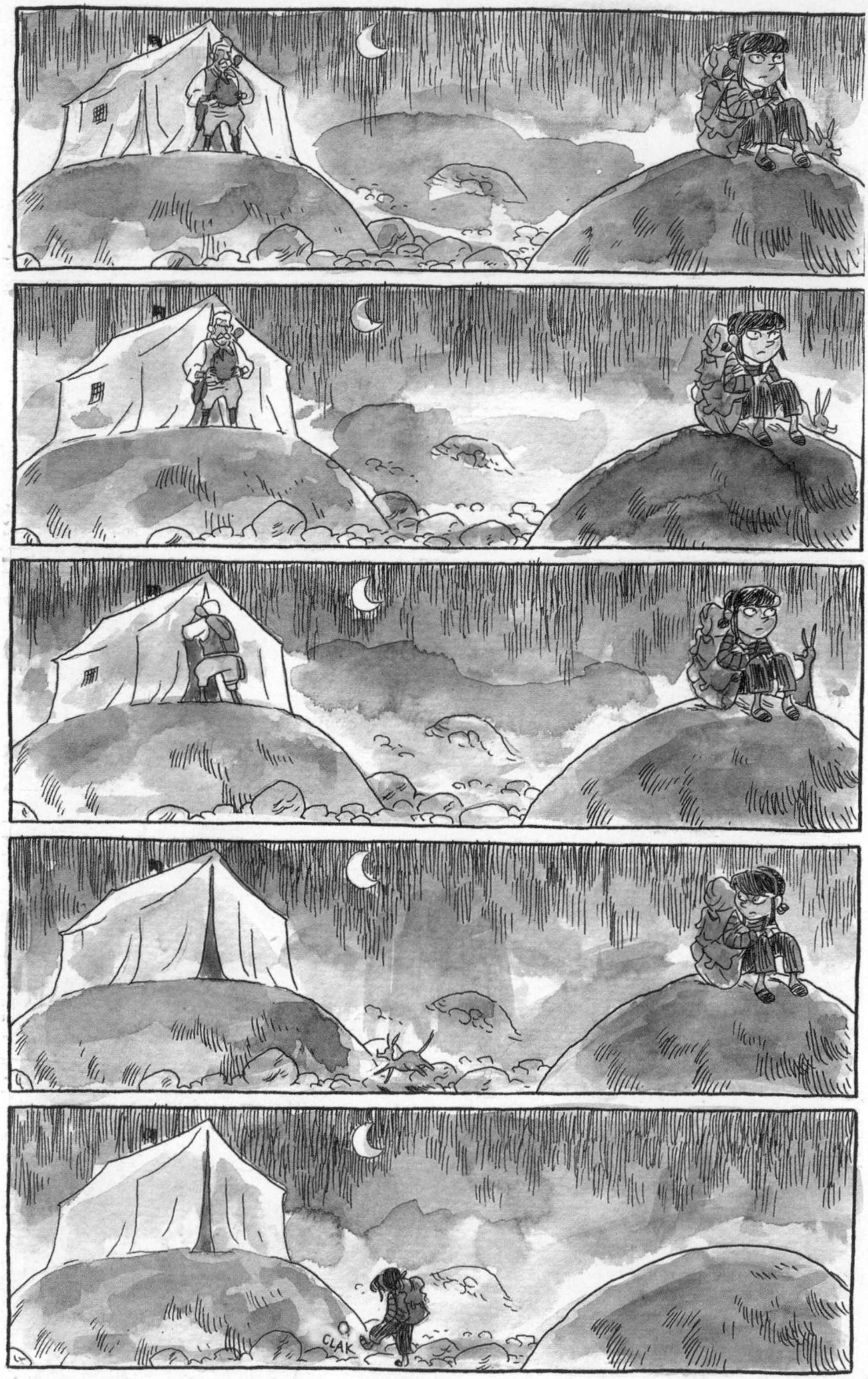
CLAK

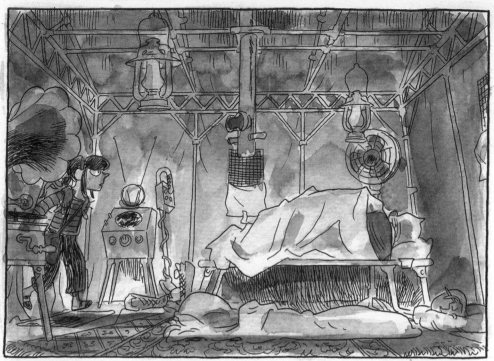

I love camping.

I love the air. It's different from anywhere else. And the sounds.

It's so quiet. Until you really start listening. Then you can hear the bugs and birds and ocean.

Stuff you never notice when you're stuck at home. Colt?

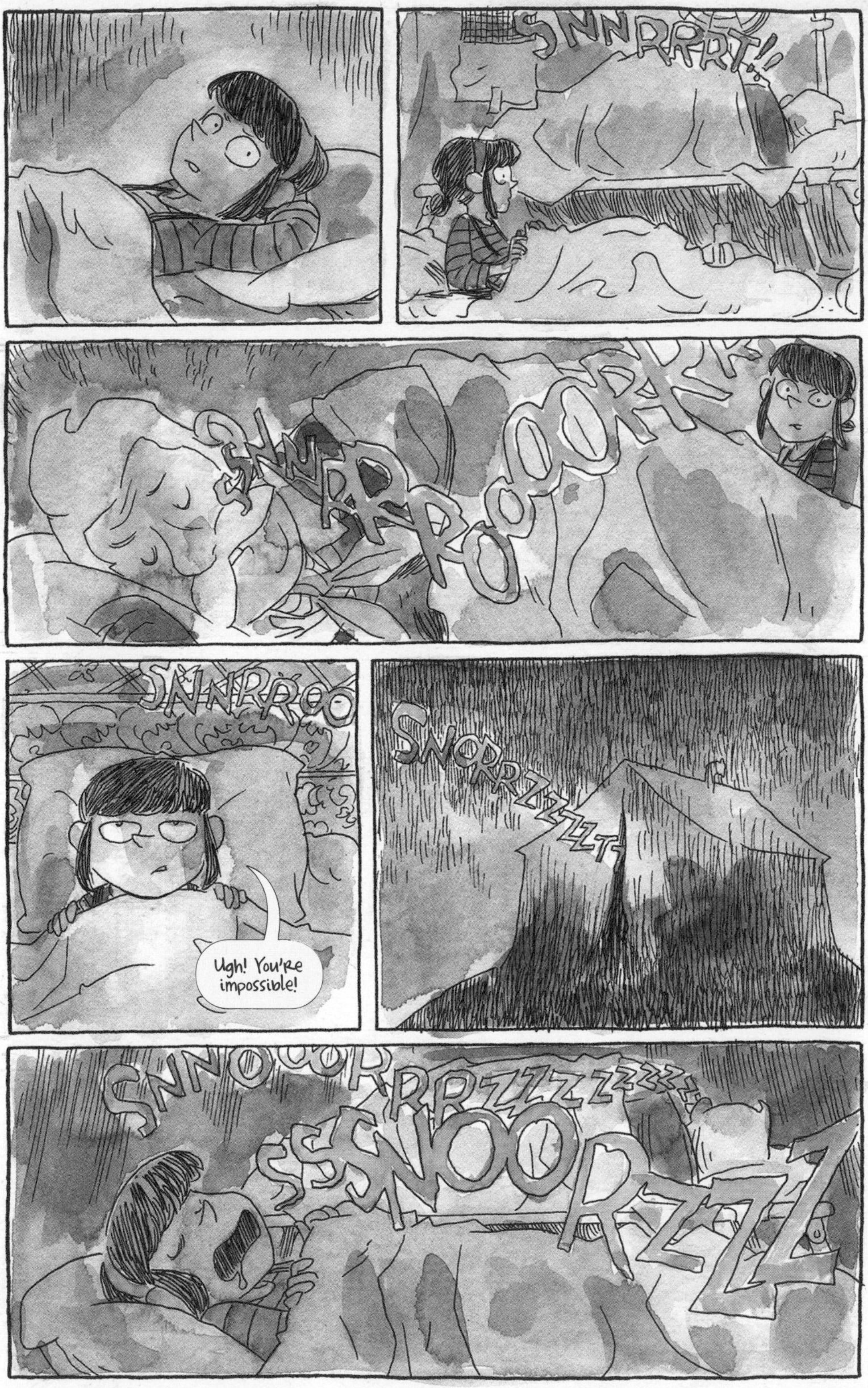
SNNRRRT!!
Ugh! You're impossible!

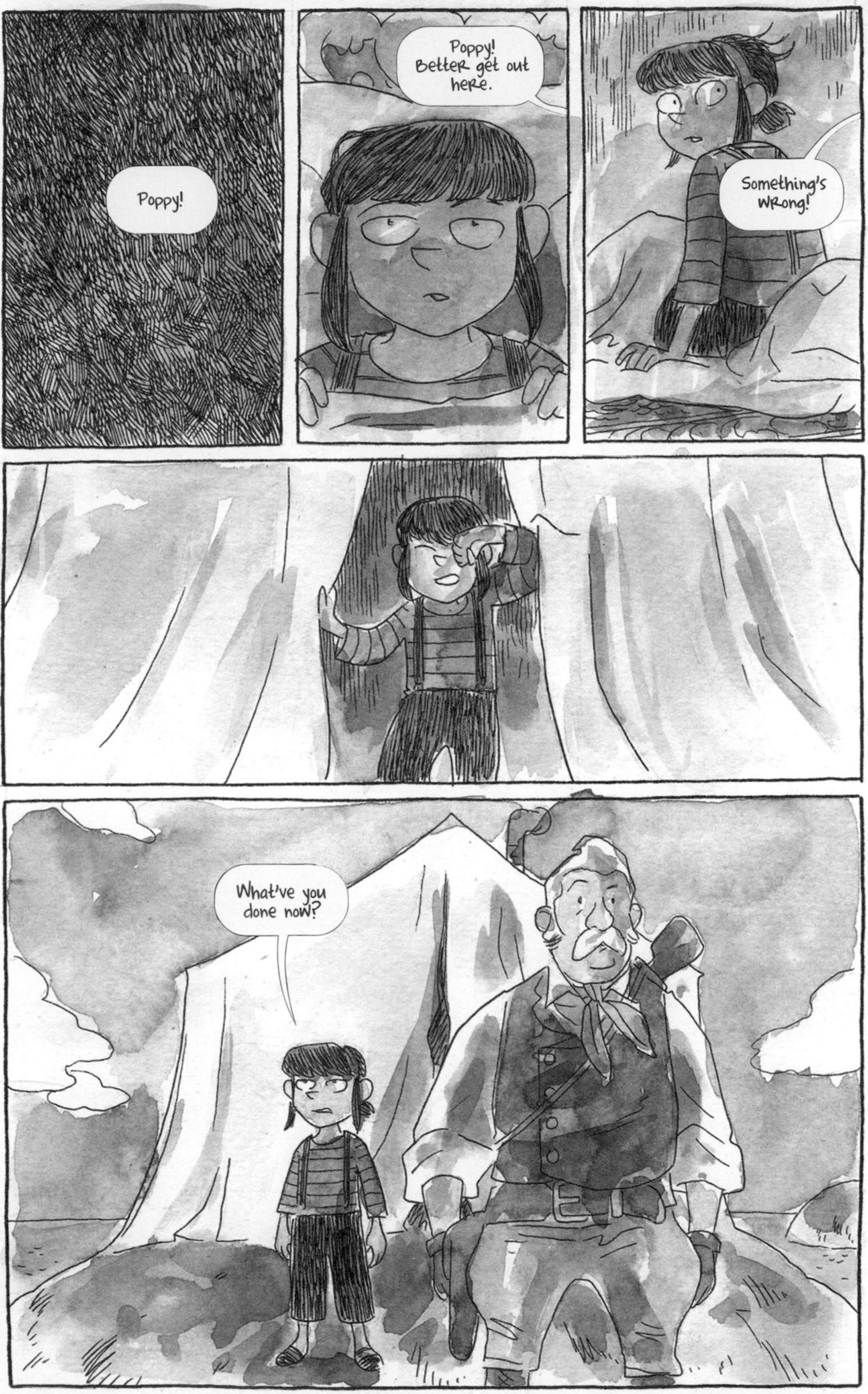
Poppy!
Poppy! Better get out here.
Something's wrong!
What've you done now?

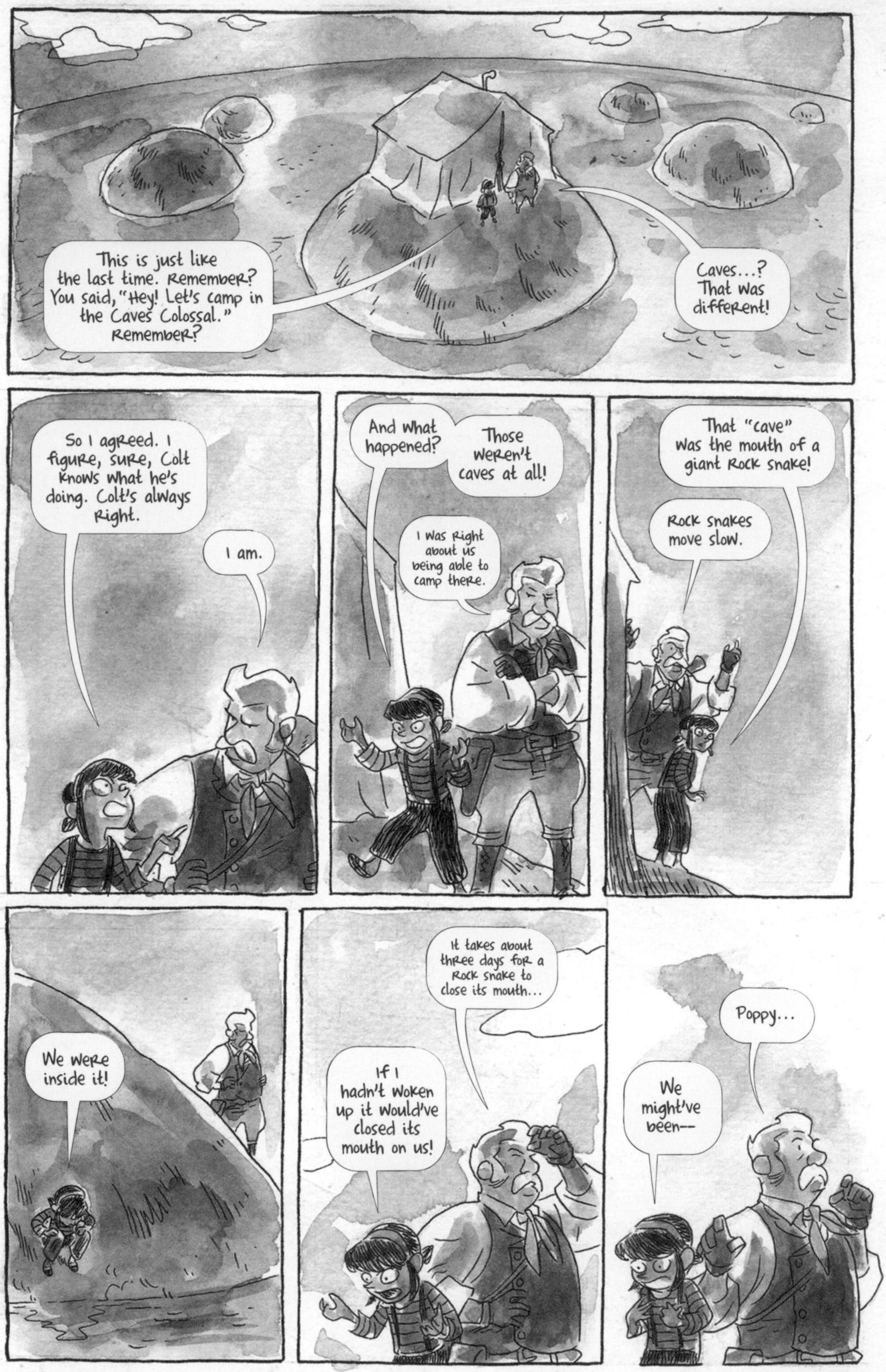
This is just like the last time. Remember? You said, "Hey! Let's camp in the Caves Colossal." Remember?
Caves…? That was different!
So I agreed. I figure, sure, Colt knows what he's doing. Colt's always right.
I am.
And what happened?
Those weren't caves at all!
I was right about us being able to camp there.
That "cave" was the mouth of a giant rock snake!
Rock snakes move slow.
We were inside it!
It takes about three days for a rock snake to close its mouth…
If I hadn't woken up it would've closed its mouth on us!
Poppy…
We might've been--

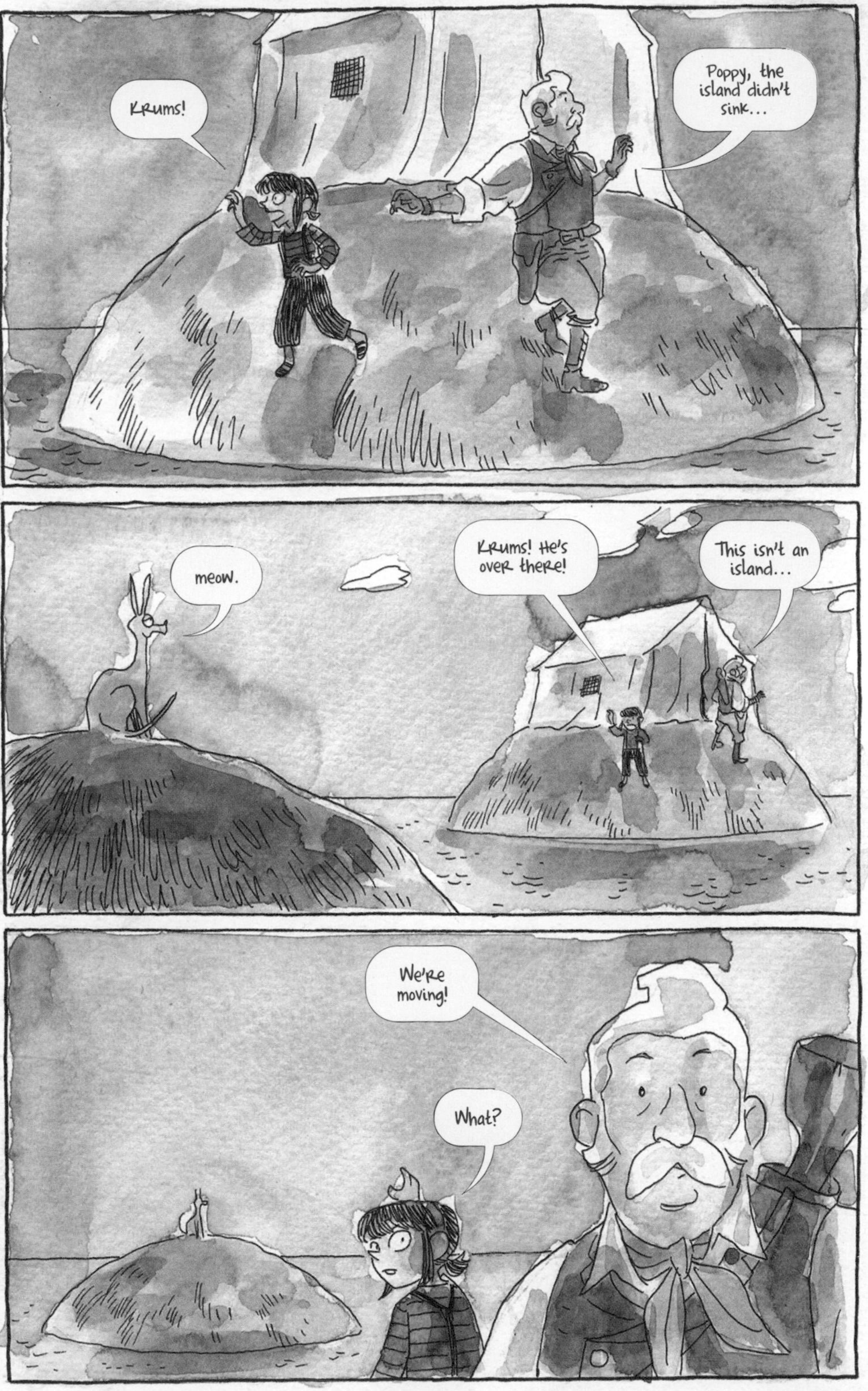
Krums!
Poppy, the island didn't sink...
meow.
Krums! He's over there!
This isn't an island...
We're moving!
What?

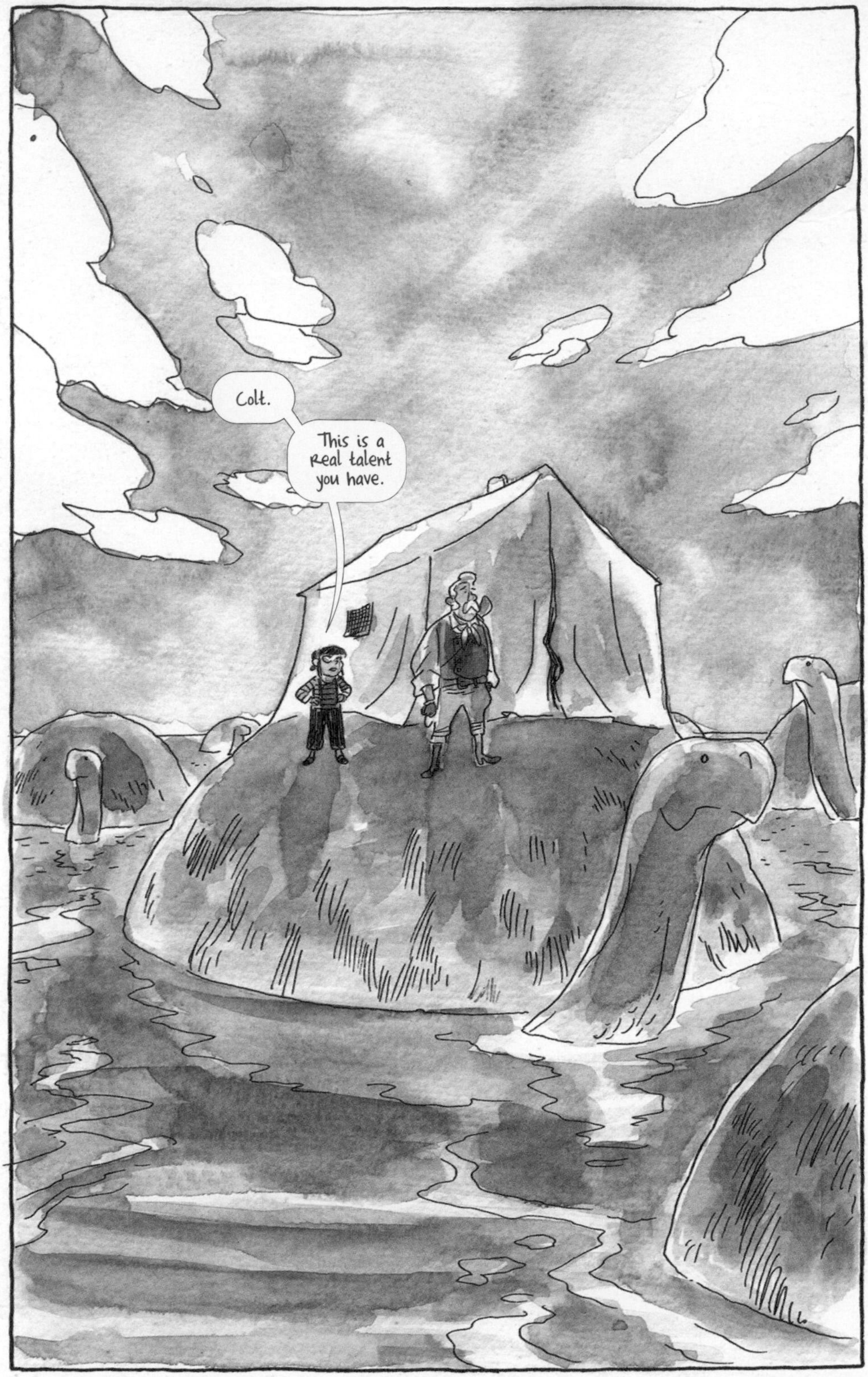
Colt.
This is a real talent you have.

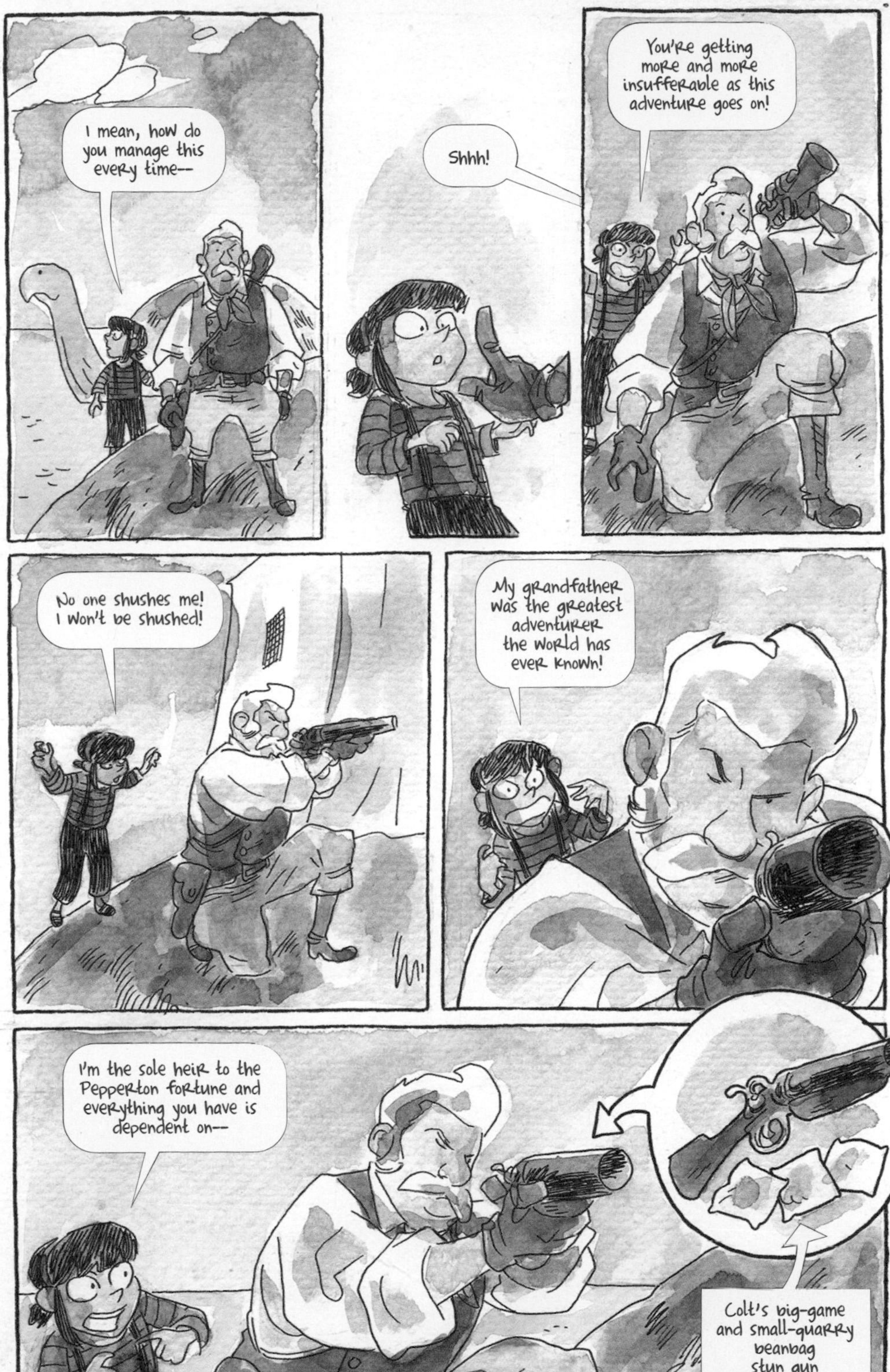
I mean, how do you manage this every time--
Shhh!
You're getting more and more insufferable as this adventure goes on!
No one shushes me! I won't be shushed!
My grandfather was the greatest adventurer the world has ever known!
I'm the sole heir to the Pepperton fortune and everything you have is dependent on--
Colt's big-game and small-quarry beanbag stun gun

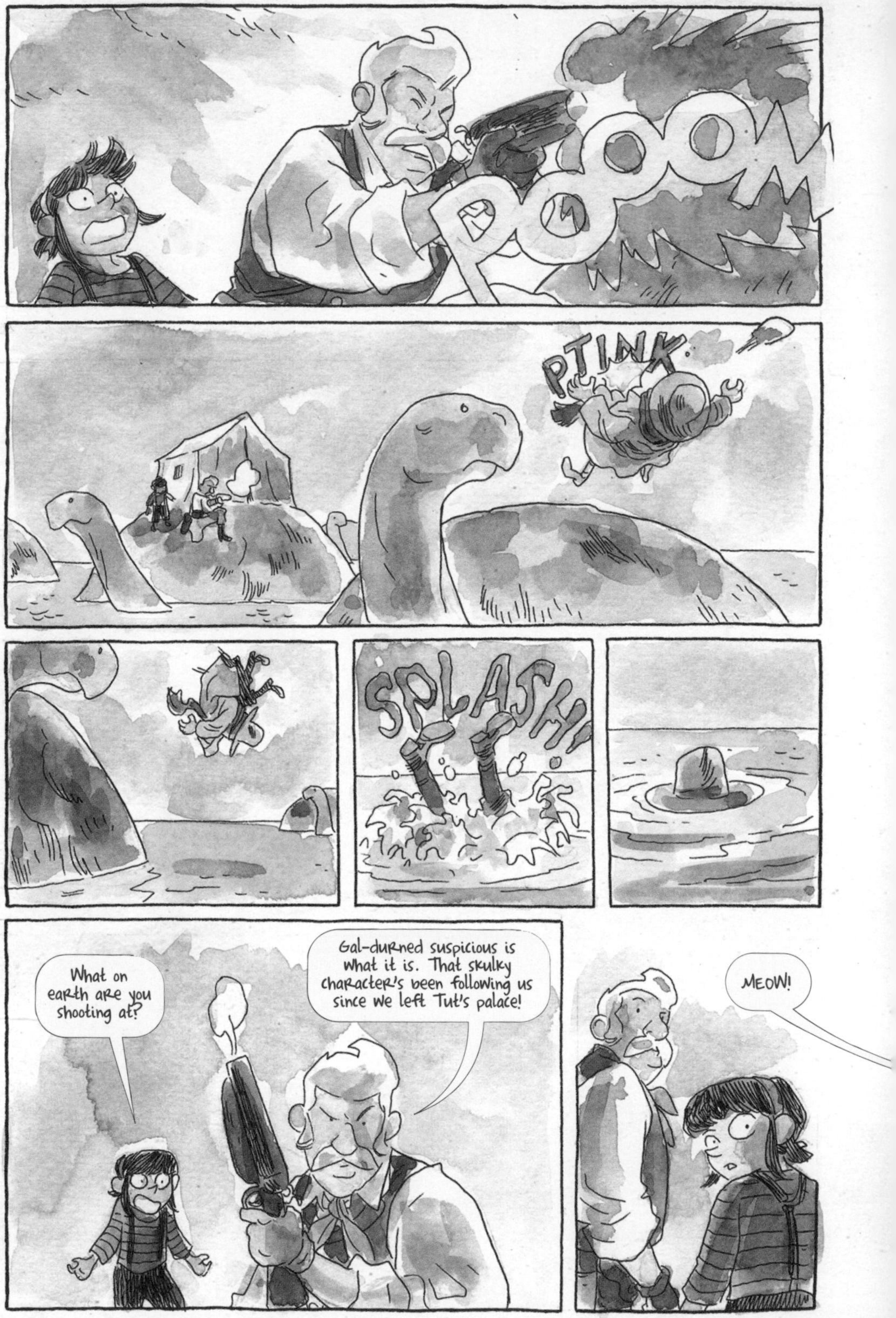
POOOOM
PTINK
SPLASH!
What on earth are you shooting at?
Gal-durned suspicious is what it is. That skulky character's been following us since we left Tut's palace!
MEOW!

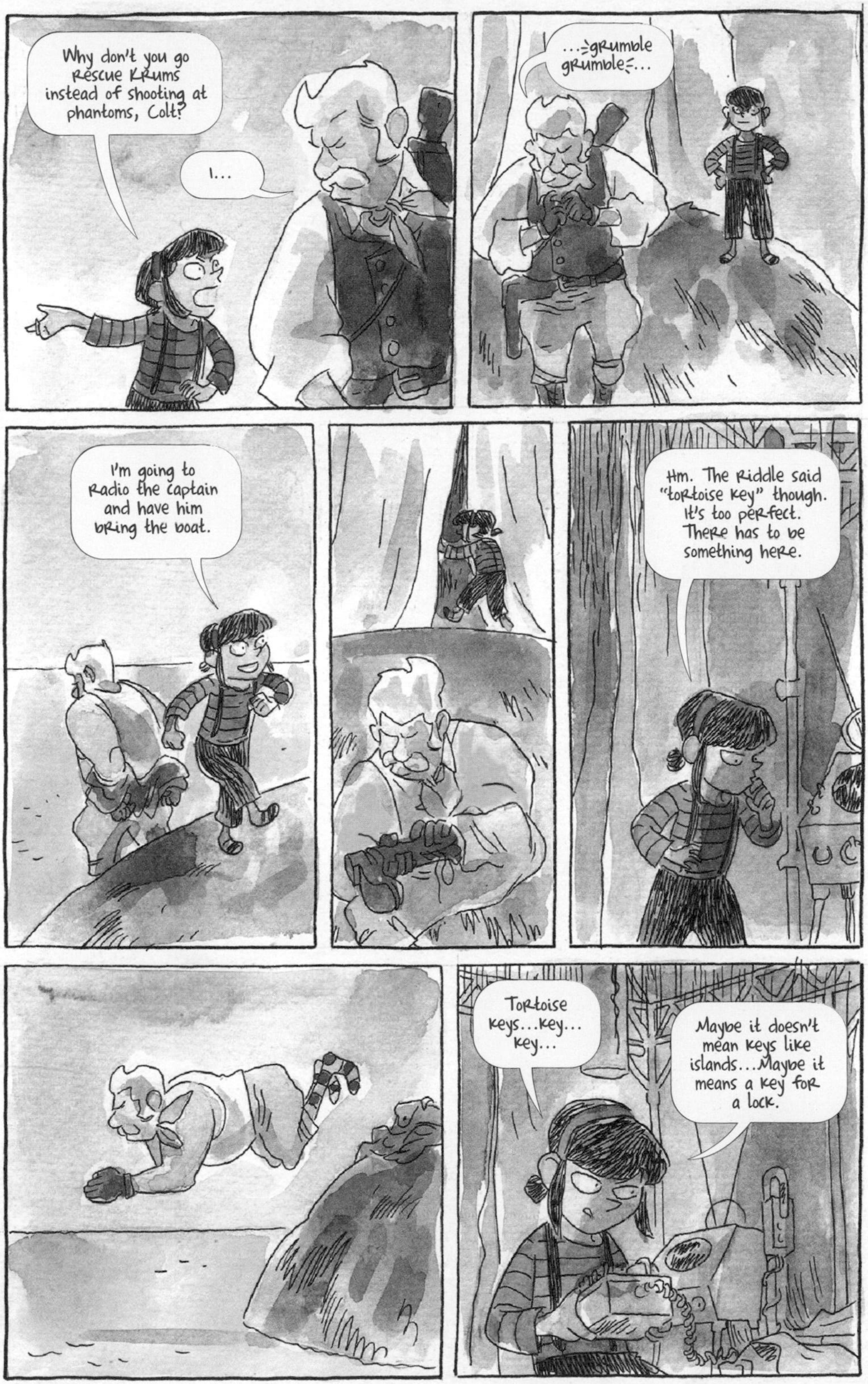
Why don't you go rescue Krums instead of shooting at phantoms, Colt?
I...
...grumble grumble...
I'm going to radio the captain and have him bring the boat.
Hm. The riddle said "tortoise key" though. It's too perfect. There has to be something here.
Tortoise keys...key... key...
Maybe it doesn't mean keys like islands...Maybe it means a key for a lock.

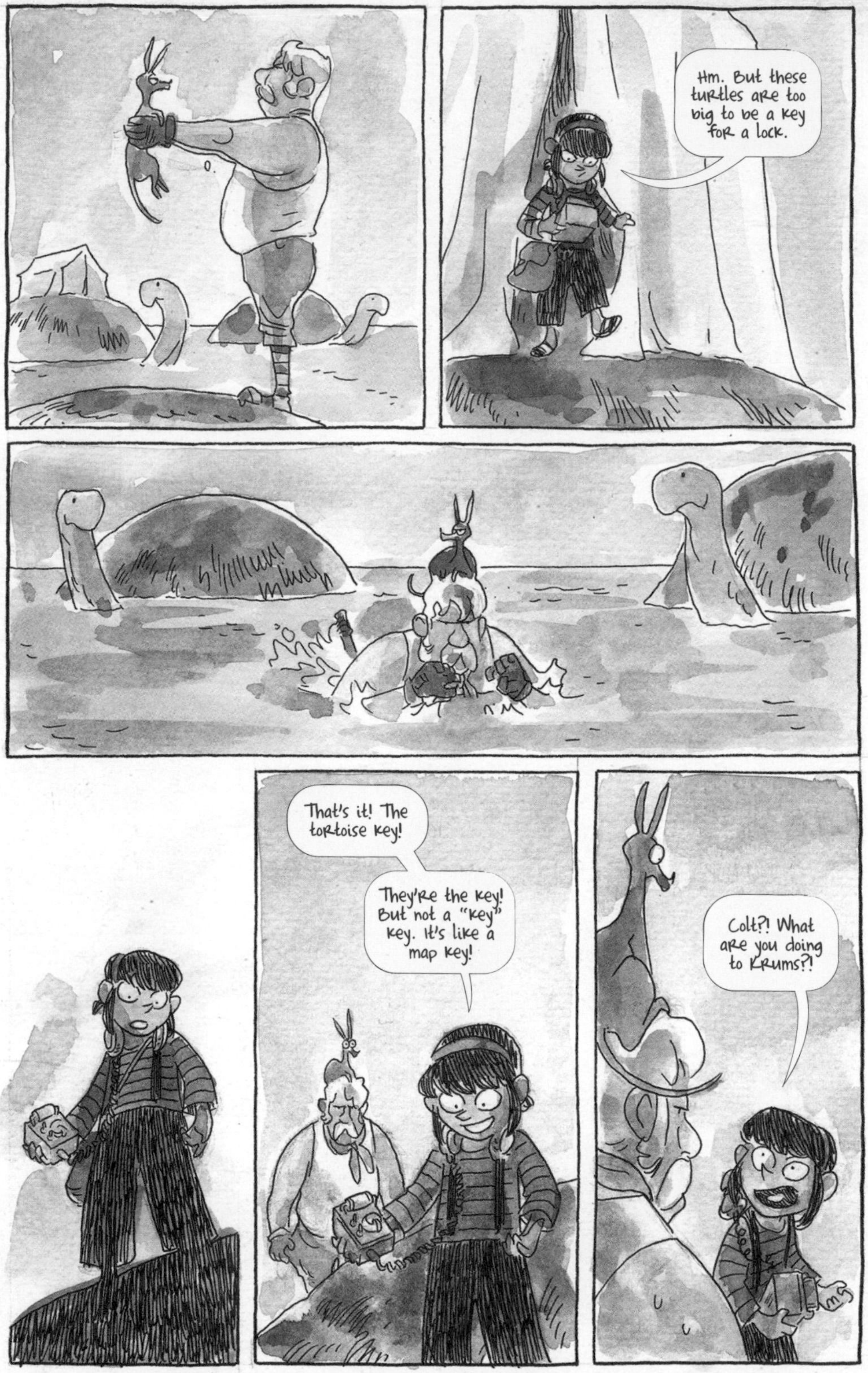
Hm. But these turtles are too big to be a key for a lock.
That's it! The tortoise key!
They're the key! But not a "key" key. It's like a map key!
Colt?! What are you doing to Krums?!

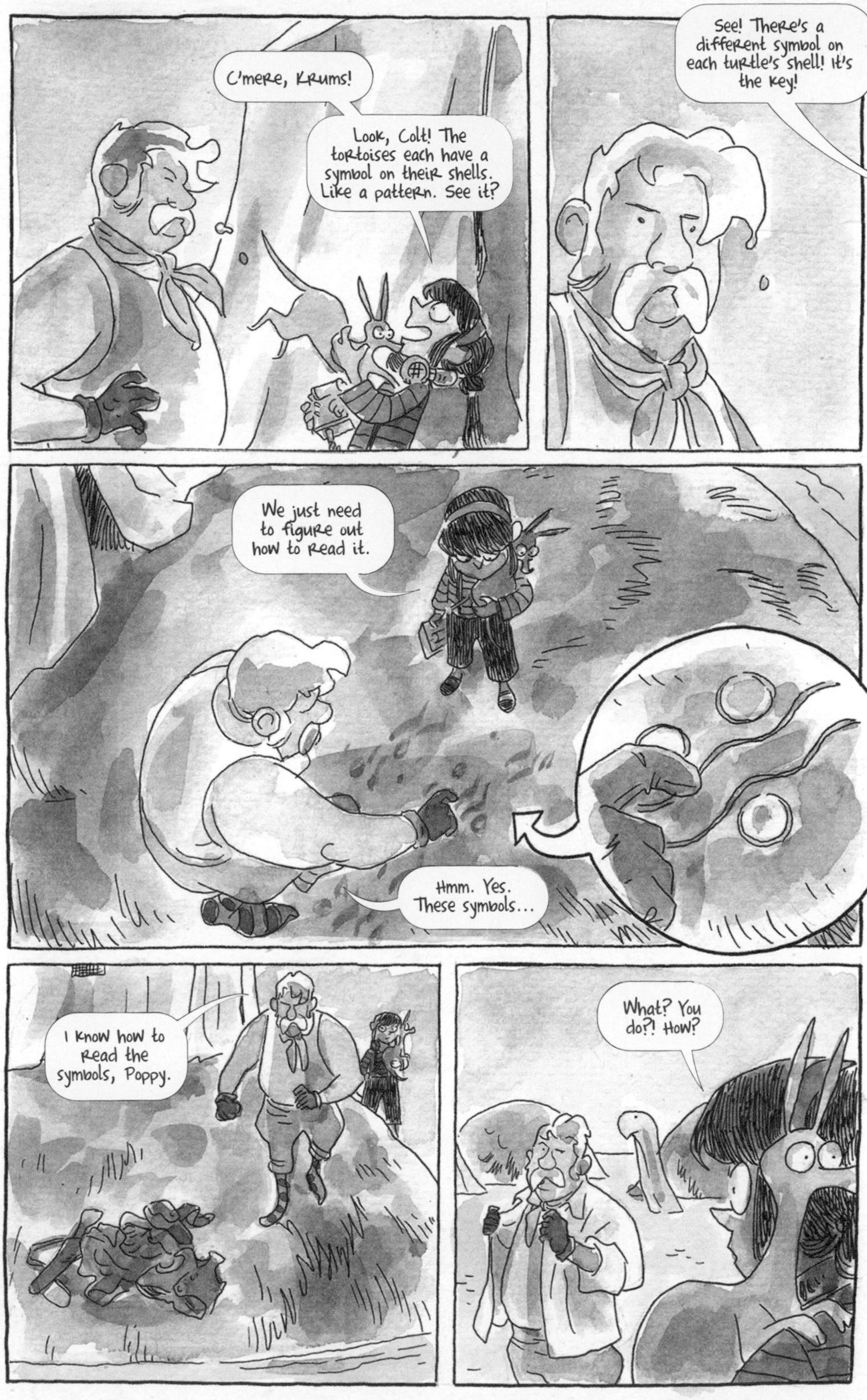
C'mere, Krums!
Look, Colt! The tortoises each have a symbol on their shells. Like a pattern. See it?
See! There's a different symbol on each turtle's shell! It's the key!
We just need to figure out how to read it.
Hmm. Yes. These symbols...
I know how to read the symbols, Poppy.
What? You do?! How?

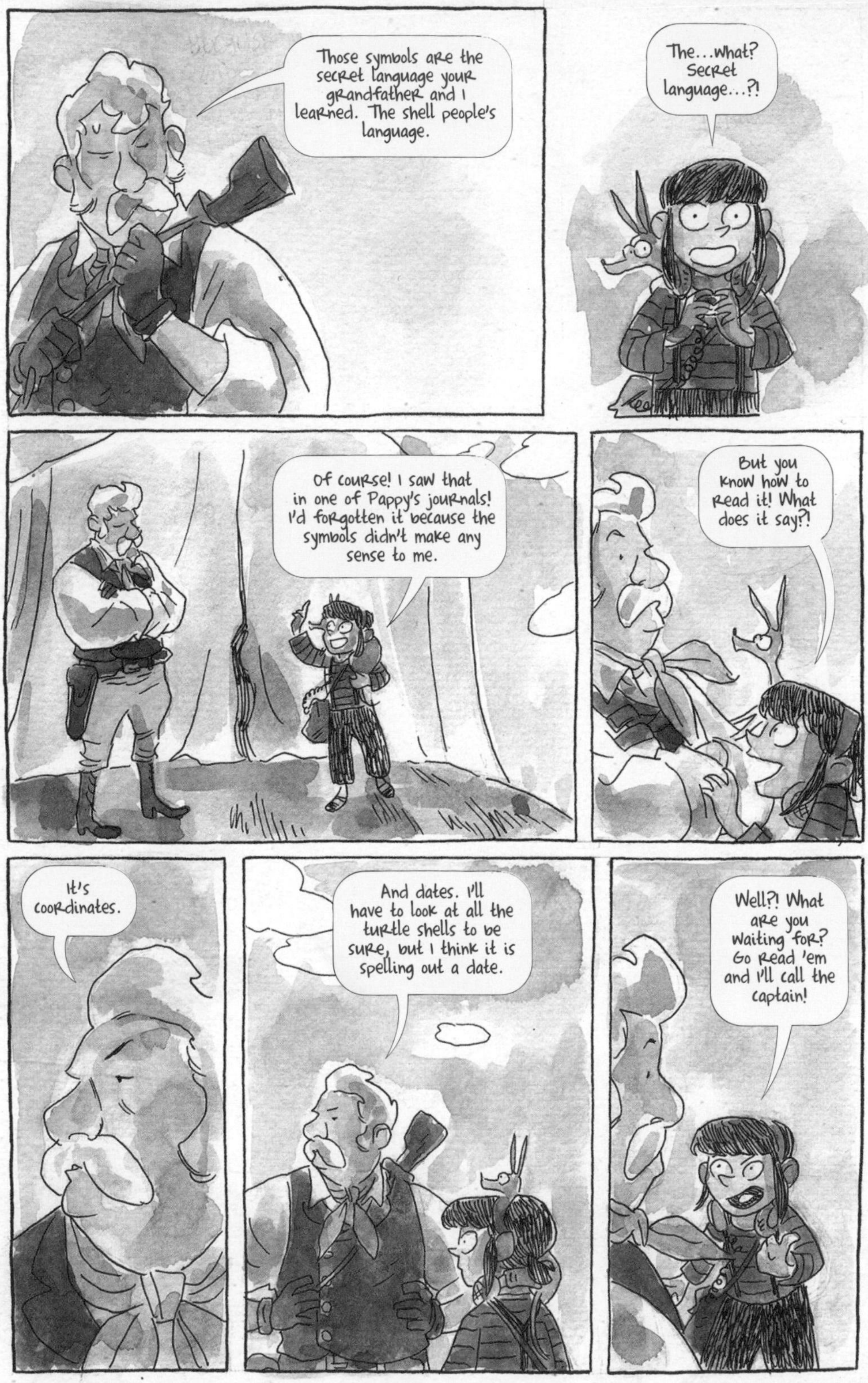
Those symbols are the secret language your grandfather and I learned. The shell people's language.
The...what? Secret language...?!
Of course! I saw that in one of Pappy's journals! I'd forgotten it because the symbols didn't make any sense to me.
But you know how to read it! What does it say?!
It's coordinates.
And dates. I'll have to look at all the turtle shells to be sure, but I think it is spelling out a date.
Well?! What are you waiting for? Go read 'em and I'll call the captain!

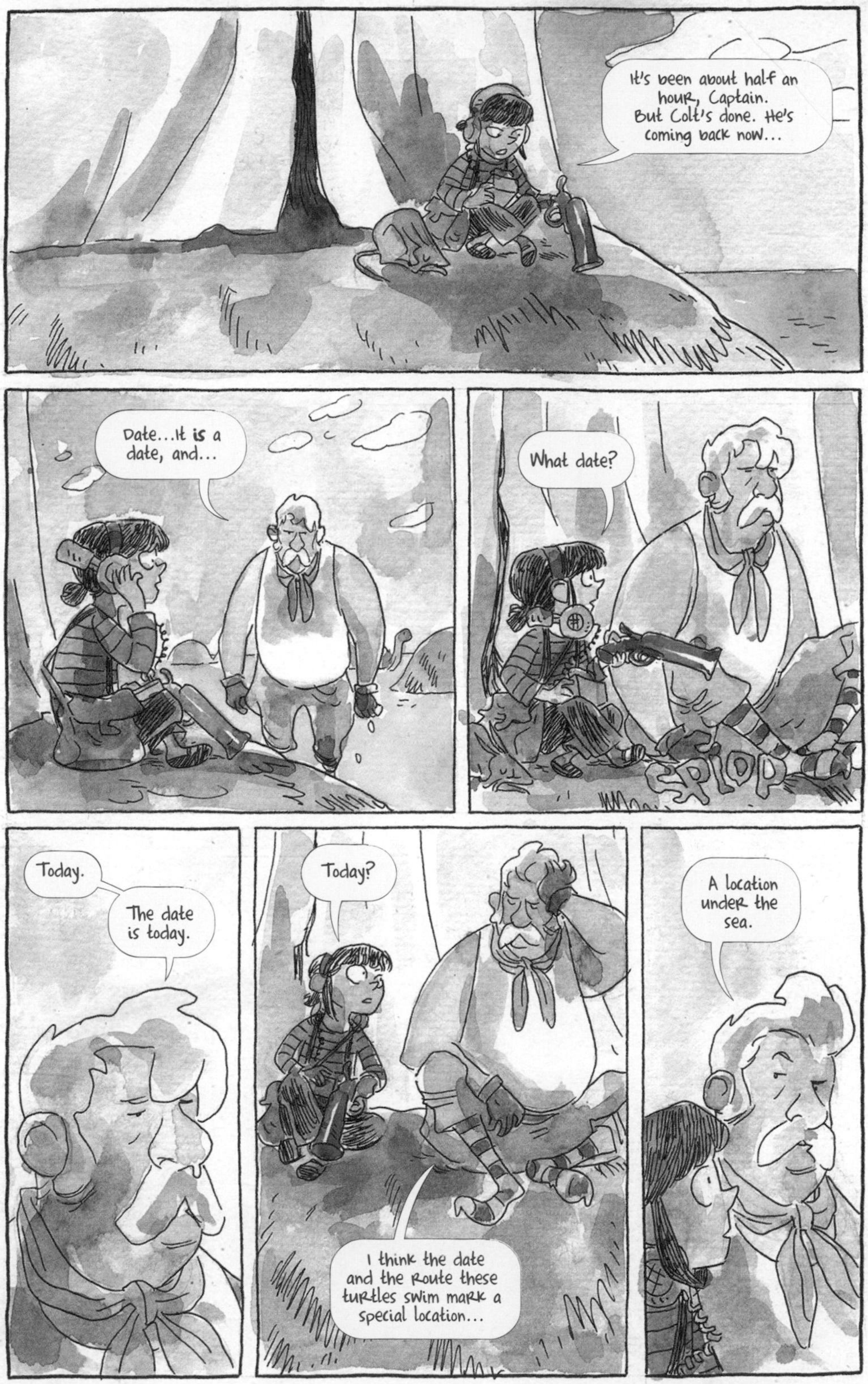

It's been about half an hour, Captain. But Colt's done. He's coming back now...
Date...It **is** a date, and...
What date?
SPLOP
Today.
The date is today.
Today?
I think the date and the route these turtles swim mark a special location...
A location under the sea.

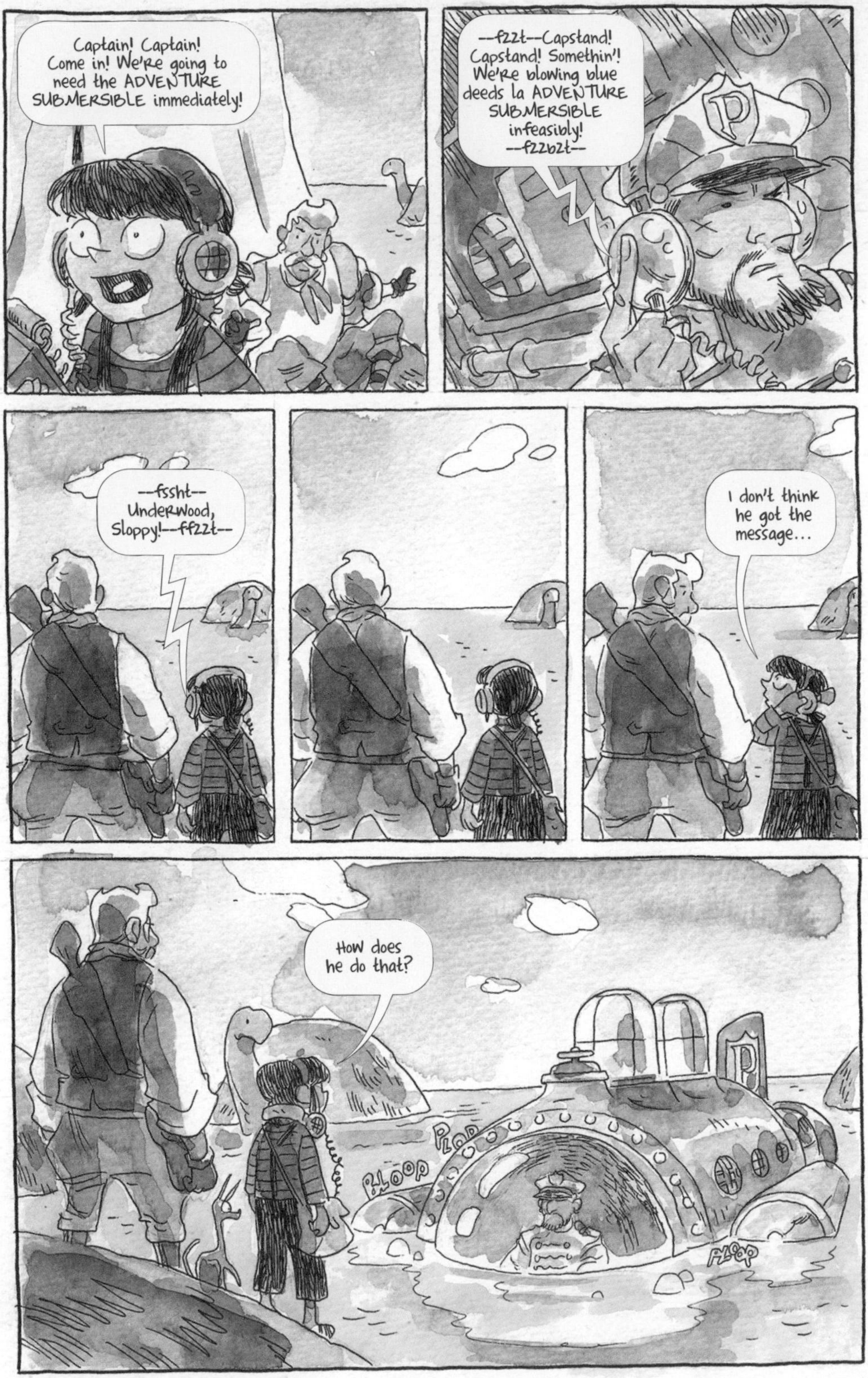
Captain! Captain! Come in! We're going to need the ADVENTURE SUBMERSIBLE immediately!
--fzzt--Capstand! Capstand! Somethin'! We're blowing blue deeds la ADVENTURE SUBMERSIBLE infeasibly! --fzzbzt--
--fssht-- Underwood, Sloppy!--ffzzt--
I don't think he got the message...
How does he do that?
PLOOP
PLOP
PLOOP

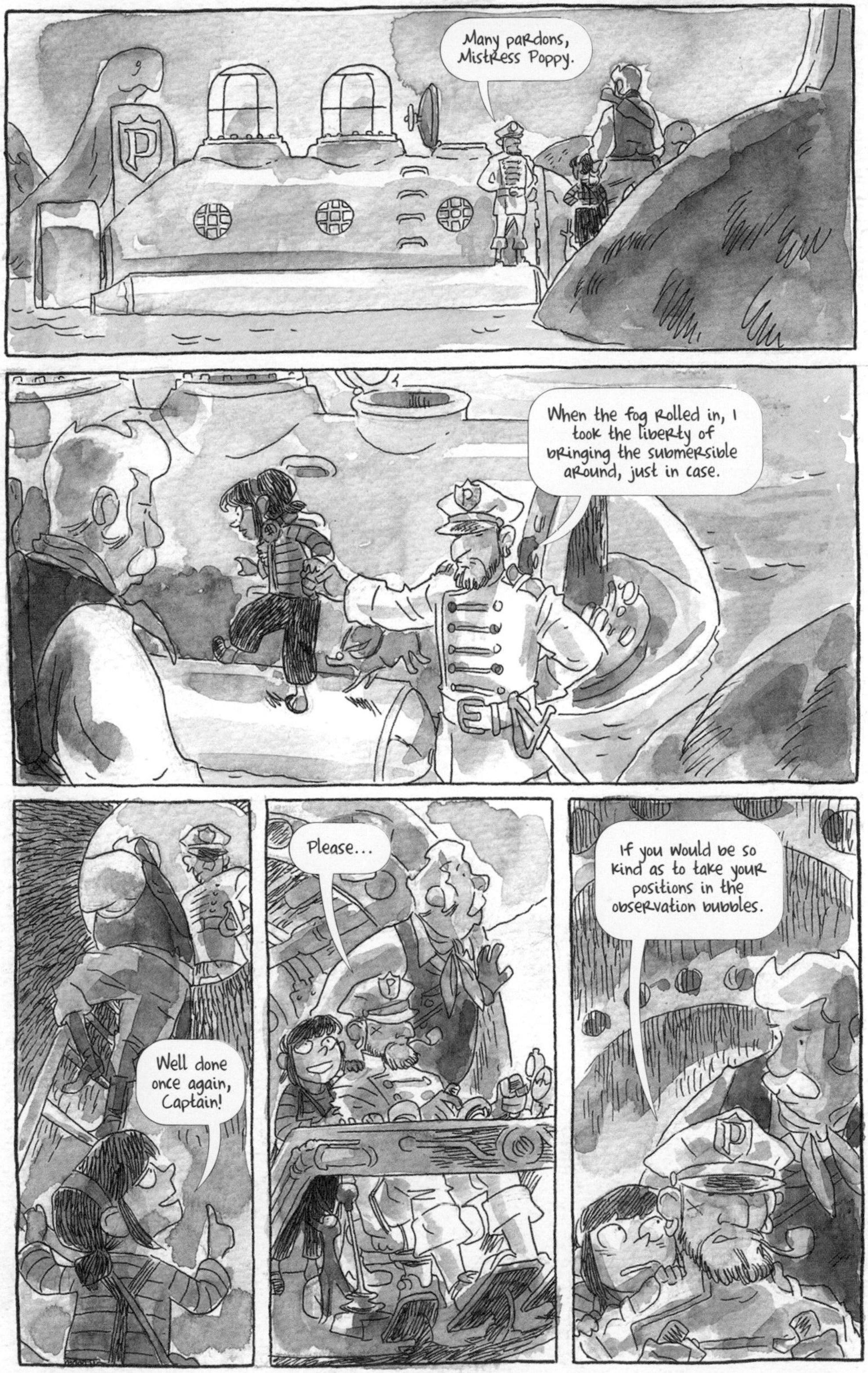
Many pardons, Mistress Poppy.
When the fog rolled in, I took the liberty of bringing the submersible around, just in case.
Well done once again, Captain!
Please...
If you would be so kind as to take your positions in the observation bubbles.

Oh man!
Look at all this stuff!

P

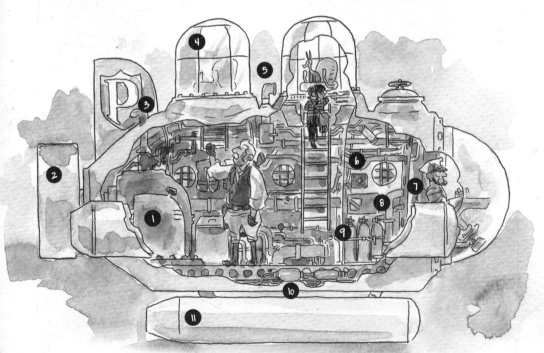

1. Bubble hush engine
2. Propeller
3. Bubble machine
4. Observation bubble
5. Stereoscope
6. First-aid kit
7. "Captains Only" chair
8. Emergency picnic lunches
9. Reserve gas options: laughing, natural, knockout
10. Musical soundtrack generator
11. Main ballast tank

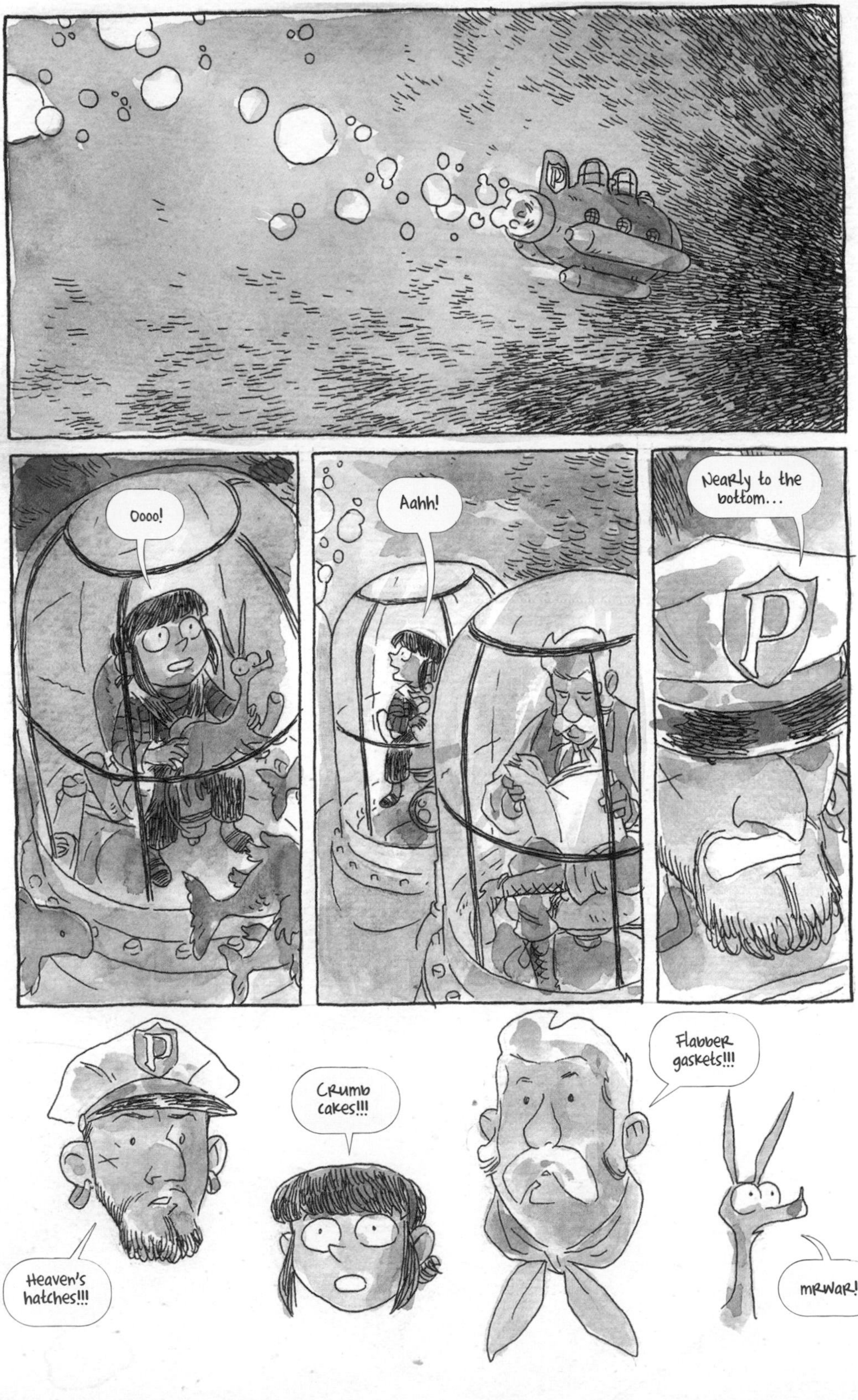
Oooo!
Aahh!
Nearly to the bottom...
Heaven's hatches!!!
Crumb cakes!!!
Flabber gaskets!!!
mrwar!

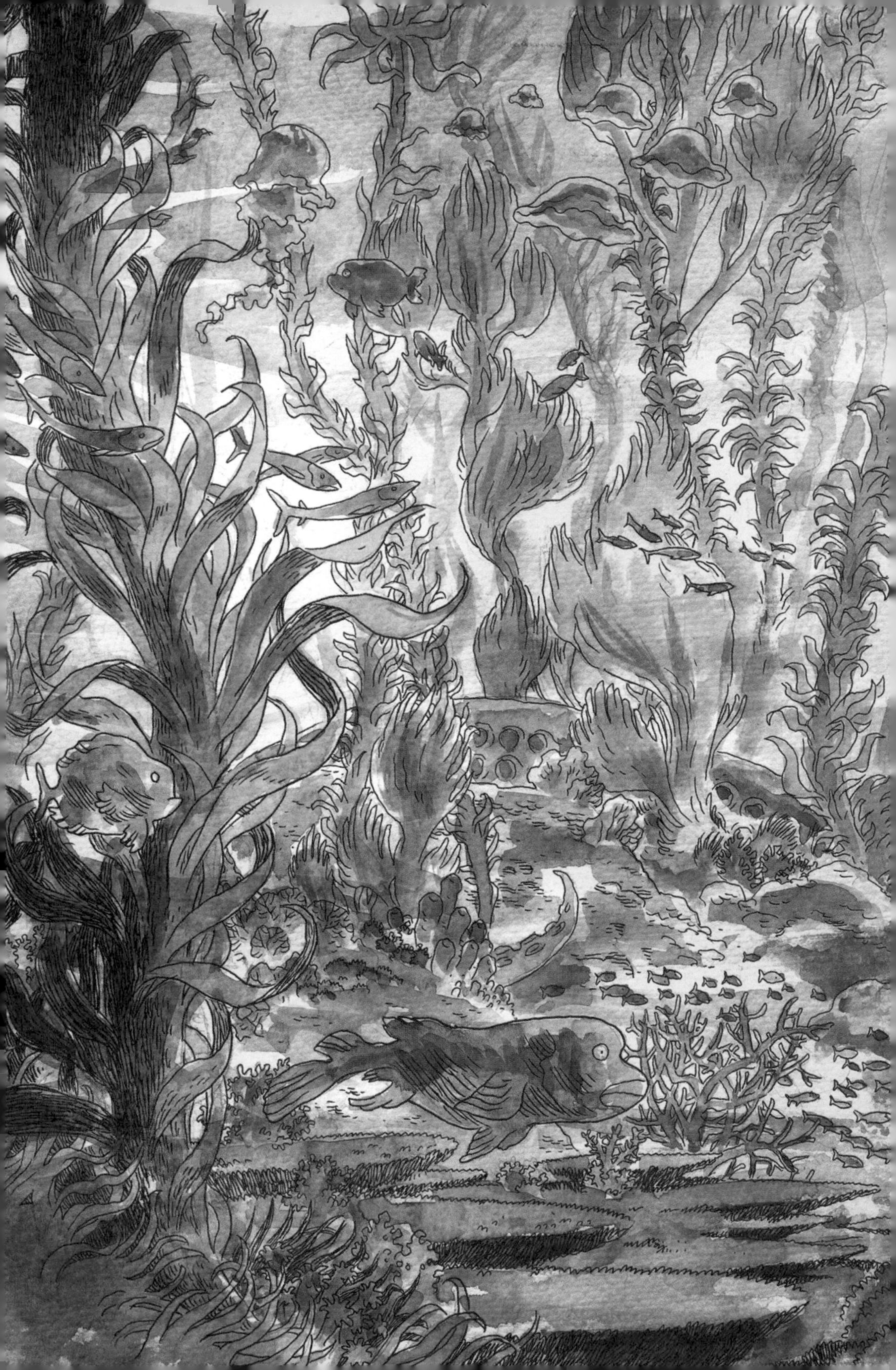

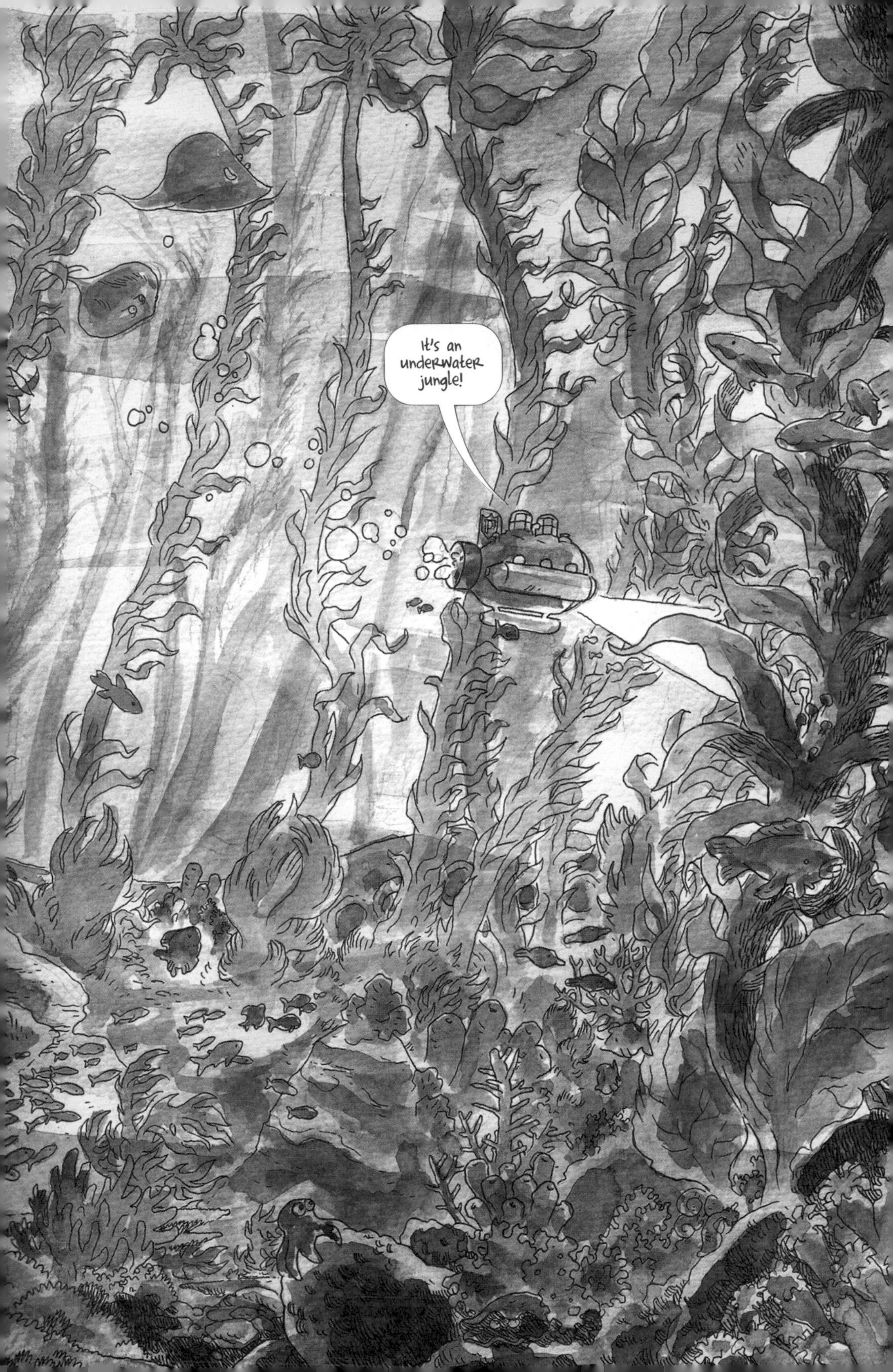
It's an underwater jungle!

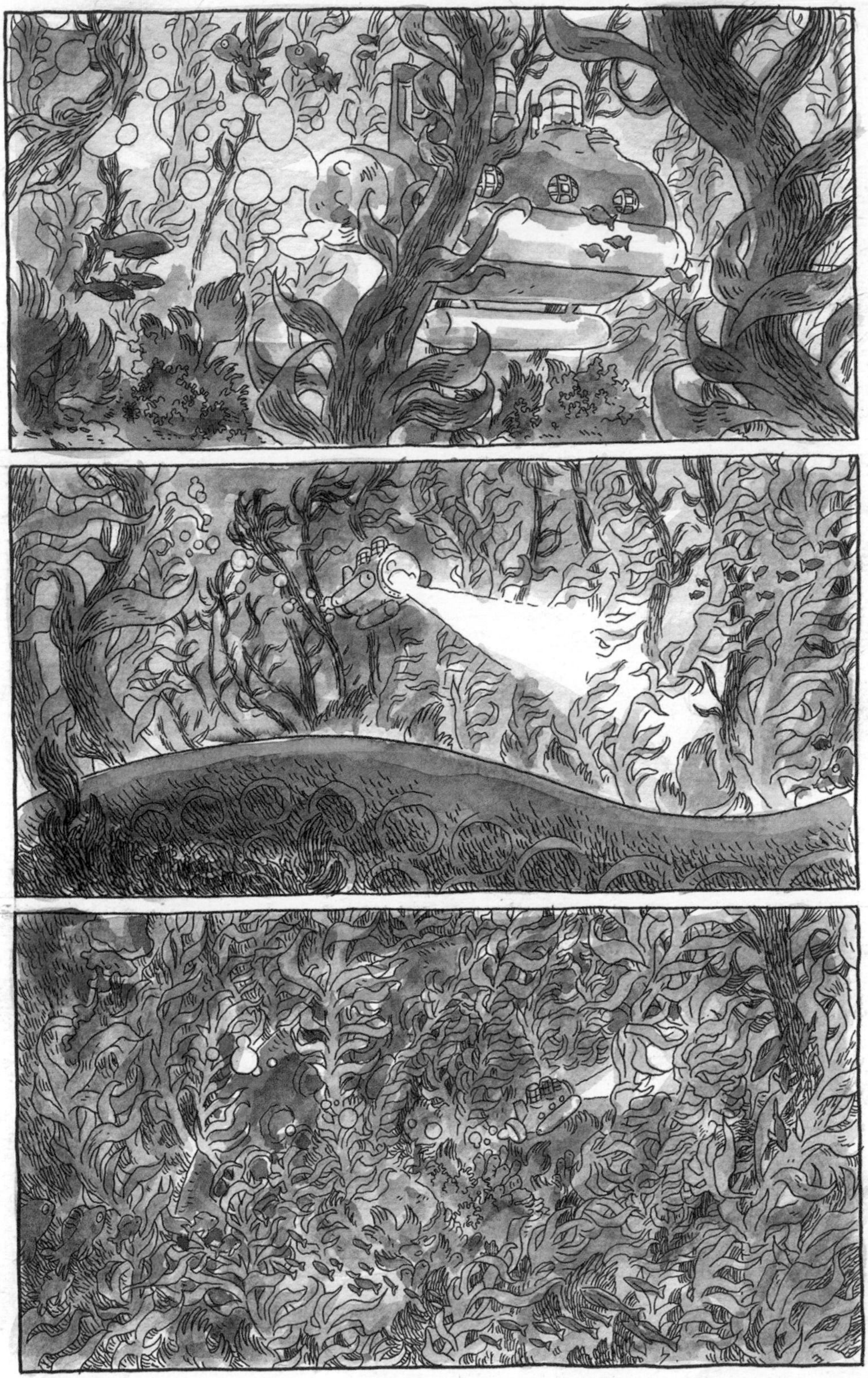

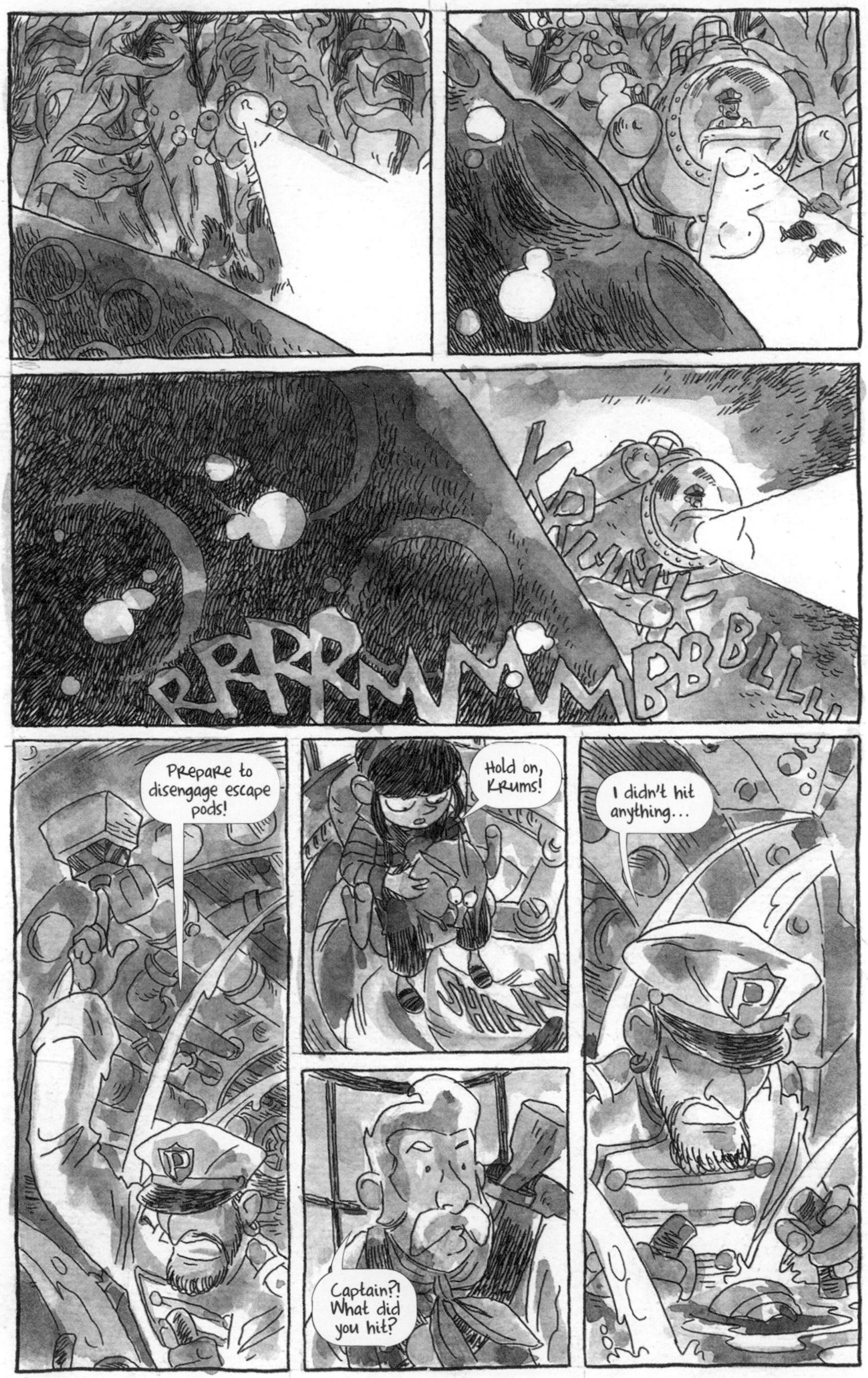
Prepare to disengage escape pods!
Hold on, Krums!
I didn't hit anything...
Captain?! What did you hit?

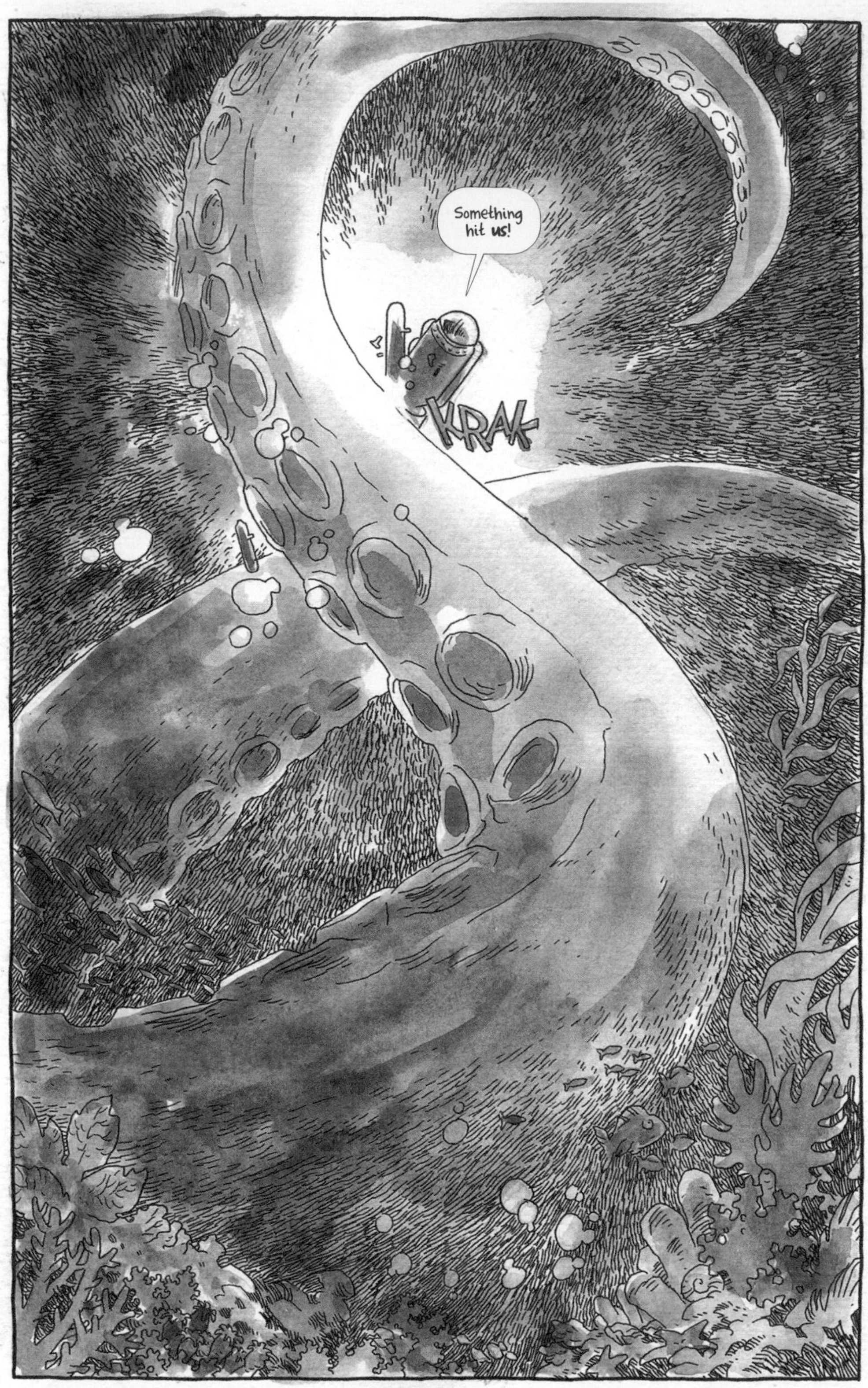
Something hit us!
KRAK

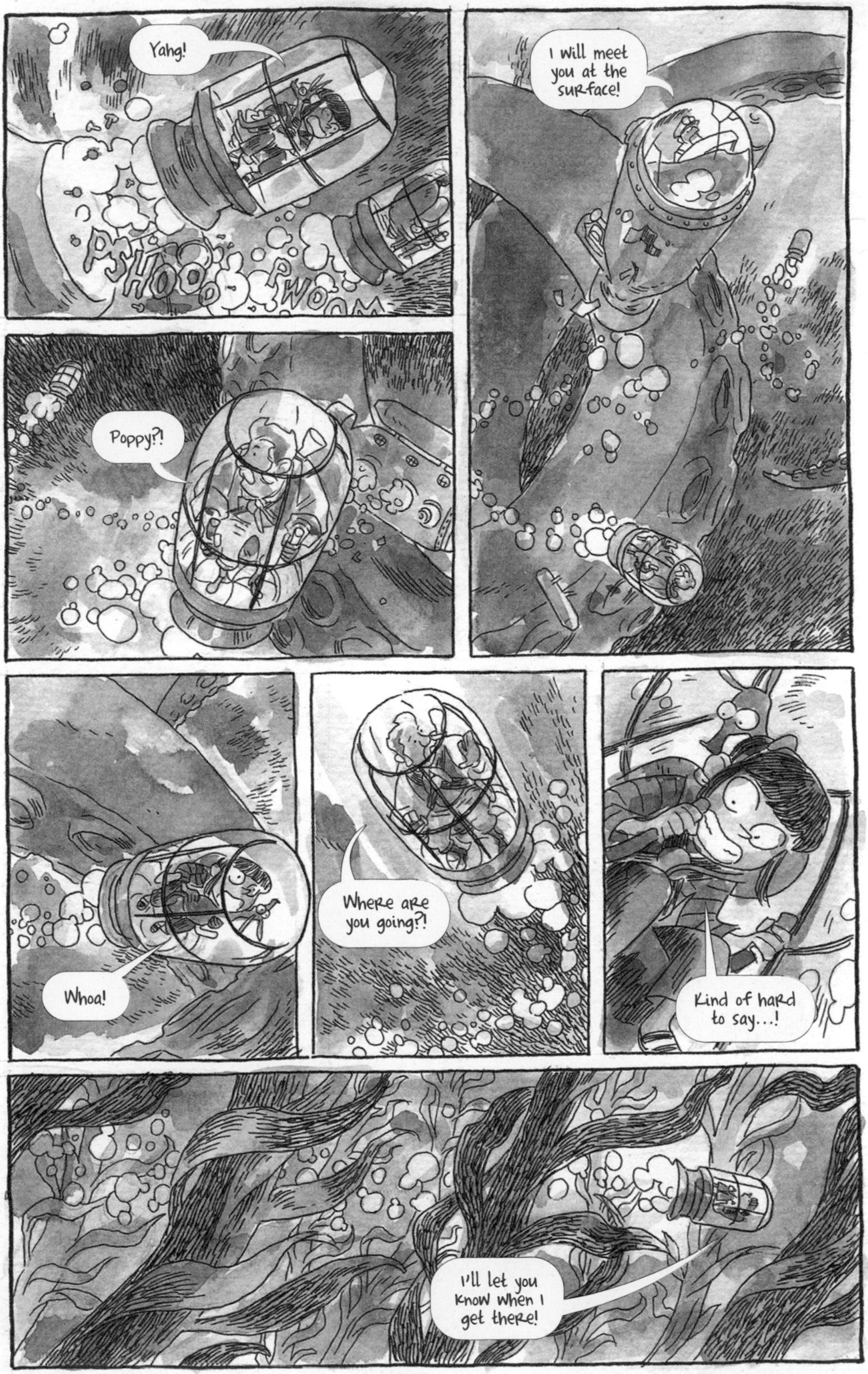
Yahg!
PSHOO
PWOOM
I will meet you at the surface!
Poppy?!
Whoa!
Where are you going?!
Kind of hard to say...!
I'll let you know when I get there!

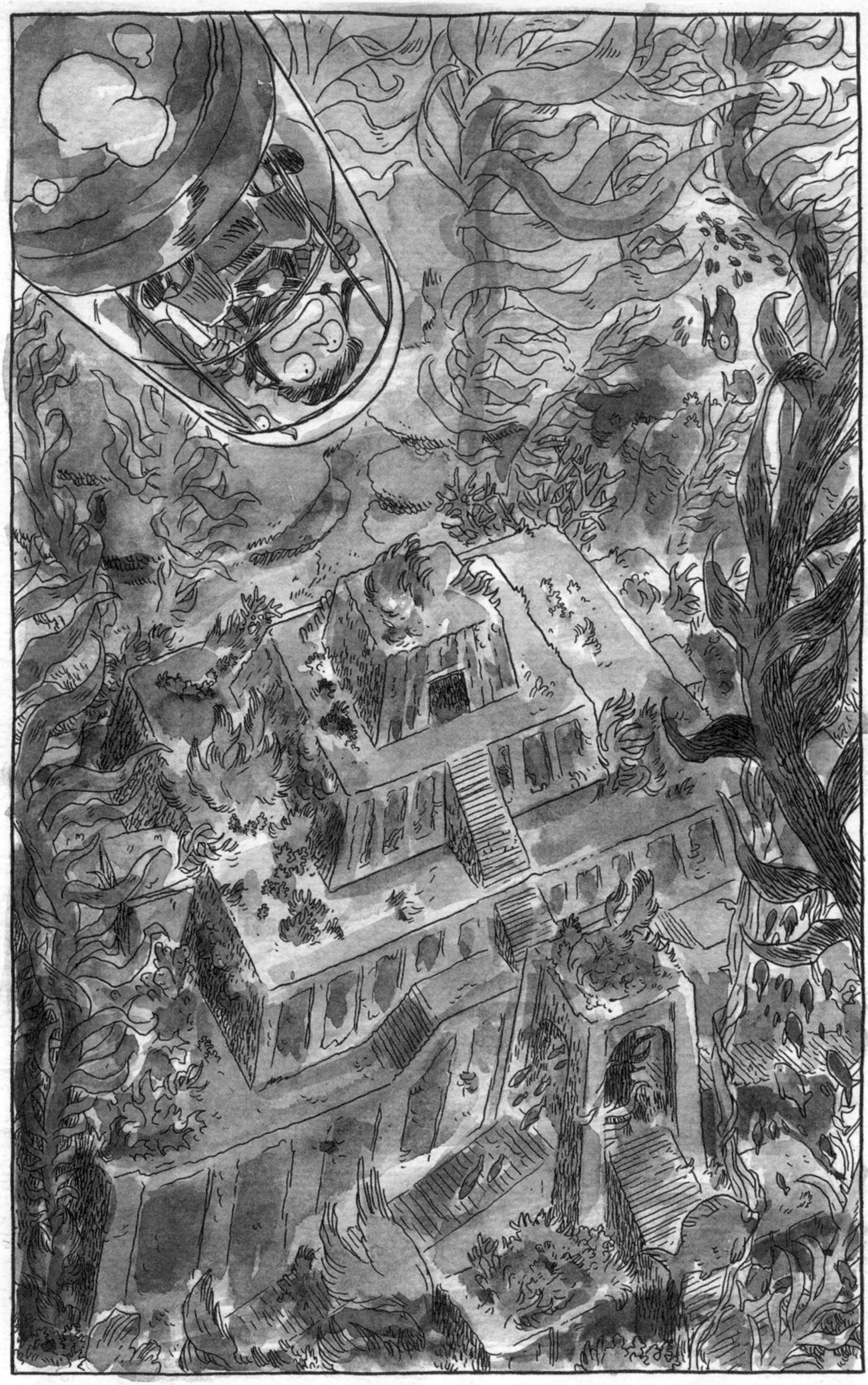

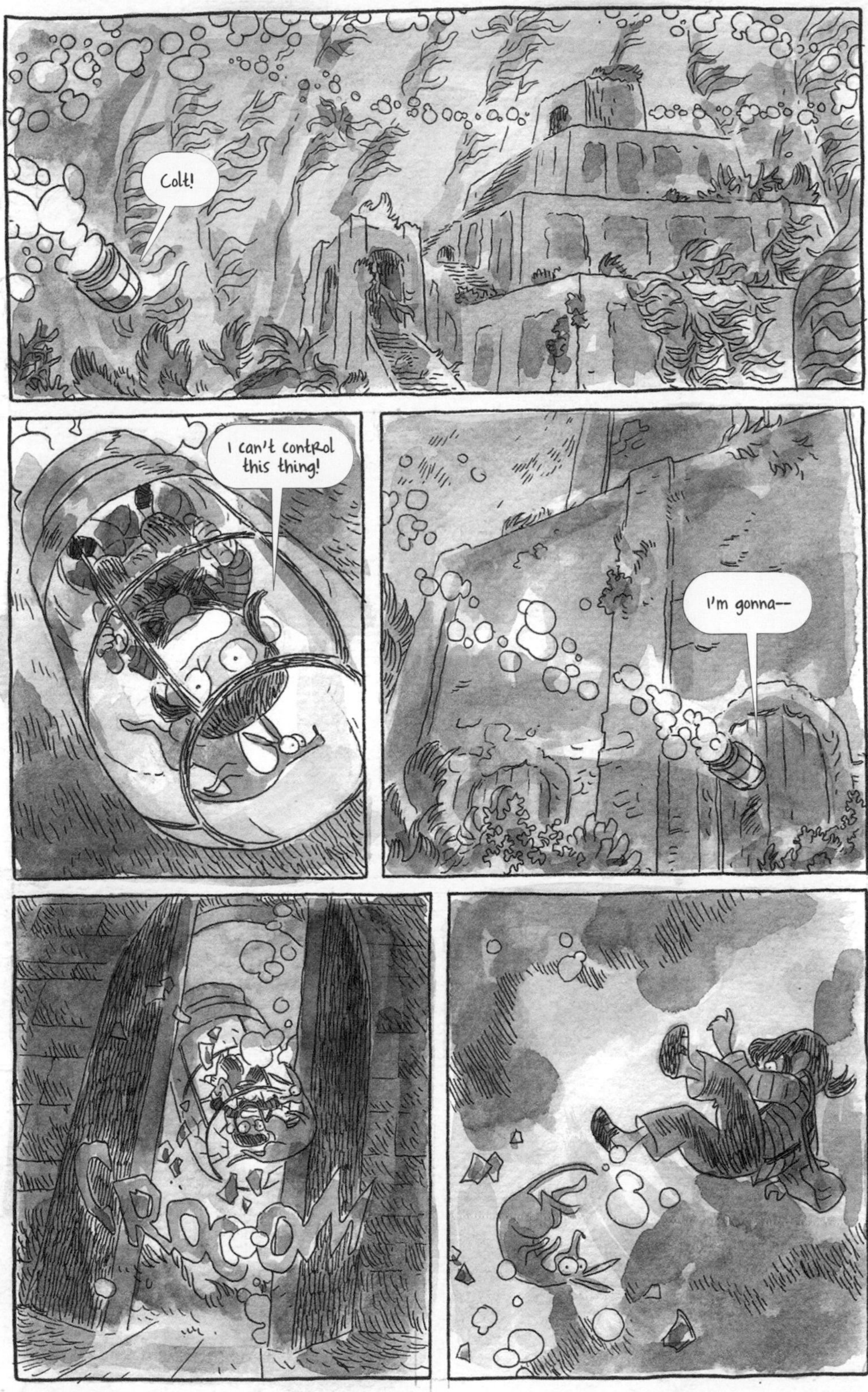
Colt!
I can't control this thing!
I'm gonna--

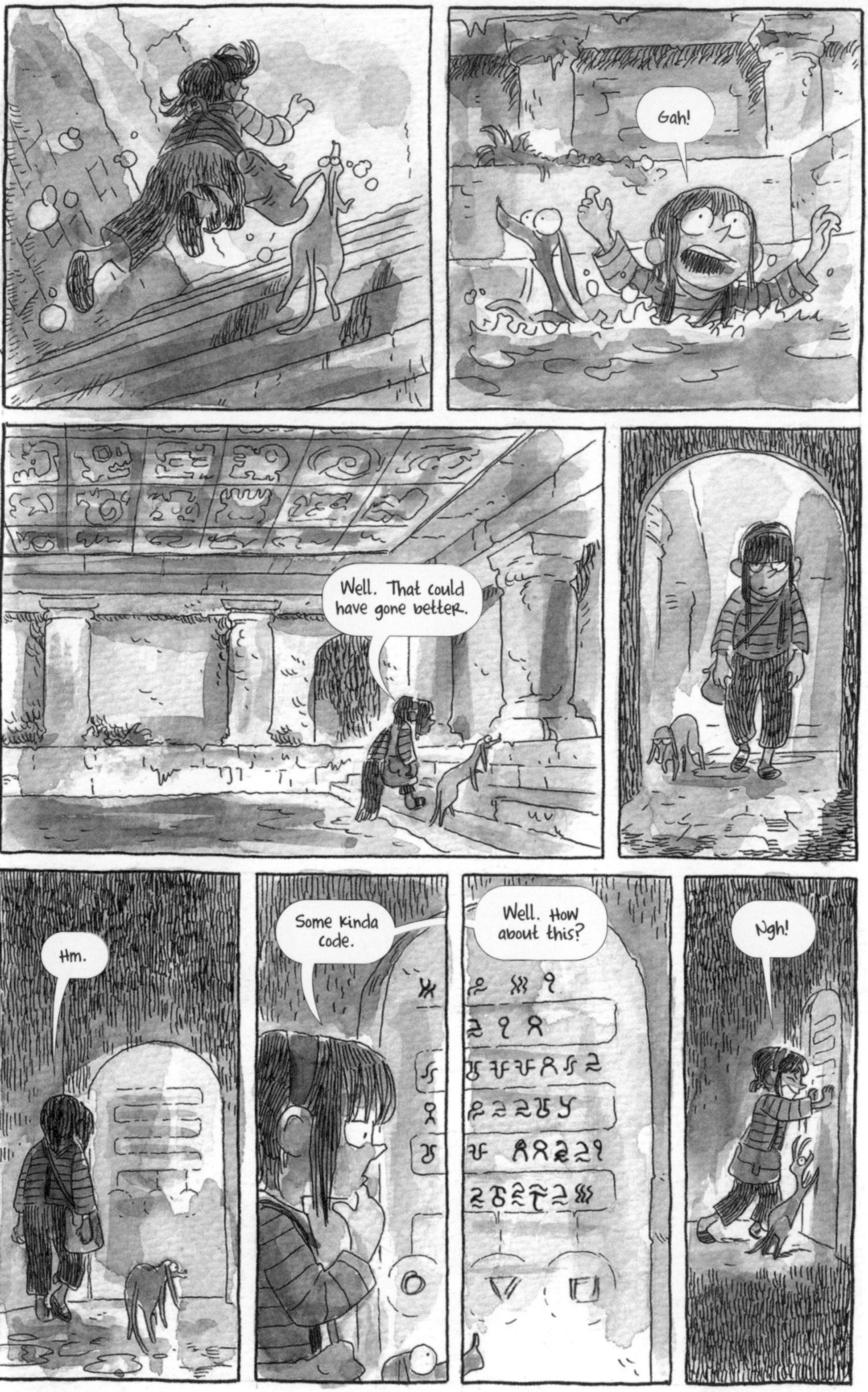
Gah!
Well. That could have gone better.
Hm.
Some kinda code.
Well. How about this?
Ngh!

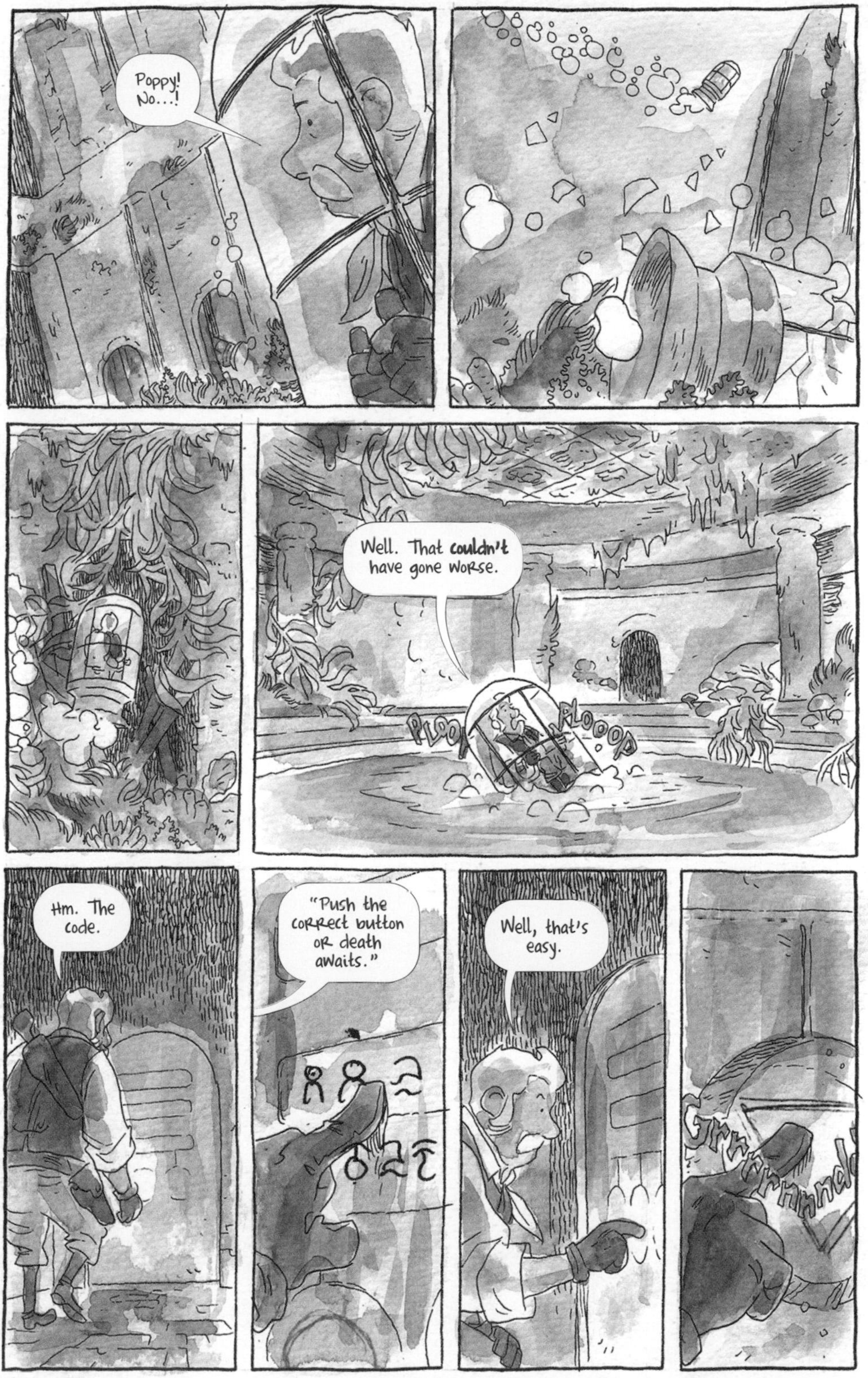
Poppy! No...!
Well. That **couldn't** have gone worse.
PLOOP
PLOOOP
Hm. The code.
"Push the correct button or death awaits."
Well, that's easy.
Grrrrrnnnd

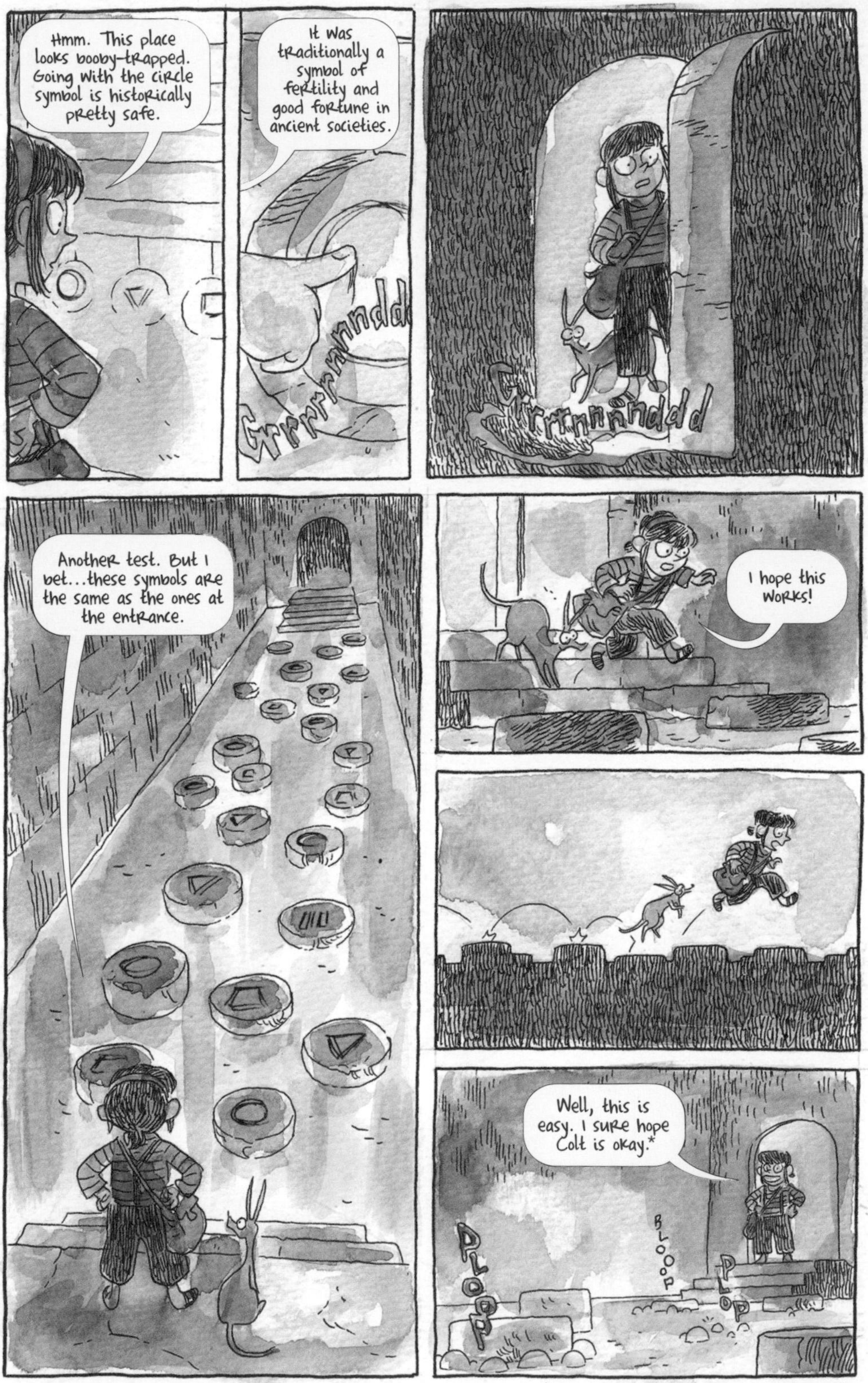

Hmm. This place looks booby-trapped. Going with the circle symbol is historically pretty safe.
It was traditionally a symbol of fertility and good fortune in ancient societies.
Grrrrrnnndd
Grrrnnnnddd
Another test. But I bet...these symbols are the same as the ones at the entrance.
I hope this works!
Well, this is easy. I sure hope Colt is okay.*
PLOOP
BLOOOP
PLOP

*See index for the solution to the puzzle.

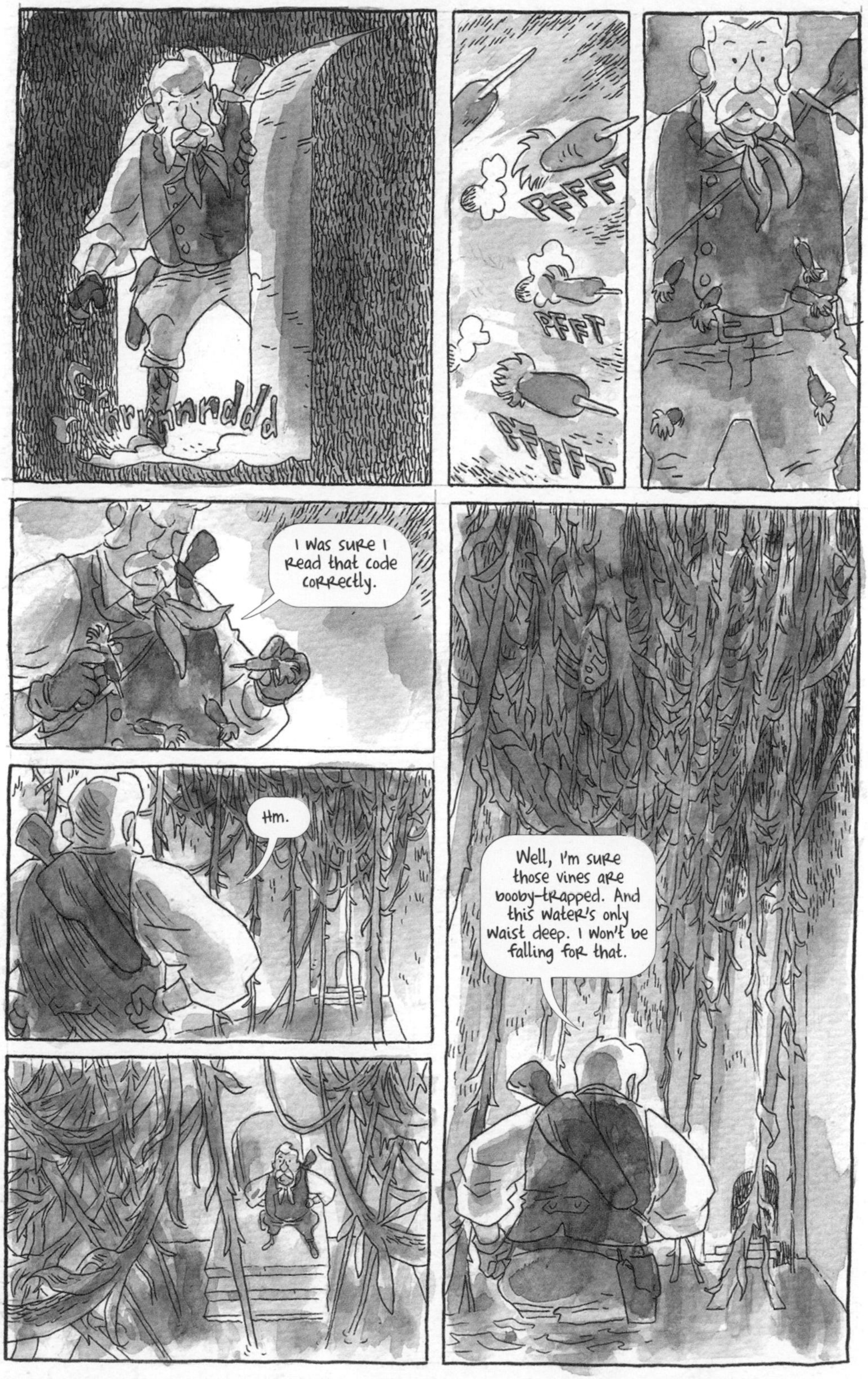
Grrrrnnrddd
PFFFT
PFFT
PFFFT
I was sure I read that code correctly.
Hm.
Well, I'm sure those vines are booby-trapped. And this water's only waist deep. I won't be falling for that.

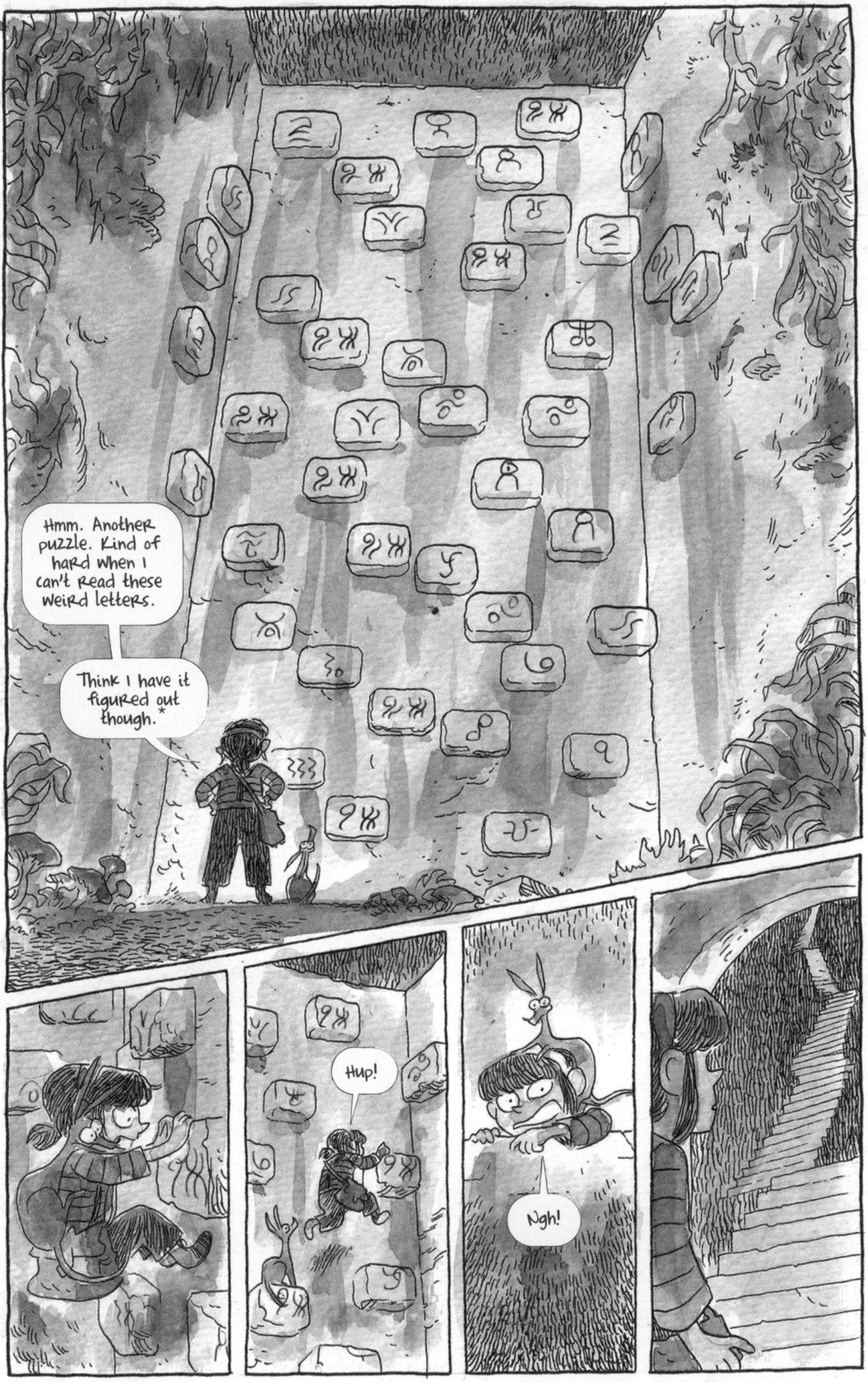
Hmm. Another puzzle. Kind of hard when I can't read these weird letters.
Think I have it figured out though.*
Hup!
Ngh!

*See index for the solution to the puzzle.

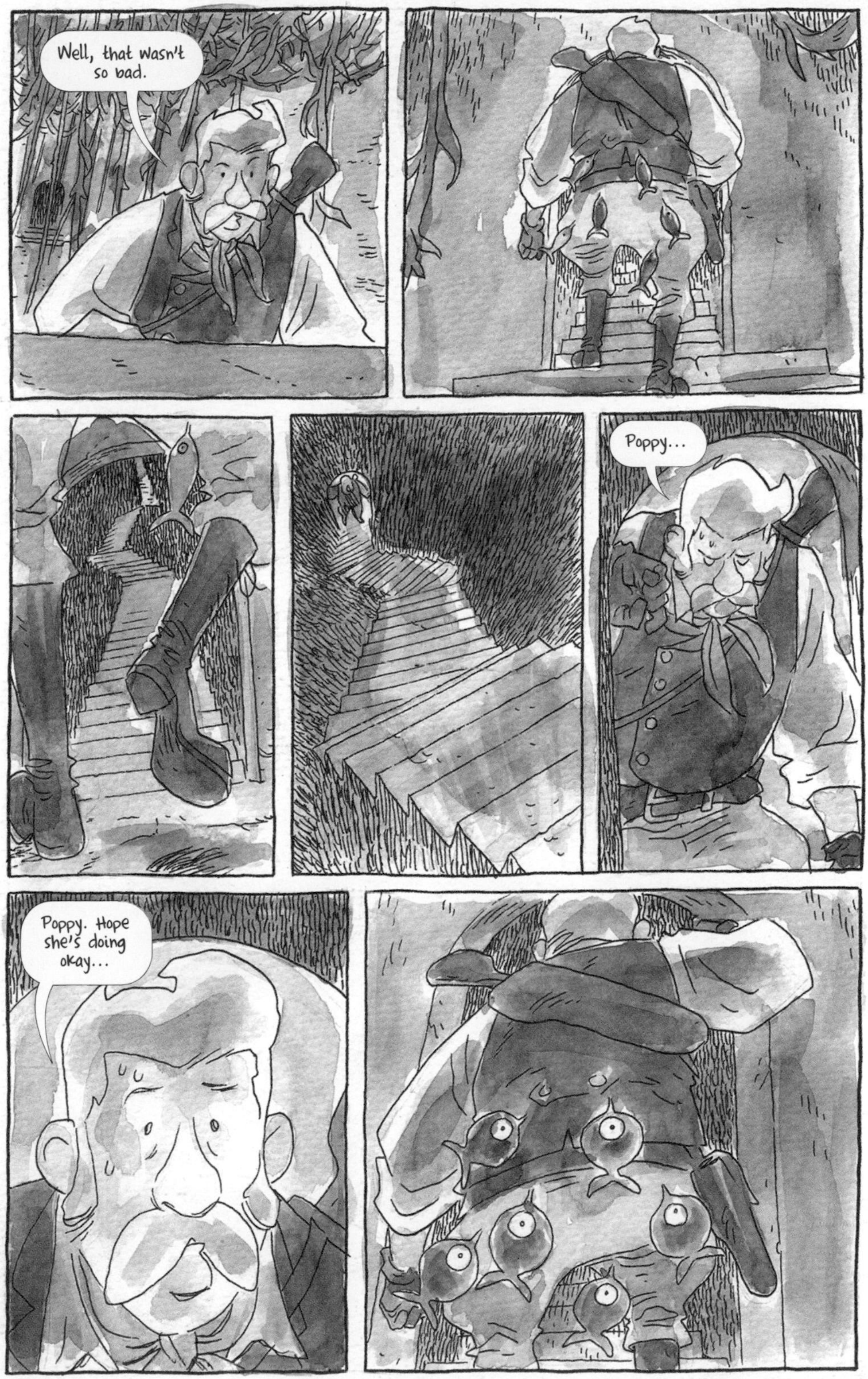
Well, that wasn't so bad.
Poppy...
Poppy. Hope she's doing okay...

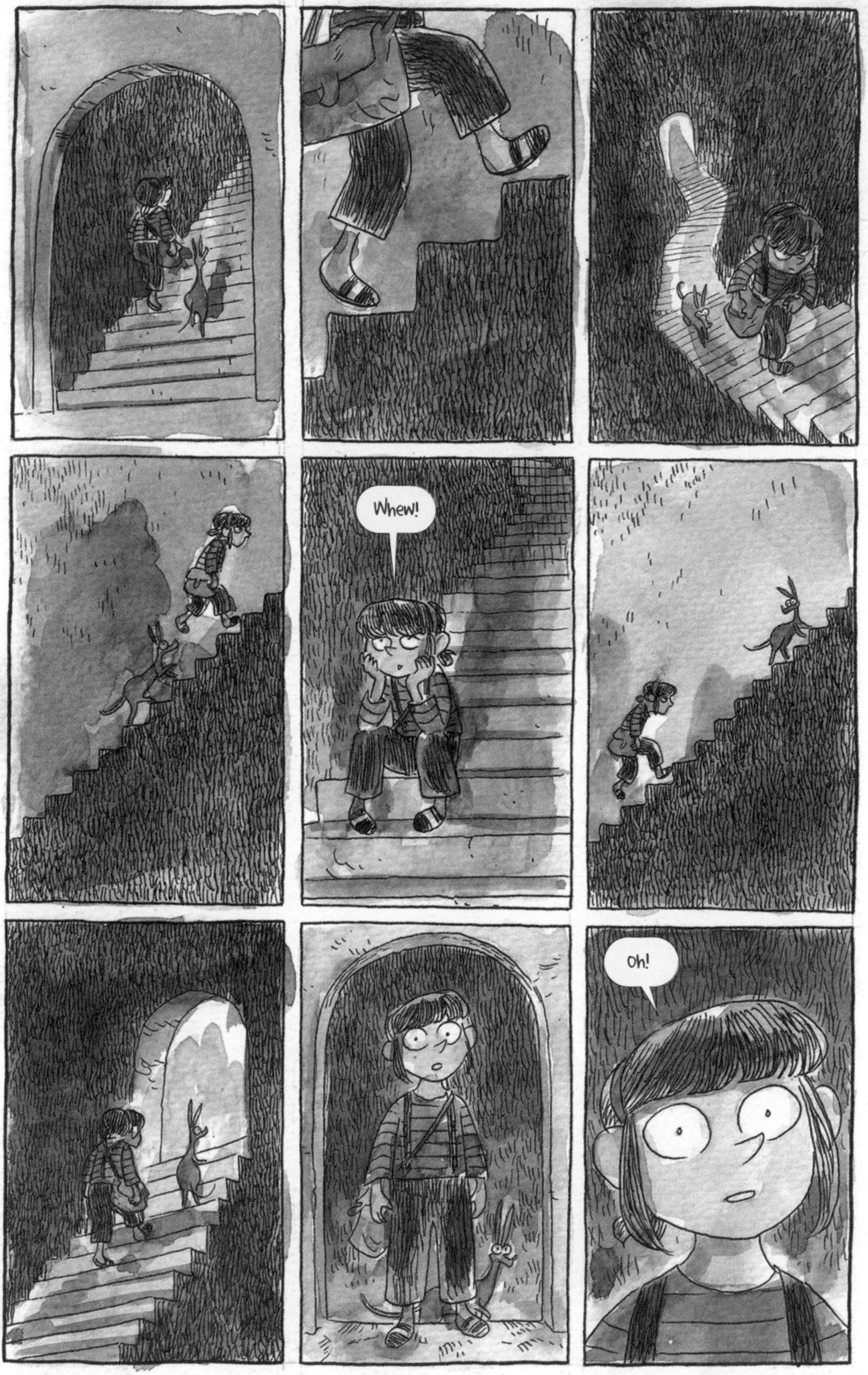
Whew!
Oh!

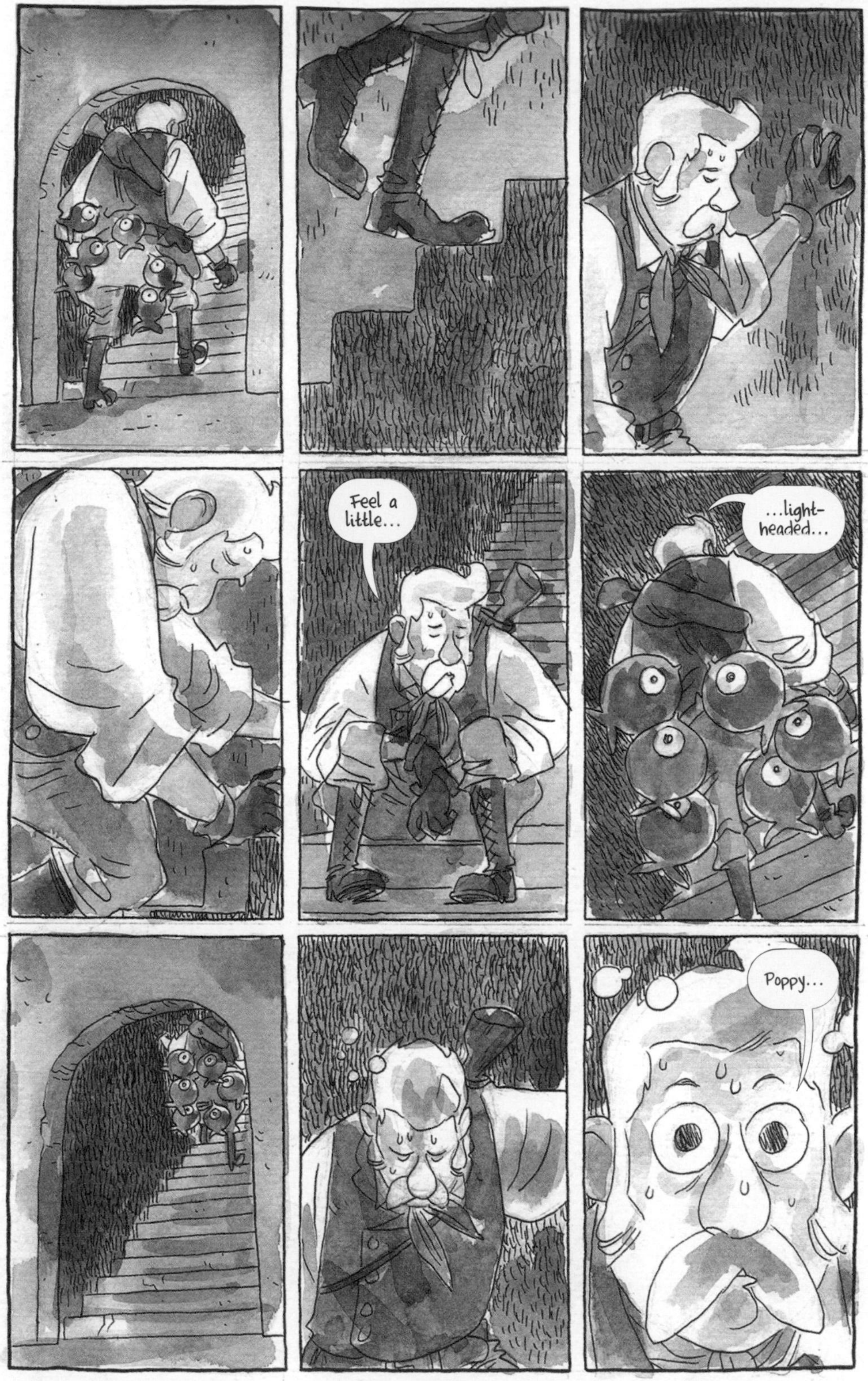
Feel a little...
...light-headed...
Poppy...

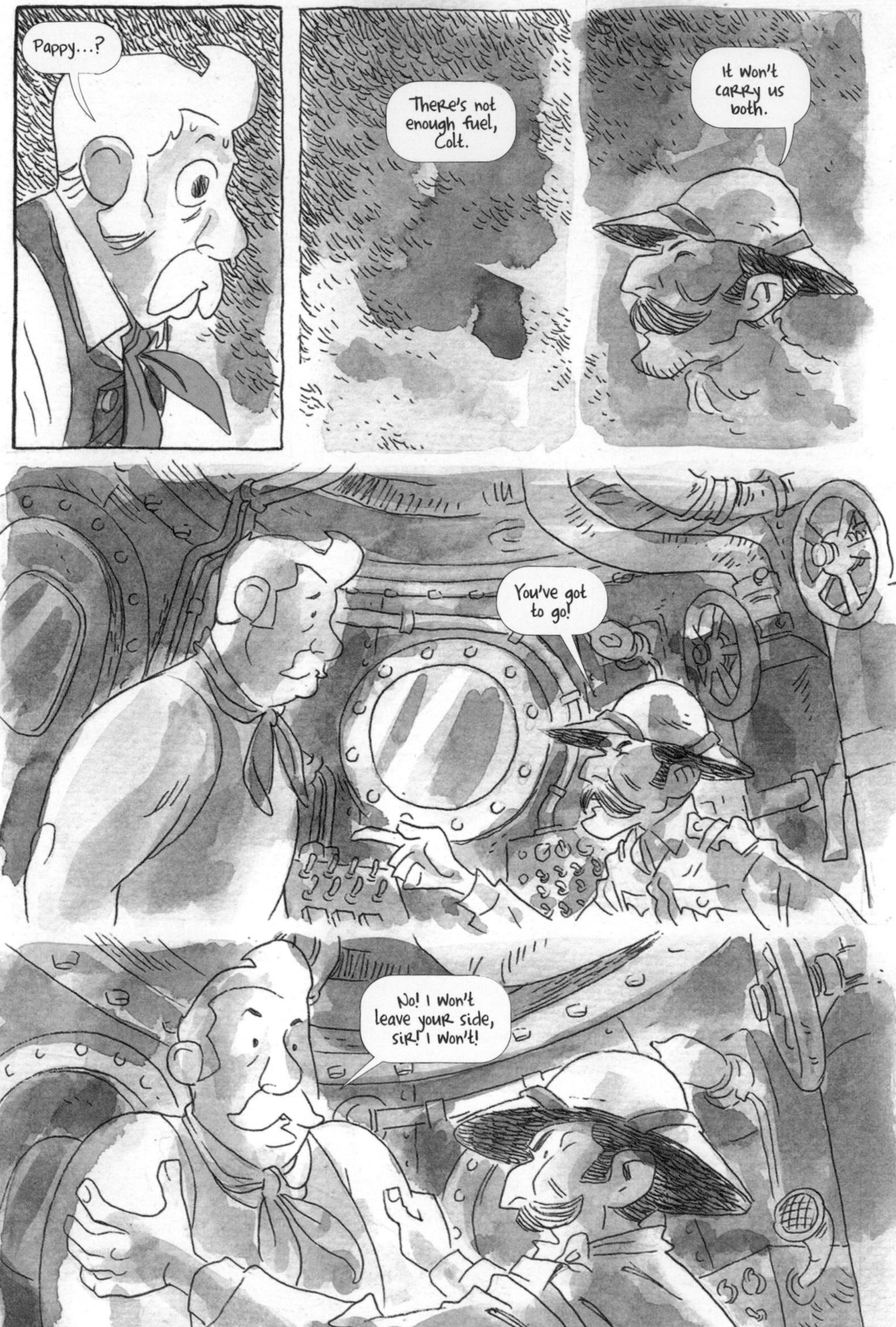
Pappy...?
There's not enough fuel, Colt.
It won't carry us both.
You've got to go!
No! I won't leave your side, sir! I won't!

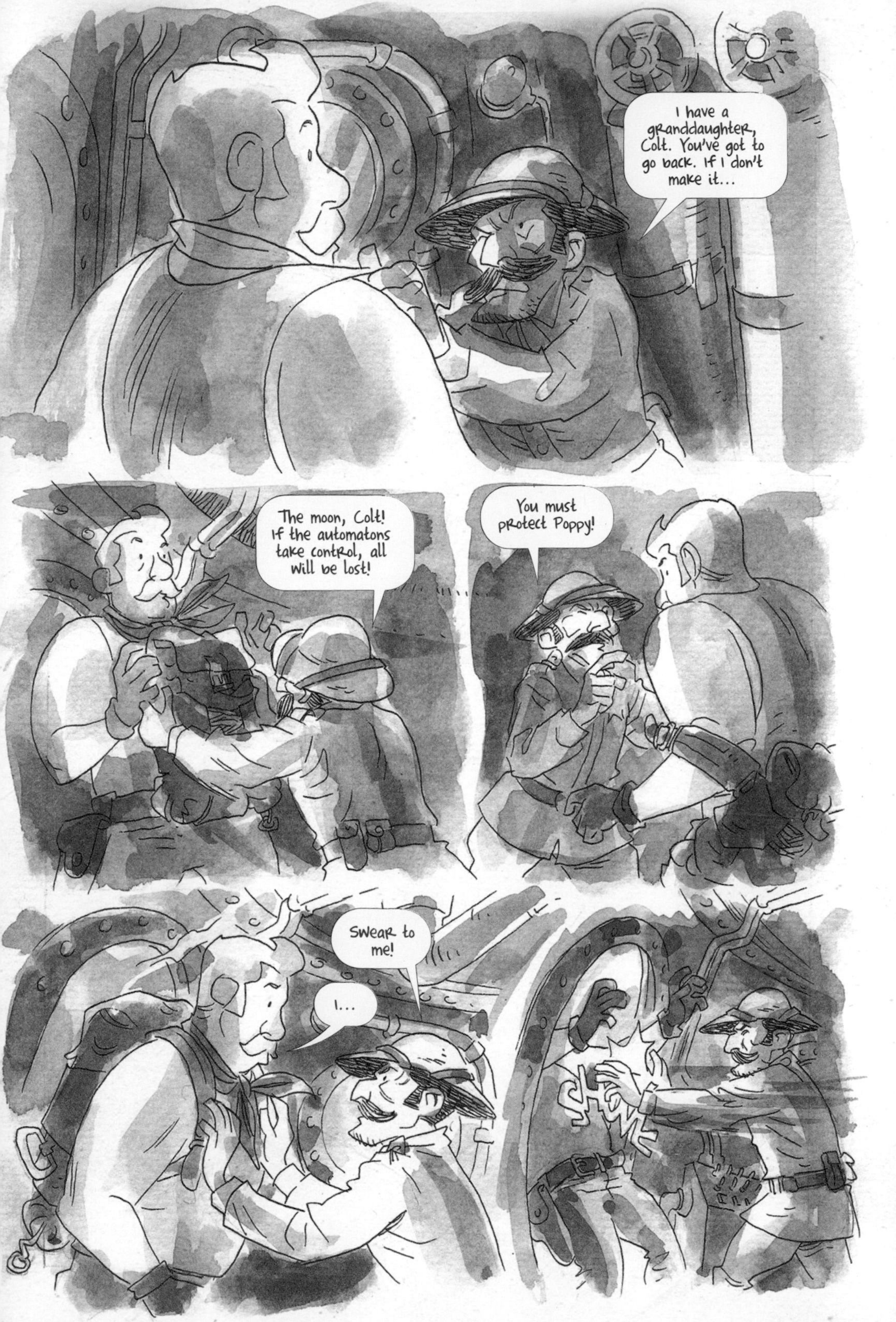
I have a granddaughter, Colt. You've got to go back. If I don't make it...
The moon, Colt! If the automatons take control, all will be lost!
You must protect Poppy!
Swear to me!
I...

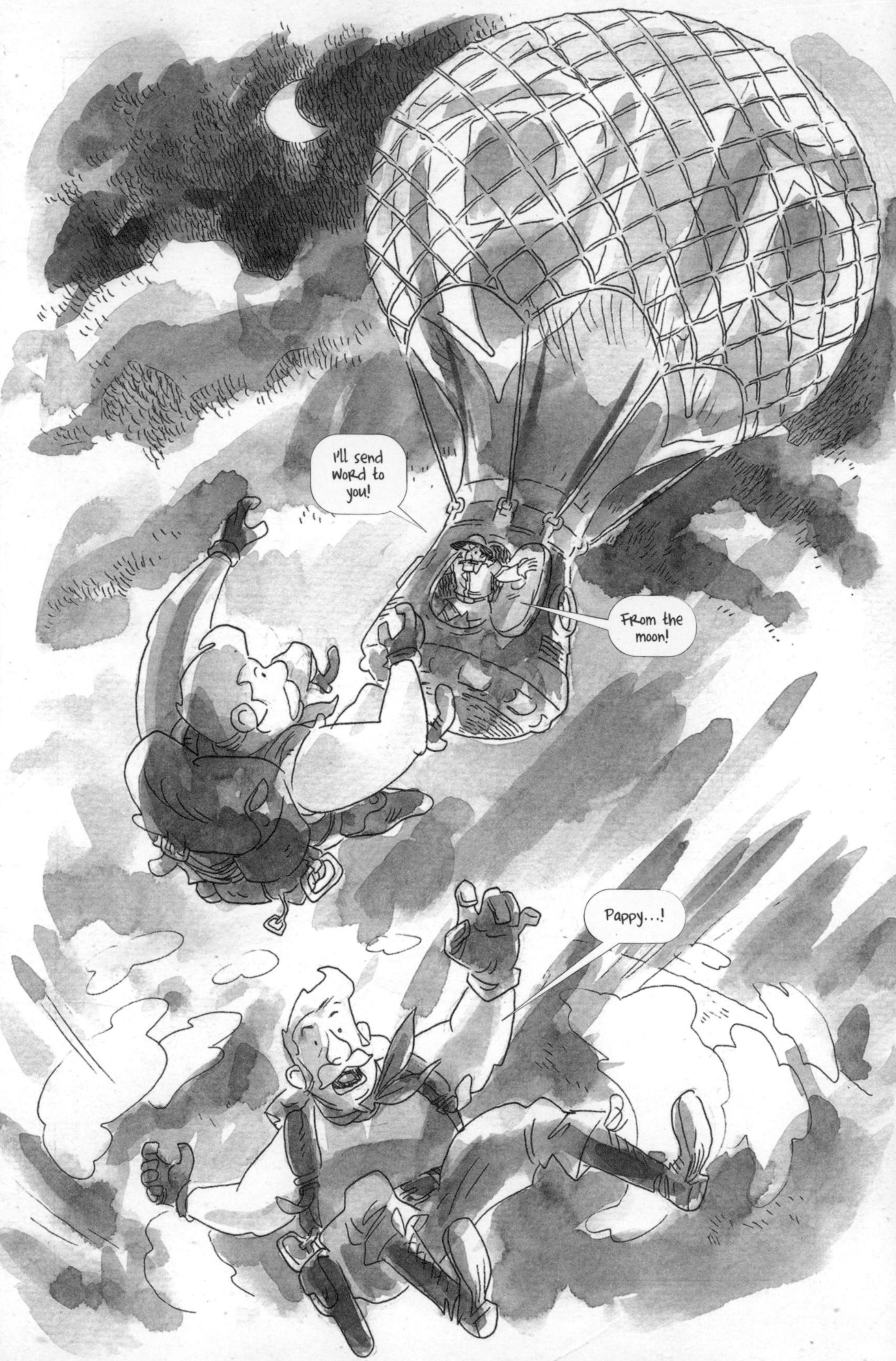
I'll send word to you!
From the moon!
Pappy...!

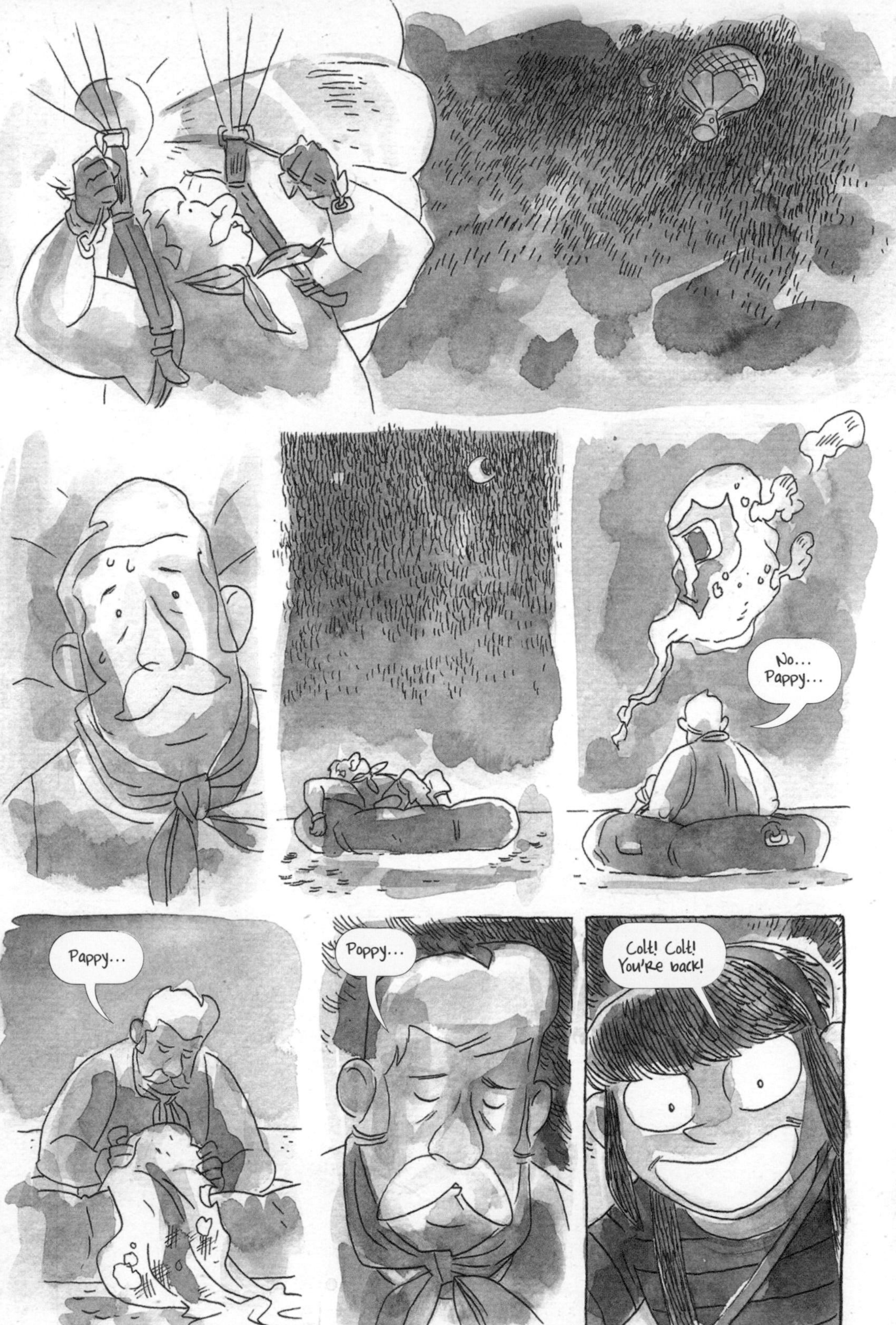
No...
Pappy...
Pappy...
Poppy...
Colt! Colt!
You're back!

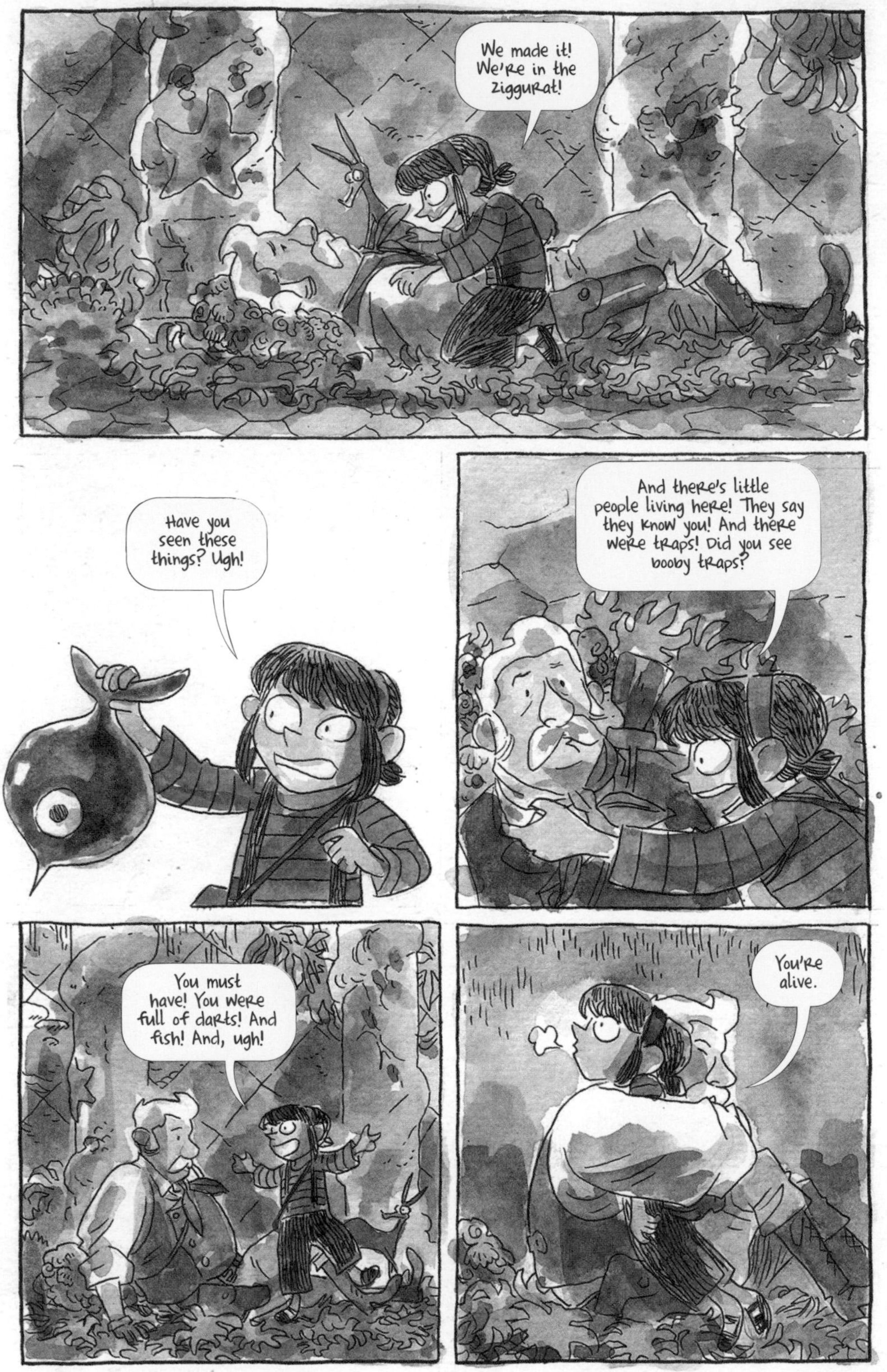
We made it! We're in the ziggurat!
Have you seen these things? Ugh!
And there's little people living here! They say they know you! And there were traps! Did you see booby traps?
You must have! You were full of darts! And fish! And, ugh!
You're alive.

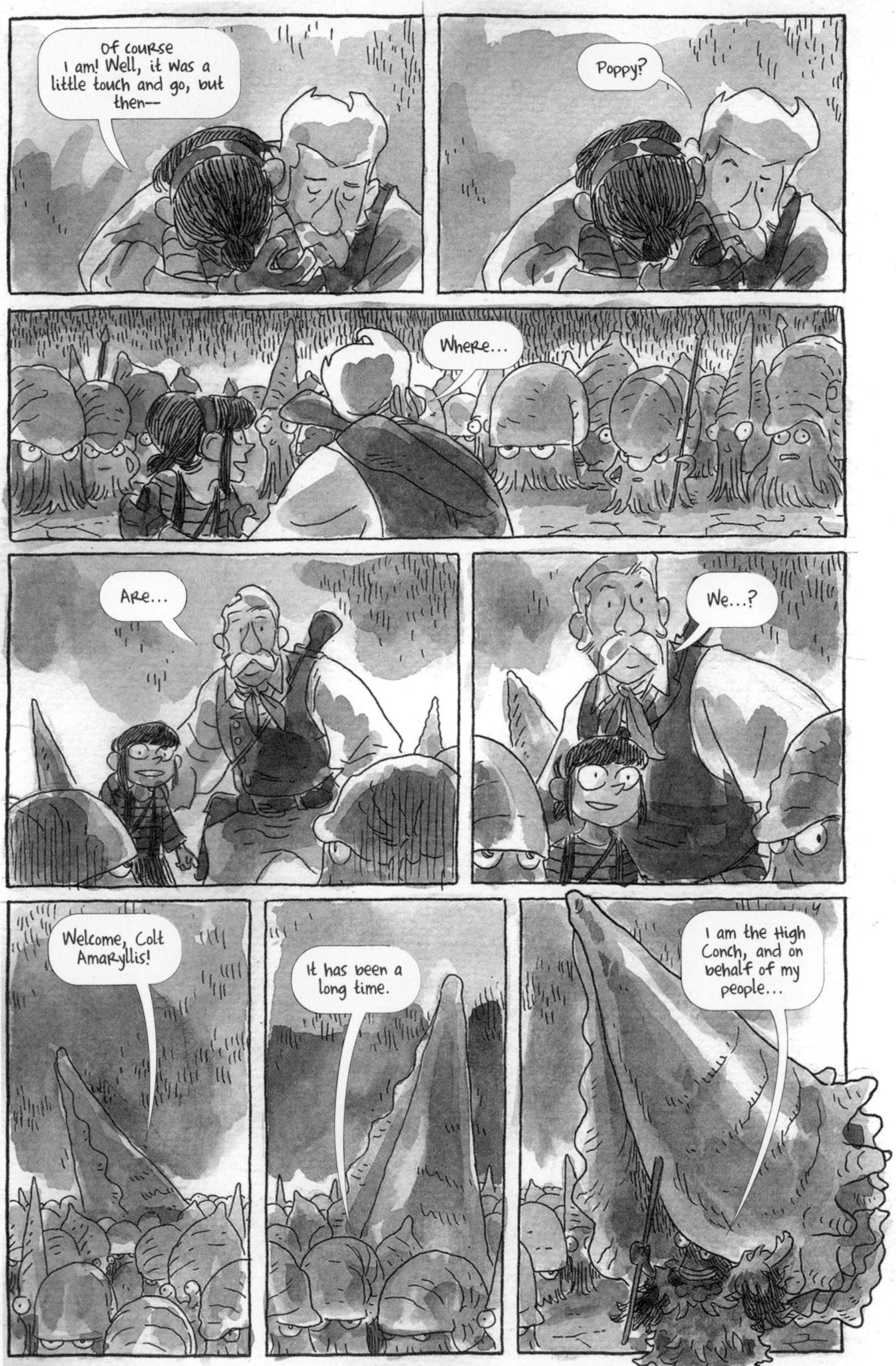
Of course I am! Well, it was a little touch and go, but then--
Poppy?
Where...
Are...
We...?
Welcome, Colt Amaryllis!
It has been a long time.
I am the High Conch, and on behalf of my people...

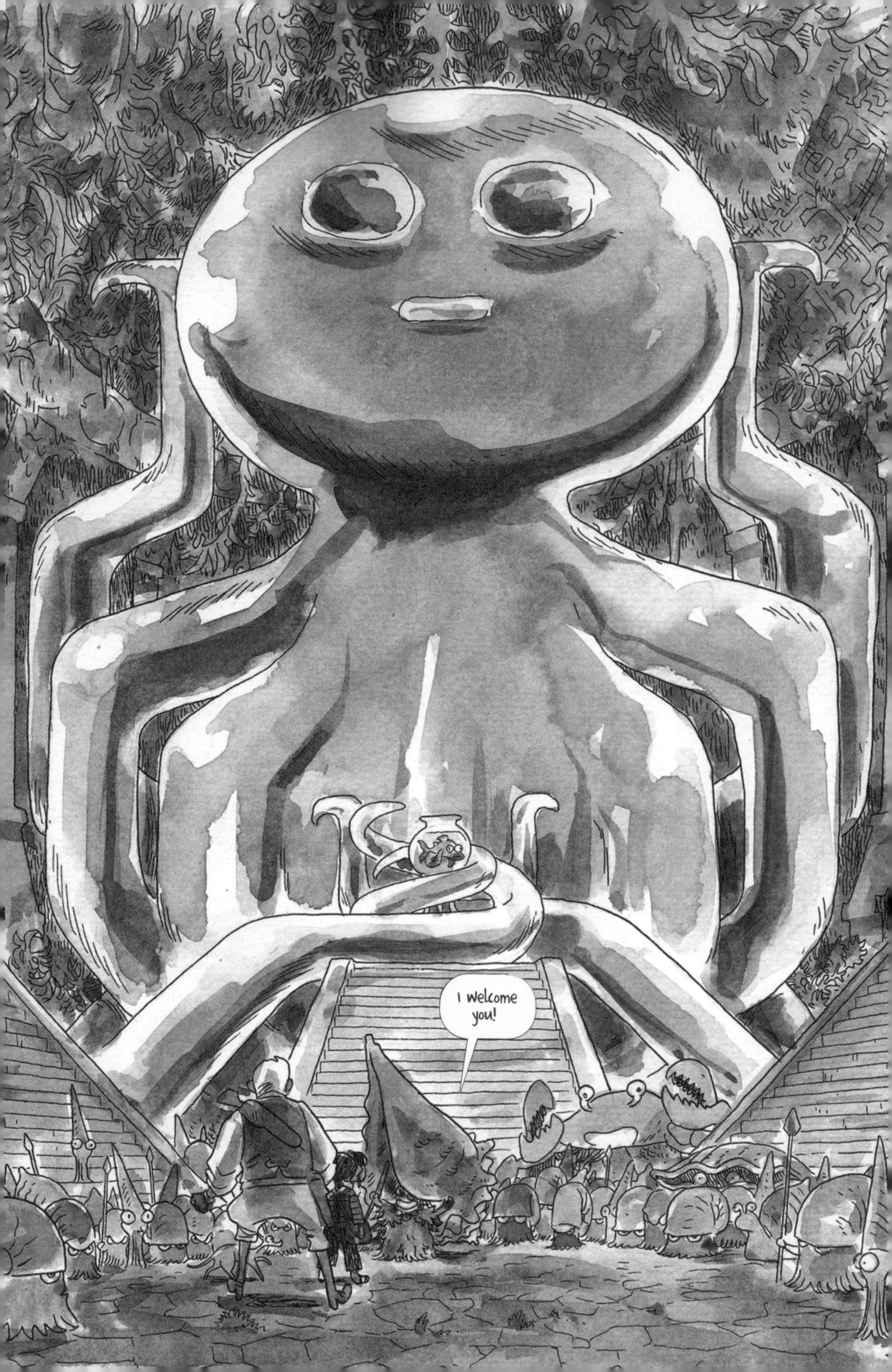
I welcome you!

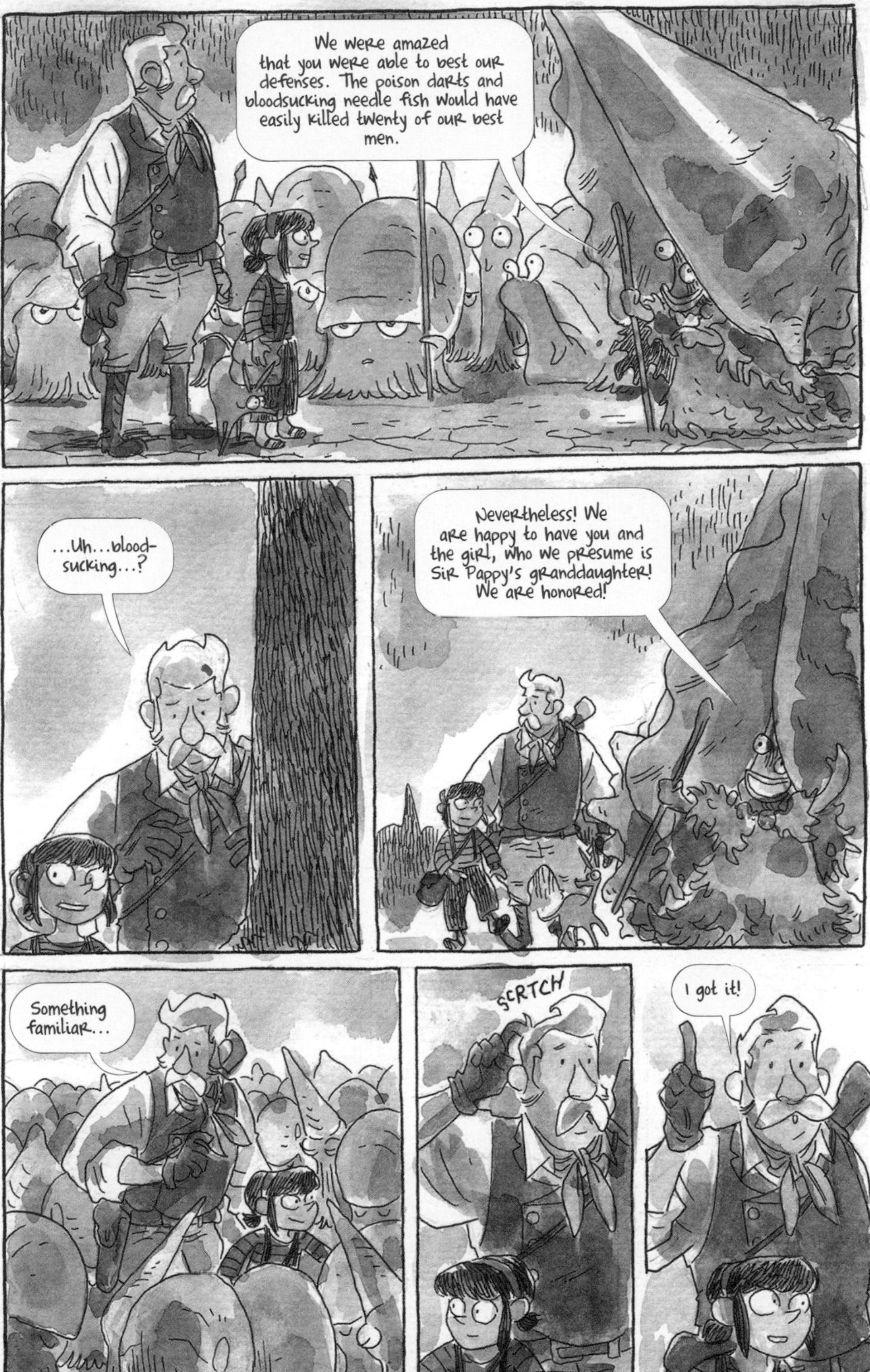
We were amazed that you were able to best our defenses. The poison darts and bloodsucking needle fish would have easily killed twenty of our best men.
...Uh...blood-sucking...?
Nevertheless! We are happy to have you and the girl, who we presume is Sir Pappy's granddaughter! We are honored!
Something familiar...
SCRTCH
I got it!

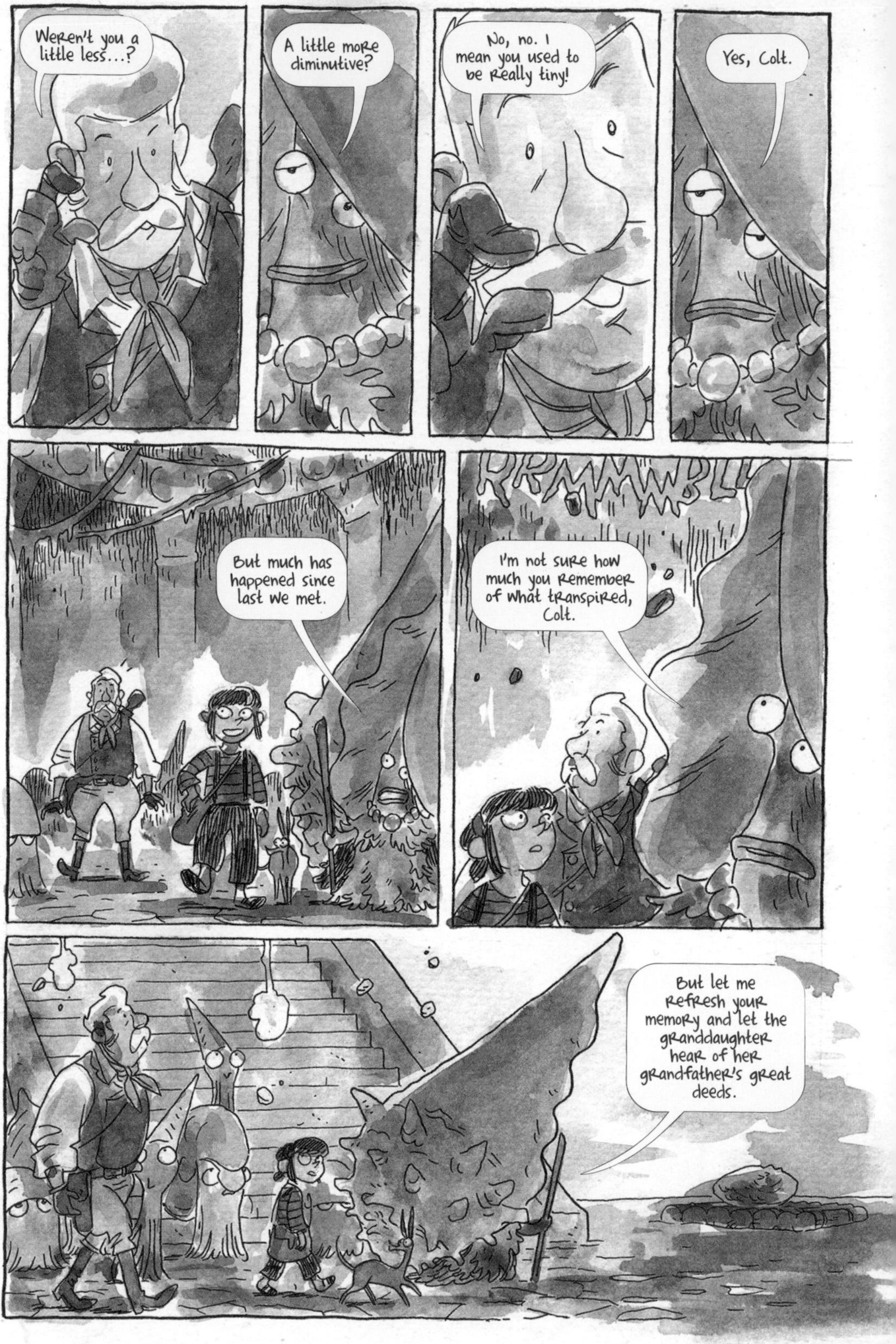

Weren't you a little less...?
A little more diminutive?
No, no. I mean you used to be really tiny!
Yes, Colt.
But much has happened since last we met.
RRMAWBL
I'm not sure how much you remember of what transpired, Colt.
But let me refresh your memory and let the granddaughter hear of her grandfather's great deeds.

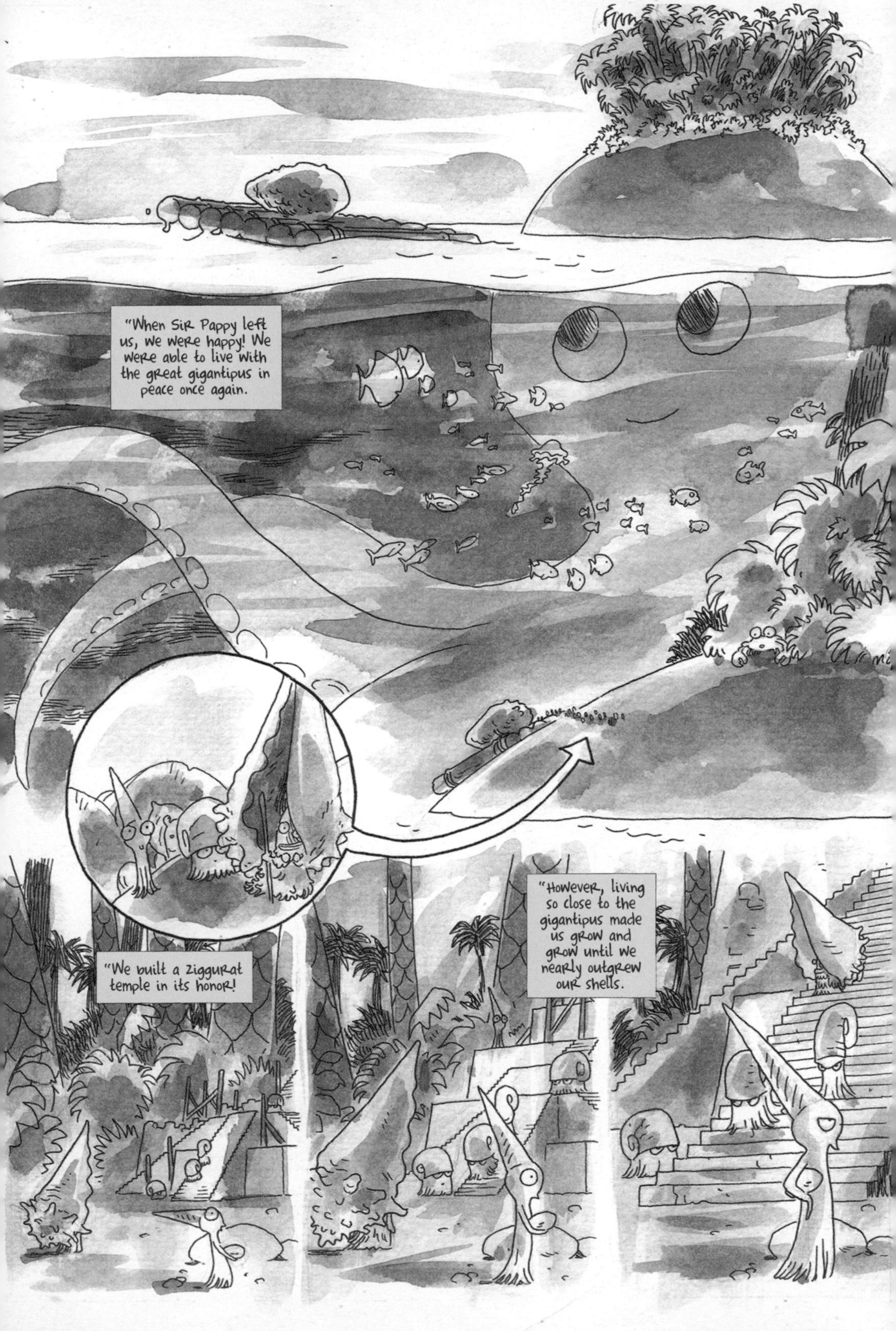
"When Sir Pappy left us, we were happy! We were able to live with the great gigantipus in peace once again.
"We built a ziggurat temple in its honor!
"However, living so close to the gigantipus made us grow and grow until we nearly outgrew our shells.

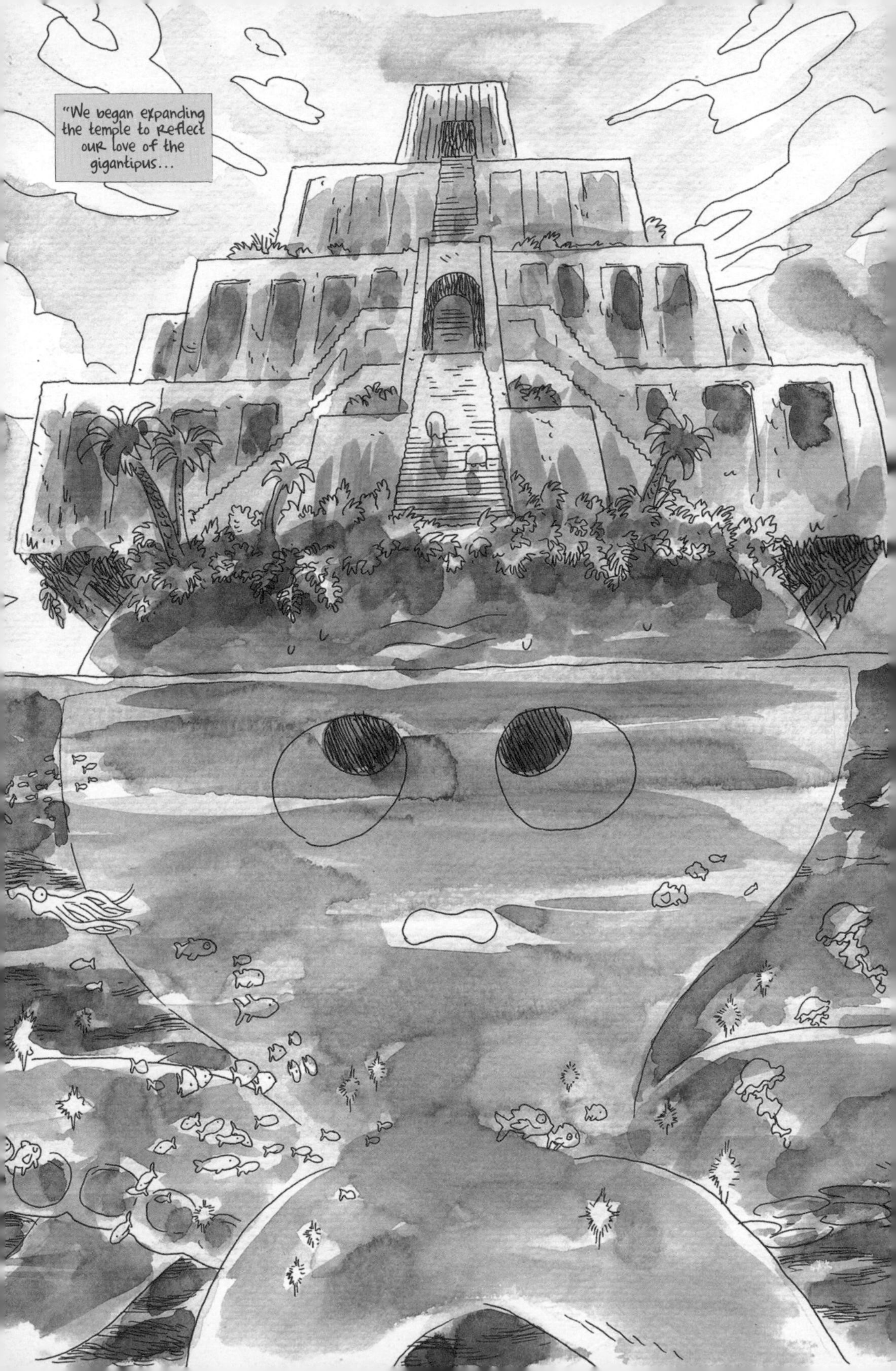
"We began expanding the temple to reflect our love of the gigantipus...

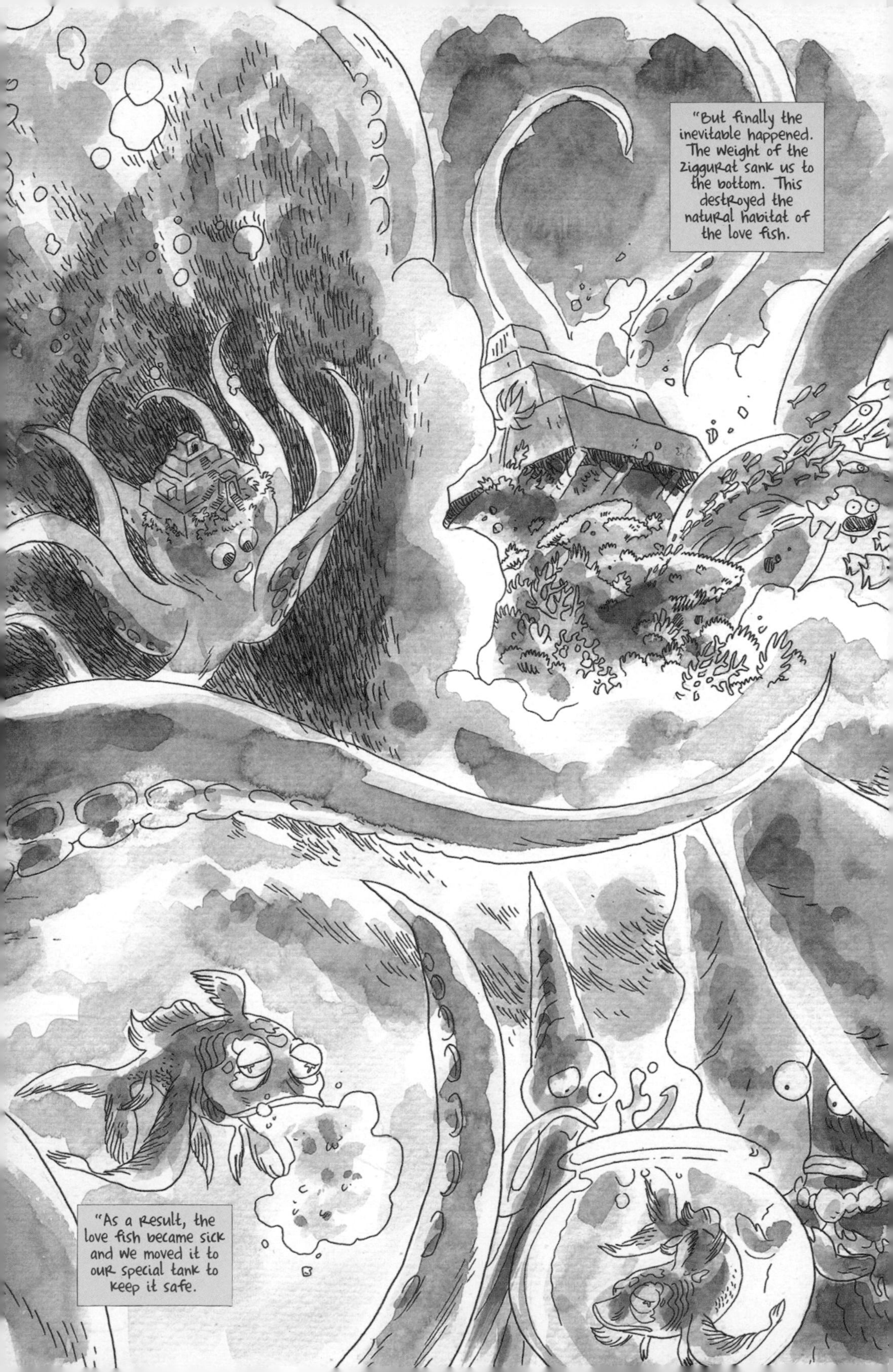
"But finally the inevitable happened. The weight of the ziggurat sank us to the bottom. This destroyed the natural habitat of the love fish.
"As a result, the love fish became sick and we moved it to our special tank to keep it safe.

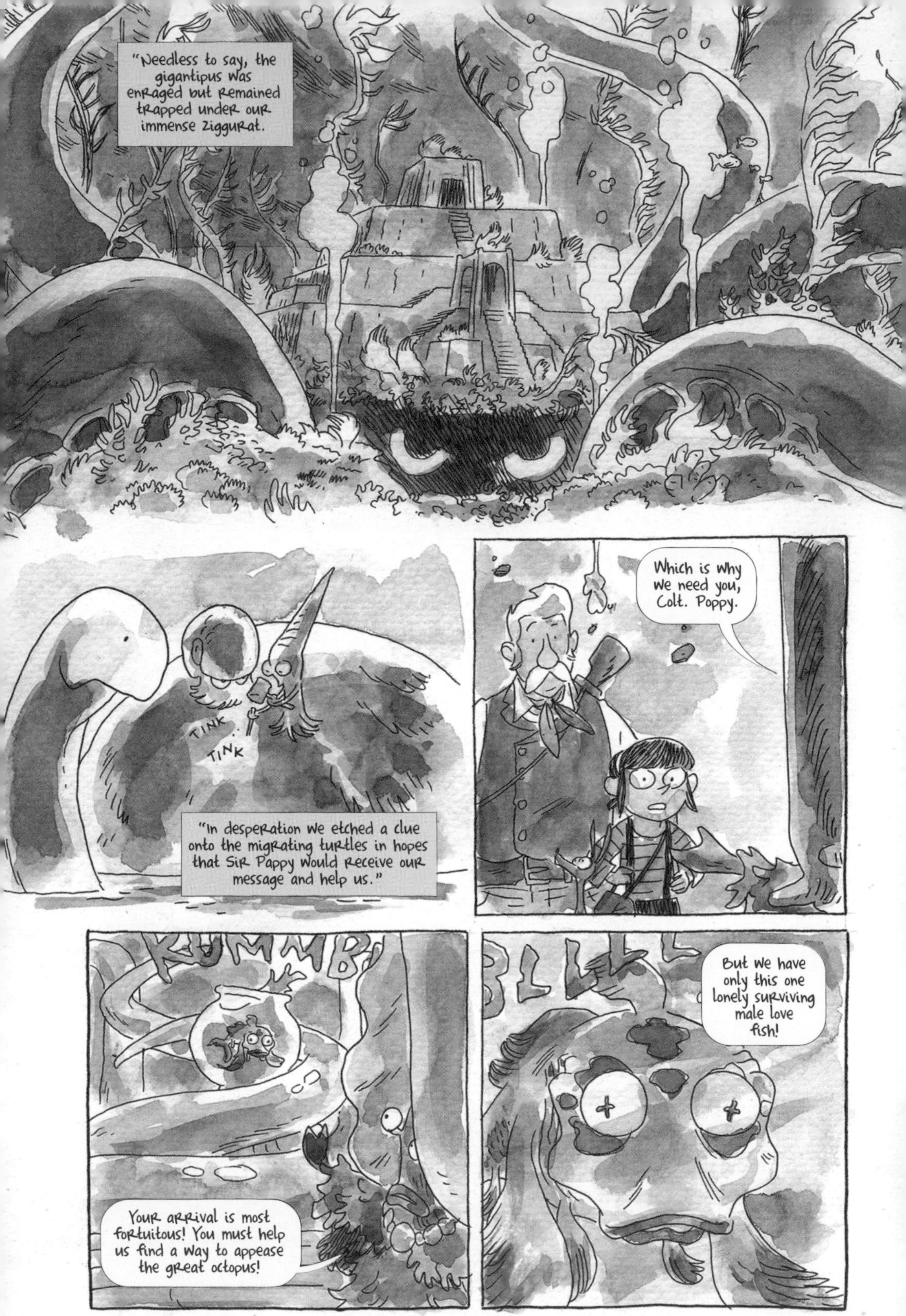
"Needless to say, the gigantipus was enraged but remained trapped under our immense ziggurat.
TINK
TINK
"In desperation we etched a clue onto the migrating turtles in hopes that Sir Pappy would receive our message and help us."
Which is why we need you, Colt. Poppy.
RUMMB
Your arrival is most fortuitous! You must help us find a way to appease the great octopus!
BLLL
But we have only this one lonely surviving male love fish!

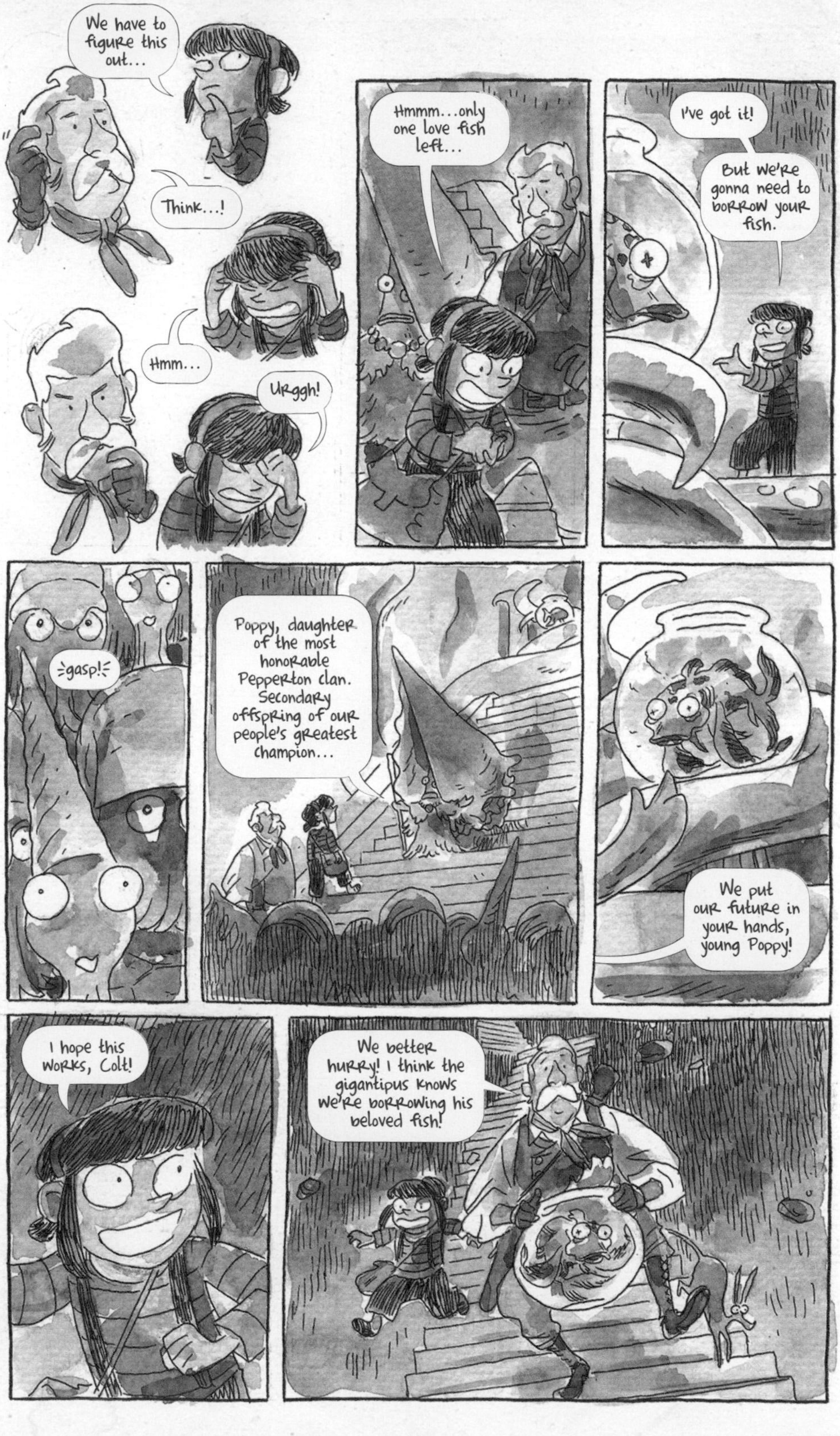

We have to figure this out...
Think...!
Hmm...
Urggh!
Hmmm...only one love fish left...
I've got it!
But we're gonna need to borrow your fish.
:gasp!:
Poppy, daughter of the most honorable Pepperton clan. Secondary offspring of our people's greatest champion...
We put our future in your hands, young Poppy!
I hope this works, Colt!
We better hurry! I think the gigantipus knows we're borrowing his beloved fish!

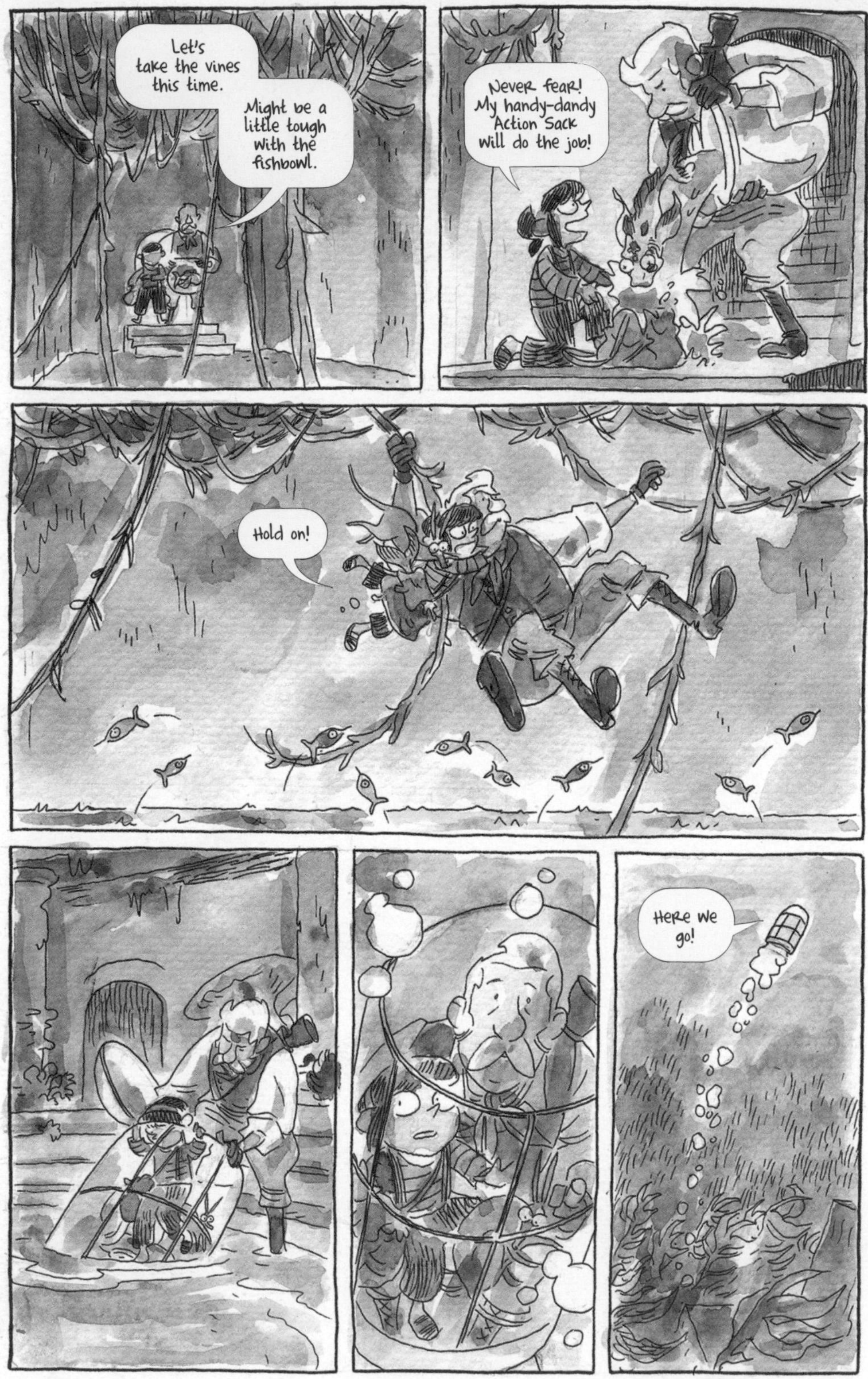
Let's take the vines this time.
Might be a little tough with the fishbowl.
Never fear! My handy-dandy Action Sack will do the job!
Hold on!
Here we go!

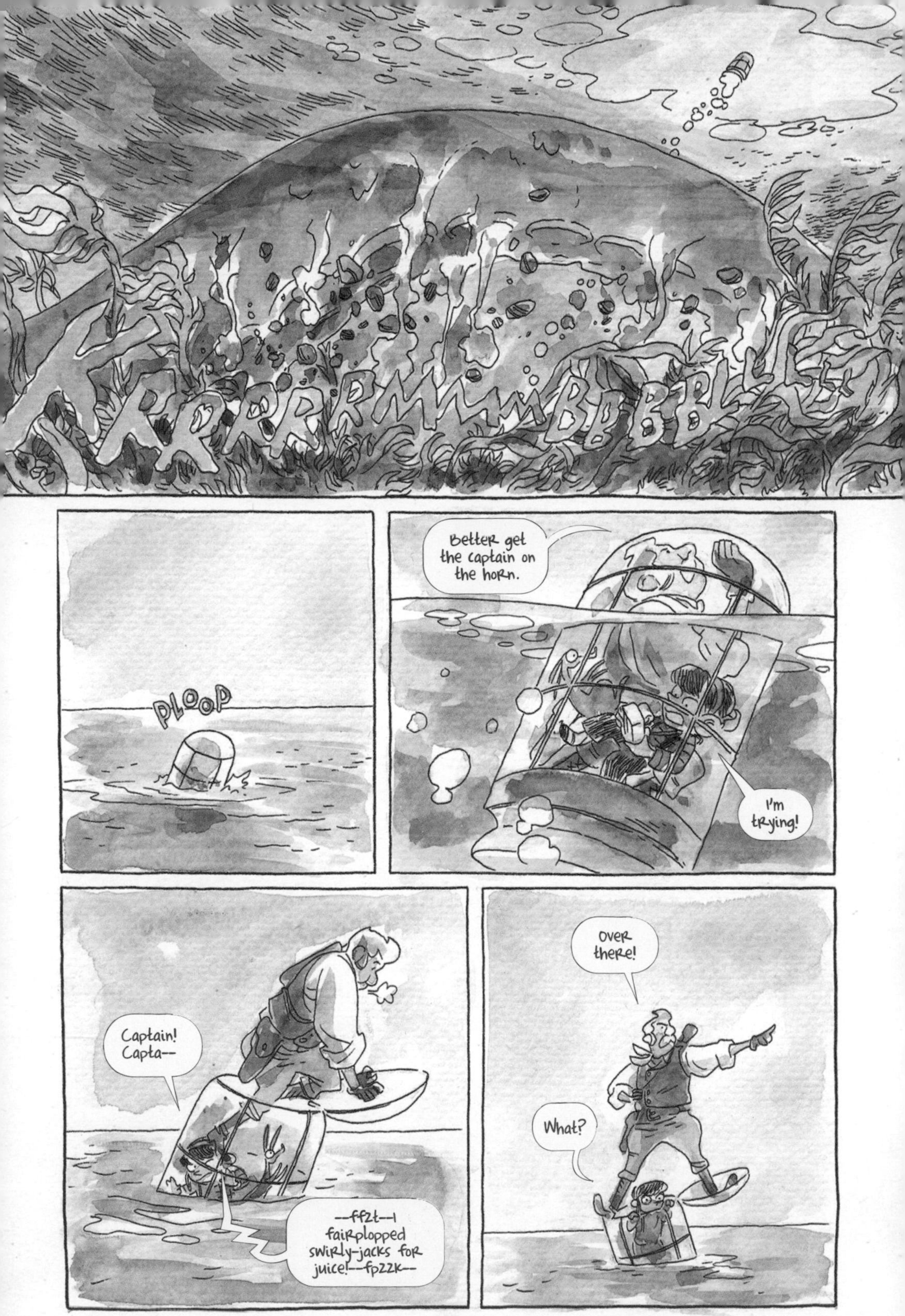
KKRRRRMMMMBBBBBLLLL
PLOOP
Better get the captain on the horn.
I'm trying!
Captain! Capta--
--ffzt--I fairplopped swirly-jacks for juice!--fpzzk--
Over there!
What?

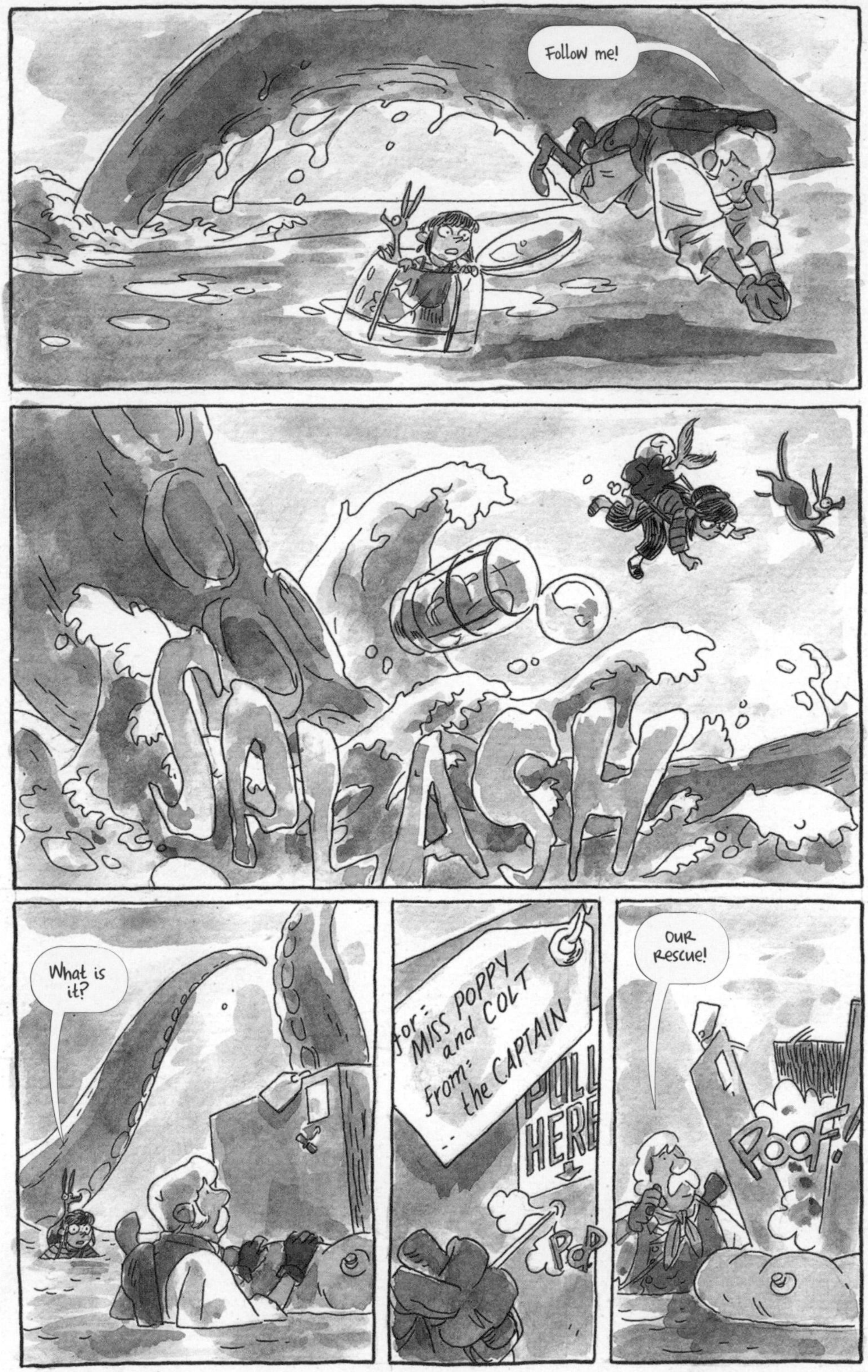
Follow me!
SPLASH
What is it?
for: MISS POPPY and COLT
from: the CAPTAIN
PULL HERE
POP
OUR RESCUE!
POOF!

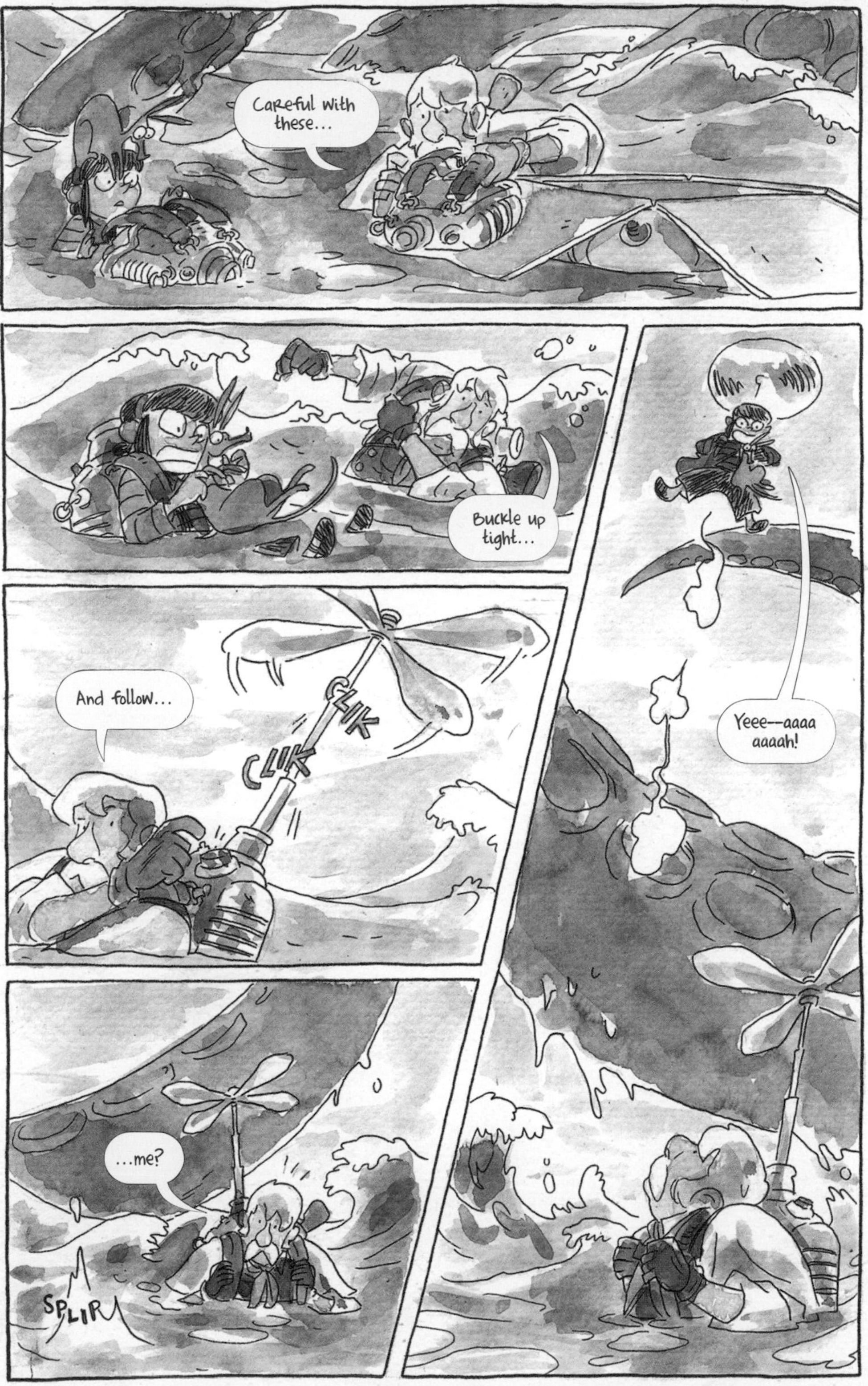
Careful with these...
Buckle up tight...
Yeee--aaaa aaaah!
And follow...
CLIK
CLIK
...me?
SPLIR

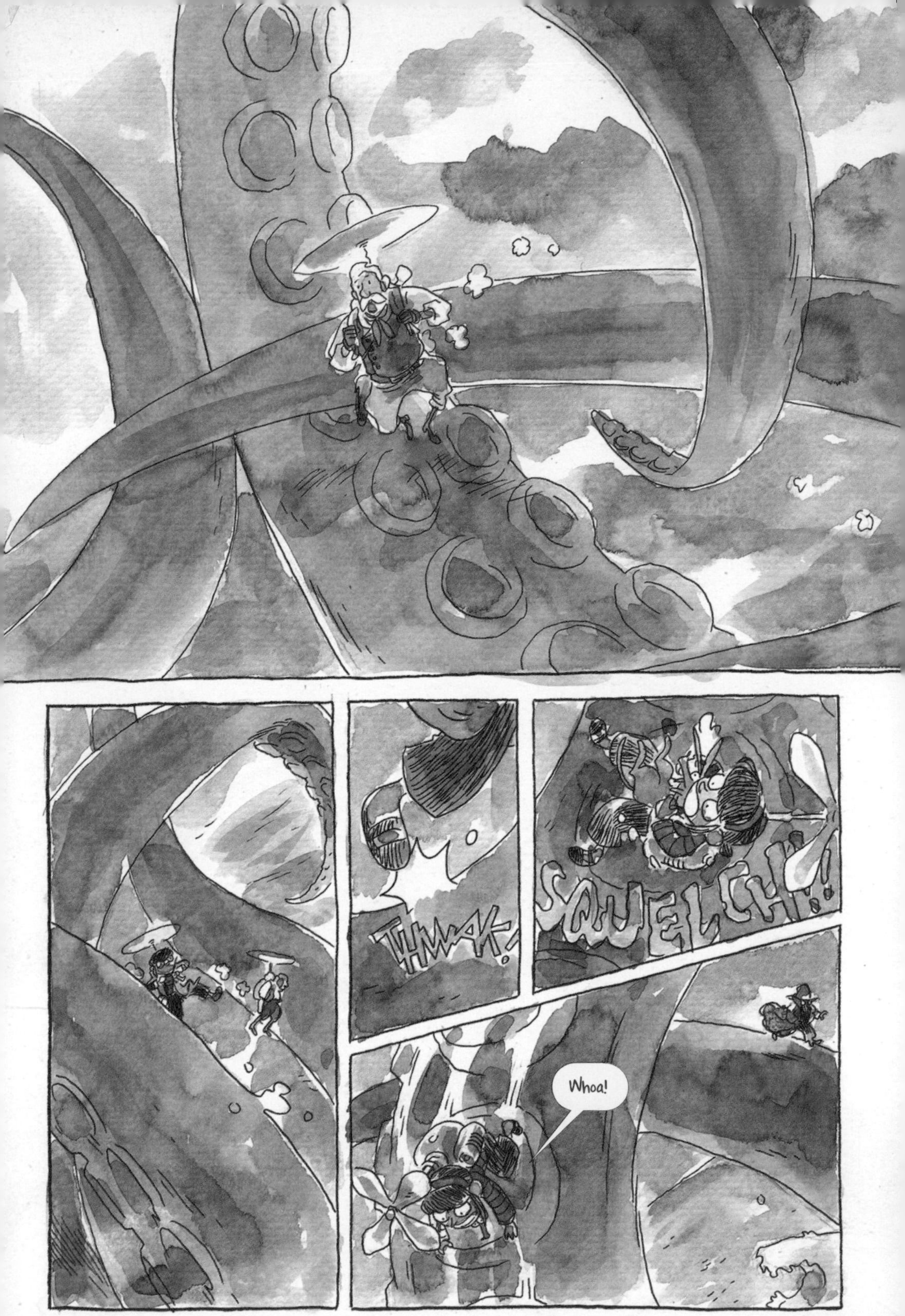
THWAK!
SQUELCH!!
Whoa!

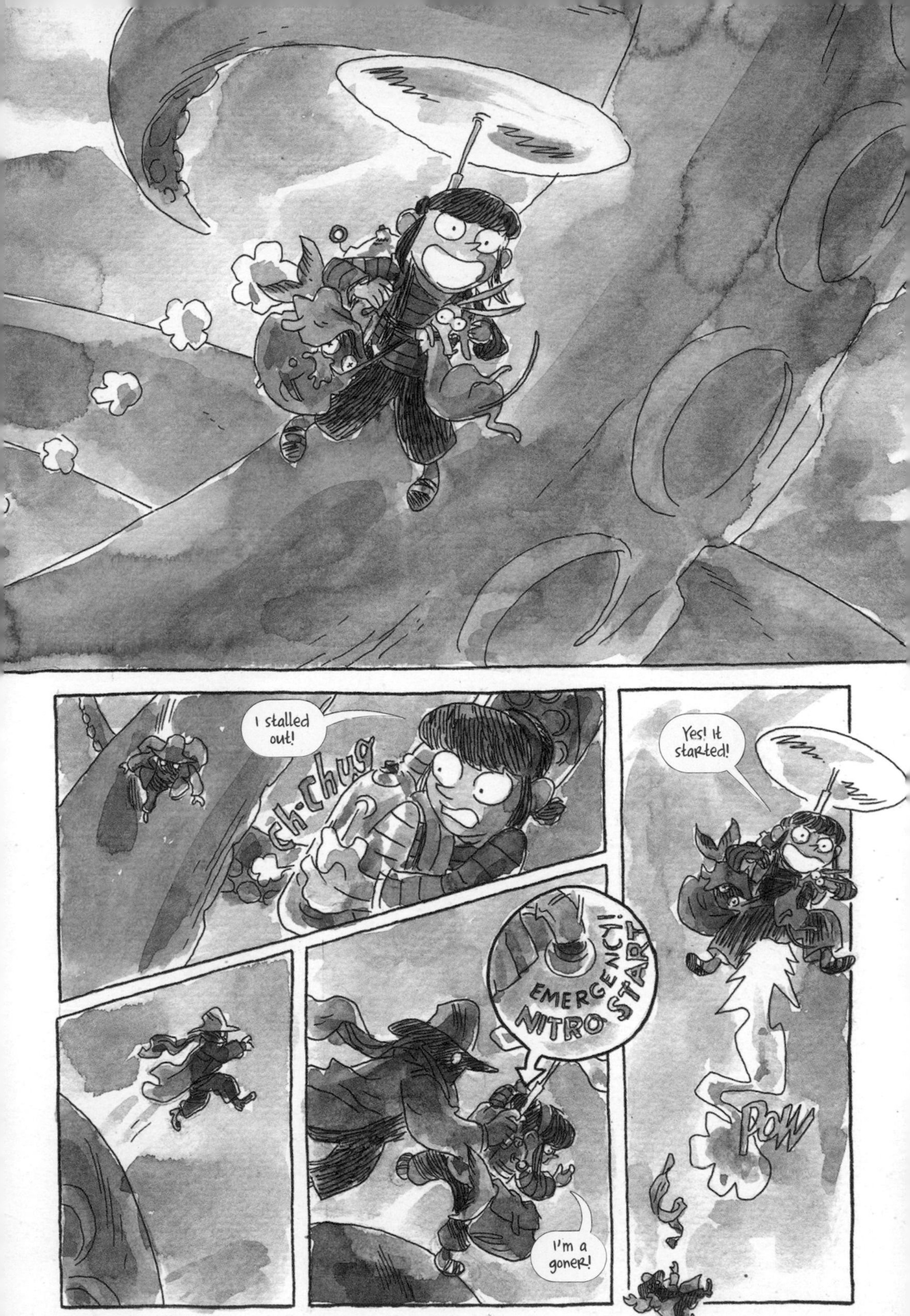

I stalled out!
ch-chug
EMERGENCY! NITRO START
I'm a goner!
Yes! It started!
POW

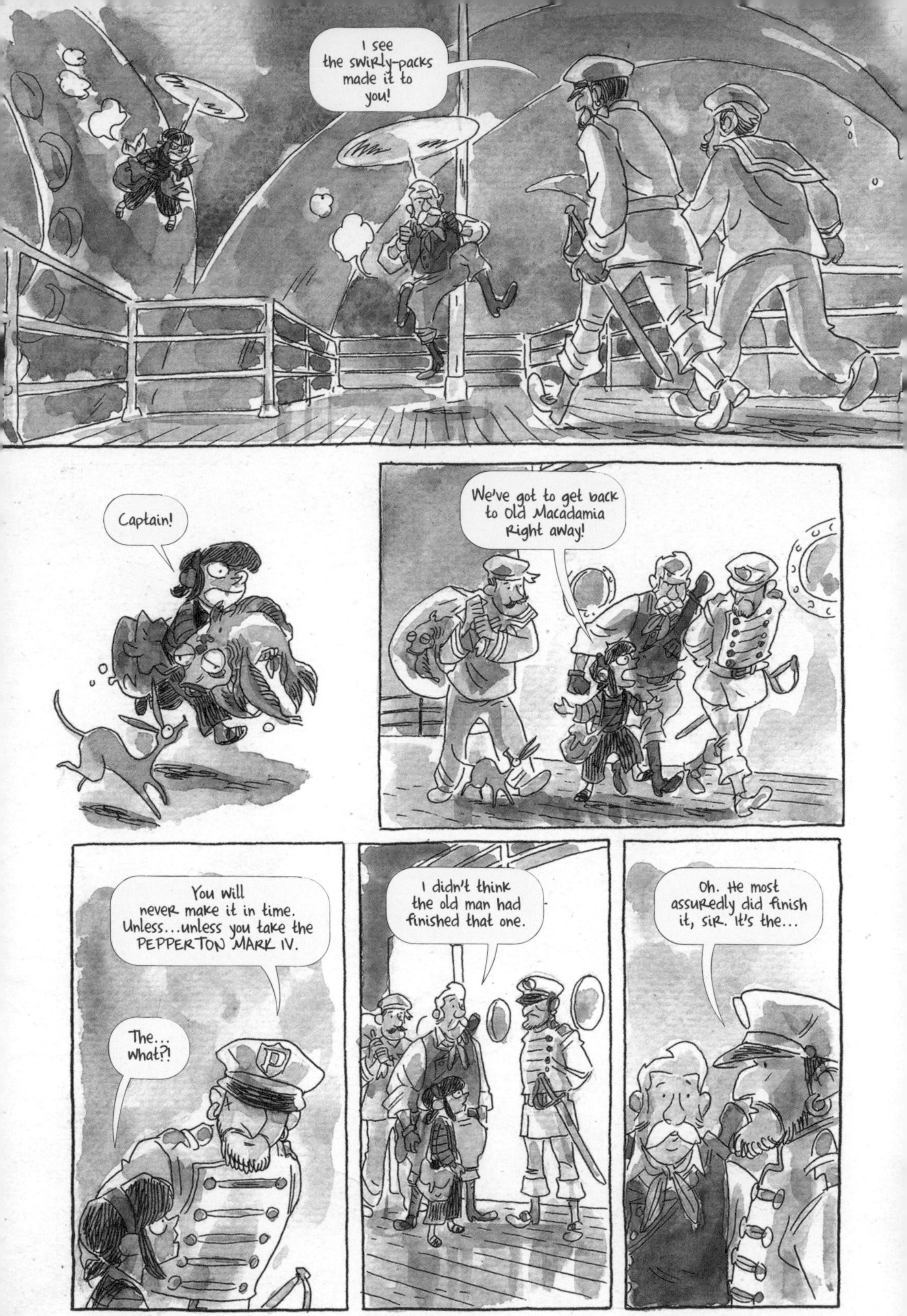
I see the swirly-packs made it to you!
Captain!
We've got to get back to Old Macadamia right away!
You will never make it in time. Unless...unless you take the PEPPERTON MARK IV.
The... what?!
I didn't think the old man had finished that one.
Oh. He most assuredly did finish it, sir. It's the...

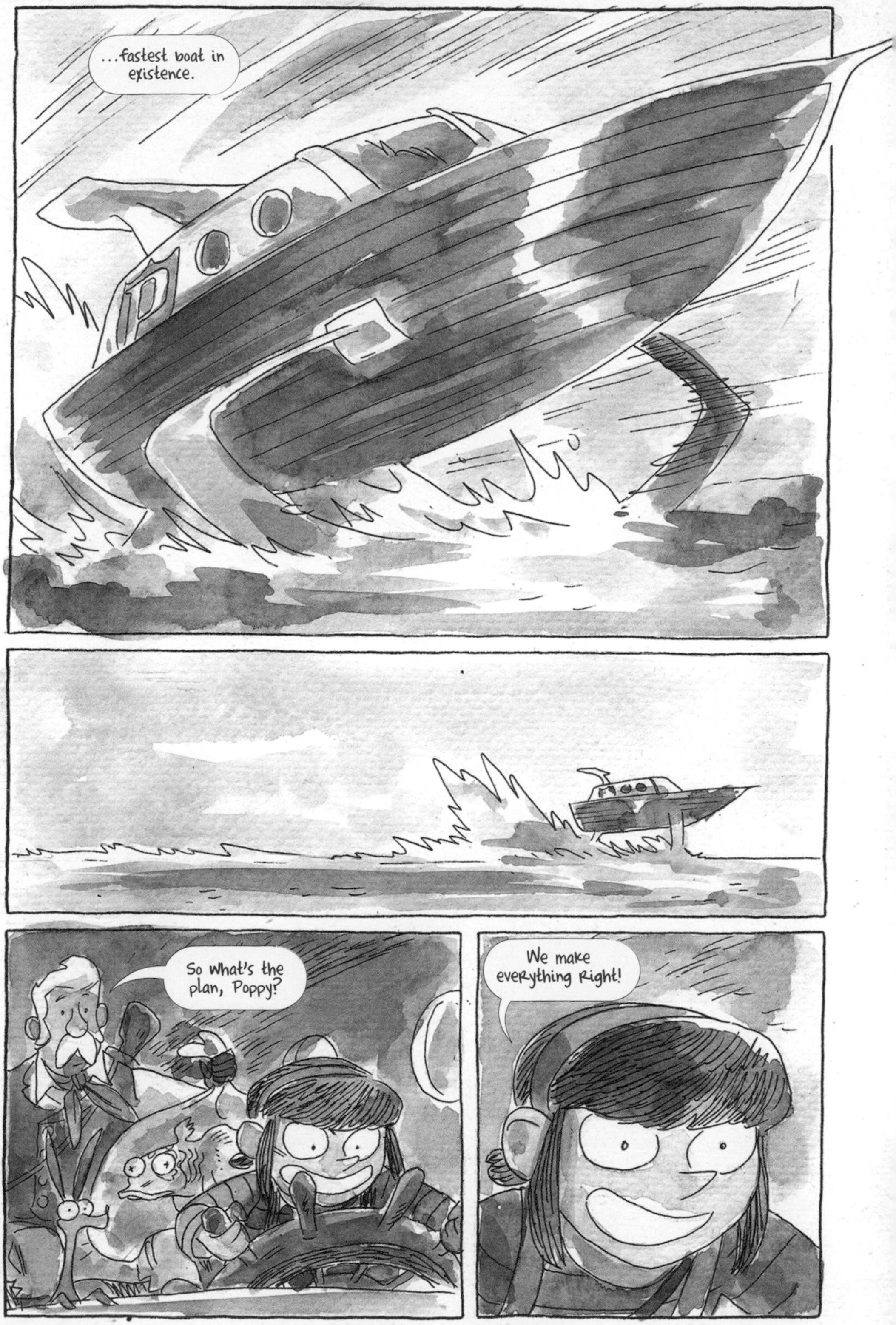
...fastest boat in existence.
So what's the plan, Poppy?
We make everything right!

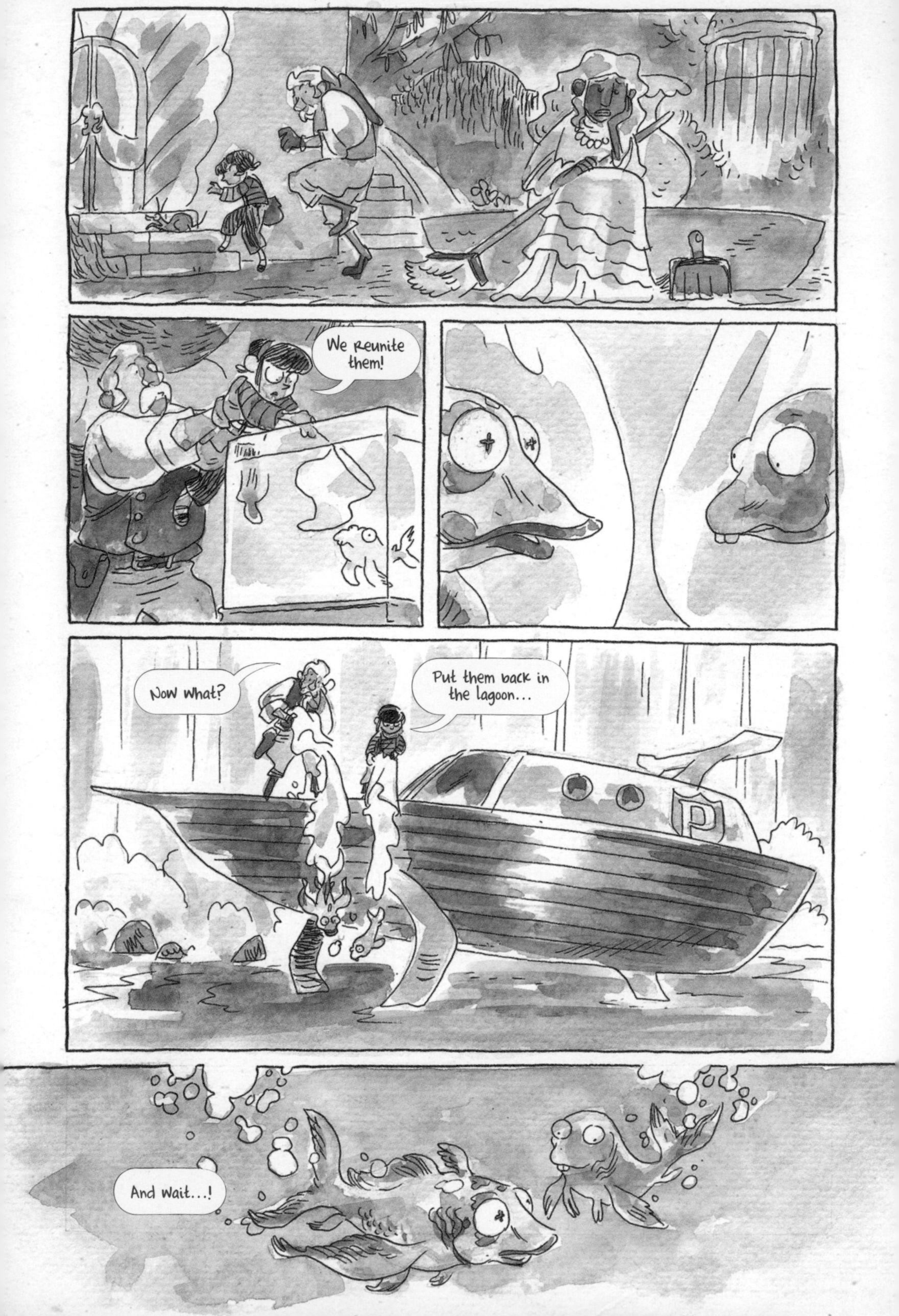
We reunite them!
Now what?
Put them back in the lagoon...
And wait...!

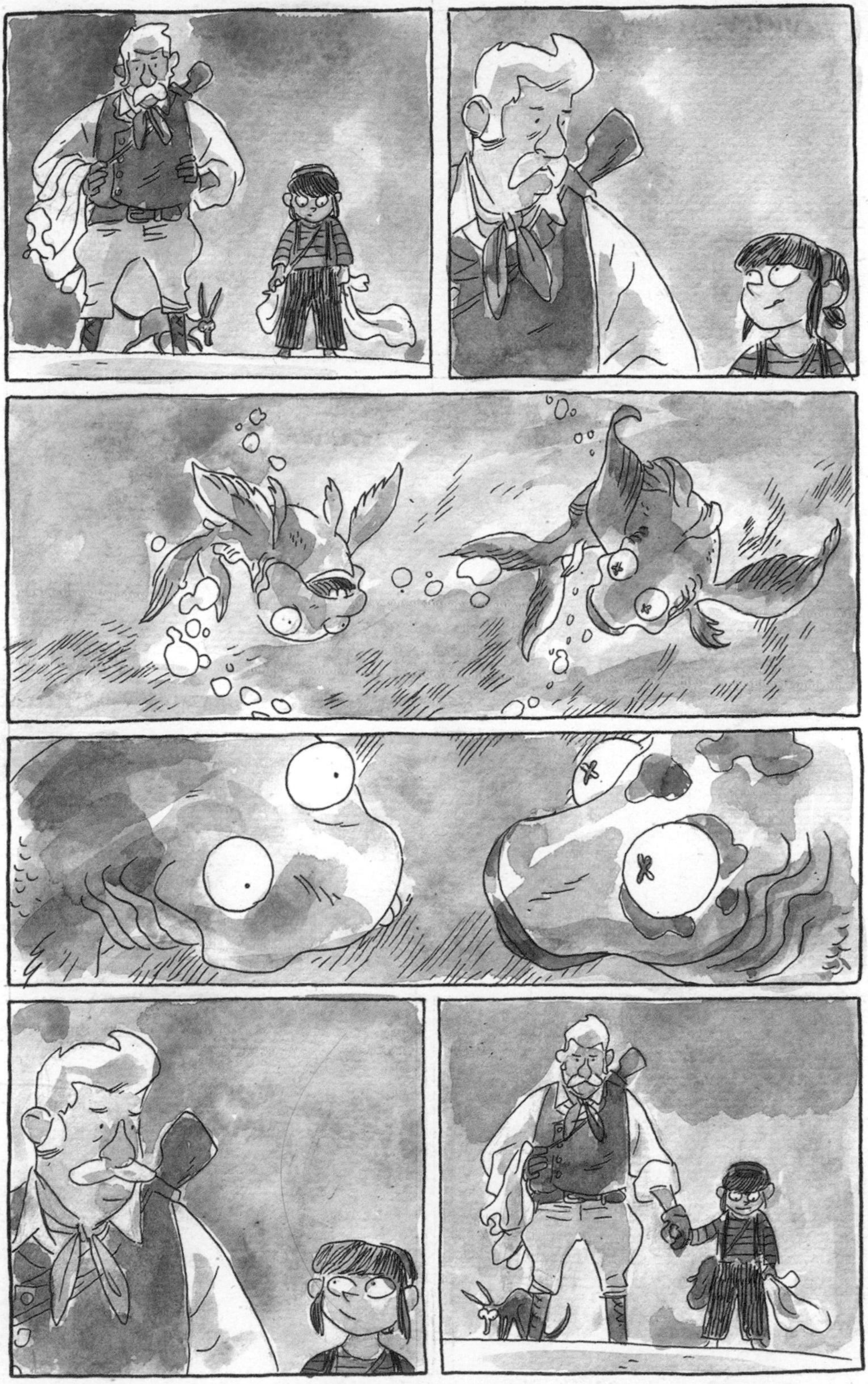

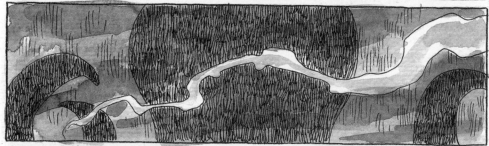

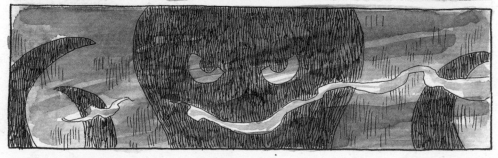

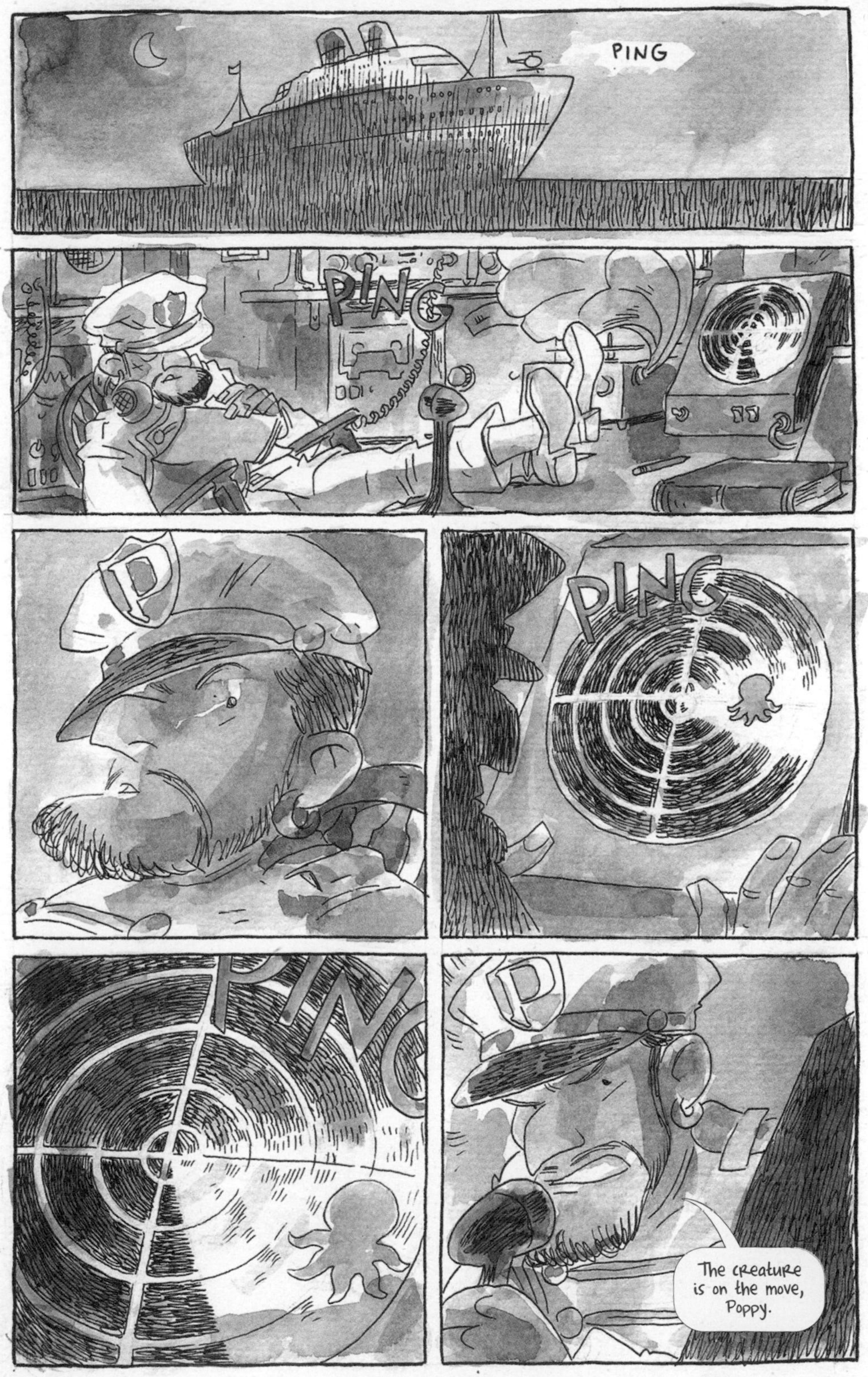
PING
PING
PING
PING
The creature is on the move, Poppy.

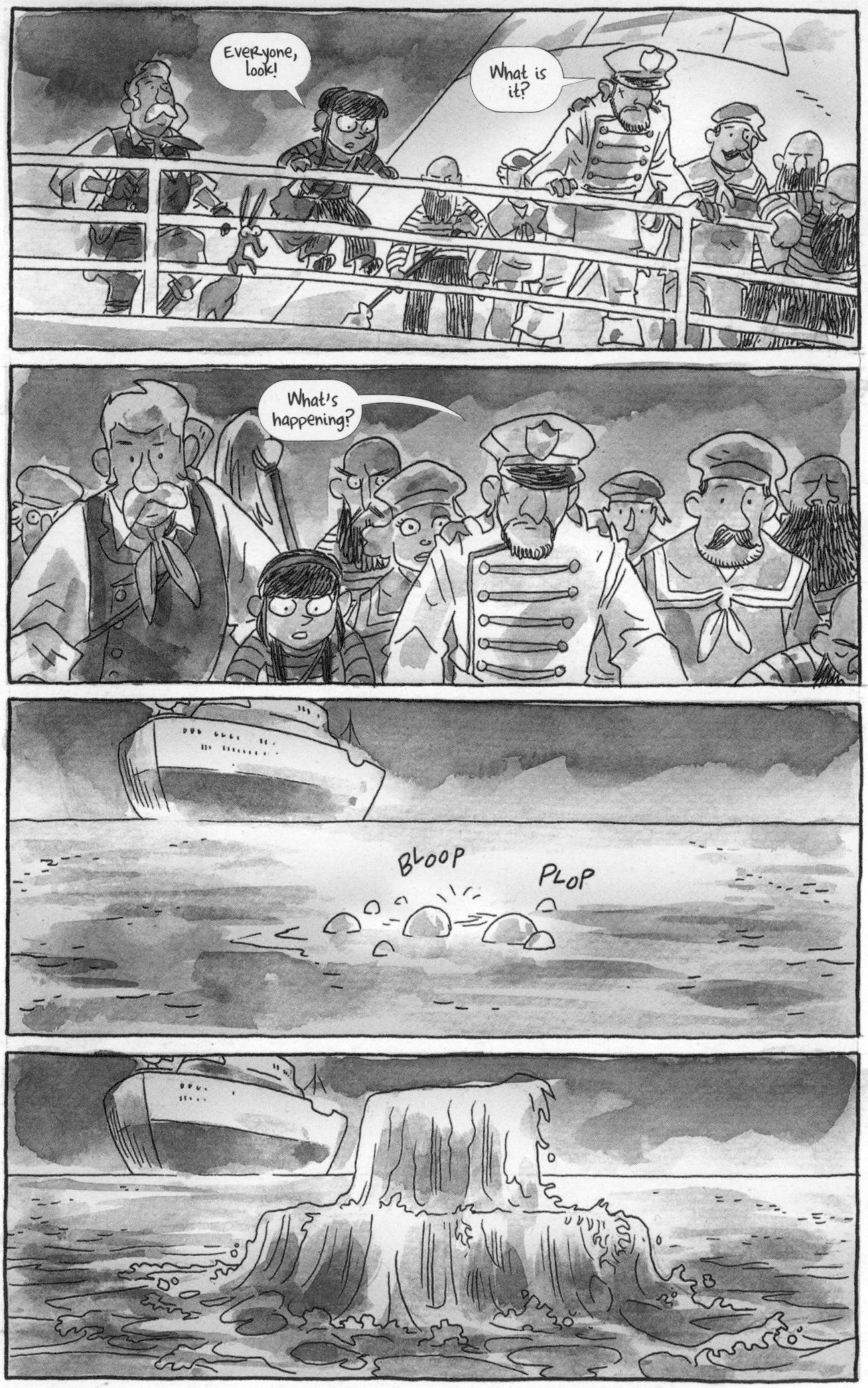
Everyone, look!
What is it?
What's happening?
BLOOP
PLOP

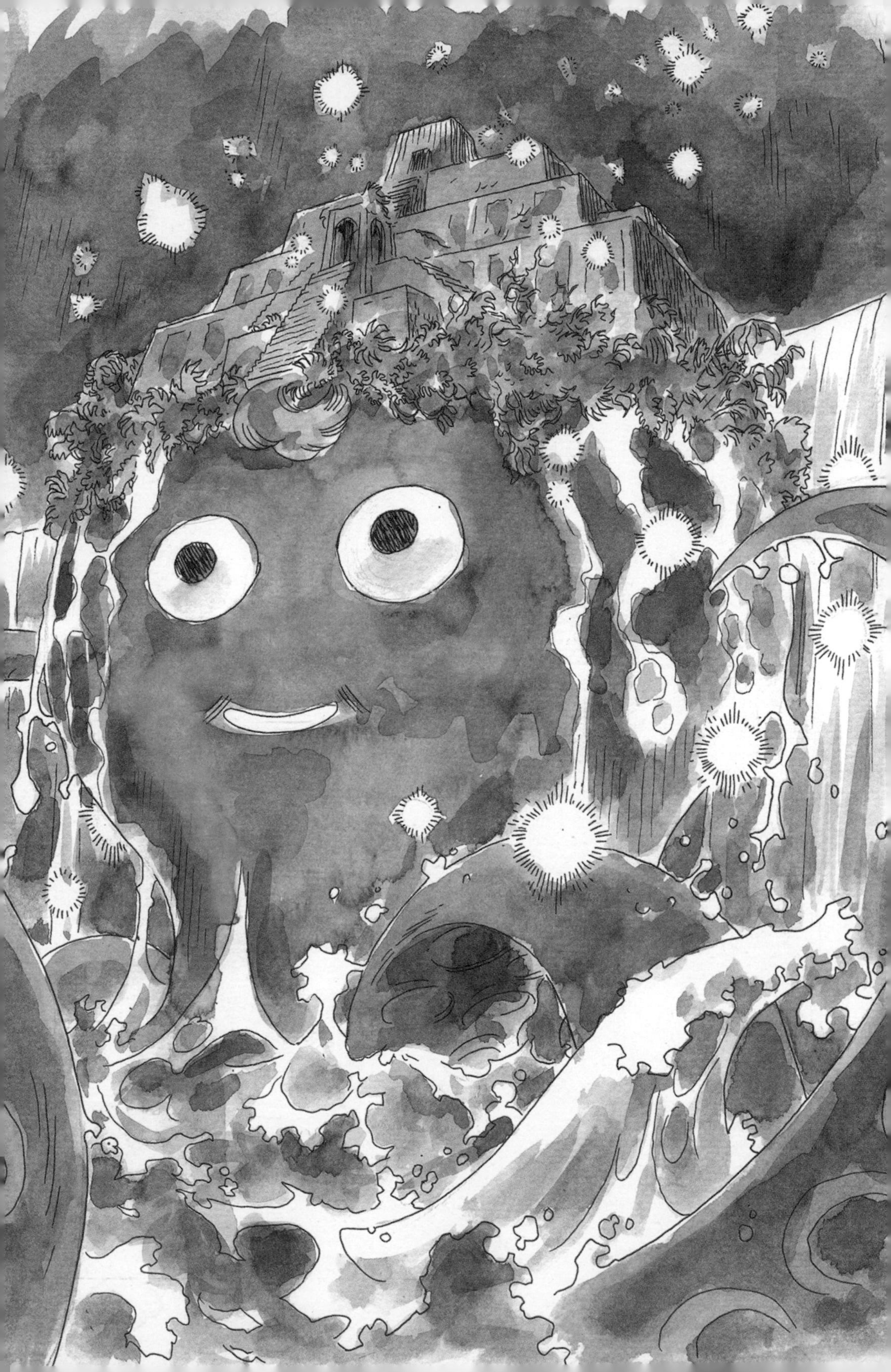

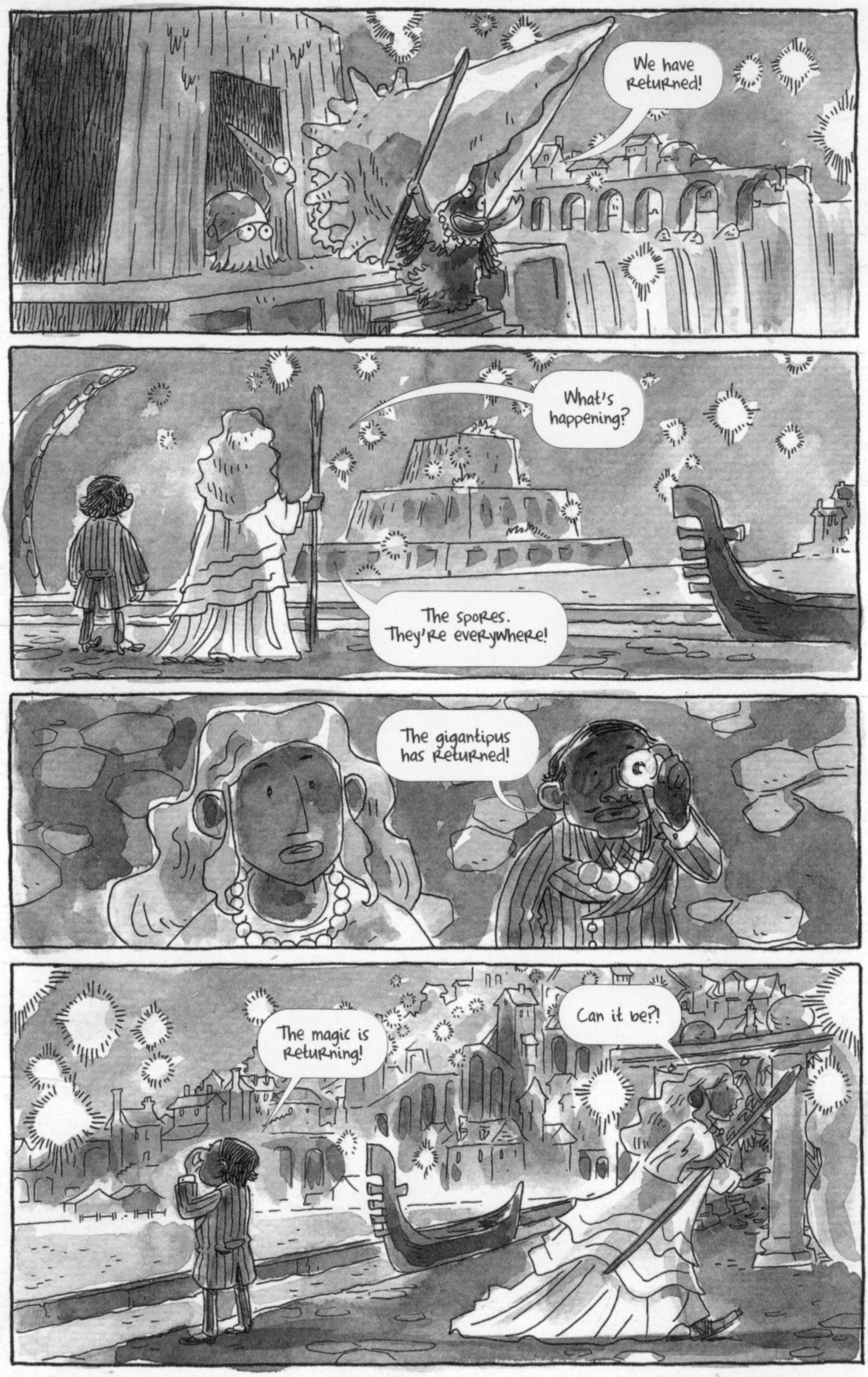
We have returned!
What's happening?
The spores. They're everywhere!
The gigantipus has returned!
The magic is returning!
Can it be?!

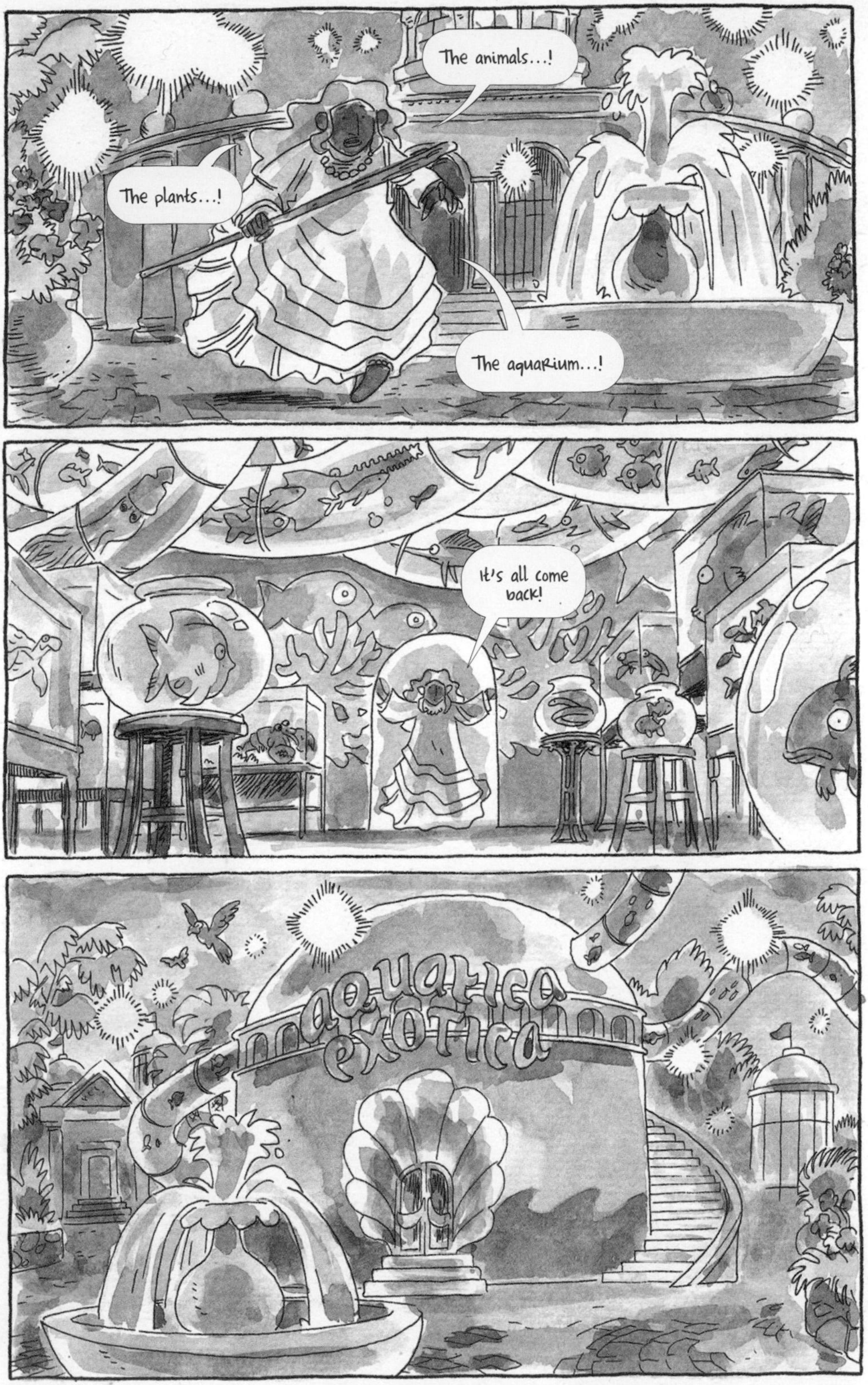
The animals...!
The plants...!
The aquarium...!
It's all come back!
aquatica exotica

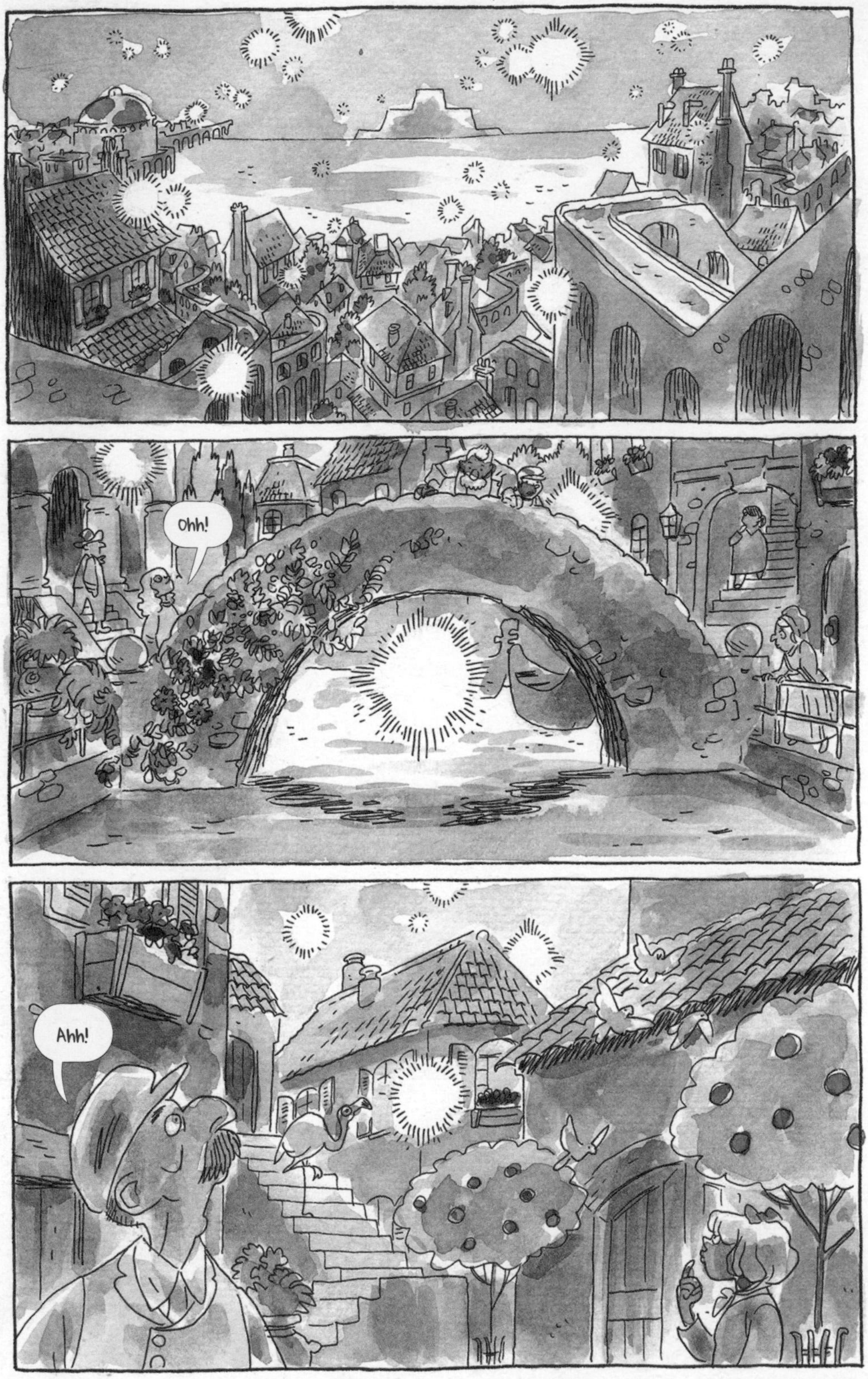
Ohh!
Ahh!

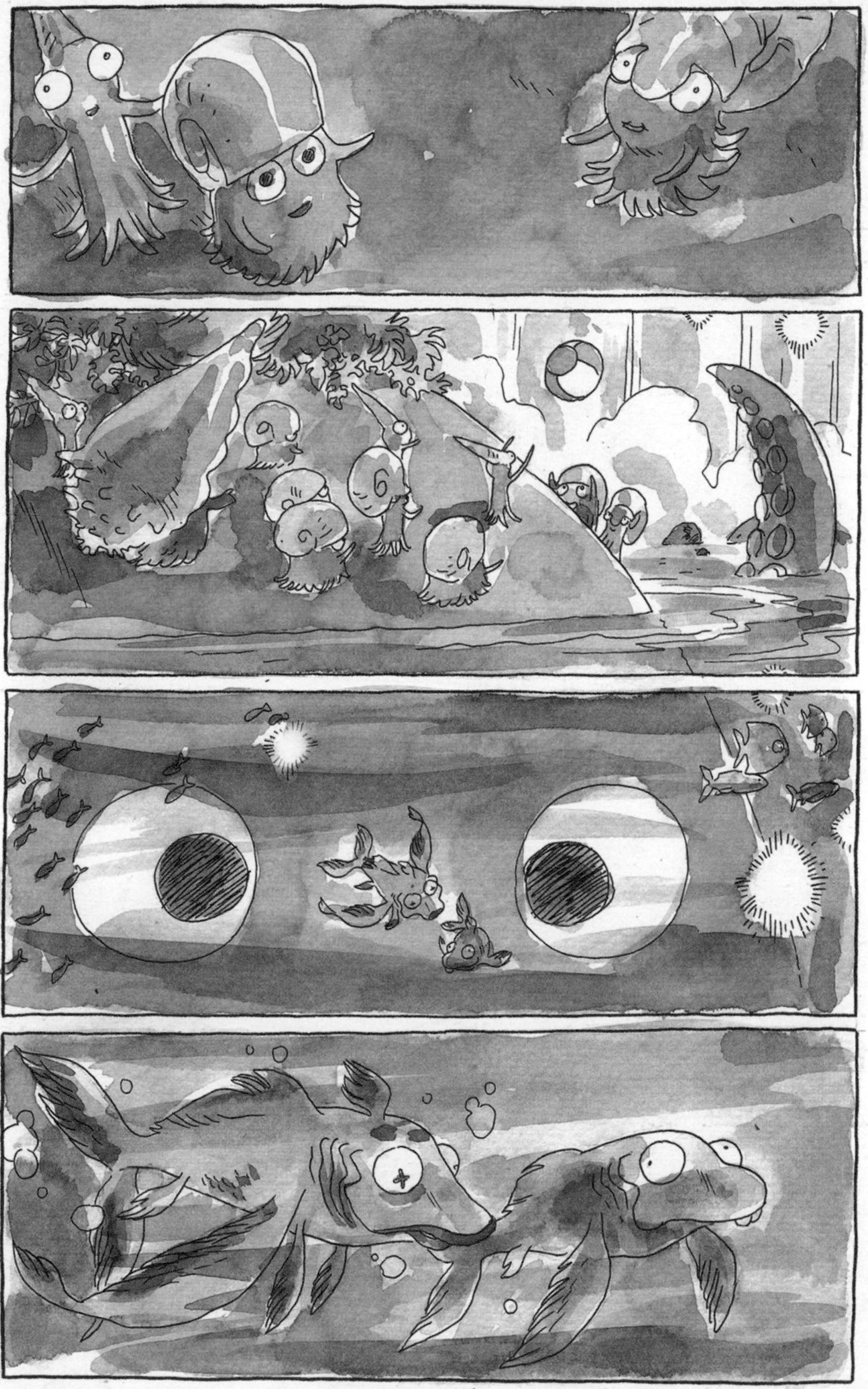

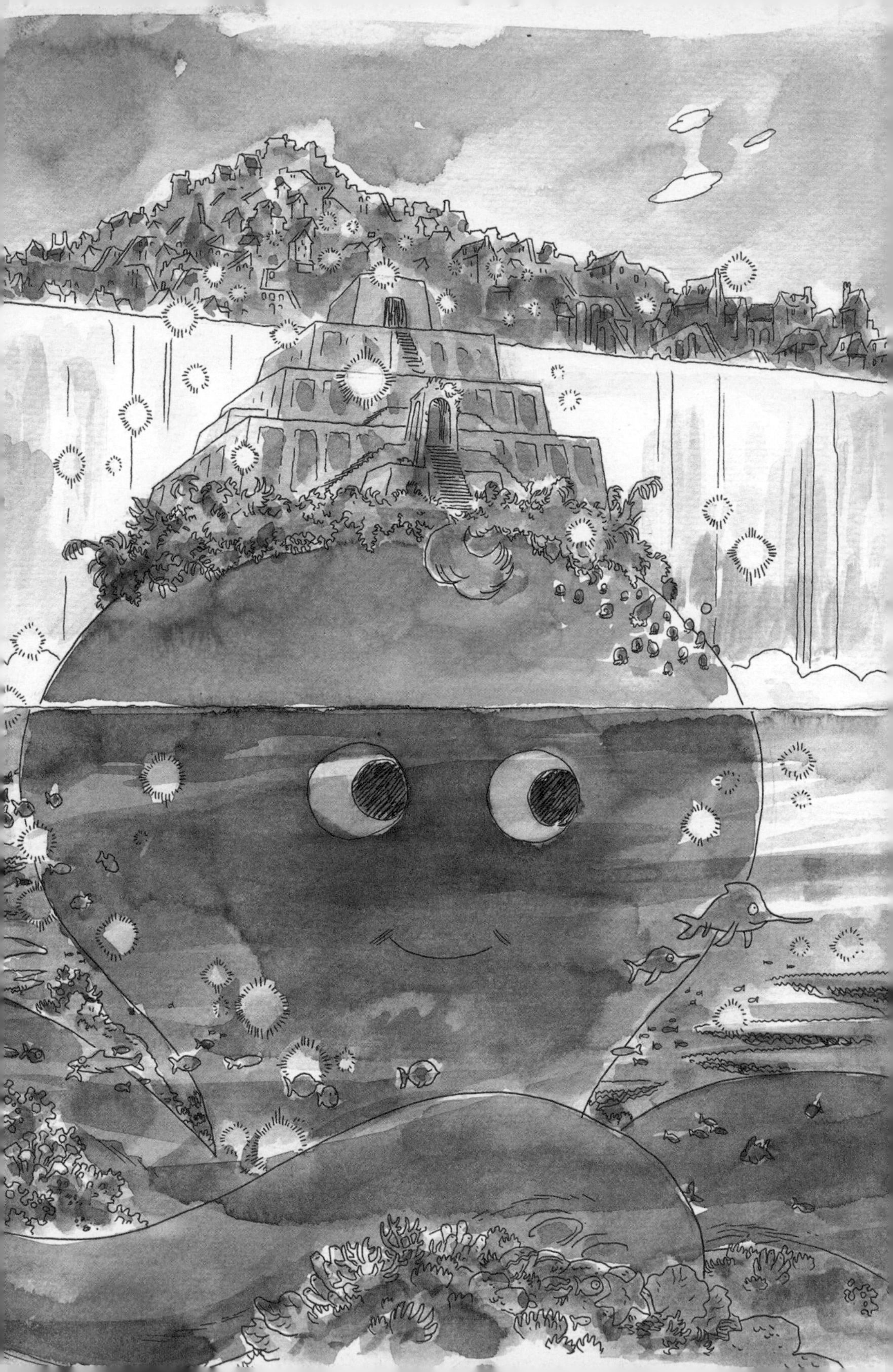

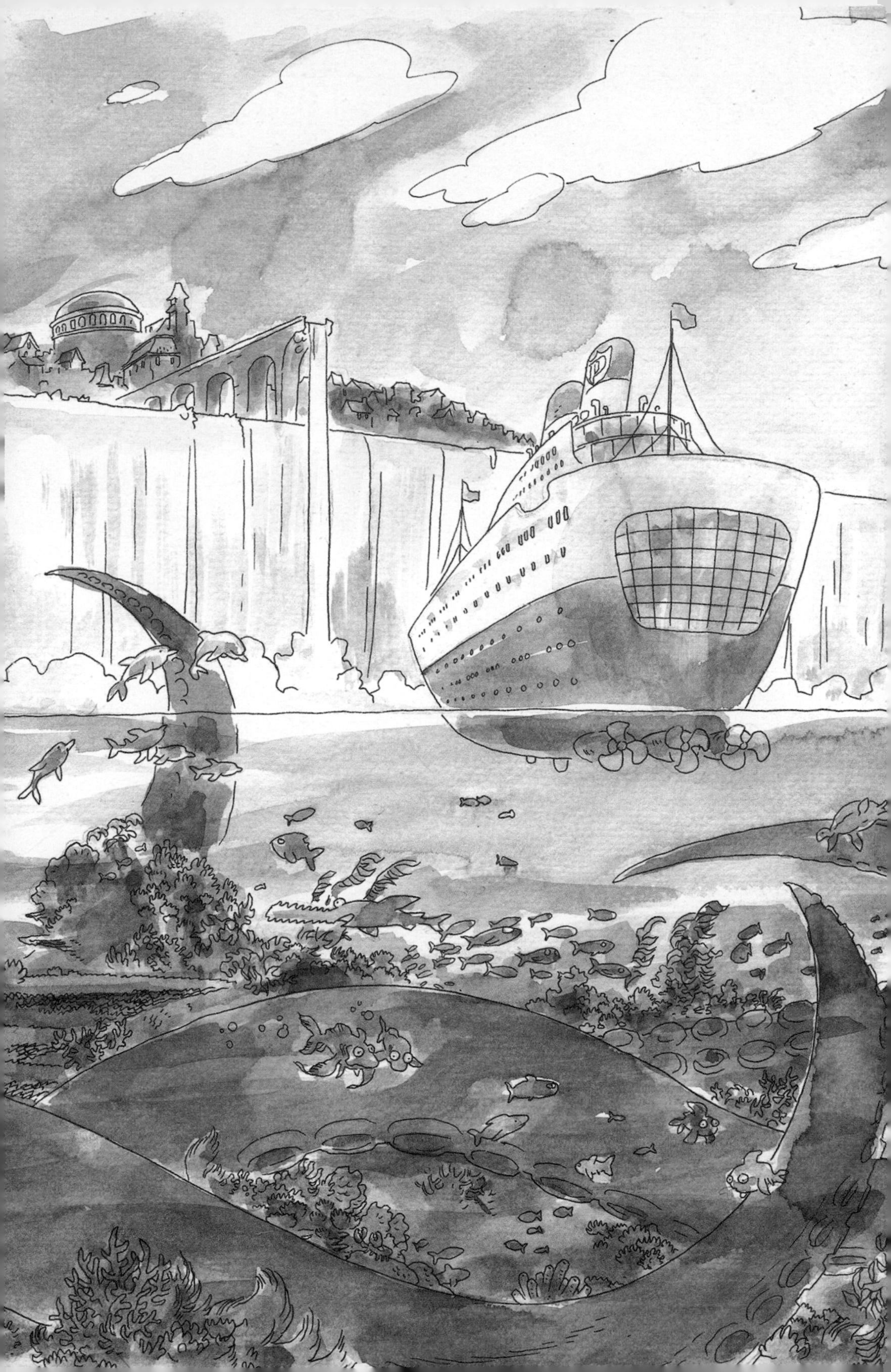

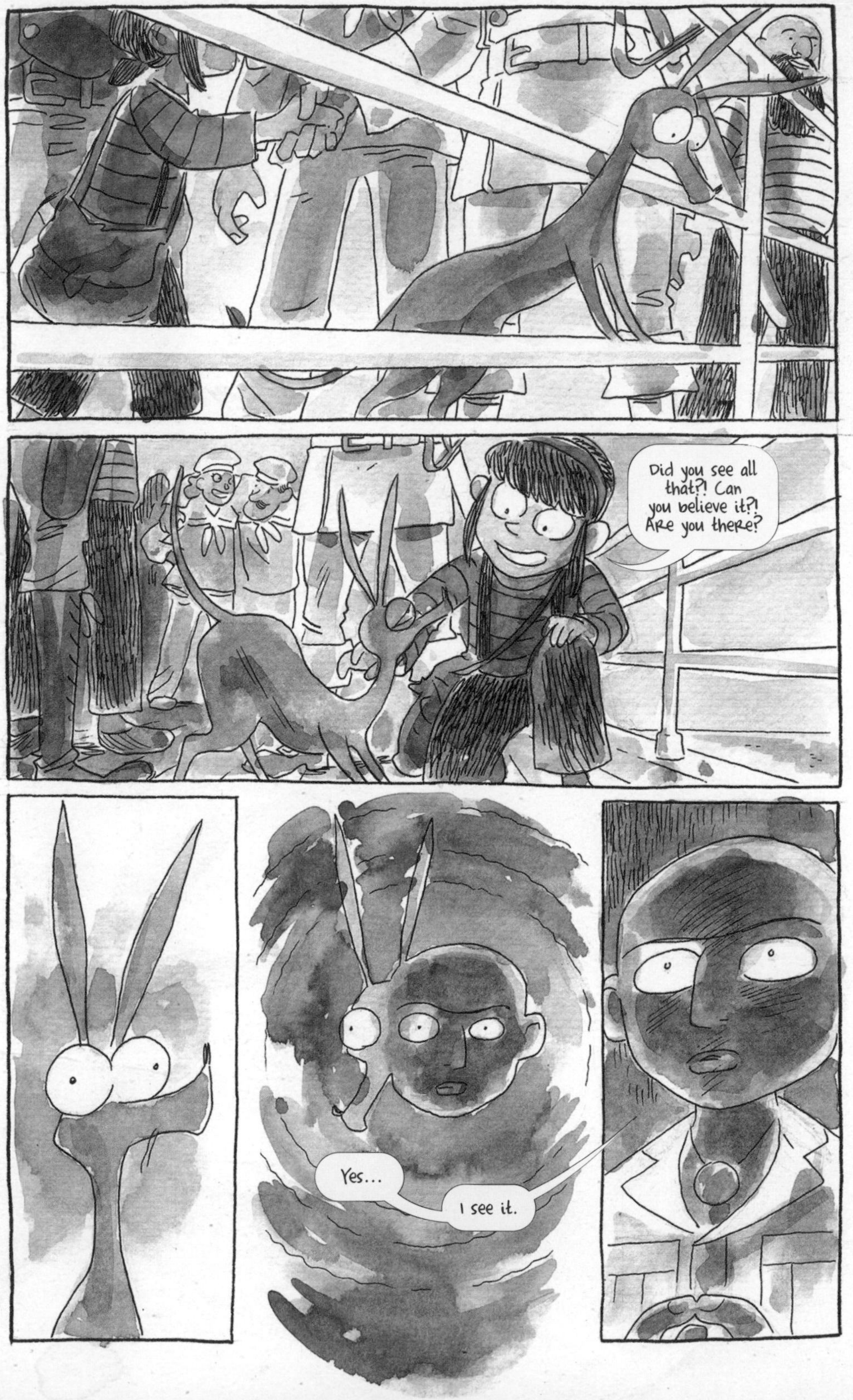
Did you see all that?! Can you believe it?! Are you there?
Yes...
I see it.

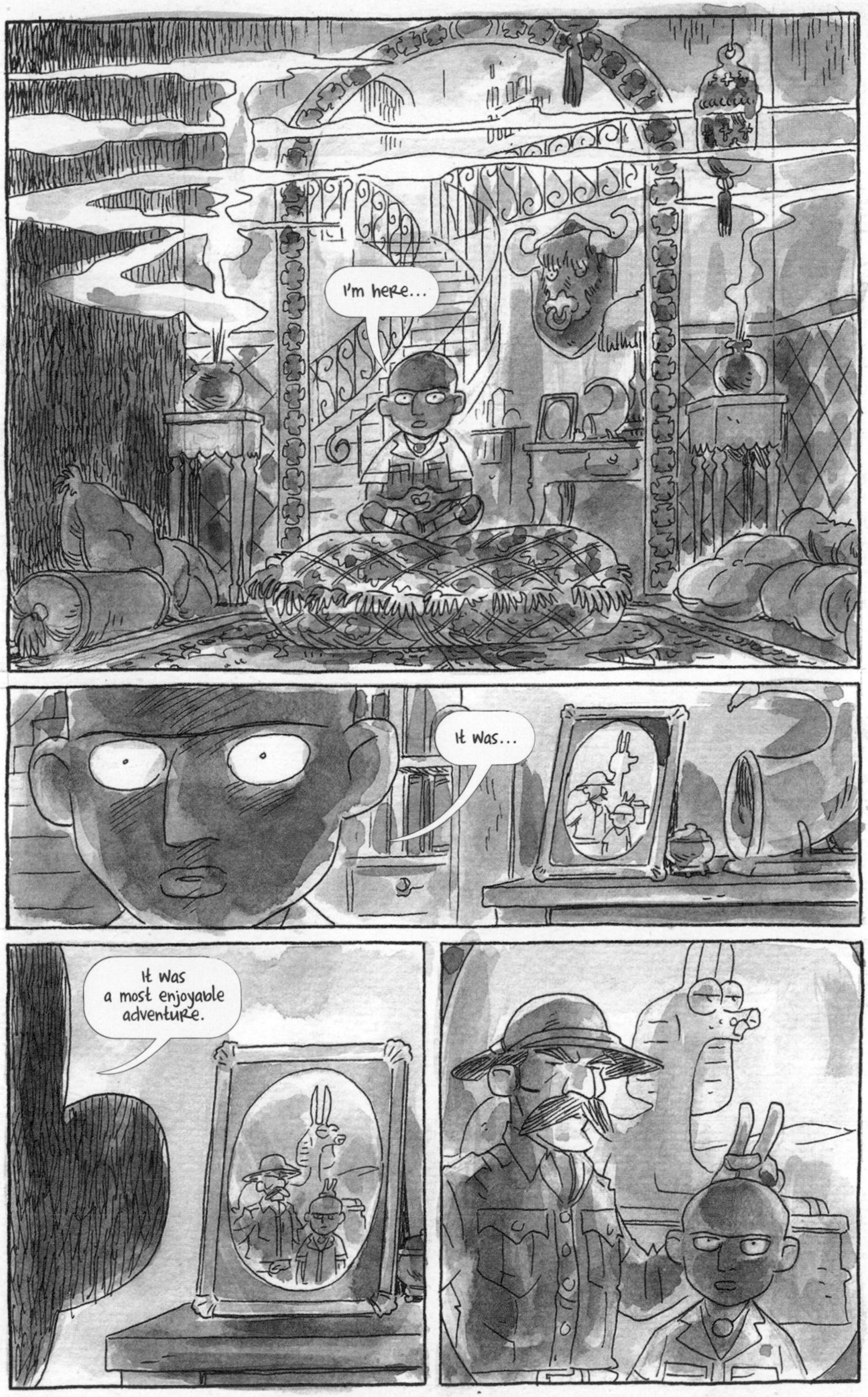
I'm here...
It was...
It was a most enjoyable adventure.

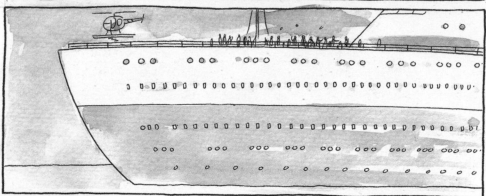

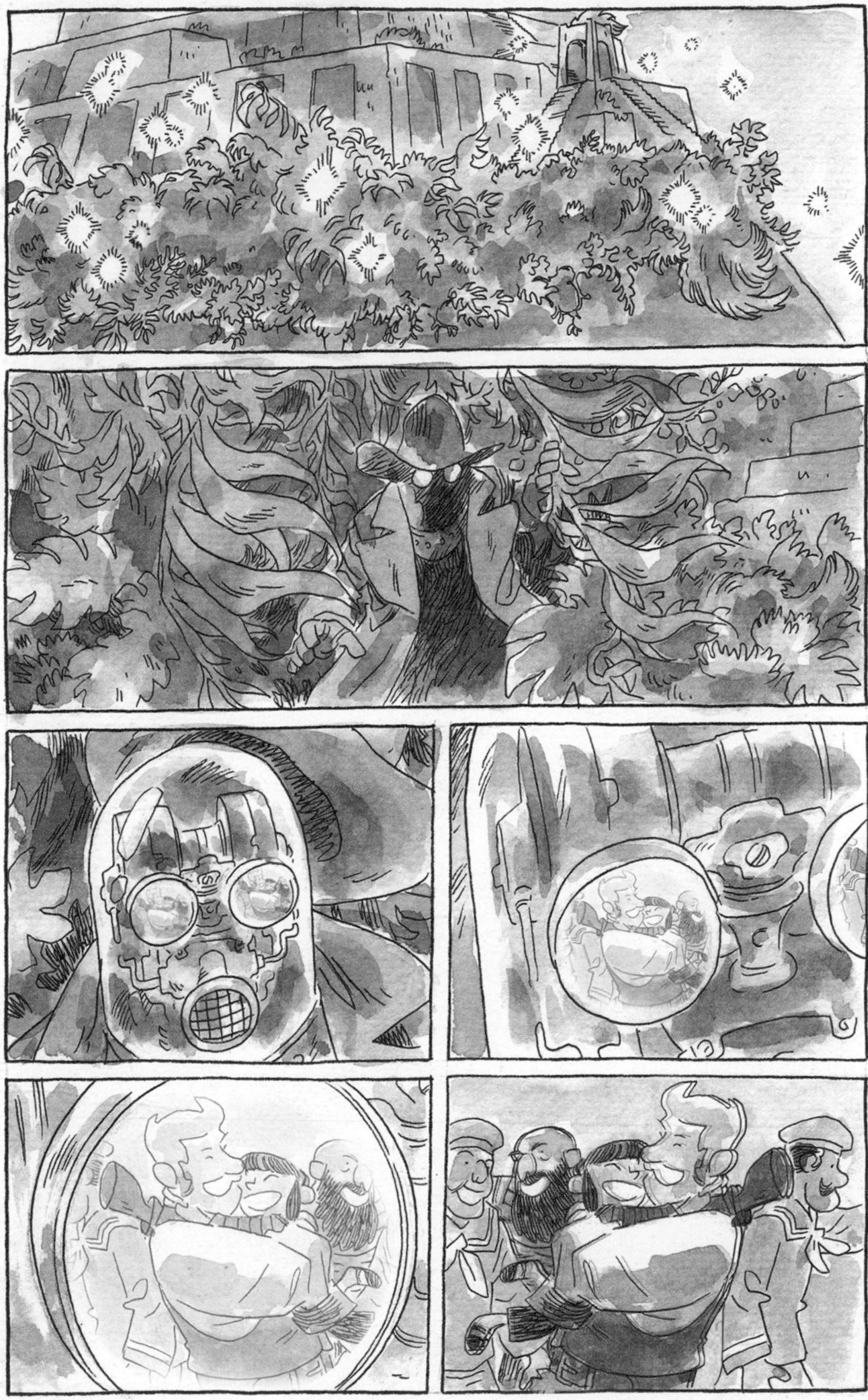

POPPY 3D VIEW-A-SCOPE: GLASSES REQUIRED

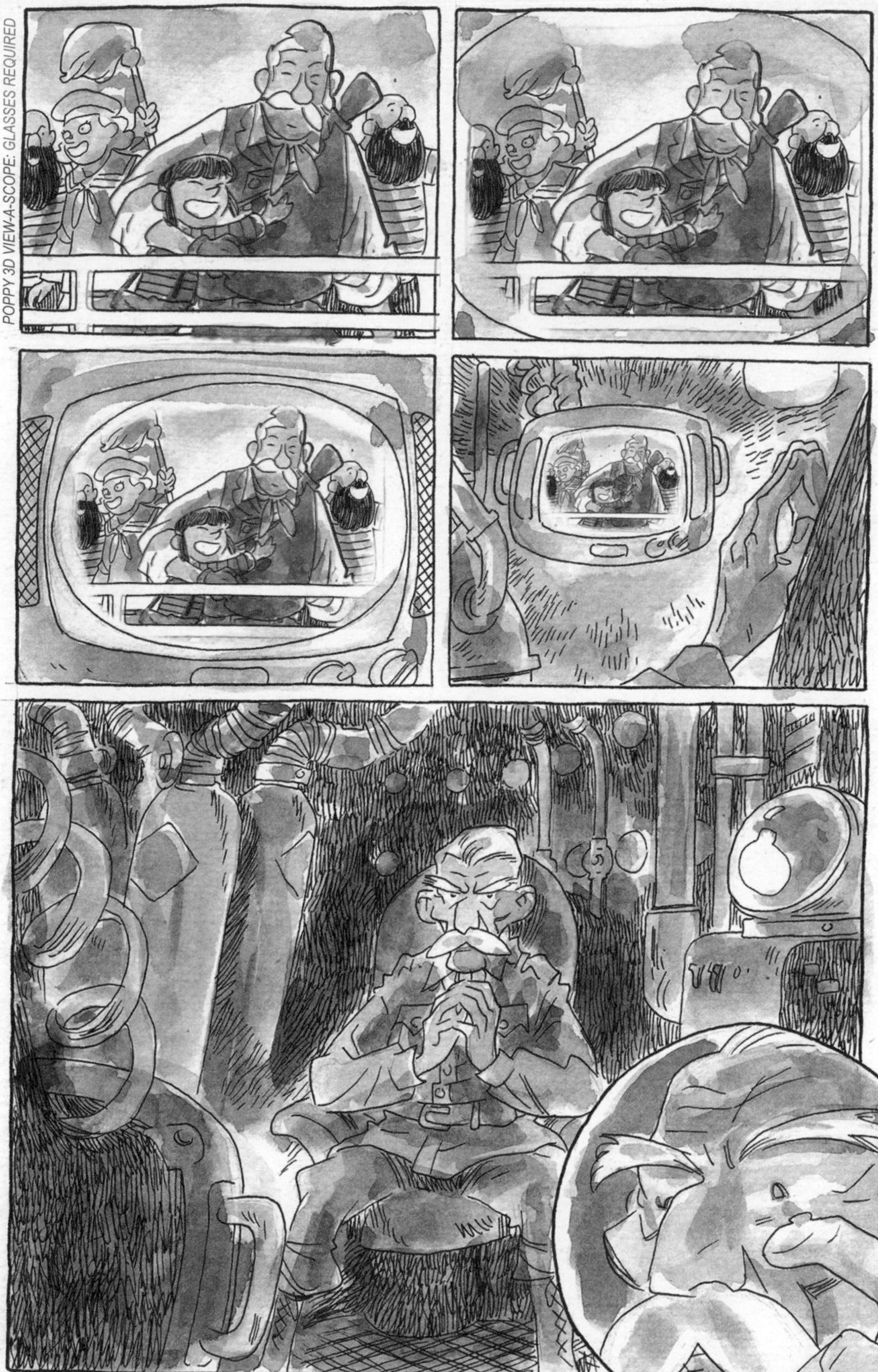
POPPY 3D VIEW-A-SCOPE: GLASSES REQUIRED

Special thanks to Karl Kindt III
for the Poppy 3D View-a-scope art.

Index of Puzzle Solutions

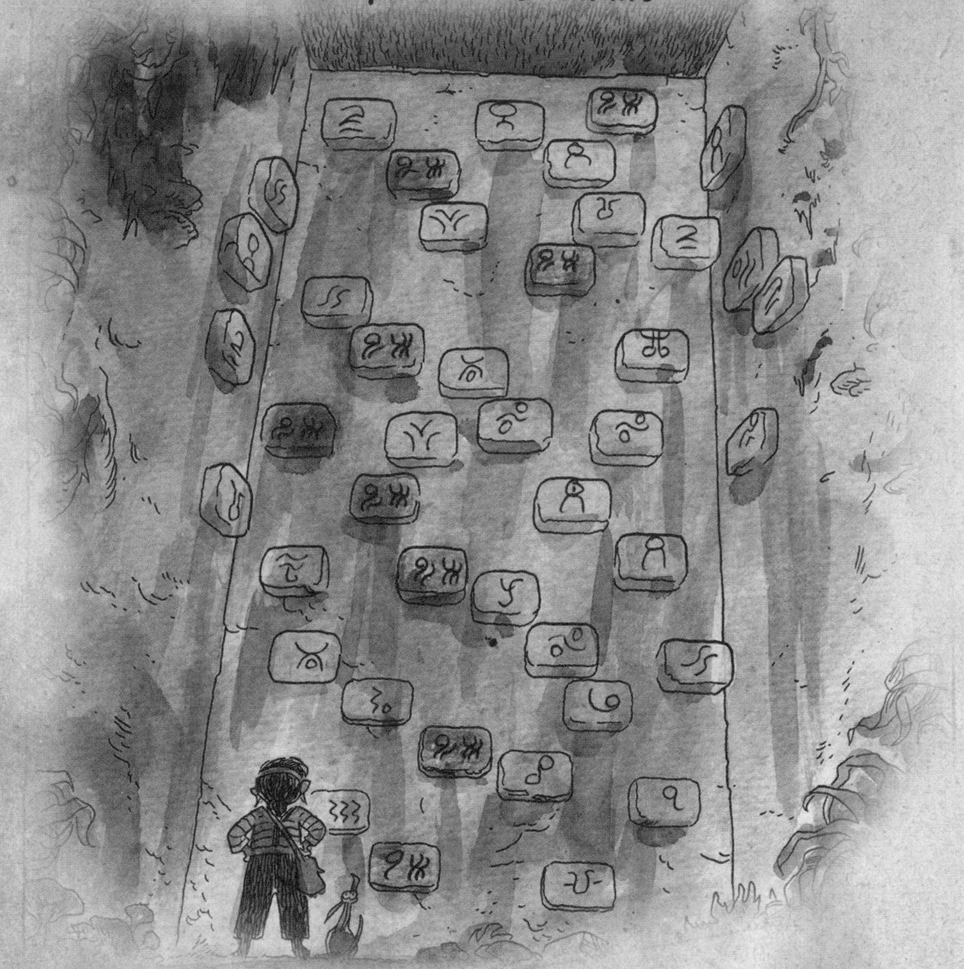

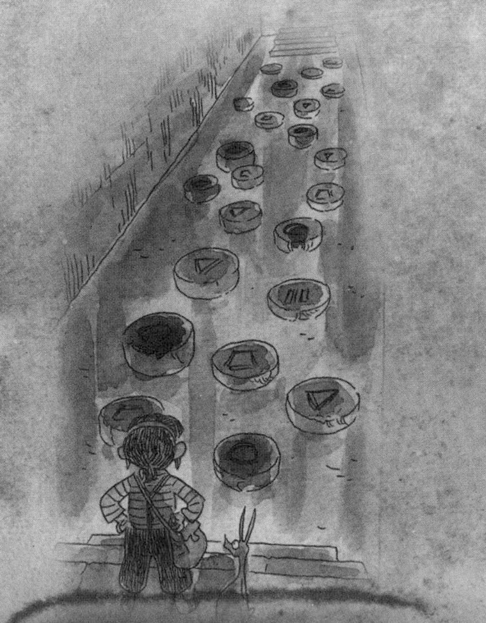

Page 94

Solution: Poppy realized that the circle from the door also marked the safe steppingstones across the water.

Page 96

Solution: Poppy noticed that only a few steps contained two symbols while the rest only had one symbol.

Can you figure out what the two symbols spell?

Language of the Shell People

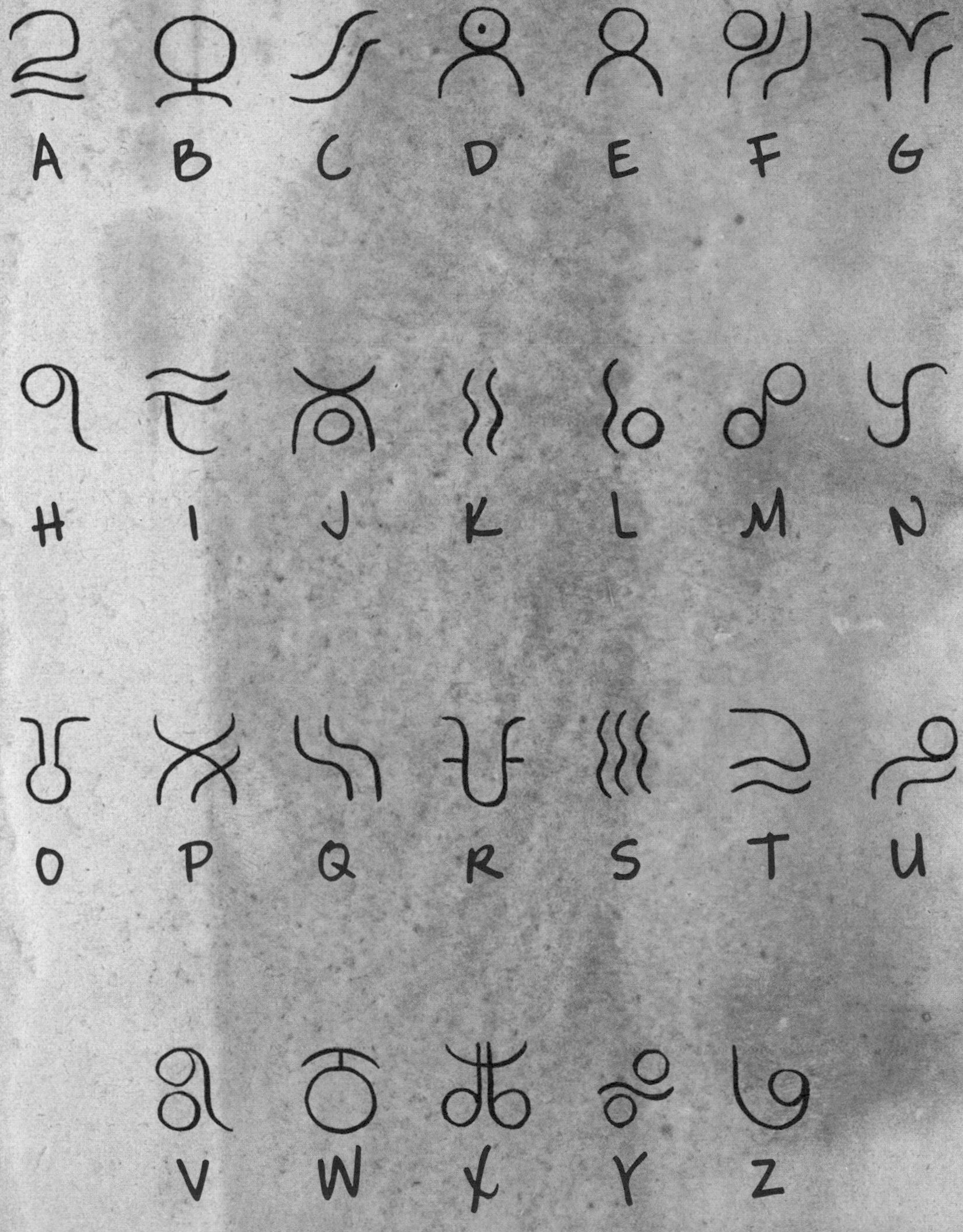
A B C D E F G
H I J K L M N
O P Q R S T U
V W X Y Z

Poppy's Action Sack!

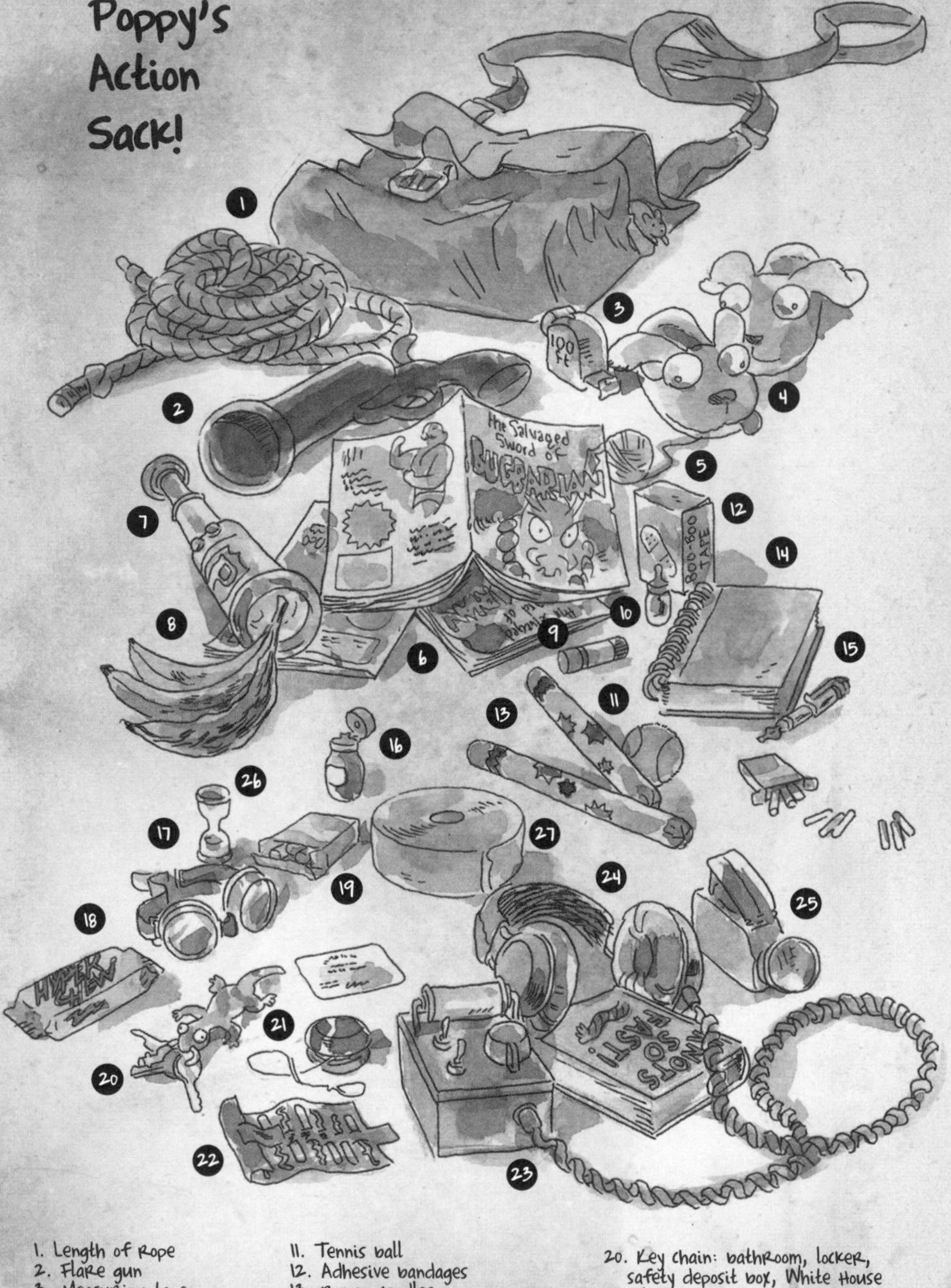
1
2
3
4
5
6
7
8
9
10
11
12
13
14
15
16
17
18
19
20
21
22
23
24
25
26
27
100 ft
The Salvaged Sword of
BOO-BOO TAPE
HYPER CHEW
NOT SO FAST!

1. Length of Rope
2. Flare gun
3. Measuring tape
4. Fuzzy bunny slippers
5. Ball of string
6. Comic Books
7. Poppy-scope
8. Bananas
9. Glue stick
10. Antivenom
11. Tennis ball
12. Adhesive bandages
13. Roman candles
14. Sketchbook journal
15. Fountain pen
16. Ink Refills: black, blue, Red, invisible
17. 3D goggles
18. Energy bar
19. Box of chalk
20. Key chain: bathRoom, locker, safety deposit box, White House
21. Yo-yo
22. Lock pick set
23. Crystal Radio
24. Headphones
25. Hand-powered flashlight
26. Minute timer
27. Duct tape

matt kindt

"I'll read anything Kindt does." —Douglas Wolk, author of *Reading Comics*

MIND MGMT
VOLUME 1: THE MANAGER
ISBN 978-1-59582-797-5
$19.99

VOLUME 2: THE FUTURIST
ISBN 978-1-61655-198-8
$19.99

VOLUME 3: THE HOME MAKER
ISBN 978-1-61655-390-6
$19.99

VOLUME 4: THE MAGICIAN
ISBN 978-1-61655-391-3
$19.99

VOLUME 5: THE ERASER
ISBN 978-1-61655-696-9
$19.99

VOLUME 6: THE IMMORTALS
ISBN 978-1-61655-798-0
$19.99

POPPY! AND THE LOST LAGOON
With Brian Hurtt
ISBN 978-1-61655-943-4
$14.99

PAST AWAYS
VOLUME 1: FACEDOWN IN THE TIMESTREAM
With Scott Kolins
ISBN 978-1-61655-792-8
$12.99

THE COMPLETE PISTOLWHIP
With Jason Hall
ISBN 978-1-61655-720-1
$27.99

3 STORY: THE SECRET HISTORY OF THE GIANT MAN
ISBN 978-1-59582-356-4
$19.99

2 SISTERS
ISBN 978-1-61655-721-8
$27.99

darkhorse
originals

"unique creators with unique visions"
— MIKE RICHARDSON, PUBLISHER